THE KILLING SEASON

JEFF STETSON

Storm
PUBLISHING

To request permissions, contact the publisher at rights@stormpublishing.co

Ebook ISBN: 978-1-80508-472-3
Paperback ISBN: 978-1-80508-475-4

Cover design: Blacksheep
Cover images: Shutterstock

Published by Storm Publishing.
For further information, visit:
www.stormpublishing.co

ALSO BY JEFF STETSON

The Stolen Girls

Blood on the Leaves

The Meeting

To those who still believe in the possibility of justice and the necessity for love

veins and then, before he could provide comfort or false reassurance, he felt the officer die.

He cradled Hoffman in his arms, gently placing the upper half of the limp body across his lap. He braced his hand against the door of his patrol car, smearing its "to protect and to serve" insignia with the blood of his colleague. He gazed at the hillside. His eyes filled with tears, causing a sprinkling of dotted lights to widen then blend to form a nightmarish haze that didn't cease when he closed them, and spoke a single word, with a trembling voice: "Matt."

TWO

Paul Henderson's feet pounded the hot pavement to the rhythm of some random song blasting through his new headphones, a birthday gift from his wife. His son, Dexter, had downloaded onto his jazz playlist Drake's *For All the Dogs* album. Dexter wanted him to catch up with the times. If the times includes music featuring someone named Bad Bunny, he'd just as soon be stuck in the past with Marvin Gaye. The things a father must do for the love of his son.

The fifth song on Drake's album, "Daylight," would be coming up in a few seconds and he'd already run past the marble and bronze statue in the playground, headed for Hill-crest Avenue, which meant he'd cut half a minute off his previous fastest time. He loved running through Beverly Hills with its clean parks, wide streets, and magnificent estates. When he was bored with the jog and needed something to distract his mind from the early morning drudgery, he'd make a bet with himself as to which luxury car would be seen most frequently—first to reach ten sightings won the contest. So far, he only needed to see one more Rolls-Royce. He'd counted seven Ferraris and four Lamborghinis. When he felt particularly adventurous, he'd run until he spotted five other African Americans jogging or walking or leaving the front doors of any of the homes in this exclusive neighborhood. (Maids were ineligible.) He didn't make that challenge often unless he was prepared to run a minor marathon.

He prepared himself for the final sprint to the finish line—the huge Mediterranean estate with the massive wrought iron gates that had a gold emblem of a lion embedded in the driveway. He breathed heavier than usual, probably from the extra birthday cake and ice cream. His gray sweats were soaked. At thirty years of age, he still had the body of a collegiate sprinter and the face of a man who couldn't grow a beard, if his life depended on it. More than once, someone had stopped and asked if he was a celebrity or sports figure or "that actor, the one who reminds me so much of a young Sidney Poitier."

He pumped his legs faster and lifted his knees higher, doing his best to work off those additional calories before he made it back to his car. He suddenly jumped to the side, barely avoiding a teen who rode his bicycle onto the curb. The near miss forced him to collide into a cluster of rose bushes. He winced as the thorns sliced across his right thigh and ripped his pants. He didn't stop to assess the damage but turned up the volume and sprinted the last quarter mile. He might start to like this Drake fella, if he could understand the lyrics.

Once he'd made it to his car, he retrieved an extra water bottle, took a sip, then poured the rest onto his leg, wiping the blood with a white towel. He removed his headphones and placed them on the passenger seat. He tossed the towel inside, turned on the car radio and drove North on Elm.

"Scores of angry Black demonstrators picketed City Hall this morning protesting last week's shooting to death of Milton Hobson by three white police officers. Hobson was the fourth unarmed Afro-American killed this year by the L.A.P.D. after being mistakenly suspected of criminal activity."

Henderson wiped the perspiration off his face with the back of his sleeve and listened to the news report. He glanced at his rearview mirror and noticed the blue and red flashing lights of a city patrol car. He checked his speedometer. It read slightly under thirty.

"Mayor Alex Palmer outraged members of the Black community by saying when it comes to police shootings, he would always give his officers 'the benefit of the doubt'."

"Hope these guys feel the same way," Henderson said wistfully and turned off the radio. He pulled his car to the side of the road and waited for the two white cops to approach. One stopped near the front of the patrol car and behind his. The other continued toward Henderson.

"License and registration," said the cop, with typical detachment.

"Is there a problem, officer?" Henderson responded, as politely as possible.

The cop gave no expression but took a moment before he issued a justification. "Your brake light," he said, as an afterthought.

Henderson looked at the officer's badge. "I didn't use my brakes until you pulled me over."

The cop gave a quick glance to his partner then returned his attention to Henderson. "License and registration," he repeated, but this time with a hint of menace in his voice.

Henderson took a deep breath and removed his license from the side pocket of the car's sun visor. He then reached across the dashboard to his glove compartment and located his registration. As he brought his arm back his hand accidentally brushed against the towel in the passenger seat, covering his headphones.

"Hold it!" shouted the cop, which caused his partner to move quickly toward the front passenger side.

Henderson did as commanded and noticed the cop staring

across the yard toward the opposite fence. Henderson was six feet behind and catching up fast, but not as fast as the dog that had no intention of letting its food escape. The dog sought to cut them off. Henderson and Calvanese made the same detour. They hurdled over a chaise longue and took dead aim on the fence. Both cops leapt high. The dog lunged higher, its teeth prepared to bite, but the chain extended a fraction too short. Henderson and Calvanese dived over the barrier while the dog appeared suspended in midair, then landed close to the fence. It barked furiously, trying helplessly to break loose from its metal leash.

The two cops were safely on the other side, face down on the lawn, out of breath but relieved. They smiled at each other, but their sense of victory didn't last. Henderson nudged Calvanese and nodded toward the rear. Calvanese could tell by his partner's tense expression that whatever was behind him wouldn't be good. He turned and saw two Dobermans from hell: big, terrifying, and from the looks on their faces, extremely pissed. They were also unfettered and as the officers were about to learn, they were exceptionally fast.

The cops sprang to their feet and raced to the next fence. The Dobermans' jaws opened, ready for the kill. One dog's nose scraped against Henderson's backside, giving the terrified officer all the motivation needed to clear the fence on his initial attempt. Calvanese dived headfirst.

The two cops landed inches from each other, faces buried in the dirt, once again. Henderson spat out turf while Calvanese removed grass from his hair and shirt collar.

"Does everybody in this neighborhood own demon dogs?" grumbled Calvanese.

"Poor man's home security system," responded Henderson.

Both men stood and brushed off their grass-stained uniforms.

"What the fuck are the fences for?" asked Calvanese.

"Good fences make good neighbors," answered Henderson.

Calvanese checked his weapon. "I see another dog, chain or unchained, even if it's a puppy, I'm shooting it." They made their way through the backyard and headed for the main street.

"You still wanna look for him?" asked Henderson.

"I'm gettin' my ass the hell outta this neighborhood just as quick as I—" Calvanese stopped suddenly, paying attention to the house on his left. The home was dark, except for the porch light. He noticed broken glass around an open door that had its screen ripped apart.

The two officers moved cautiously. Calvanese motioned for Henderson to go around to the front while he headed for the rear. Henderson crept past the side of the house peering inside the windows as he went. Calvanese inspected the door and avoided stepping on the glass. He entered the home through the kitchen and noticed furniture damaged and chairs overturned.

Calvanese unsnapped his holster, withdrew his gun, and then moved into the living room, where he found additional signs of a struggle. He looked down the hallway and saw a door partially opened with light filtering from the room, low, close to the floor. He'd been in enough similar situations to know this wasn't likely to end well. Calvanese wondered how many bodies he'd find this time, hoping the answer would be none, but the odds weren't in his favor. Instinctively he prayed there wouldn't be any children among the victims. Those images always haunted him the longest. He'd almost quit after seeing the body of a six-year-old girl, raped and mutilated. That was less than a year ago—ten months and three weeks, to be exact.

He snuck down the hallway headed for the light, pausing in front of the door before pushing it open all the way. An elderly Black woman lay on the floor, clothes ripped, half-naked, bleeding, beaten badly. A table lamp lay on its side, near the foot of the bed, casting an eerie combination of light and shadow across the bloodstained carpet. Calvanese moved to the woman and knelt near her. He gently turned her over and discovered she was still alive.

"He... He..." she whimpered.

"It's all right," he reassured her. "I'll call an ambulance. You're gonna be okay."

She looked at him, dazed, confused, but mostly terrified. "He's still here."

Calvanese felt a sharp blow to the back of the head, immediately followed by a second more devastating punch thrown by a powerfully built Black man dressed only in his underwear. The assailant kicked Calvanese in the left kidney, knocking him to the floor next to the woman.

"I'm done with the bitch. You can fuck her now," uttered the man, before rushing out of the room. He raced through the living room and out the front door where he crashed into a surprised Henderson who tumbled over the entryway railing. The officer rolled to his feet and chased the assailant across the lawn, tackling the man into the street. Henderson punched the man in the face without any perceptible impact.

They struggled in the darkness, but Henderson was no match for the much stronger man who outweighed him by at least seventy pounds. The assailant lifted Henderson in a crushing bear hug and then drove him to the ground. The man pummeled Henderson with fierce punches to the stomach and head and then viciously stomped the fallen officer's chest and ribs.

After one last kick to the face, he raced down the street as Calvanese rushed out of the door and past Henderson.

"Freeze!" Calvanese screamed. The man stopped. He kept his back toward the officer, his body now concealed in the darkness except for a dim streetlamp that reflected off his white briefs.

Henderson groggily rose to his feet and stood next to his partner.

"I said freeze!" Calvanese commanded again.

The man turned quickly. Calvanese fired three times, striking him in the upper chest, violently thrusting him backwards against a tree. The man remained standing for a moment, made a weak motion with his right hand. Calvanese fired one final shot. The man collapsed to the ground.

Calvanese stood motionless in the middle of the street, his arm extended, gun still aimed at the assailant.

Henderson stared at him in disbelief, and then looked at the man's body, slumped at the base of the tree. "What the fuck did you do that for?"

"I was defending myself," Calvanese said calmly.

"From what?" responded Henderson incredulously. "Some half-naked guy?"

"There's only one person out here half-naked, Henderson," said Calvanese, returning his weapon to its holster. "And it's you." He walked away, disgusted, and returned inside the home.

Henderson hesitated then looked at his holster. Empty. He slowly approached the lifeless body to render assistance. He removed his flashlight from his belt, aimed the light at the fallen figure, and discovered his gun, still clutched in the dead man's hand. "Shit," he said.

FOUR

Calvanese sat impatiently in the audience watching Police Chief James Gibbs pin a medal on Henderson, who stood uneasily on the outdoor stage, next to a dozen racially and ethnically diverse police officers, waiting to receive their awards and commendations. Gibbs used to be a cop's cop, but the silver-haired veteran had long ago become a shrewd politician and public relations specialist who cared about his officers only when it served his political ambitions. His most pressing goal now was to maintain a healthy relationship with Mayor Alex Palmer; an alliance that existed primarily as a marriage of convenience. He'd make Palmer look good enough to run for governor, with the expectation that the favor would be returned. Gibbs would benefit from Palmer's endorsement to be the next mayor of the City of Angels.

Calvanese stole a look at his watch and wished he'd put on some sunscreen. He could smell his own flesh starting to roast under the sun. The ceremony took place outside City Hall, and the inept planners had neglected to erect enough tents to protect the guests from downtown's arid heat. It was only April, but climate change had made yearly calendars useless, as if you

could ever really tell which month it was in sunny Southern
Cal.

A large gathering of police officers, their families, and well-
wishers, had assembled throughout the makeshift arena along
with the usual number of dignitaries, politicians, and members
of the media. Gibbs also had seen fit to personally invite leaders
from the major civil rights organizations, paying special attention to their seating arrangements. They were placed prominently in the front center rows in direct view of the nightly
news cameras. Everyone and everything served a P.R. purpose,
thought Calvanese, whether alive or dead.

Mayor Palmer had opened the event with his typically
uninspiring homage to the "finest police force in the world," and
then called for a moment of silence for "our fallen brethren lost
in the line of duty." Palmer knew how to make his voice break
convincingly and, more importantly, he knew when to time it
for maximum effect. A consummate politician, the three-term
mayor could kiss a baby while ruthlessly cutting childcare benefits and then kicking the infant's mother off public assistance.
Having accomplished that, he'd take great pleasure in giving the
poor woman re-election material with a request for a campaign
donation. And with that famous puppy-dog look of his, she
would gratefully donate all she had and offer her sincerest
apologies for not being able to contribute more.

After his contrived choked-up moment, which Palmer
ensured the news cameras captured, the mayor regained his
composure long enough to excuse himself from the proceedings
saying that he had "urgent business requiring my immediate
attention." Calvanese assumed it had something to do with
meeting the demands of Palmer's breast-implanted clerical
assistant whose long, slender fingers weren't wasted simply
caressing the smooth surface of her computer keyboard. In fact,
he seriously doubted that the woman knew how to take fast
notes, let alone type.

Once, he had jokingly invited her to join him surfing the internet and she excitedly agreed, indicating it would give her a chance to wear her new yellow string bikini. She quickly canceled the potential tryst fearing that her boss might have overheard the conversation or, worse, would learn about it. "There are no secrets in political office," she whispered, looking over her shoulder several times before summoning enough courage to smile and hand Calvanese her private number which, at his first available opportunity, he wisely discarded.

Gibbs shook Henderson's hand, posed for a photo, and then moved to the next officer in line, a Latina, daughter of former illegal immigrants, who were proudly seated next to their son, also a member of the force. Captain David O'Ryan, Area Commanding Officer of the 77th Street Community Police Station, handed Gibbs a medal attached to a red, white, and blue ribbon. The chief placed it around her neck and shook her hand. Calvanese yawned widely and thought the colors of the ribbon ought to be black, brown, yellow, red, and pink in keeping with the department's affirmative action goals. The last color could serve the purpose of representing solidarity with women.

Henderson's wife, Nicole, seated in the third row, blew him a kiss. Dexter, their seven-year-old son, excitedly waved a small American flag, occasionally striking the back of the police chaplain's head, preventing the minister from either snoozing, or praying with his eyes closed. Calvanese cut across the middle row to get a head start on the buffet.

After the ceremony, awardees mingled with their families and friends. Reporters busily interviewed the chief while a mariachi band played off-key in the background.

"Smile, Dad!" yelled Dexter as Nicole snapped a photo of her husband.

"Go stand next to your father so I can get a picture of the two of you together."

Dexter ran to his father's side and pointed proudly to the medal pinned just above Henderson's shirt pocket.

Nicole focused the lens of her camera, adjusted the aperture, and took a shot. "Don't leave yet. I want to take one more." She aimed but Calvanese approached from behind and took the camera from her before she could press the shutter button.

"Why don't you join them," he suggested, "and I'll take one of the whole family."

Nicole stood in between her husband and son. She and Dexter smiled. Henderson didn't.

Calvanese fumbled with the switch and refocused. "Everybody say: 'Hands up against the wall and spread 'em.'"

Henderson gave a pained expression as Calvanese took the shot and then returned the camera to an appreciative Nicole.

"Thanks very much, that was extremely considerate of you," Nicole said as her husband stood silently next to her. She gave him a sharp nudge followed by a quick nod in Calvanese's direction.

"Nicole, I want you to meet Tony Calvanese," he said listlessly. "Tony, my wife, Nicole."

They shook hands. Calvanese had another reason to feel a little envious of Henderson. Nicole was a knockout, large almond-shaped eyes, great figure, but the thing that impressed him most—the woman had class. She dressed in a certain style, had a sexy elegance about her. The warmth of her hand matched the radiance emanating from her genuine smile. *Henderson—you're one lucky son-of-a...*

"I was hoping we'd get a chance to meet," she said pleasantly. "My husband's told me so much about you."

"Your husband doesn't know that much about me, so it must have been a brief conversation."

"Some of your more endearing qualities take a long time to describe," replied Henderson. "Let alone understand," he added somberly.

floor. "Sister Mary Ellen Bonaventure would strike you on the top of your head with a ring full of keys. Paul, you ever been hit by a ring full of keys?"

"No, sir. I'm Baptist. We use old-fashioned leather."

O'Ryan flashed Henderson a look as if the officer were from another planet. "That was a rhetorical question, Henderson. That means you're not supposed to answer it."

"Sorry, Captain."

They reached the elevator and O'Ryan pushed the button and then checked his wristwatch. "Sometimes, she would hit an innocent kid. She'd take the boy aside and look into his eyes and say, 'You may not have done anything wrong today. But accept this punishment for the bad things you did do but got away with.'"

O'Ryan leaned close but dropped the fatherly tone. "Henderson, accept the award for the times you didn't fuck up but went unrewarded."

A hollow signal chimed the arrival of the elevator and the end of the discussion. The green arrow flashed pointing up and the door glided open.

"We understand each other?" O'Ryan asked.

"Yes, sir."

O'Ryan entered the elevator and turned to face Henderson, fashioning a priestly smile. "Bless you, son. Now, go with God."

Henderson remained motionless, watching the sliding metal door close with a final thud.

FIVE

Reverend Donald Jeremiah Wilson stood in front of Milton Hobson's open casket and spoke with a combination of righteous indignation and mournful eloquence. A former star linebacker in high school, Wilson had forfeited a college scholarship after having been accused in a sex scandal involving several teammates and one, apparently unwilling, underage cheerleader. The charges were dropped after the girl refused to testify against the players. Some said she was threatened while others said she and her family were paid off.

Whatever the truth, Wilson's chance at fame on the gridiron had vanished. A few years later, destitute, and drug-addicted, he found God or, as he sometimes related the story, God finally found him. The born-again preacher had not only discovered a new life but inherited a glamorous starring role, one that replaced the football field with an altar not as large but far more impressive. He tackled the holy word with the same ferocity he used in protecting the line of scrimmage. Those who studied the Bible believed he was as innovative in interpreting the scriptures as he had been creative at inflicting illegal hits on wide receivers and avoiding any subsequent penalties.

"Milton was dedicated to this community and this church." The overflowing congregation murmured agreement with their pastor.

"He loved his wife, Laura. He loved his precious children, little Donnice and her big sister, Gwendolyn." Wilson stepped away from the coffin and with his palm facing upward, made a graceful gesture toward Hobson's widow who had her arms around her two grieving daughters. "And with every fiber of their being, they loved him back."

The church elders uttered "yes they did," and for good measure repeated the sentiment.

"He didn't break any law," shouted Wilson, "and yet this innocent man was slain—murdered—by the very people this city employed to protect him!"

Hands reached high in the air. Heads shook side to side. Lips moved, praying aloud the words, "Amen," and "Praise God."

Wilson displayed a set of keys and held them near the casket. "His only crime was having a set of these in his hand." He jingled the keys briefly as if ringing a small church bell or summoning a servant, then tightly clutched them inside a powerful fist.

Eyes were lowered in grief and then raised in anger.

"The mayor says the police who shot him acted reasonably." Wilson elongated the last word with bitterness and cynicism, his six-foot-three body crouching slightly. "He said that he would always give the benefit of the doubt to his police over this or any other dead Black man!"

Wallace Reeves listened intently. His muscular arms were chiseled from years of lifting heavy metal in his auto repair and body shop. He established the business after returning from his second tour in Afghanistan, dishonorably discharged for striking a white soldier, his superior officer. Reeves regretted that he hadn't "killed the racist bastard." Those were the exact words he used at his court-martial. After the tribunal announced their verdict, he grabbed his crotch, laughed, and then spewed out a steady stream of hate-filled profanities while being forcibly removed from the proceedings.

"Well, Mr. Mayor..." Wilson issued a warning and made it sound ominous. "I give the benefit of the doubt to the Bible, and God's word is both reasonable and just."

The organist underscored the pastor's comment with tantalizing music, and several women in the center section rose to wave their prayer towels in rhythm to the inspirational beat syncopated with an occasional, but deeply felt, "halleluiah."

Wilson moved behind his pulpit and positioned himself in front of the large stained-glass window which shimmered from the sun. Spreading out his arms, he embraced his adoring flock. "I say to you and to all those murderous thugs who operate under the color of authority, you shall reap what you sow!"

The church members in Reeves's pew nodded in affirmation. Reeves didn't bow his head for anyone, not his preacher, his congregation, or even the dead man being eulogized.

"And we shall not rest," Wilson pounded the podium, his voice reaching a climatic shrill, "till God's work is done!"

The membership rose in unison and shouted, "Yes! Speak the truth, now! Speak the truth!"

* * *

The end of the funeral service coincided with Mayor Alex Palmer agreeing to take three final questions at his press conference, which had grown increasingly heated.

"Mr. Mayor!" yelled a reporter who'd managed to get Palmer's attention by screaming the loudest. "How do you respond to increased calls for the Justice Department to conduct investigations into the practices of the L.A.P.D.?"

The feisty mayor looked unswervingly at the television

camera. He had an uncanny ability to find the one belonging to the station with the widest viewing audience. "Maybe you should direct that question to the family of Matt Hoffman who, until he was murdered last week in the line of duty, spent three decades protecting the citizens of this city. You ask them, or any of his nine thousand fellow officers, if they deserve to have their practices investigated."

"Mayor," shouted another reporter, "what do you say to your critics, largely from minority communities, who accuse you and your police department of racial insensitivity?"

Palmer swallowed hard and answered condescendingly. "We've dramatically reduced homicides within minority communities. The fact they're alive to criticize the very people who protect them is testimony to our effectiveness." His chest expanded slightly as he pointed to a Black reporter. "Last question," he announced with obvious contempt.

"Do you regret your statement that when citizens are shot by police you would always give the 'benefit of the doubt' to your officers?"

Palmer contained his anger but exhibited his displeasure by wagging his finger at the reporter who dared ask the question. "There's no finer police department anywhere in this country. I'm proud to support them. I do so completely, enthusiastically, and without any reservation or apology. I'll continue to do so regardless of the demagogues who demand otherwise."

Palmer hurriedly left the room as photographers competed with one another to capture the best photo.

SIX

Calvanese drank coffee at his favorite café, a small hideaway in Culver City, not far from his home. He appreciated the fact that he could order coffee without having had to study French. It also helped that he didn't have to pay six bucks for steaming hot water poured over ground beans topped off with whipped cream and cinnamon. He loved the ambience of this place. It didn't have any. No Starbucks customers typing away the next great screenplay on two-thousand-dollar laptops. No sockless men wearing eight-hundred-dollar Ferragamo loafers. No surgically enhanced trophy wives searching through Louis Vuitton bags for platinum charge cards to pay for extra-large lattes that they would graciously bring home to their faithful undocumented housekeepers. This oasis, squeezed in between a large mall on one side and the future on the other, somehow had managed to remain real by catering to folks who enjoyed their java hot and their Styrofoam cups devoid of corporate logos. Perhaps that was why the welcome sign had been replaced by one that read: "Going out of business."

Calvanese thought about progress for a moment and then

released a sigh. He wondered if it always had to come at such a heavy price, and then questioned if he could make any with his disenchanted partner. He studied a brooding Henderson, sitting across from him, finishing a glass of juice, and decided it was worth the effort. "Look," he explained, "it doesn't matter that I shot a guy who raped and tortured an elderly woman. I'm white. That means I'm a vicious racist who victimized a Black man in his shorts." He dumped another packet of sugar into his coffee. "So, if you get a medal for being a hero, there's no community protest. No civil rights lawsuits. Everybody's happy and the guy I shot stays dead." He tested the new sweetness, appeared mildly satisfied, and hoped that progress could be achieved without destroying everything that came before.

Henderson leaned back in the booth, stretched out his legs and balled up the paper sleeve that had protected his plastic straw. "And I'm supposed to just go along with that," he said with dismay. "Politics as usual."

"Hey, if it bothers you that much, next time you shoot a white guy, I'll take the medal." Calvanese shrugged. "I'm not racist."

"You could've fooled me," mumbled Henderson.

"Don't take this the wrong way," warned Calvanese, "but fooling you is about as difficult as telling the difference between black and white."

Henderson stared at Calvanese in amazement. "Now what possibly could have given you the impression that I might take that the wrong way?"

"'Cause you got a chip on your shoulder about this race thing," answered Calvanese smugly.

"I've got a chip on my shoulder?" asked a mystified Henderson.

"About race," clarified Calvanese. "You saw a Black man in underwear whereas I saw a rapist with a gun." He rubbed his shoulder against the back of the chair. "If it wasn't for his color, you might've seen the danger, too."

"I don't believe this," said Henderson. "I'm getting a lecture on color from you."

"Just be grateful you didn't keep your dick in your holster, or the guy might have stolen your manhood along with your weapon." Calvanese whistled serenely, not a care in the world. He motioned to the waitress for another coffee.

Henderson glared at an unflappable Calvanese. "So, let me get this straight."

Calvanese stopped whistling and smiled with feigned interest.

"You're telling me that I should be more like you and every time I see a Black person, I need to automatically assume he's a dangerous criminal? Is that what you're suggesting?"

The waitress poured coffee into Calvanese's cup. When it was halfway filled, he nodded that it was enough and waited for her to leave. He ripped off the tops of three packets of sugar and spoke confidentially. "You ever study one of those ologies at that fancy university you went to?"

"Those what?"

"Ology. You know, psychology, sociology, shit like that." He poured the sugar into his coffee.

Henderson released a deep sigh and looked around the café. "I took some courses."

"You remember that famous test they did with the dog and bell?"

"Pavlov's experiment," Henderson answered, perfunctorily.

"Yeah. The one where the guy would ring-a-ding then feed a dog. After a while the bell was enough for the dog to slobber all over itself."

"Do you have a point or is this your way of conducting a new experiment?" asked an annoyed Henderson.

"My first partner was shot in the throat by an eleven-year-old Black kid. Just before I saw the gun go off, I remember thinking the kid had the face of an angel, like he should be singing in the choir. My first rape case was a nine-year-old who watched a group of Black men gangbang then murder her mother. After they passed their crack pipe around, they took turns on her." Calvanese drank the rest of his coffee, then placed down the cup closer to Henderson.

"I had to notify her father that his wife was dead and that his daughter would never be a child again. I see Black people, a bell goes off. You wanna think of me as a racist? Fine. But you ought to blame that Pavlov fella."

A Black customer walked past the table and acknowledged Henderson. "Say, brother."

Henderson nodded. Calvanese looked away and rubbed the corners of his mouth uneasily.

The waitress returned and placed the bill on the table. "Can I get you gentlemen anything else?" she asked.

"A bell," answered Calvanese without looking at her.

Henderson and Calvanese walked to the cash register and waited for the hostess. Henderson grabbed a mint from a large plastic bowl and pointed to the wall mirror. "You should be thankful you never arrested Charles Manson or Jeffrey Dahmer," he said casually.

"Why's that?" asked Calvanese.

"Hate to think you'd have ringing in your ears every time you looked in the mirror." Henderson placed the bill on the counter. "It's your turn to pay." He tapped the service bell and left.

Calvanese's waitress approached, took the bill, and calculated the total on the register. "Well, I see you found what you were looking for."

He appeared puzzled.

She motioned toward the service bell. "That bell you

wanted. I wish you'd take it with you. Damn thing lasts a minute every time it's rung."

Calvanese handed her a ten-dollar bill. As he waited for his change, he stared at his image in the mirror and listened to the bell's chime gradually fade to silence.

SEVEN

The corner of Crenshaw and Stocker suggested an era of renewal. But like most inner-city intersections, looks were oftentimes deceptive. A gun could be fired from that spot and the bullet could reach a luxury home, or a thriving arts center, or an enterprise zone supported by a sports celebrity. It might also violate a church or ricochet off a mortuary or shatter the storefront glass of any one of the competing bail bondsmen's offices in the neighborhood. In all likelihood, the bullet would find its way into the body of a child or a passenger in a car or truck or bus who happened to be in the wrong place at the wrong time, or some teenager who hadn't heeded their mother's warning not to wear red or blue or anything of value, like jewelry or expensive sneakers or a leather jacket.

Yes, on the surface, this was a corner that made certain promises, all of which would be broken over and over and over again. This afternoon would be no different as members of two rival gangs engaged in a stare-down contest on a street where making eye contact was tantamount to a challenge that could lead to death. On this occasion, it simply led to a shoving match that escalated into a brawl which necessitated an emergency call to the police. By the time the patrol cars arrived, bodies were on top of each other in an all-out war. Henderson and Calvanese joined several other police and quickly put a halt to the disturbance.

Calvanese grabbed one of the more notorious members of the gang known as MC5, a thug called Hard Candy, a term applied to anyone targeted for death while in county jail for a serious violation of unwritten prison rules – no snitching, no child molestation. He was guilty of both. He not only survived behind bars, but he also managed to greatly enhance his reputation, achieving near rock star status. The Asian inmate who had issued the hit wasn't quite as fortunate and now found himself under rocks and stars, buried in a potter's grave.

Calvanese slammed Candy against the wall of a liquor store. He clutched him by the throat and moved his face closer to his own. "It's so inefficient to fight with your hands when you're perfectly capable of putting a permanent end to this hostility by using your Uzi."

Henderson took Calvanese's hand and eased it off Candy's neck. Calvanese gave Henderson a warning look and then decided to handle it later.

"You're hilarious," Candy said to Calvanese. "Ever think of doin' stand-up or your own Netflix comedy special?"

Calvanese acted extremely interested. "You know somebody? Can you put in a good word for me?" He snapped his finger. "But then again, I can't afford the monthly subscription on a cop's pay. So, if I was on it, could I come by your place and watch? Since I'm sure you're stealing cable for free."

Candy turned his attention to Henderson. "You need to watch who you hang with. This Clint Westwood motherfucker could get you hurt."

"Eastwood," corrected Calvanese. "His name is Eastwood."

"Eastwood, Westwood, Southwood, Peckerwood," Candy

responded. "Don't take it personal, ain't nothin' but a 'G' thang."

Candy shared two things in common with the near dozen young men involved in the confrontation. They were all under twenty-one and each had at least one felony conviction. Candy, between juvenile detention and county jail, had spent more than one-third of his young life incarcerated. Although, in street years, twenty-one was old, much older than most had expected to live.

"You three face the wall," instructed Henderson.

Three of the gang members turned and did as ordered.

"Everybody put your hands in the air," added Calvanese. "Wave 'em like you just don't care." He glared at Candy. "Ain't nothin' but an L.A.P.D. thang," he explained.

Henderson patted down two of the teens. Calvanese checked Candy by running his hand inside his leg.

"A little higher and to the left," Candy requested, smiling in defiance. His expression changed quickly as Calvanese's hand closed tightly around the groin area.

"He ain't packin' nothin'. And I do mean nothin'." Calvanese grabbed Candy by the shoulders and spun him. "Turn around and give me that gold-capped smile again."

"Somebody needs to put you on a chain," Candy said dangerously.

"He's not that bad," said Henderson, defusing the situation. "You just have to ring a bell before you feed him."

"Then somebody please go ahead and give him some Alpo and a litter box," pleaded Candy.

"Alpo's for dogs. Litter boxes are for cats," snapped Calvanese.

"He's right, you know," said Henderson. "You're mixing metaphors."

"Meta-fours, meta-threes, meta-twos, if it oinks like a pig, it ought to be put out of its misery," responded Candy. "'Nuff said."

"Everybody listen up!" announced Henderson. "We can take you downtown, update your mug shots, use precious tax dollars to feed and clothe you for the night. Or you can promise to go home, watch Dr. Phil and learn how to channel your hostility in a more constructive manner. What's it gonna be?"

"Long as we ain't got to watch Oprah," announced Candy.

"Self-hate is a terrible thing," replied Calvanese, shaking his head sadly.

"So's ugliness," said Candy. "But you wear it well."

The teens dispersed after exchanging a few threats to each other. Cops returned to their cars. Henderson and Calvanese remained behind to ensure everyone left peacefully.

"You sure you don't wanna kiss them goodbye?" remarked Calvanese, snidely.

"If you show them respect, they give you respect in return," replied Henderson. "Maybe you should try it for a change."

"Not interested, but you still got time to take 'em to Camp-Hug-A-Thug, or maybe you'd like to invite them to your home for brunch," commented Calvanese.

"Didn't clean up before I left."

"I forgot you had this *Good Housekeeping* seal of approval fetish." Calvanese moved Henderson to the side. "And don't ever take my hand off a punk's neck again," he threatened.

"You have any children?" asked Henderson calmly.

"No."

"Good."

They didn't look at each other. They didn't need to. Calvanese climbed behind the wheel and started the engine. Henderson hesitated for a moment before entering the passenger side. Neither one spoke another word for the rest of the shift.

EIGHT

Henderson didn't have much of an appetite, even though his wife had prepared a feast fit for a king and had spent all afternoon arranging the food and decorating the dining room with celebratory ribbons and balloons. This was his favorite space in their home. Most men preferred their dens or family rooms or basements or, in some cases, even their garages with built-in work areas and sturdy metal tool chests. Not Henderson. For him, nothing was more satisfying than a dining room. He'd never had one as a child.

He'd usually eat by placing his food on top of a small glass coffee table in front of the large console television in the living room, or on the small desk in his bedroom while watching the portable T.V. His mother and father worked long hours and seldom dined together. Even when they did, it consisted of different meals cooked at different times and served in separate areas of their modest home. His father was a meat-eater, preferring heavily salt-laden fried foods, no vegetables, plenty of junk, store-bought snacks, sweets, and carbonated sodas to wash it down. The ideal diet if you want diabetes and high blood pressure. "Treats from the Colored man's menu," his father often joked before taking his heart medication along with forty milligrams of Lipitor before his first big meal of the day.

Nicole brought Henderson his most recent favorite dessert, warm peach cobbler with a sprinkling of cinnamon and a generous scoop of French vanilla ice cream on the side. He placed his spoon inside the bowl and watched the ice cream melt.

"Is something wrong with the cobbler?" Nicole asked, attempting to conceal her disappointment.

"I'm sorry, honey. Everything's perfect, I guess I'm just not in the mood for celebrating."

"Daddy, can I take your medal to school? I'll pin it on my shirt, so it won't get lost."

Nicole gave a proud but bittersweet smile.

"Dexter, I shouldn't have won the medal. I was just doing my job." He pushed away the bowl of dessert. "And the truth is, I didn't do it that well."

"Then why'd they give you a party?" asked his son.

"Politics," his father answered, disheartened. "You know what that is?"

Dexter thought about it and then guessed. "Something grown-ups do for fun?"

Henderson nodded in agreement. "If you've got a weird sense of humor."

Dexter laughed as if his father was making a joke he fully understood. He stopped and looked at his parents. "How come no one else is laughing?"

"Because sometimes adults can't accept success and won't allow anyone else to enjoy it either," said a miffed Nicole. She abruptly got up from her chair and left the area.

Dexter looked at his father, who finally took a taste of the cobbler and enjoyed it, immensely.

"This is really great," said Henderson. "You should try some."

Dexter didn't need any additional encouragement. He grabbed a bowl and gulped down the ice cream first.

* * *

Calvanese unlocked the door, entered his living room, and flicked on the light switch. Home. He used to love coming inside to find his wife cooking or asleep on the couch or watching T.V. or, best of all, lying in a hot bubble bath reading a romance novel. She'd learned a lot from those books and did her best to teach him the finer points, particularly what to do with handcuffs and whipped cream.

They'd made love in every room of this two-story colonial. The mortgage hadn't been approved by the bank when they convinced the real estate agent to leave them alone for an hour to do their own inspection. They inspected all right, every square inch of skin they both had to offer. They had a forty-five-day escrow and, before it officially closed, they found a reason to further scrutinize their prospective home as often as possible. By the time they had moved in the furniture, they knew the location of every creak and squeak and uneven spot throughout the entire 2,750 square feet of living space, including closets, laundry area and the two-and-a-half bathrooms.

She'd left him the house when they divorced three years ago. He initially believed her generosity reflected an act of extreme kindness, but once he saw the mansion she'd moved into with her new husband, he recognized it for what it was: diabolical revenge.

It allowed him to feel inadequate while at the same time constantly reminding him of her absence. On second thought, it wasn't her absence that bothered him, it was something far worse. The place simply reminded him of her: her presence, the things they did together, the arguments they had that ended up in lovemaking or two days of refusing to speak to each other—

silent pouting that usually culminated in laughter, but not always. Sometimes the silence lasted longer, not because they remained angry but because they had nothing to say, no more desire to speak or argue or reconcile.

He thought marriage was forever. She told him it wasn't marriage that lasted forever, but love. As usual, she was right. He still loved her even though the marriage ended long before the divorce proceedings commenced. And although he'd accused her of every conceivable betrayal, he knew she didn't leave him for another man, wealthy or not. She left him because she needed someone to hold her, to tell her she felt good, that she was necessary—that she was loved. Somehow, he'd lost the ability to do that. So, she gave him the house and all the memories that went with it and now, instead of being welcomed by a warm body and gentle smile, he was greeted by those memories every night; and to top it off, they bid him farewell each morning with the promise to wait for his return, no matter how late his arrival.

He removed his gun belt, laid it across the back of the sofa, and made a disgusted face. His nose led him to a foul odor in the kitchen, burned scrambled eggs stuck to the surface of a frying pan soaking in the sink, filled with rancid water. He took a long wooden ladle, searched the bottom of the basin, lifted the rubber stopper, and turned on the disposal. He replaced the stopper, turned on the hot water, rubbed a scouring pad across the chipped Teflon and rinsed it. He dropped the pan into a new tub of water, added some dishwashing soap, and ran a bit more liquid.

In the refrigerator he discovered three bottles of beer and a pizza box. He grabbed a bottle and the container and set them down on the counter after using his elbows to clear aside various bags of snacks and jars of peanut butter. He flipped open the lid and removed both slices of pizza covered with a variety of discolored meats. After testing the rock-solid leftovers with his finger, he placed the slices into the microwave and set the timer for ninety seconds. He snatched the bottle of beer, took a quick swig, then moved to the living room and checked his tape machine. No messages. Unconvinced, Calvanese pushed the button and heard the recorded voice announce: "You have no new messages."

He lifted the receiver and listened for a dial tone. No problem with the phone. He dropped the receiver in its place, opened his tattered address book, and flipped through it. He glanced at a few names, decided on one, dialed the number, and waited patiently.

"Hi, is Deanne there?" He gulped down another three swallows of beer. "When?" He nodded twice. "Over a year ago. Married?" He nodded again. "No, I don't need the number. If you talk with her, just tell her the police called."

Hanging up the phone, he leaned back against the chair and flipped through the book again. Finding a number that he thought could be interesting, he reached for the phone just as the timer rang. Returning to the kitchen, he retrieved his pizza. Instinct and prior experience forced him to put his nose near the food where he sniffed it once, twice, and then dropped it into a trash receptacle.

He finished the first beer, reopened the refrigerator, and grabbed another bottle. Before closing the door, he stood motionless, stared at the empty shelves, and watched the door close slowly. I gotta get a life, he thought, or another job. He wondered if he should just sell the house but then realized that would be like divorcing his wife a second time, and once was enough, far more than he wanted or could ever be expected to reasonably handle.

* * *

Henderson and Nicole finished devouring each other. She held him tenderly, his head rested gently over her heart. He kissed her breast and she stared at the ceiling, concerned, afraid.

"It always scares me when you make love that way," she said.

"I thought I was pretty good," Henderson replied defensively. "Scratch that. I was damn good... wasn't I?"

"I didn't say I didn't like it. I just said—"

"It scares you," he answered her.

"You act as if it might be the last time. Like you want to say something to me but can't. So, you let your passion say it for you."

"Is that so wrong?"

She stroked his back and looked away. "I don't know what I'd do if I ever lost you. I know that sounds clichéd, and I wish I could come up with something more original. But I think about it a lot. Every time you leave the house to go to work. Whenever I hear a news report about an incident involving the police, a shooting, a car chase, anything that makes me wonder if I'll be the next widow having to attend a funeral surrounded by my deceased husband's fellow officers dressed in blue and lined up around a coffin draped in the—"

He placed his fingertips over her lips and eased his body on top of hers. He moved his hand away from her mouth and touched the side of her face to experience skin that had never failed to excite him. He had met her ten years ago at a party thrown by his ex-girlfriend, who had remained a close friend, despite her new husband's unfounded jealousy. She stood in the kitchen with her back turned toward him, wearing a red-striped tube top and a tight-fitting pair of jeans. She was helping to rinse dishes before carefully placing them in the dishwasher. It impressed him how she organized the dishes, using all the available space. He hated it when water was wasted to clean three dishes and two cups spread out unevenly.

The music coming from the living room caused her to move to the rhythm of Smokey Robinson's "I Second That Emotion."

When she faced him, he did more than second Smokey's emotion as well as his own. Their eyes met immediately and, as they say in the movies, time froze. She smiled and he thought she had the most perfectly formed mouth he'd ever seen, made more tempting by her rose-colored lipstick that, before the evening was through, would leave an imprint on his shirt collar that he'd never want to remove. And he never did. It now shared a space next to the pound of sand he brought back from a Jamaican beach where they spent their honeymoon.

"Hi," she had said after her mesmerizing smile. "My name's Nicole."

"Are you married?" he asked, not realizing his inner thoughts had betrayed him with a public utterance. He should have just spied her ring finger—but why be secretive when you can totally lose self-control and blurt out your true feelings and appear a fool?

Her eyes darted toward the ceiling, and she fidgeted with her belt loop. "Not at the moment," she responded after a long uncomfortable pause.

Well, that was an indication that she hadn't ruled it out. He'd already jumped off the diving board and was headed straight for the pool. It was far too late to worry about getting wet now. "Would you like to be?" he asked cordially.

She shifted her body to one side, then the other. She moistened her lips with a nervous flick of her tongue and then looked around the room. He feared it was for help or to locate the quickest exit. "I'm Paul, by the way, and obviously a bit of an idiot."

"Paul... would you like to play backgammon?"

He nodded yes, forgetting that he didn't know how. He felt like a little boy too anxious to be embarrassed. She taught him and he won the first six games. Did she let him win, or was his luck that good? He approved of both possibilities.

Someone asked her to dance. She politely declined. In fact, she did so graciously. If he was ever rejected, he hoped it would happen that way, but not by her. Never by her. The music changed to a slow dance. She reached out and grabbed his hand and led him to the dance floor. He held her tight, felt his heart against her body. He prayed he wouldn't step on her foot, so he used the excuse to move more slowly, barely at all.

When the song ended, he suggested they go outside to catch some "fresh air." After a lengthy stroll, they decided to ditch the party and see a movie— "back at my place," she offered. When he left her that morning, she gave him a long, slow kiss, an extra set of keys to her apartment, and a remote control that would open her garage door. They were married six months later. All of that and so much more flashed through his mind as he lay on top of her now and tried to reassure her, alleviating her fears.

"I don't want Dexter to lose his father," she said. "He adores you, you know that. Don't you?"

"And I adore his mother." He kissed her softly on the forehead and then her lips. He wiped away a tear from her eye. "I'm a cop, Nicole."

"And a husband and a father," she reminded him gently.

"The luckiest one there is," he said. "I'm not going to let anything bad happen to me, to us."

"How can you be so sure?"

"Because I've got a brand-new shiny medal, and they only give those to people who know what they're doing."

"That's not the only reason they give them," she countered, then turned away, moving her face to the side. "And sometimes they can't give the medals to the person who earned it, so they award it to his family, in his name."

He sat on the edge of the bed. "You knew this is what I wanted to do before we got married."

"I thought you had given that up once you went to law school."

"I can do more being a cop. And I can do it a lot more quickly."

"You can die faster, too."

"Is this about Matt?"

"He was going to retire in two days. Two days! What happened to him could happen to any cop, anytime. And you haven't said anything about him. Not a word. It's like it never happened."

"What do you want me to say?"

"Anything. Just acknowledge it. Tell me how you feel. Are you sad, afraid? The man was in our home. He played with our son. He was your friend."

Henderson shook his head. "He was a cop I worked with, that's all. I'm not sure it's possible for cops to have friends. You get too close, start caring for another cop, and..."

"And what?"

"You can't do your job the way you should. We need to protect the public. We start thinking about protecting a friend, each other, that's when it all begins to fall apart."

Yes, the murder of Matt Hoffman was every cop's nightmare and Henderson's reason for grief and frustration that had nothing to do with a medal. He wanted to believe it was possible to finally have the time to enjoy life, to retire without the uniform that made him a target, the gun that never really protected him, and the badge that drew contempt from the very people he tried to protect. He knew it could happen at any time, for any reason. A bullet could end his life and destroy the lives of the family who loved him. He'd try not to think about Matt or the ones who would inevitably follow.

She held out her arms and drew him closer to her and then held him tightly, whispering, "I love you so much." He wanted to tell her how much he loved her in return but couldn't. He realized making love was another way to avoid dealing with his pain and her fear. It suspended enough time that when they were through, they could act like the problem had been resolved, better yet never existed. He knew why she held him in her arms, and it wasn't to make love, but rather to be loved.

NINE

The Santa Ana winds wreaked havoc throughout the day downing electrical power lines and sweeping debris onto yards and streets, causing numerous accidents, and contributing to short tempers and long arguments along with far too many calls to 911. As if L.A. needed any more excuses for weird behavior, a full moon sparkled in the sky, a sure sign that emergency rooms would be busy tonight. Werewolves might exist only in the imagination, but predators were real and for some strange reason their activity increased with the lunar cycle and the summer months. June sucked. July was worse. And no one wanted to see August. But it was still April, so everything should be normal, except for the effects of the moon.

A patrol car pulled into an alleyway behind a series of interconnected row houses, cheap dwellings that would be torn down in any other state, but in Southern California's real estate market they were considered far more valuable than the people who lived in them. Arthur West, the senior officer, searched the area while his partner, Neil Andrews, crossed the lawn looking for the correct address.

Most of these places had been converted into multiple residences, top and bottom floors rented to different tenants; front and back rooms were often further subdivided. Each unit had the same address, except there might be fractions added to the end: a ¼ or ½. Or else the letters A through D would be reflected on the mailboxes, and you had to guess the right door—not an easy task since the people who lived here sought anonymity from bill collectors and other unwanted visitors.

Officer Andrews pressed a door buzzer and discovered it was broken or disconnected. He used the knocker, or what was left of it: a small, thin scrap of metal loosely attached to the door that served no useful purpose when tested against thick wood. West walked two steps toward the entrance; based on his waistline he'd rather fight doughnuts than bad guys, and he'd had more than his share of both.

"Bell doesn't work?" he asked.

"It never does," answered Andrews. "Don't know why they bother installing them."

Jennifer Goode, a Black woman in her early thirties, opened the door as far as the chain lock would allow and studied the officers through the six-inch clearance. "My husband's not here," she said.

"What makes you think we're looking for him?" asked Andrews.

"'Cause I been lookin' for him for over six months," she answered, then ran her tongue over her front teeth. "Ain't found him. Maybe you'll have better luck."

"Got a call you had a domestic problem," West notified her while trying to sneak a peek inside.

"I got lots of problems, domestic and imported," she said, and then adjusted the front of her bra.

The two officers exchanged amused glances. "Mind if we come in, take a look around?" asked Andrews, politely.

She evaluated them for a moment. "You thinkin' of rentin' or buyin'?"

"You're a pretty funny lady, you know that?" said West.

"I make myself laugh all the time." She undid the chain lock and opened the door wide. "Don't track no dirt on my carpets. Just had 'em cleaned."

The cops entered, after wiping the bottom of their shoes on the filthy welcome mat.

Three adorable girls, ranging in age from two to seven, gathered in the living room and stared at the white men in uniform.

"See, I told you if you didn't clean your rooms, I was gonna call the police," she warned her children.

The girls looked at each other, not knowing who to blame or where to hide.

"Okay if I open some doors?" asked West.

"You can dust and polish the furniture if you like."

West shook his head and sighed. "You should have your own sitcom," he said. He nodded to his partner and then proceeded down a hallway and entered a side room. Andrews winked at the oldest girl and her two sisters giggled and tried to wink back.

"They're gonna be heartbreakers one day," he said to their mother.

"Done broke everything else," she informed him. "Can I get you something to drink?"

"No thanks. I'll be home in a half-hour. Hopefully, I'll get there before my little girl's asleep."

"How old?"

"Eighteen months," he announced proudly. "They're magic at that age."

"Except they don't disappear," she joked and nudged the officer. "I hope they never do."

"Amen to that."

The woman smiled. "You a religious man?" she asked, impressed.

"In my line of work, you pray as often as you can."

"Don't matter what your job is, pays to have the Lord on your side."

West re-entered the room, nodded to Andrews. "Everything checks out. Sorry to trouble you, ma'am."

"No trouble, I enjoyed the company. Just hope you can find your way back here when I really do need you."

"You can count on it," assured Andrews. He pinched the youngest girl on her cheek and left with his partner.

They took a relaxing breath and observed the moon, high in the sky, a cloud moving slowly to partially conceal it. They leisurely cut across the lawn and headed for the alley.

"Cute kids," said Andrews.

"Nice lady," added West.

They reached their patrol car but had no time to react to the gunman who moved quickly from the rear, firing his shotgun at close range. Their faces contorted in pain and trauma. Their bodies twisted as they fell to the ground. West was dead on impact. Andrews squirmed then barely managed to crawl before collapsing on his back. He tried to lift himself but stopped when he saw the barrel of the shotgun inches from his face. He murmured "please," but wasn't allowed to finish his appeal as the shotgun exploded again.

The gunman's footsteps rapidly faded in the night, leaving behind a moment of deadly silence interrupted by electronic chatter transmitted over the police radio, human voices intermingled with static.

Doors slammed shut or banged open. Neighbors exited their homes or rushed into them hurriedly. Dogs barked. Voices filled the air with hushed warnings or panicked speculations. A crowd gathered near the patrol car and then slowly surrounded the fallen bodies.

Jennifer Goode slowly moved away from her front door and then raced toward the activity screaming, "No, Jesus! Oh no, dear Jesus!" Her three girls followed. The two-year-old stopped and stood still, watching her sisters cry. Frightened, she placed her tiny arms up in the air and cried, too: a terrifying, hungry wail, worse than any she'd previously experienced in her brief existence on this earth.

Her mother rushed to her and desperately attempted to shelter all her daughters from the horrible carnage. But her oldest child had wandered too close to the officers and now stood in a pool of their blood, her body shivering in fear and shock. And then she screamed and kept screaming long after she was lifted by a neighbor and carried inside to the safety of her mother's home.

TEN

Wallace Reeves sat at his workbench wearing a grease-stained mechanic's uniform listening to the news report on a car radio turned up to full volume.

"Tuesday's killing of two L.A.P.D. officers in South Central Los Angeles marked the third such shooting death in the past ten days."

Reeves spread out a newspaper and used a razor blade to cut around the edges of an article and its accompanying photo.

"A spokesperson for the state's Department of Justice refused to comment on widespread reports that the killings may be racially motivated and in retaliation for the recent upsurge of police shootings of unarmed African American males. All three slain officers were white."

Reeves heard rap music blaring through bass speakers and peered outside his shop window, where he noticed a vintage customized metallic cherry-red 1975 Ford Thunderbird pulling into the rear parking lot. He shook his head in disgust and placed the newspaper clippings inside a cabinet drawer. "Dumb motherfucker," he mumbled and then turned off the car radio.

He walked past his tool shed, picked up an old worn tire,

and tossed it on top of a stack of retreads. He flicked several switches activating a compressor which automatically lowered a sports car perched atop the center lift. He placed five-gallon paint cans on a metal shelf and cleaned the attachments to a spray gun with a pungent turpentine solution.

The front door opened, setting off the security alarm that buzzed twice. Five-Dollar-Rock, a twenty-four-year-old Black man wearing sagging denim pants and a ripped white muscle shirt that revealed his bare chest, strutted inside. Short, rail-thin, and immensely unattractive, he compensated for his inadequacies by wearing as much jewelry as his underdeveloped body could carry. He didn't so much walk as glide, aided by sweeping arm gestures and wide semicircular shoulder movements that demanded much more space than any normal person required. His gold- and diamond-inflated ego was accentuated by the single word "MANSLAUGHTER" tattooed prominently over his heart in blood-red letters. Next to the inscription was the number "5" representing both his name as well as time served for his felony conviction. He tugged at his black nylon stocking cap and admired himself in a smoke-tinted mirror.

"You were right," he said, then approached Reeves, who ignored him.

"Always am," Reeves said nonchalantly. He grabbed a wrench and placed it in its proper slot in a heavy-duty steel tool chest that he slammed shut.

"Shoulda picked the gold trim," said Five-Dollar with a noticeable degree of regret.

"I'll fix it," mentioned Reeves. "But it's gonna cost."

"You ain't never done nothin' for free, old man."

"Call me old man one more time and I'll put your fuckin' head in a vise and squeeze till your brains squirt out your ears, assumin' they ain't all plugged up from that damn music you play." He moved behind the counter and grabbed an order form. "You understand me?"

"Ain't no need for all that drama." Five-Dollar picked up a heavy chunk of iron and struggled to complete a set of curls. Ten for the right arm, then he alternated and repeated the number for his left. "I know you got a rep, and if you wanna keep it don't go disrespectin' mines."

"Difference between my rep and yours," remarked Reeves, "is that I don't havta put mine on my chest like I'm some goddamn walkin' billboard."

"Yeah," countered Five-Dollar, "but we come from a different time and place. People need to know who they dealin' wit'." He pointed proudly to his chest. "Pays to advertise, saves a lot of trouble down the line. You feel me?"

Reeves released a disapproving grunt and then wrote down some information on his pad. He observed Five-Dollar looking at a series of old framed photos of Black Marines dressed in uniform and holding their weapons. The pictures were plastered on the rear wall, lined up neatly next to military paraphernalia showcased inside a dirty glass cabinet. Several medals and awards rested on a velvet cloth which hadn't been dusted in quite some time.

"You served in Afghan?" asked Five-Dollar, impressed.

"I ain't served nowhere."

"Then who are all these soldiers?"

Reeves answered without looking up. "Just some dead niggers."

Five-Dollar stared at Reeves curiously. "Why keep a bunch of dead men on your wall?"

"'Cause they're the lucky ones," Reeves said without any discernible emotion.

"You a strange dude," remarked Five-Dollar, falling somewhere in between admiration and contempt.

"Strange is a word used by ignorant folk who got trouble figurin' out what they can't understand," said Reeves, eventually looking up long enough from his work to glare at Five-Dollar.

"I understand you're a better mechanic than a philosopher, so save your advice and do what you do best, change oil, fix and custom-paint my motherfuckin' ride."

Reeves smiled for the first time, an unusual smirk that appeared to momentarily unnerve Five-Dollar.

"You got something against pickin' up a trade, boy?" asked Reeves. "Doin' something useful with the talents God gave you?"

"Ain't got a problem wit' that at all. It's cool with me," said Five-Dollar, trying to find an area of agreement, if not reconciliation. "You learn how to be a mechanic in the war?"

"No," said Reeves impassively. "That's where I learned how to look at a dead body and not give a fuck." He ripped off a sheet of paper and handed the receipt to Five-Dollar. "Leave the key."

Five-Dollar tossed him the car keys. "You a friendly motherfucker, ain't you?"

"You wanna friend"—he pointed to the photos of the Marines on the wall—"take one of those pictures with you. That's how useful friends are gonna be to someone like you."

"You don't know anything about me, brother," asserted Five-Dollar with defiance.

"I know you ain't my kin, so don't be callin' me brother." Reeves moved from the counter and stood face-to-face with Five-Dollar. "Nothin' else I need to know except you'll be here a week from next Tuesday and you'll pay in cash."

"I can't wait that long. I need my ride."

"Quality takes time. You don't give a shit about how your ride looks? There's a nice white auto shop in Westchester I can recommend. But they might check the VIN number and have the police waiting for you when you come to pick up."

Five-Dollar took a step forward and then waved him off as if he didn't matter. He walked out of the garage and entered a waiting car. When he turned, Reeves was glaring at him through the window. He flashed the old man a gang sign as the car sped off.

Reeves crossed to a thick wooden cabinet and unlocked the door. He reviewed a group of keys hanging on a plastic display. He studied the ignition key belonging to Five-Dollar and compared it with the blank keys on the bottom row. He selected a key and lined it up, matching it to the original and then brought both keys to a cutting machine where he made a duplicate.

When he finished, he put the new key in a small combination safe and turned on the car radio, changing the channel to an oldies-but-goodies station. After returning to his workbench, he retrieved the newspaper clippings he'd cut out earlier. He studied the articles of the two dead police officers with interest bordering on admiration. Flipping the pages to the front, he paused to read an article on the policeman murdered in Hollywood Hills. Officer Matt Hoffman, who was scheduled to retire after two more shifts, left behind a wife, four daughters, and a grandson.

The front door alarm chimed its double warning and Max Oliver entered carrying a brown paper lunch bag and a silver thermos jug. Reeves glanced up at the oval-shaped clock hanging above the heavily dented refrigerator, an old-fashioned one-door unit with a broken handle that had to be twisted inward then pulled hard to function. He hastily gathered the newspaper cuttings. He balled up what remained of the shredded pages and dumped them into the wastebasket underneath his bench.

"You're late," Reeves said.

"My car wouldn't start so I had to take the bus," replied Oliver, lamely.

Reeves rose from his seat and stood in front of his workstation blocking a full view of the material on the bench. "A mechanic who can't start his own automobile," Reeves pondered aloud. "Now that's one hell of an ad slogan."

Oliver struggled to open the refrigerator and then placed his bag and thermos inside. "When you gonna get a new fridge?"

"Ain't nothin' wrong with that one," snorted Reeves. "Keeps things cold, which is why I got it in the first place."

Oliver grabbed his toolkit and carried it to his stall. He moved gracefully for a tall, lanky kid who looked closer to eighteen than twenty-four. He had crooked teeth that added personality to his smile. A dimple sometimes appeared but seldom lasted long. His freckles were out in full force, aided by the bright red shirt that hung from his body like a sheet on a clothesline. He wore clunky hiking boots that increased his six-three frame by an extra inch or two. Why someone would wear those shoes in hot weather remained a mystery to Reeves.

You could read this kid from a mile away. Another white boy who had his anchor tossed in the wrong river. That's what Reeves concluded ten months ago but decided to hire Oliver anyway. Maybe that was the only reason Reeves offered him employment. He looked like a wounded canary whose mother had just died. Even an injured bird can be saved or serve a useful purpose if it's guided toward the proper nest. And, as Reeves knew all too well, if you can't find or make your own nest, then you take someone else's. That's the law of nature, which was a more polite way of saying jungle.

"Need to redo the Thunderbird with gold trim," Reeves informed his employee.

"Thought that's what you recommended in the first place," responded Oliver, now fully engaged with repairing an engine in a Subaru that had seen better times.

"Advice don't cost nothin' till you ignore it," Reeves quipped. "Made an extra key for the ignition, just in case you wind up losing the original."

Oliver glanced up, annoyed. "I told you, I never lost any key. So just drop it, all right?"

"Whatever you say," Reeves snickered. "Wasn't accusing you of anything worth a fuck, so don't go gettin' your panties in a bunch."

Oliver shook his head in resignation then gave a terse smile. "Forget it. Guess I'm just a little upset with my car and all."

"Bring it in and let a real mechanic work on it. I won't charge you for labor."

Oliver flashed a surprised look.

Reeves folded his arms across his chest. "I meant to say, won't charge you as much for labor."

"Now that's the man I know," replied Oliver.

"You don't know me," said Reeves gravely. "Not hardly." He unpacked a large crate of chrome rims and turned up the volume on the car radio. It played one of his favorites from back in the day, a song by Isaac Hayes that Reeves hadn't heard in years. His head moved to the rhythm of the music, and he listened nostalgically to the sultry voice that introduced himself as "Chocolate Chip" and then volunteered the prophetic refrain: *You ain't never had a nigger like me.*

ELEVEN

Across town a far different type of music played. A sole bugle
sounded the haunting melody of "Taps" in tribute to Andrews
and West, veterans of both the military as well as the L.A.P.D.
Wreaths were solemnly laid on two coffins as their families and
friends wept and their fellow comrades watched stoically.
Andrews' young widow held their daughter in her arms; merci-
fully, the little girl had fallen asleep under the unbearable heat
made worse by the grief and torment of her mother, who she'd
never seen suffer.

Mrs. West looked much older than her forty-five years on
this earth, more than half of which she'd spent loving her
husband. Grief will change the way you look more quickly than
how it makes you feel. She stood with her three teenaged sons
who had cried all the tears they had available and were now
drained of emotion and, seemingly, of life.

Dozens of police stood at attention as the bugler finished
his farewell song. Hundreds from all over the state had taken
part in the traditional salute to their fallen heroes earlier in the
week. Motorcycles and patrol cars lined the streets traveling
slowly in a funeral procession with their vehicular beacons and

flashing lights paying tribute to Andrews and West. Henderson lowered his hand from his heart while Calvanese stared ahead and tried to remember the number of funerals he'd attended since he first put on a uniform and swore to uphold the oath. He used to bring his wife with him to these events but after attending the fourth or fifth "fallen hero" memorial in less than eighteen months, she told him she'd had enough. He thought she meant funerals, but he learned much later that she'd had enough of him, or to be fair and more precise, she couldn't take any more of his job and what it had done to him.

Mourners listened to the police chaplain as he spoke his final tribute, stopping several times to regain his composure only to have his voice break near the end, barely releasing the prayer which ended with the words, "May God welcome them to His glorious kingdom and grant them both everlasting life."

Some white officers wore photo buttons of the two slain policemen, given to them by Mike Stevens, a thick-necked former Marine and twenty-five-year veteran of the force who had once partnered with West. He approached Calvanese and handed him one of the buttons he was carrying and placed the rest in his pocket. "Where's your dark Tonto?" he asked, looking around for Henderson.

"You're being politically incorrect," warned Calvanese, not amused by the comment.

"Kept me alive this long," Stevens said. "Don't see any reason to change now." He removed his cap and ran his fingers through his sandy blond hair or what was left of it.

"There's always a reason to change," said Calvanese reflectively, "and most of the good ones aren't your own." Calvanese squinted in pain then shielded his eyes with his right hand.

"What's wrong with you?" asked Stevens.

"Put your hat back on, will ya? The sun's reflecting off that bald spot, damn near blinded me."

Stevens put on his cap. "Baldness is a sign of virility," he said in response.

"Then you could have a lot of bald children runnin' around somewhere."

"This ain't the appropriate place to be jokin'," said Stevens.

Calvanese turned serious, observed the line of officers offering condolences to the widows. "Got to laugh to keep from cryin', Mike," he said quietly. "'Cause when the tears finally do come, they stay an awfully long time, and that's the gospel truth."

Stevens nodded his head in agreement. "Speaking of the truth, you hear the news?"

"Not unless I made it."

Several other officers joined Stevens and waited for him to finish his business with Calvanese. "Buzz on the street is a Black group set 'em up. Called 911 and then waited for them to check it out. Once their guard was down, they never had a chance."

"Anybody suggest a motive?" Calvanese asked, then noticed Mrs. Andrews being comforted by a Black woman, Jennifer Goode, accompanied by her three daughters, the oldest of whom offered the widow a small bouquet of flowers.

"I believe the motive's called justice," commented Stevens.

"We don't know what the fuck happened out there or why," said Calvanese.

"Two more white cops are dead. Ain't nothin' else to know," responded Stevens, looking at his comrades seeking and receiving their support.

"You start spreadin' some wild speculation and the shit will really get outta control," warned Calvanese.

"Speakin' of wild speculation, what do you and your partner talk about?"

"The size of our dicks."

"Joke if you want to but you're being talked about. And it

ain't good. Which means it ain't safe." Stevens saw Henderson. "Speak of the devil. You need to choose a side, or it'll be chosen for you."

Henderson approached and acknowledged the group with a nod, then turned his attention to Stevens. "Mike," he said, without much warmth. "Heard you were handing out buttons, got any extra?"

"All out of 'em," he lied.

Calvanese handed his button to Henderson. "Here, you can have this one." He gave Stevens a dissatisfied look. "I know where I can get some more."

Henderson stared at Stevens; there was no love lost between the two men. He turned his attention back to Calvanese. "You ready to go?"

Calvanese nodded at his fellow cops. "Gentlemen, I must leave to make America safe."

"If you wanna keep your own ass safe," said Stevens, adding as much suspense as possible, "my advice is stay really close to you-know-who." He nodded to Henderson as the other cops shared in the amusement.

"What the fuck is that supposed to mean?" responded Henderson angrily.

"Means you're a good luck charm," said Stevens. He nudged Calvanese. "Tony, maybe you can make some extra bucks and let us borrow your partner as an insurance policy."

"He doesn't own me, asshole," Henderson confronted Stevens. "So, he can't rent me out."

"Come on, Paul," intervened Calvanese, "this isn't the place to start trouble."

"I didn't start it," said Henderson and glared at Stevens. "But I'm prepared to finish anytime you like."

Stevens smiled and nodded. "I'll look forward to that occasion."

"Count on it." Henderson walked past Calvanese. "I'll be in the car."

Calvanese watched him leave then turned toward Stevens. "Why you wanna bust his balls like that?"

"When you'd get so protective of that jig?" replied Stevens. "You know the only reason they assigned him to you was fuckin' politics."

"I don't give a shit how I got him. He's my partner and that makes me protective. You got a problem with that?"

Stevens studied Calvanese for a moment, uneasy, and then softened his tone. "I got no problem with you, Tony. But there's gonna come a time when you'll learn the only partners those people have are the ones they can stab in the back. You remember that." Stevens looked away and saw something that caused him to appear disgusted. "Ain't that motherfucker been to enough funerals in the last week?"

Calvanese turned and noticed Officer Dawson offering his condolences to the two women.

"Matt was gonna retire in two fuckin' days. He deserved a whole lot better than some rookie who dived to save his own black ass," said Stevens.

"He could've stayed on his feet," commented another officer. "You're not in any danger long as your skin's the right color."

"How do you know that?" asked Calvanese, aggravated.

Stevens tapped Calvanese on the chest with the back of his fist. "Solidarity among the brothers," he said contemptuously. "We better get over there. That kind of sympathy she doesn't need." Stevens and the rest of his crew proceeded toward the young widow.

Calvanese watched Dawson walk away from the women and join other Black officers who were patiently waiting for him.

TWELVE

Calvanese willingly submitted to Henderson's demand for the keys, hoping that he'd calm down once he got behind the steering wheel. But after ten minutes, the driving became increasingly erratic.

"We just left a funeral," Calvanese said. "I'm not in the mood to attend another one, especially my own. You wanna slow down on the turns?"

"You've got nothin' to worry about, remember? Mike said you'd be safe with me, so keep your mouth shut and enjoy the view." Henderson took a right onto Western Avenue, ignoring Calvanese as much as possible.

"You need to lighten up," Calvanese said unapologetically and then glanced at Henderson. "In a manner of speaking," he added, tentatively.

"I'm getting pretty sick and tired of your jokes," snapped Henderson.

"That wasn't a joke," protested Calvanese. "It was an expression. Like 'flesh tone' bandages. It's not sinister. It's life. Why you always got to see the negative in the world?"

Henderson looked at Calvanese with incredulity. "This coming from Mr. Pavlov himself."

"Be careful what you say, you might be comparing yourself to a dog." Calvanese glanced at a sedan pulled over by a patrol car. A Black man dressed in a well-tailored business suit was being cuffed by two white officers. A woman, presumably the man's wife, consoled their two young children who were crying desperately.

"Let's check it out," said Henderson.

Calvanese gave it a quick assessment. "Looks under control to me."

Henderson gave him a look that suggested he thought otherwise, then turned around the car and headed for the disturbance. Calvanese released a groan and raised his window. Henderson parked behind the other police car and exited with his reluctant partner. They approached the two officers.

"Need any assistance?" Henderson asked.

"Not anymore," one of the cops answered, dismissively.

"What's the problem?" Henderson continued.

"Don't have one," the same cop said, annoyed, then addressed his comments to Calvanese. "Routine traffic stop. He decided not to cooperate."

"That's a damn lie!" shouted the man's wife. "He just wanted to know why you were stopping us!"

The cop turned to her with disdain. "Look, I can haul your ass in, too."

"You don't need to talk to her that way," intervened Henderson. "Not in front of her kids."

The cop took a step toward Henderson, but Calvanese pulled the officer to the side. "Look," he said confidentially, "isn't there a way to reconsider?"

The cop looked away stubbornly.

"It's your call," continued Calvanese congenially, "and I'm not trying to run interference, you're in the best position to know." Calvanese glanced at Henderson and then nodded at the cop's partner who remained with the cuffed man. He returned his attention to the officer and spoke in a friendly and supportive manner. "It's just, we got enough headaches going on right now, it's hot outside, you got a lot of paperwork to fill out. In the greater scheme of things, this shit ain't really worth it. Now, you gotta admit that's true, don't you?"

The cop thought about it, studied the Black family, then looked at Calvanese. "Just tell your partner to stay out of this. I don't appreciate his attitude."

Calvanese gave the cop's shoulder a sociable tap. "I'll talk to him. He means well, just a little pushy sometimes. You know the type."

"Yeah, I know," the cop answered resentfully.

"Meanwhile, can't you cut the guy some slack?" Calvanese said encouragingly. "I'd appreciate it." He nodded and spoke conspiratorially. "One cop to another. Give the dude a break, for the sake of his kids. What'd ya say?"

The cop glanced at the Black man and then walked a few steps with Calvanese. "If he apologizes." He stopped walking and stood defiantly. "The guy's got to apologize, that's the only way. Otherwise, I take his ass in, paperwork or no paperwork."

Calvanese walked back to the scene with the cop. "All right, we can settle this," he said sternly to the man. "You can be on your way home with your family."

"That's all I want," said the man, relieved.

"Just apologize," Calvanese recommended casually, trying to alleviate the sting.

"Apologize?" the man repeated incredulously. "For what?"

Calvanese softened his voice. "Show your kids a good example, then we—"

"What kind of example am I going to show them by apologizing for standing up for my rights?" The man looked at his wife and kids and then tried to reason with Calvanese. "He had no call to pull me over and treat me like some common criminal!"

"If he takes you in, that's what you're gonna be. You want a record?" asked Calvanese.

The man looked at Henderson, who provided no assistance. He looked at the cop who waited impatiently for the apology. "You wanna arrest me, then do it!"

"Fine," said the cop, who took a step forward but was cut off by the man's oldest son, about seven years old, who rushed to his side and held onto him, crying, and pleading with his father.

"Daddy! I don't want you to go away with them! Please, Daddy, don't go! Don't leave us alone!"

The man looked helplessly at his child, unable to embrace him because of the handcuffs. His wife cried and tightly held onto their daughter. He turned to Henderson once again and this time received a weak and embarrassed nod. Tears welled up in the man's eyes. He looked down at the ground and spoke softly. "I apologize."

* * *

Calvanese drove while Henderson sat quietly in the passenger seat staring out the window. Although they were separated by less than three feet, Calvanese felt isolated, miles apart. He knew if he said anything it would come across the wrong way. But he didn't want the silence to continue any longer; that could cause even more damage. "Hey," he said, encouragingly, "he let him go, didn't he?"

"It shouldn't have gotten to that," Henderson spoke sullenly without looking at him.

"He wouldn't have stopped him without cause."

Henderson angrily confronted Calvanese. "You have no idea what the fuck you're talking about! So, do what you always do, use your reflexes and not your mind. Just drive the car."

Calvanese felt his own anger surge, but he handled it the way he did best, with sarcasm and humor. "No harm. No foul." He didn't get a response. "Just another day in the neighborhood." Still nothing from Henderson, so he decided to push it. "Give peace a chance. Let my people go. Mama's little baby loves short'nin', short'nin'." He glanced at Henderson, trying to evoke a smile, then sang in a childlike voice: "Mama's little baby loves short'nin' bread."

Henderson turned slowly, giving him a pathetic look. "Is that what you whispered to the cop to let them go?"

"Actually, I told him Obama was your cousin. He was really impressed." Calvanese tapped Henderson on his arm. "Wanted your autograph and everything," he said, keeping his eyes on the road, driving carefully. He stopped to allow an elderly Black woman to cross the street. She nodded in appreciation. He smiled politely and tipped his hat.

Henderson massaged his temple in slow, ever-expanding circles.

THIRTEEN

The Outlaw Bar & Grill was a popular police hangout, conveniently located halfway between City Hall and Skid Row and untarnished by the substantial redevelopment that had occurred around it. During the last decade, there had been a major governmental effort to attract young professionals to the previously blighted area. Warehouses had been converted into million-dollar lofts, designed by a new breed of architects who enjoyed displaying their contempt for the familiar. These "open-spaced, high-ceiling" playgrounds allowed decorators to "experiment" in ways made possible by the extravagant desires of those who had inherited their wealth. Yet, somehow, in the middle of this voyeuristic residential and business district, the O.B.G., as it was affectionately known, managed to remain inconspicuous despite the constant presence of police cars that helped to ward off the public and other "undesirables." If you weren't a cop, related to a cop, or retired from the force, then you didn't know what went on behind the large oak door that had no welcome mat, no name, no address, and no need for security.

And that was precisely how its owner and operator, Jasper

Campbell, preferred it. Campbell, a former homicide detective, had had the good fortune to work on a murder case involving a well-known celebrity athlete. Despite an extraordinary amount of circumstantial evidence pointing to his guilt, the star defendant was acquitted of all charges. In appreciation for the decision, the freed prisoner invited the jury to his Newport Beach mansion for a catered affair in their honor. "A Tribute to Justice," was the phrase engraved on the crystal souvenirs contained in each personalized gift bag. In a typically flamboyant move, the grateful host rewarded the jury foreman with a pair of season tickets, center courtside seats.

Campbell resigned shortly after the verdict and wrote a bestselling book detailing the facts of his investigation. He received a handsome advance for the movie rights and used the funds to buy the establishment. On opening night, the athlete arrived in grand style with his entourage of gorgeous women and supplicant men hanging onto every word and laughing on cue. He bought a round of drinks for everyone at the bar. Campbell took the money, five crisp one-hundred-dollar bills, and burned it at the athlete's reserved table. The ashes from that memorable moment were on permanent display in a specially designed "prison cell" glass cabinet built into the wall behind the bar and illuminated by a single fluorescent light.

Officers from the South Bureau, overrepresented by the 77th Street Station, were scattered throughout the restaurant enjoying their meals and boisterously swapping war stories from the past week's shift. Black cops sat at a long table in the rear section participating in their monthly union meeting. A few policewomen celebrated a promotion of one of the officers in their group. Mike Stevens and his crew held court around their regular table, having gone through two large pizzas, a tray of hot chicken wings, three baskets of cheese sticks, several liters of draft beer, and two thoroughly harassed waitresses—one of whom had ended her shift early, having had more than enough hands groping her behind.

Calvanese entered the club and walked directly to the bar. By the time he took his seat, Campbell had a frosted mug of beer waiting for him.

"You're late," Campbell said. "I was worried about you."

"You worry about me," Calvanese droned. "You prepare my drink just the way I like and have it waiting for me when I arrive. People will think we're in love." He quickly drank half the beer.

Campbell laughed and slid a bowl of chips down the bar toward him. "You're not my type."

"Why?" asked Calvanese. "You got something against cops?"

Campbell stared at the table of attractive policewomen. "If they were around while I was still in uniform, I'd have something against them, you'd better believe it." He took a damp cloth and cleaned the countertop. "And it would be stiff and hard."

"Regulations don't allow you to use your nightstick that way," responded Calvanese. "It's considered police brutality."

"Excessive force ain't always a bad thing," confided Campbell.

"Hey, Calvanese," yelled Stevens from across the room.

"What's up, Mike?" shouted Calvanese.

"You the man," Stevens approached Calvanese and hugged him and then sang softly into his ear. "Ebony and ivory, live together in perfect harmony."

Calvanese jokingly pushed him away. "You sing like I hear you fuck."

"Damn straight," said Stevens proudly. "Loud and all over the place." The men laughed. "Just wanted to say no hard feelings about the other day. Just a little on edge. I'd never question your loyalty. You know that."

"Didn't realize that you had."

"We're okay, then?"

"I can't speak for you, but I'm a damn sight better than okay." Calvanese raised his mug, gave a half-hearted toast, and downed the rest of the beer.

"How's your dad?"

Calvanese's mood changed; he became more distant. "Hangin' in." He gave Campbell a signal to hold off on any more drinks. "I'll let him know you asked about him. Make him feel good he hasn't been forgotten."

"Nobody's ever gonna forget Big Lou. Now that was a cop."

"He showed me the way."

"You and half the folks who are still worth a damn," Stevens said broodingly. "Tell him I might join him the end of this year."

"Thought you wanted to do thirty?"

"Twenty-five is five too many. We used to know who the fuckin' enemies were. Now, we got to work with 'em." He nodded in the direction of the doorway. "Take him, for instance."

Calvanese watched Allen Davis, leader of the Black police officers' organization, walk through the entrance.

Davis was a tall dark-skinned man with a stern disposition, made even more imposing by a ten-inch scar that began on the top of his bald head and disappeared around his left ear to resurface at his jawline and end halfway down the front of his neck. Conflicting rumors had circulated for years regarding how he got that mark of distinction. Despite the various speculations, there was general agreement among his colleagues that the person or persons responsible for inflicting the visible wound were no longer available to be interviewed. It also was known that Davis rejected cosmetic surgery, preferring to wear the scar as a badge of honor, or more probably as a warning to friend and foe alike. Davis waved at some of the Black cops, who returned the salute. He gave Stevens an icy stare and then strode directly to Calvanese.

"Tony, where's Henderson?"

"Call Dionne Warwick," Stevens said sarcastically. "If her psychic friends can't tell ya, refuse to pay."

"Gee," said Davis, surprised, "I didn't know I was talkin' to you."

"You don't know a lotta shit but that's never stopped you from runnin' your mouth."

Davis took a step toward Stevens, but Calvanese quickly defused the situation. "What'd you want with Henderson?" he asked. "You still tryin' to recruit members?"

"You gentlemen have the Protective League," replied Davis, keeping his eyes on Stevens. "We need an organization to protect the interests of Black officers."

"The League's for all of us," Stevens said. "You weaken the union, we might as well turn in our badges."

"Might be a better place if some of you did," Davis said, and let the implication linger. "Tony, when you see Paul, ask him to give me a call, will ya?"

"I'm a servant of the people," responded Calvanese. "I have no other purpose in life but to relay your messages."

Davis dismissed the comment with a derisive grunt and walked away to be greeted by a white policewoman who kissed him on the lips followed by a friendly hug. Stevens made no effort to hide his disgust. "Fuck this. I definitely ain't puttin' in thirty."

Calvanese watched Davis greet his fellow Black officers using their special handshakes, before taking a seat at the head of the table and conducting business as if he were royalty. Calvanese considered him a good cop; tough, hard as nails. But he was also a bit of a peacock, thought he deserved some type of special treatment because of his "leadership" position—elected spokesman for the officers of color. Wasn't white a color, too?

Calvanese nodded at the bartender who brought him another cold draft. He sat on the stool and looked up at the overhanging television. "Jasper, do me a favor and turn that up. Our leader's speaking."

"Who the fuck wants to listen to that asshole this time of night?" Campbell asked.

"He might be talkin' about cutting your pension," Calvanese warned.

"I'm still licensed to carry, so he better not mess with my grandchildren's college fund."

"Or your mistress's vacation money," quipped Calvanese.

"Especially that," agreed Campbell as he turned up the volume. Calvanese listened to Mayor Palmer over the din of the bar.

"I, along with Police Chief Gibbs, am working closely with other law enforcement agencies throughout the state in a coordinated effort to find and convict those who may have had any involvement in these brutal, senseless, and cowardly slayings."

Calvanese tasted the beer and decided he needed something stronger. He signaled Campbell, putting his thumb and index finger an inch apart. The bartender poured a shot of whiskey and slid it down the bar to Calvanese who downed it in one gulp.

* * *

"Now let's hear the pitch for more money," said Henderson, seated on the couch with his family closely watching the news report on a wide-screen television.

"This afternoon, I personally spoke with the governor and formally requested additional budgetary resources as well as an increase in administrative personnel, to ensure that these murderers are apprehended swiftly," Palmer said with as much confidence as he could convey.

"Told you," said Henderson.

"He has assured me that his office will fully support any measure to capture and bring to justice those responsible for these cruel and heinous acts." Palmer stared directly into the camera and concluded his statement in dramatic fashion. "How can the citizens of this great city feel secure, if the people entrusted with their protection are not safe?"

"If Mayor Palmer's going to ensure our safety, then I think we should buy some property in Bosnia," said Henderson who used the remote to change the channel to the Nickelodeon network, much to the delight of his son.

"Dexter, you wanna live in Bosnia-Herzegovina?"

"Do I have to go to school?"

"Yeah. But you don't have to learn anything."

Nicole punched Henderson in the arm. Henderson grabbed a couch pillow and retaliated. Nicole grabbed a bigger pillow and escalated the battle. Dexter grabbed one and joined the fight. The battle was on.

FOURTEEN

Calvanese remained the lone soul seated at the bar. Campbell lined up the last row of liquor bottles, meticulously organizing them in front of the mirrored cabinet. Once that was accomplished, he placed the clean glasses on the shelves underneath the bar and then turned his attention to polishing the stainless-steel basin.

"Want anything else, Tony?"

"Yeah," sighed Calvanese, "but it ain't here."

Campbell looked up and froze. "Damn if it ain't," he muttered.

A stunning blond strolled in and took a seat next to Calvanese. He guessed she was five-ten without heels. She wore a dark gold designer jacket with a matching skirt and light brown stiletto boots. Calvanese assessed her gorgeous tanned legs but he was far more interested in another part of her anatomy: a particular finger on her left hand.

"Hello," she said in a voice that would melt ice.

"Hi," he responded, hoping his voice wasn't quite as high-pitched as it sounded. He discreetly glanced at her left hand

and found a Rolex watch on her slender wrist that had to be worth more than five months of his salary, including overtime.

Campbell winked at Calvanese and walked away, giving him some privacy.

She placed her purse on the empty barstool next to her and he finally saw the unobstructed hand. Not married. Either that or she was concealing the fact, which was just as good, if not better.

"What brings you here, tonight?"

"Always wanted to see the inside of this place. Whenever I drive by, I can't help but notice all the police that come in and out all hours of the night. Thought this might be the safest place in the city."

"I've learned from personal experience that what you believe is safe can break your heart." He slid a bowl of peanuts toward her and tapped the side of the container. "Would you care for some?"

Campbell approached. "Can I get you something? We're closing in a few minutes, but I'll make an exception for you."

"Won't you get in trouble with the law?" she asked coyly.

"I've got friends in high places," Campbell said sheepishly. "I assume my friend here hasn't asked you your name yet, so please, allow me to do the honors." He placed his hand on Calvanese's shoulder. "Tony Calvanese, a prime example of L.A.'s finest, please let me introduce you to my newest, most important and, might I hope in the near future, most frequent customer..." Campbell waited for several long moments while his wide smile began to wear off.

"This is where you're supposed to tell us your name," said Calvanese, with a cold detachment that successfully concealed his growing excitement.

She looked closely at the enchanted bartender. "Do you think they're stale?"

"Do I think what's stale," asked a perplexed and overheated Campbell.

She slid the bowl of peanuts toward the bartender and tapped the side of the container. She leaned closer toward Calvanese, and he stared into her light blue eyes that had a tint of green and a streak of passion. "Next time you want to know a woman's name, ask as if you weren't demanding her license and registration." She flashed a sparkling smile, grabbed her purse, and walked out of the bar under the watchful gaze of both men.

"Who the hell was that?" asked Calvanese.

"I have no idea," answered Campbell. "But I'd like to find out."

"She ever been in here before?" asked Calvanese, his eyes still fixed on the doorway.

"If she had been, I would've remembered. Hell, I would've taken a picture and hung it up behind the bar, after I made copies and distributed them to all my friends."

"You don't have that many friends," Calvanese quipped.

"I would've made a lot more with those pictures," responded Campbell, "you can bet your last dollar on that."

"I wonder what she wanted," said Calvanese whimsically.

"Tony," Campbell touched Calvanese on his hand. "You've either been drinking too much or it's been way too long in between dates."

"What'd you mean?"

"I mean, she wanted you. Wasn't that obvious?"

"You think so?" asked Calvanese, containing his excitement.

"Let me tell you what I really think," said Campbell. "If I thought she wanted me"—he leaned halfway over the counter—"I'd leave my wife. I'd sell my bar. And I'd..."

Calvanese left before Campbell could complete the statement.

"Follow her wherever she led," Campbell said to himself, lovestruck. He took a mouthful of peanuts and chewed slowly.

Calvanese stood outside and searched the area, but he found no trace of the woman. Another lost opportunity, he thought. He decided to go home and face his punishment like a man. He'd made his bed a long time ago, so it was only fair that he slept in it—alone.

FIFTEEN

Calvanese exited the 101 Freeway and drove his Jeep down Ventura Boulevard. He regretted not taking his patrol car; the siren and flashing lights would have enabled him to cut forty-five minutes off the trip. He could have also pulled over that redhead who smiled at him on the 405 at the Westwood ramp. He hated traffic, especially the slow crawl through the San Fernando Valley caused by young, arrogant talent agents who handled their cell phones better than their steering wheels. Wannabe starlets applied make-up instead of brakes. And undocumented aliens with fake licenses were the only ones driving under the speed limit, way under—usually in the left lane.

Every fender bender generated the rubbernecks who'd slow down to observe a minor accident and, in the process, create several major ones. And don't let it rain! California drivers and wet roads don't mix. If it ever snowed, half the population in the county of Los Angeles would die on roads and highways reduced to hazardous bumper car arcades. And the other half would succumb to frostbite and be buried the way they lived—in designer chiffon wearing no underwear.

He reached the Tarzana town line and drove another mile to his parents' home, a modest three-bedroom in an overpriced neighborhood, although all neighborhoods were overpriced in Southern California. His father purchased the house thirty years ago for the price of one of today's low-end family SUVs. Today it was worth over a million, without a pool! Only in the land of frequent earthquakes would people place such value on a two-thousand-square-foot brick and mortar structure with aluminum siding and roofing covered with burnt-orange Spanish tiles. He pulled into the driveway and smiled when he saw the recently planted flowers leading up to the front entrance; they were a sign that his mother had purchased a new gardening book and read at least the first chapter, or perhaps thumbed through the glossary.

She opened the door before he reached it and even from that faraway distance, he could smell the aroma of homemade sauce and baked garlic bread. Isabella Calvanese was in her late fifties but to her son, except for the faded blond hair with ample strokes of silver and gray, her appearance hadn't changed significantly from the day she helped pack his bag and sent him off to the police academy. She had the same smooth skin, her sparkling hazel eyes hadn't dimmed with time, and her smile still dazzled—a perfect complement to the laughter that usually preceded it.

She placed her arms around him and squeezed hard. "Tony, we've been so worried about you."

"Mama, I'm indestructible." He flexed both arms. "It's all that olive oil and oregano you fed me as a baby. Bullets slide off."

She threw up her hands and issued a stern warning. "Don't joke about bullets." She took him by the arm and continued the scolding. "Also, don't joke about my cooking."

They entered the home and walked into the living room.

"I'd rather insult the Pope," he said with deep sincerity.

"That's 'cause the Pope can't make marinara like your mother makes marinara. Only one other person came close." She stopped suddenly and got that look on her face, the one that suggested to Calvanese it would be a long visit.

"Speaking of which..." She paused, with dramatic reflection.

Here it comes.

"When are you and Susan getting back together?"

I knew it. "I guess she has to leave her husband first," he said, knowing that wouldn't put an end to the matter.

"*You're* her husband. You get married once. Anything else is living in sin."

"Well, sin pays. You should see the house she's in. Even *you* might leave Pop for a country estate that magnificent."

She pointed her finger at his chin and gave him the *don't go any further* curse. "Don't you dare say such a thing."

"Sorry, Mom," he said, sounding like a young boy.

She turned and flashed a sly smile. "Of course, if it had a really big kitchen with a double oven, gas not electric, I might consider weekend visits." She thought about it for a moment, smiled, then became serious. "But I'd return to your father first thing every Monday." She moved to the kitchen. He followed dutifully.

"Now, back to your wife and your life, you should arrest her. Keep her locked up until she comes to her senses." She approached the stove the way a priest would approach an altar. She carefully removed the lid covering the eight-quart copper pot and used a long wooden ladle to stir and then taste the sauce. She added a pinch of seasoning and stirred again.

"When did you become such a fan of Susan's?" asked Calvanese. His mother stuck a sample of sauce in his mouth which he accepted gratefully and then nodded his approval. "First five years we were married, you never let me forget she was *just* half Italian."

"But she was the *right* half," his mother acknowledged while opening the oven door and checking the manicotti. "I taught her how to make lasagna. She took to ricotta the way a duck takes to water." She closed the door and thumped her son's chest. "Those women are hard to find. Trust me. She was a natural."

"Not anymore."

"What are you sayin'?"

"She dyed her hair blond."

She thought about it and shrugged. "So, blond is better than gray." She pointed to her hair.

"She also got a boob job."

Mrs. Calvanese frowned. "What kinda job is that to have for such a smart and pretty girl? She could be working anywhere."

"It's not an occupation, Mama." He watched her prepare a salad and wondered if he should continue. "She got implants."

She stopped chopping tomatoes and looked at him, obviously confused.

"Enlargements," he said, but she still didn't have a clue. "For her breasts." He placed his hands on his chest then extended them a foot and a half.

His mother's jaw dropped in amazement then she quickly recovered and sliced cucumbers. "Leave me alone and let me finish my work. Go surprise your father."

He snuck up behind her. "You mean I should go boo?"

"I didn't tell him you were coming."

"Afraid he might hightail it out of here?"

She gave a mother's sigh then whacked him with a dish towel. "Go. Or I'll call Susan and invite her over. I have her number."

"I don't," he said, offended.

"If you want, I'll give it to you. I'm sure she won't mind."

Calvanese raised his hands and signaled no thank you. He

escaped from the kitchen and walked down the hallway filled with family photos: his father dressed in a police uniform, Calvanese as a young boy at his side. He knew his dad would be behind his desk in the den, his favorite room. He stopped at the closed door. His father enjoyed privacy. Calvanese feared that he was beginning to enjoy it too much. He knocked gently.

"Tony, come in," said the voice immediately.

Calvanese smiled and entered the room, which adorned with police awards. Photos of cops were scattered throughout the den, on the walls, tables, and bookshelves. As he predicted, he found his father seated behind the desk fiddling with God knows what type of paperwork, possibly old police files of unsolved cases. "How'd you know it was me?"

In his early sixties with pure white hair, Louis Calvanese still looked formidable: the type of cop you wouldn't say no to more than once. "Your mother doesn't knock," he said wryly. "She also doesn't run around smiling all day like a young girl except for when she knows her baby's coming."

"Ain't I your baby, too?"

Mr. Calvanese motored his wheelchair from around the desk and headed toward his son. "What's wrong?"

"Every time I come over something must be wrong. Can't I just want to see my old man?"

"Is it the job or a woman?" he asked, cutting through the bull.

Calvanese turned away, trying to avoid the human lie detector.

"I was hoping it was a woman," Mr. Calvanese said disappointedly. "Your mother wants grandchildren. Me? I'll settle for someone to listen to my stories." He wheeled the chair closer. "When you gonna find someone makes your face wide open?"

"Nose, Pop." He leaned closer to his father. "The expression is having your nose wide open."

"Is your nose on your face?" he asked, annoyed. "Is it already big? If it stretches, you tell me, how much face you gonna have left?"

Calvanese ignored the questions and asked the one that concerned him most. "How you feeling?"

"Numb," he joked for the hundredth time. "But then you know that."

"That's not funny. It never has been."

"Who you tellin'? Thirty-five years I'm a cop. Not a scratch. I retire. I fall off a freakin' roof tryin' to fix an antenna. Your mama wanted me to get cable. Tony, always listen to the woman who loves you." He tapped his son on the knee. "But not while you're on the roof."

Calvanese kissed his father on the cheek. Mr. Calvanese flinched, both touched and embarrassed.

"It's okay for two men to kiss especially when they're Italian and related."

"That's how confusion starts," Mr. Calvanese responded defensively. "All tradition ain't good."

"Doesn't he look good, Louis?"

The two men turned and saw Mrs. Calvanese at the doorway.

"Isabella, how long you been standing there?"

"Just got here," she said unconvincingly. "Didn't see nothin'. Not even the kiss. And if I did see it, my lips are sealed. Dinner's ready in five minutes. Plenty time to get in another hug or two." She left with a bounce in her step.

The two men glanced at each other.

"Now, if only I could find a woman like that," said Calvanese lovingly.

"Forget it," his father snapped. "She's taken. But, if you want, you have my permission to take her out for lunch once in a while."

"How about you? Can't I take you out, too?"

Mr. Calvanese's eyes deadened. He touched his face, rubbed the corner of his mouth. "I don't like goin' out. Too hot."

Calvanese knew it had nothing to do with the weather and everything to do with pride. His father didn't want his friends to see him confined to a wheelchair. He also feared running into some ex-con that he'd put away; under no circumstances would he give his enemies such a high level of satisfaction.

"We could go at night." Calvanese offered the compromise. "It's cooler."

"I go to bed early," huffed his father.

"You're a piece of work, you know that don't you, Dad?"

"Yeah," Mr. Calvanese agreed. "And I created another great work of art, just as good. Maybe better." He extended his arms and spread them as wide as possible. Calvanese knelt by his side and felt the strength and warmth of his father's arms embracing him. "Every time the phone rings, we worry it might—"

Calvanese pulled back quickly, unwilling to allow his father to go down that road. "Pop, I was taught by the best. Nothing's going to happen to me. I'm a great cop and great cops like—"

"Great chefs, work from instinct," said Mr. Calvanese as if the words were ingrained. "Cookbooks are for those—"

"With no imagination," agreed Calvanese. "Rules are—"

"For those with no balls," Mr. Calvanese finished and then grabbed his son's shoulders and spoke with a father's concern. "The rules have changed, Tony. Used to be people respected a blue uniform. Now, it's a target. And when you can't depend on your own partner to protect your back, the only thing left to do is pick out your coffin."

"If this is your way of building up my confidence," said Calvanese, "it ain't workin'."

His father gave him the stare, the one that used to make knees buckle. "We've never bullshitted each other, Tony. How well do you know him? This partner they gave you."

Calvanese released a deep sigh.

His father moved the wheelchair back a few inches, raised then tilted his head, and took a good look at his son. "More importantly, can you trust him with your life?"

SIXTEEN

Calvanese dreaded large-chain book retailers; in truth, he wasn't that fond of the independents, but they were better than those used bookstores that smelled old, looked dusty, and caused you to itch or sneeze or both. He'd sneezed three times thus far and hadn't yet made it halfway down the back aisle in search of the Black studies section. Segregated books, he thought. There was a lesson in that, but who would dare teach it? He looked at the rows of books stacked on shelves from floor to ceiling. Nobody but a librarian would climb that high for a work of fiction.

He perused a variety of titles. The older or more militant-sounding books had the word BLACK prominently displayed while the newer or more scholarly works used AFRICAN AMERICAN. Calvanese wondered why books by white authors didn't plaster CAUCASIAN on the cover or at least somewhere on the spine. He figured *Black Beauty* must have confused a lot of potential readers who were looking for either positive role models or cosmetic tips for women of color only to be confronted with a story about a kid and her horse. His left arm started itching but he didn't scratch. He knew it would only make matters worse. If he gave in to the temptation soon his whole body would be screaming for similar attention.

He examined a few more titles to jog his memory. He'd heard Henderson quote a particular author several times and figured that would be as good a place as any to start. He ran his fingers across the bindings of dozens of books until he found the "Bs" and then discovered Baldwin, James. God, this guy was popular—a regular Stephen King. *Go Tell It on the Mountain* sounded too religious. *Giovanni's Room*, too Italian. He picked up the thickest volume, something called *The Price of the Ticket*. Probably would be a good choice if he were a traffic cop. He thumbed through it anyway and discovered it was an anthology, which would save him the trouble of having to buy two or three of these books. He'd skim it later until he found something of interest, and if he didn't like anything, he could always use it as a footrest or a small step stool. Given its weight it would make one hell of a weapon; might be poetic justice if he used it only against minority suspects. Of course, he'd leave himself open to claims of excessive force. Damn. He knew Blacks had issues, but did it really take this many pages to make white people feel guilty?

Okay, he'd do his part, accept his share of the blame, and invest a few dollars for the cause. He brought the book to the counter and waited for the bald guy with Benjamin Franklin glasses to finish picking his nose.

"Did you find everything all right?" the man asked.

Did you? Calvanese decided not to embarrass the man or himself by asking. "Yeah, thanks. I'll take this." Calvanese opened the front cover and studied the numbers penciled in small figures—$135.00—and then next to it, the word "mint." He looked at the back and then returned to the inside front cover and held the book under a light to get a better look.

"Is something wrong?" asked the cashier.

"I think there's a mistake with this price," said Calvanese and then handed the book to the man who glanced at it quickly.

"That's the correct price," he confirmed.

Calvanese chuckled and leaned on the counter. "A speeding ticket doesn't cost that much." He waited for the joke to sink in. "Price of the ticket." Calvanese paused for a reaction but didn't get any. "The title of the book," he continued. "Speeding ticket, get it?" Maybe it would have worked better if he'd been wearing his uniform, he thought.

"It's a first edition," the cashier informed Calvanese, with a certain degree of religious fervor.

Calvanese stared, unimpressed.

"It's out of print," the man said haughtily.

"Then shouldn't it cost less?"

The man licked his lower lip then folded his hands together. "It's a book, not a bakery good."

"For 135 bucks, after I read it, I ought to be able to eat it."

The man studied Calvanese carefully. "Something tells me you're not a bibliophile, am I right?"

"If it's any of your business, I'm a Catholic but I'm non-practicing." Calvanese looked at the man suspiciously. "I hope that's what you meant."

"You want to buy the book or not?"

"Can I rent?"

The cashier shook his head.

"What's your return policy?"

The man pointed to a large sign directly behind him. NO RETURNS.

Calvanese reluctantly removed his wallet. "It better have a good story with lots of sex and humor."

The man snickered. "Oh, it's got sex all right. And I'm sure it's the type that'll make you laugh." The man displayed a self-amused smirk.

Calvanese moved his jacket to the side and deliberately

revealed his gun in his holster. The man's eyes widened nervously. "If not, I'll be back," Calvanese warned then smiled politely.

* * *

During his drive home, Calvanese contemplated whether he was a racist and concluded, in rather short order, that he wasn't. The fact that he'd considered it at all was proof positive that he couldn't be. And if he needed further evidence to support the claim, beside the fact that he'd just shelled out over a hundred bucks for a book he'd never read, he remembered he'd once dated a Black woman—granted, a very light-skinned, hazel-blue-eyed Black woman with hair that flowed down to her last vertebra—but Black, nonetheless. And although she only dated white men—a fact that he learned on their first encounter under the sheets—he remained free of any such prejudice. It bothered him that she held such negative views of her male counterparts, although they weren't together long enough for him to raise his disapproval more formally.

She was his first affair following the disintegration of his marriage. The day he received the finalized divorce papers, he bought a red sports car and had a relationship with an African American who shared his taste in music—Bruce Springsteen—and beer—anything cold, bottled, and domestic. He wrecked the car one morning when he skidded into a garbage truck, and later that night, he managed to ruin their brief romantic encounter when he called her Susan, not once but twice, while making love.

But it was fun while it lasted. In a mere three weeks he'd managed to have two accidents. One he attributed to a slick intersection, the other he blamed on painkillers. Veronica more accurately described the condition when she screamed: "You still love the bitch! Admit it!" She slammed the door, or maybe he did. Okay, he did. In any event, both the auto crash and the breakup of a predictably doomed relationship were due to human error rather than any sinister motives generated by prejudice or racial hostility.

Most reasonable people know that if it rains you put on your raincoat and carry an umbrella. Those same people roll up their windows, lock their car doors, and keep a weapon nearby when driving through most Black neighborhoods. That's not racism. It's common sense. At least, that's what he was prepared to say tonight if the subject came up.

SEVENTEEN

Baldwin's book rested on Calvanese's coffee table. In fact, it was the only thing on the table, centered squarely in the middle. Henderson sat on the couch and stared at the book then gave Calvanese a curious peek. He picked up the book as Calvanese casually glanced away.

"You read James Baldwin?"

Calvanese appeared puzzled. "Doesn't everybody?"

"No," Henderson said, then opened the book and ran his fingers across the inside binding. "It's got a new feel to it. The pages are still stuck together, like they've never been read."

"I take care of my books," Calvanese said proudly. "It's a first rendition, you know."

"Edition," corrected Henderson.

"When a book really sings, you don't just read—you perform." Calvanese leaned back, exceedingly pleased with himself. "I wore out my first copy, so I ordered another."

Henderson studied the barren room. "I don't see any other books in your extensive library."

"You don't see my underwear. Don't mean I ain't wearin' any." Calvanese studied Henderson.

"What?" Henderson asked, self-consciously.

"I think you've got a problem with me reading that book."

"Why would I have a problem with you reading Baldwin?"

"You're nervous 'cause I'm reading something that might help me understand you."

Henderson smiled like a hunter who'd just trapped his prey. "The purpose of the book is for you to understand yourself. Obviously, you haven't gotten to that part, yet." He inspected Calvanese with a growing sense of admiration and wonderment. "Although, I do have to admit, Baldwin's the last author I expected you to be reading."

"Why?" asked Calvanese, feigning emotional injury. "Just 'cause the guy happened to be Black?"

"No," answered Henderson, with a certain academic smugness. "Because he happened to be gay."

Calvanese's lips moved to form words but were unable to complete the task. He rubbed his hands together uncomfortably and felt as if his body had been invaded by microscopic insects that made his skin itch. He scratched the corner of his right eye. "Bald... Baldwin's gay?" he asked, his voice breaking slightly.

Henderson studied the dreaded expression that overtook Calvanese's face. "I would've thought that was obvious to anyone who read past the opening few pages."

Calvanese searched for a response and settled on the first excuse that came to mind. "I start from the back."

"I imagine, so did he," remarked Henderson, giving Calvanese an amused look.

Calvanese's eyes turned dark. "Don't even go there, okay," he threatened. "It's just a book." His shirt collar suddenly felt tight, even though it wasn't buttoned at the top. "Truth is, I didn't buy it. It was a gift."

"From whom?" asked Henderson, waiting patiently for a response.

"From one of the many Black citizens I've helped in my

illustrious career," he answered rapidly. "Is that all right with you?"

"If you say so."

The two men avoided looking at each other. The awkward silence was broken when Calvanese tossed a bag of chips to Henderson.

"Thank you," Henderson said.

"You're welcome," Calvanese replied, tartly.

Henderson took a chip out of the bag and scooped up some dip. "Is there a reason you invited me over?" he asked offhandedly.

"Some law against us getting to know each other better?" Calvanese responded innocently. "I just wondered how we'd get along outside the patrol car."

Henderson gave him a peculiar glance. "You're sure Baldwin was a gift?" he teased. "And not a way of life?"

Calvanese shifted his weight to one side and glared at Henderson. "I warned you once already, so just drop it. I'm not tellin' you again."

Henderson smiled, mumbled something under his breath, ate the dip, and scowled. "The dip's too salty," he announced with displeasure.

Calvanese dug his finger in the dip and tried some. "It was all right a few days ago." He licked his finger again for a second opinion. "You think I should have put it back in the fridge instead of leaving it out?"

Henderson suspiciously studied the remaining half of the chip he hadn't yet tasted and placed it down on a paper plate. He put his hands on his knees and nervously drummed his fingers, stopping periodically to survey the room. "Nice place," he said unconvincingly.

"I decorated it myself," replied Calvanese.

"I could tell," said Henderson, drumming his fingers against the side of his legs now.

Calvanese stared at Henderson. "This remind you of something?"

Henderson thought about it and looked around the room. He didn't have a clue.

"I'll give you a hint," offered Calvanese. "It's a movie."

Henderson tilted his head to the side, uncertain. "*Night of the Living Dead*," he guessed.

"*In the Heat of the Night*," Calvanese answered, solving the mystery.

Henderson appeared puzzled. "The television show?"

"The movie," Calvanese said, in exasperation. "Tibbs visited the redneck sheriff's home."

"Are you admitting you're a redneck?"

"No. I'm sayin' you got a certain Sidney Potter thing going on. Anybody ever tell you that?"

"It's possible that you meant Harry Potter, but I doubt it, so you must've meant Sidney Poitier."

"Poitier?" Calvanese said, astonished. "What the hell kind of name is that for a..." he hesitated, then spoke under his breath, "actor."

"Whatever," Henderson said, surrendering to the spirit of the occasion. "I'd rather be thought of that way than compared to Archie Bunker, the character whose distinct qualities you so adamantly cherish."

Calvanese stared at Henderson, confused. "Rod Steiger never played Archie Bunker."

"I was speaking about the television series."

"Fuck the television series. It was a great movie."

"I never saw the film."

"The white guy was the hero." Calvanese set the record straight. "Sidney was all right, a little arrogant in a black, three-piece suit sorta way. But Rod won the Oscar, so what does that tell ya?"

"Tells me there aren't many Black voting members of the Academy."

Calvanese rolled his eyes and munched some pretzels. "Why'd you become a cop, Henderson?"

"Is there some mystery in that for you?"

"As a matter of fact, yeah."

"Why'd you become a cop, Tony? If you can answer that for yourself, you can answer it for me."

"I just meant you had more choices. That's all. Went to a good college, finished graduate school, went to law school, you coulda..." He hesitated, then gave a sly smile. "You coulda been a contender."

Henderson gave Calvanese a sympathetic look then shook his head sadly. "You watch too many movies? You should read more." He pointed to the thick book on the coffee table. "You can start with your first rendition of Baldwin."

"I'll wait till he sells the film rights."

"Hate to be the one to break the news to you, but Baldwin's dead."

Calvanese considered the information. "Guess that explains why the book cost so much." He rose from the couch and stretched his arms over his head. "You want some lemonade?" he asked with a thick Southern accent.

"Is it fresh?"

Calvanese turned up his nose, offended. "Made from the best stuff on earth." He paused dramatically. "You want Snapple pink, regular or extra sour?"

"What the hell," Henderson shrugged. "I'll try the pink."

Calvanese headed for the kitchen. "I know it's late, but if you're up to it, we can play a little B-ball under the night sky." He stared at a wide-eyed Henderson. "You play, don't ya?"

Henderson displayed a superior smile.

Calvanese strutted to the refrigerator, singing loudly and off-key. "IN THE HEAAAT OF THE NIGHT."

Henderson shook his head in resignation and tightly tied the shoestrings on his Nikes.

Henderson drove on a tired Calvanese who hacked him across both arms preventing a lay-up and knocking the ball out of his hands. Calvanese's oversized sweatshirt was drenched with perspiration. He bent over and breathed heavily.

"It's basketball, Tony. Not hockey!"

"I barely touched you. If you hadn't pumped up your Air Jordans, you wouldn't have jumped into my defense."

"Defense?" exclaimed Henderson. "You call that pitiful game of yours a defense?"

"Yeah, what would you call it?"

"Assault and battery. Look it up in the penal code." Henderson retrieved the ball. "And while you're at it, see if there's anything in there that comes close to describing how you play offense. Start with the section on reckless endangerment and driving under the influence of having NO GAME."

Calvanese regained his second wind and readied himself for the competition. "Hey, give me someone to throw the ball to. I'm a passer, not a shooter."

"You wanna throw me the ball, cracker?" said an ominous voice from across the court.

Calvanese turned and saw five young Black gang members flashing their eastside hand signals, emerge from the dark and walk slowly toward him, menacing and large. The most muscular in the group pulled out a long stiletto knife and cleaned his fingernail with it. He stopped several feet in front of Calvanese and then slowly twirled the blade. The sharp steel glimmered under the glare of outdoor lighting.

"What, white meat, you ain't a passer no more?"

"Actually," Calvanese said apologetically, "I misspoke." He calmly walked toward the gang. "What I really meant to say was I'm not a passer..." He removed his gun from underneath his sweatshirt and his badge from his belt. He pointed the gun at the youth that had done all the talking and displayed the badge to the group. "I'm a shooter."

Calvanese imitated the gang members and flashed a west-side signal and then twirled his weapon. "You got next?" he asked in a friendly challenge. "You can be skins, we'll be shirts."

"Maybe some other time."

"Look forward to it," smiled Calvanese.

The teen put away his knife and backed off with his friends. Calvanese watched them leave, giving them a warm-hearted wave as they left.

Henderson looked at him in astonishment. "You're out here playin' me one-on-one with a gun stuck in your sweats?"

"I was thinking of shooting you in the leg during your lay-up. But I figured you'd punk out and cry foul." Calvanese took a wild shot at the basket and missed everything. "Play you a game of freeze-out. A hundred bucks to the winner." He retrieved the ball.

"You're gonna challenge me?" Henderson snickered. "Have you lost your—"

Calvanese took a thirty-foot right-hand hook shot with his back to the basket. Henderson watched the arc of the ball climb and then slowly descend, hitting nothing but net.

Calvanese grinned at a stunned Henderson. "If it makes it easier for you, I'll do it left-handed off the backboard."

"Better get out of here before that gang comes back," Henderson said meekly. "Lucky for you, too," he added with more vigor.

EIGHTEEN

"You play sports other than basketball?"

Henderson drove the patrol car down Western Avenue and glanced at Calvanese wearily.

"What?" Calvanese said defensively. "I'm just asking a simple question."

"At least you know it's simple," said Henderson flippantly. "Yeah, I play other sports."

"Let me guess. Baseball? No, that's not a popular sport anymore with... with certain folks. Football? Naw, probably too violent. You college types are probably into tennis. You get to shout out numbers and talk about love."

Henderson rolled his eyes. "Where is all this leading?"

"I was trying to find a sport you might be good at. Based on your performance last night, I'd remove B-ball from your résumé, if I were you." Calvanese folded his arms across his chest and leaned against the door. "I wanted to find an appropriate sports analogy to inspire you to do better in your job and in life. Let's use baseball as an example."

"Even though that's not popular anymore with... with certain folks?"

"Let's imagine, for the sake of argument, you're a player with the old Negro League.

Okay? So you're up at the plate, bottom of the ninth, two outs, full count, bases loaded, score tied nothin' to nothin'. The next pitch looks like it'll be just wide. If you're right, the winning run scores on a walk. If you're wrong, the umpire calls you out on strikes, the game goes into extra innings and the other team has the advantage."

"Why do they have an advantage?" asked a perplexed Henderson.

"Because it's my story," Calvanese snapped, annoyed. "You need a better reason?"

"Now that you ask," snarled Henderson, "yeah."

"Fine," Calvanese replied stubbornly. "They got a great bullpen and yours sucks."

Henderson tapped the siren, which was sufficient incentive for two prostitutes to move their business elsewhere. "I thought it was a scoreless game. We must have a great pitching staff."

"No," corrected Calvanese, politely. "You've got a great pitcher and he's finished for the night. All you've got to rely on now are a bunch of third-rate, overweight, underperforming losers. Like those hookers you just chased away. May I continue with my story, now?"

Henderson shrugged. "Whatever brings you joy."

"Thank you," Calvanese said condescendingly. "So, do you take the risk of being called out with the bat on your shoulders or do you swing and try to get the game winning hit?"

"I take ball four and win the game."

Calvanese made a sucking sound and glanced out his window. "Figures."

"Hey, I play the percentages," Henderson said indignantly. "If I get the call, we win. If not, we extend the game, and get another chance next inning. We're playing at home, that must count for something."

"It means you won't have to travel far after you lose the game and, trust me, whatever the score, you'll still be a loser."

"That makes as much sense as anything else you've said. And for the record, there were no third-rate, overweight, under-performing losers in the Negro League. Ever!"

"You don't get it, do you? If you're gonna win, deserve to win. Don't let the other guy's mistake give you the victory, 'cause that's not some major triumph to feel proud about. It's a chicken-shit defeat disguised as success."

Henderson checked out the alley behind a convenience store and then proceeded across the front parking lot. "I know you don't appreciate this. But balls and strikes are part of the rules of the game. And if you play by the rules, you earn whatever success you achieve."

Calvanese studied Henderson closely. "Do you have to do everything by the book?"

"Yes, I'm a police officer and that's what we're trained to do. Does that present a problem?"

Calvanese opened a package of gum and removed a stick which he carefully unwrapped.

"Let me tell you something that might save your life one day or better yet, save mine." He stuck the gum into his mouth and offered Henderson a piece, which he refused. "Great cops, like great chefs, work from instinct," Calvanese dutifully explained as he chewed. "Cookbooks are for those with no imagination. Rules are for those with no balls. When somebody needs a cop, they better pray they get one who isn't working from someone else's recipe."

"I hadn't realized the Constitution had a footnote that read: 'Season to taste.'"

"It's right next to the section on all men being created equal, which is also subject to much experimentation and debate." Calvanese smiled smugly but his body jolted forward at the sound of a shotgun blast.

Henderson slammed on his brakes and looked at his rearview mirror. Calvanese turned and saw a police motorcycle slide across the street and crash into a storefront. A white officer lay motionless in the middle of the road. A burgundy Cadillac sped off, hitting several parked cars as it raced away from the scene.

Henderson made a rapid U-turn and headed for the fallen victim. Calvanese grabbed the radio transmission and barked instructions. "Officer down! Officer down! Western and King! Need immediate attention. In pursuit of suspect."

Henderson's patrol car pulled up near the body as two security guards from a local bank rushed to the officer's aid. Calvanese could tell it was too late by the amount of blood and brain matter scattered across the area. The bullet had struck full impact through the back of the head; the helmet had exploded away.

One of the security cops knelt next to the slain officer, shaking his head sadly. He looked at Henderson. "We'll stay with him."

Henderson floored the accelerator and took off in hot pursuit while Calvanese provided the police dispatcher with details requesting backup.

The Cadillac burst through the business district headed for the Harbor Freeway. Cars and pedestrians barely avoided the getaway vehicle. Calvanese tried to get a look inside but couldn't see through the Cadillac's heavily tinted windows.

The Cadillac sideswiped one car, forcing it into a collision with a small van. Henderson quickly maneuvered the patrol car around the accident but lost control momentarily, sliding onto the sidewalk. Calvanese saw the Cadillac take the nearest ramp unconcerned with cars waiting to merge into freeway traffic.

Henderson regained control of his vehicle and cut across the avenue toward the exit blocked by a series of vehicles that had piled into each other. He steered the patrol car along the island kicking up dirt and uprooting small bushes.

Calvanese managed to spot the car. "It's in lane three, quarter mile ahead," he said, and detached the shotgun from the console. The Cadillac recklessly maneuvered its way through traffic, merging in and out of lanes and cutting off vehicles.

Two highway patrol cars joined the chase with their sirens blasting. Henderson led the way and tried to keep pace with the assailant's getaway car, but the driver of the Cadillac disregarded their own safety, intentionally ramming other automobiles to create obstacles behind him.

One of the highway patrol cars swerved to avoid a school bus but crashed into a series of disabled vehicles causing a chain reaction of additional accidents. Henderson's car and the remaining highway patrol unit raced parallel to each other as they narrowed the gap between themselves, and the Cadillac headed toward an exit ramp. In anticipation of the move, Henderson sped toward the exit but at the last moment the Cadillac rapidly veered away from the ramp and continued down the freeway.

The police cars quickly followed. Calvanese glanced at the speedometer. "He's doin' more than a hundred, where the fuck is the air cover?" Calvanese searched overhead looking for a police helicopter but noticed something ahead that alarmed him. "Shit!"

Construction workers were repairing a stretch of the center divider, and the Cadillac crossed the lanes, headed straight toward them. The workers dived for cover.

The Cadillac crashed through the median divider, still under construction, and drove the opposite direction into northbound traffic. The police cars came to a screeching halt and attempted to back up to the opening but were prevented by dozens of automobiles and trucks, now part of a massive and chaotic traffic jam.

The Cadillac zigzagged across the four lanes as cars slammed on brakes, colliding with each other. A supermarket tractor trailer swerved and struck two cars. The back door of the truck swung open releasing a stream of produce, groceries, canned goods, and frozen meats, flying onto the freeway, bouncing off cars and smashing windshields.

A second tractor trailer, carrying a fleet of new luxury automobiles, tried to avoid the wreckage but didn't have a chance. It struck a sedan, flattened a sports car, and then careened off the railing, spinning out of control. Two cars on the top railing were unhinged and the pair of four-thousand-pound projectiles flew across the freeway into oncoming traffic. One of the cars barely missed Henderson's patrol car, sailing over the hood, bouncing over traffic. The second car landed onto a sedan flattening it like a tin can.

The skidding trailer swerved into the guardrail, slid a quarter of a mile destroying everything in its path, culminating in an explosion that sent a fireball across all four lanes.

The Cadillac headed the wrong way toward an exit ramp and disappeared.

Henderson's patrol car headed south on the freeway taking the closest exit. Calvanese peered out the rear window and discovered nothing but freeway wreckage for as far as the eye could see.

A half-hour later, several police vehicles, including Henderson's, surrounded the abandoned Cadillac in a vacant lot near the old Fox Hills Mall. Staff from the police lab busily searched the car looking for evidence. One technician removed a registration slip from the glove compartment and held it up before his colleagues.

Henderson nudged Calvanese. "You think he's paid his registration fee?"

Calvanese shrugged. "Don't know, but I hope he's current with his insurance."

NINETEEN

Henderson stood motionless in the shadows of a stairwell, alert, and tense; perspiration dripped from his forehead onto the cracked, faded linoleum. His eyes signaled Calvanese, who moved steadily down a poorly lit, dingy hallway that reeked of alcohol and urine. Henderson followed behind, gun drawn, carefully targeting every dark corner. Behind him, a dozen members of SWAT took up their positions preventing access in or out of the building.

Calvanese tentatively approached an apartment door and stationed himself on one side, gun ready. Henderson joined him on the opposite side. The two men faced each other, and Calvanese searched his partner's eyes for a sign that betrayed more than nervousness but suggested outright fear. He wasn't certain what he found, and in any event, it was too late now. He was forced to depend on this man, but for reassurance, he glanced at the leader of SWAT, who signaled his readiness. Henderson prepared to knock but Calvanese shook his head and moved closer to the door, listening intently.

Inside the apartment, Linda Watkins wore a see-through lavender teddy and was slowly coming off a drug-induced high. She wiped white powder from her nostrils with her fingertips and licked the residue. Her drug use had taken its toll on her appearance, looking much older than twenty-seven and far less attractive than her photo perched on the ledge over the fireplace mantel. When she heard loud knocks at the door she turned to her part-time lover and full-time supplier, Derrick Nixon, a Black ex-convict whose arms and chest were overly developed from pumping iron during his last two prison terms. He looked at the door, more annoyed than concerned, and then motioned for Linda to check it out. Her eyes glazed over in resignation as she walked unsteadily toward the door, kicking off one fluffy pink slipper in the process.

"Who is it?" she asked, in a raspy voice, trying to clear her dry throat. "I said who the hell is it?"

Calvanese glanced at Henderson then spoke with a poor accent. "Youa orda Chinese food?"

Henderson gave his partner a weird glance and shook his head in disapproval. Calvanese shrugged and tightened his grip on his weapon.

Linda turned around, still a bit disoriented, and addressed Nixon who had just finished a second line of coke. "You order Chinese, baby?"

"I ain't ordered shit," he grumbled. "Motherfuckers always knockin' on the wrong door. Tell 'em to take his fuckin' ass back to China 'fore I bust a cap in his fortune cookie!" He inhaled two quick bursts of air, and his head kicked back, releasing a low groan. His eyelids flickered; his body shivered—a hot, spastic reaction hit him hard in the center of his belly bending him over in ecstasy. Both his hands tightened into fists then opened slowly in apparent surrender.

"You got the wrong fuckin' address!" she yelled, then looked for additional drugs.

Henderson spoke softly. "You shoulda said pizza."

Calvanese raised his gun shoulder high, pointed at the door, and responded firmly. "Everybody says—"

Both cops shouted, "Pizza!" and kicked open the door, rushing inside followed quickly by several members of SWAT.

Nixon lunged for his gun and then grabbed Linda from behind, using her to shield himself. He put his massive arm around her neck and squeezed hard, pressing the weapon against the side of her head.

Calvanese and Henderson aimed their guns at Nixon and his terrified hostage.

"Let her go, Derrick!" ordered Henderson as he inched closer.

"Back the fuck off!" ordered Nixon. "Or I'll break the bitch's neck!"

"Help me, please," begged Linda. "He'll do it. He's crazy."

"Hey, you're not related to me," said Calvanese casually. "Why the hell should I care?"

"You piece-a-shit flatfoot," cried Linda.

"I don't walk. I ride," said Calvanese. "Technically, that makes me a flat ass."

The SWAT members stood at the doorway and focused their weapons on Nixon, waiting for a clear shot or a command from Calvanese.

Henderson looked at Calvanese and motioned toward the corner of the room. Calvanese moved slowly toward an artillery warehouse; machine guns, grenades, and explosives were all lined up against the wall along with boxes of ammunition stacked on top of each other. Calvanese feared one misplaced bullet could collapse the whole apartment building. He signaled the SWAT team to back off.

"Expecting a war, Derrick?" asked Henderson.

Nixon pointed the gun at the stack of explosives. "I'll blow up this fuckin' place and everyone in it!"

"Then you'd be dead," answered Calvanese. "Think of all

the sorrow and grief you'd cause the people who depend on you —pimps, prostitutes, junkies." Calvanese took a small step to the side. "Your mama."

"My mother's dead," Nixon said angrily.

"You wanna visit her?" warned Calvanese. "I'll be happy to arrange it."

"I didn't visit her when she was alive," huffed Nixon, "sure ain't plannin' on seein' her anytime soon." He brought Linda closer and inched his way toward the back wall.

"Give it up, Derrick," said Henderson. "Let your girlfriend come over here and nobody has to get hurt."

"Put your guns away first," said Nixon. "Then I'll let her go." He pressed the gun against her head again.

"Doesn't work like that," said Calvanese. "We give the orders, you follow them."

Nixon stared at Calvanese. "You just want an excuse to blow me away, don't you?"

Henderson slowly moved toward Nixon on the opposite side from Calvanese. Nixon became increasingly anxious and tried to track the movements of both cops as they steadily encircled him.

"You've given me all the excuses I need," responded Calvanese. "Lucky for you, I don't like filling out the extra paperwork. Cooperate with me and you can be back in the cell with your sweethearts who miss you very much."

Nixon pleaded with Henderson. "You ain't gonna let him kill me, are you brother?"

Henderson started to reassure the man but was cut off.

"I hate to break up this family reunion," interrupted a peeved Calvanese, "but I got a house with nobody in it waiting for me to come home. So, to use your expression, 'break the bitch's neck' or let her go. Now!"

Henderson looked disapprovingly at Calvanese. Nixon violently pushed Linda into Calvanese and fired a shot into the ceiling, exploding the ceiling's light fixture. He raced across the living room and leapt through the closed window, shattering glass. Calvanese shoved Linda off him and glanced at Henderson.

"Your brother just got away." He motioned SWAT and the team rapidly exited the apartment and sprinted down the corridor.

Henderson rushed to the window and noticed that Nixon had landed awkwardly, injuring his leg. Henderson knocked away some jagged glass jutting out from the window frame and looked at the two-story drop. He climbed on the windowsill and jumped to the ground.

Calvanese moved to the window and looked out. He decided he'd rather take the stairs. He proceeded to the door, then stopped and smiled at the frightened woman.

"What's your name, darlin'?"

"Linda."

"Linda, be a love and call 911."

"Fuck you."

"I'm lonely, but not that much." He exited the apartment, leaving Linda alone. She picked up a vase and angrily threw it against the wall and then looked around the room for any usable drugs.

Nixon hobbled toward a car, but Henderson grabbed him around the neck. Nixon threw two elbows that struck Henderson in the ribs, and then tossed the officer over his shoulder into some tall hedges. Henderson fell onto the wet lawn face first and slid several feet.

Nixon opened the car door, but two gunshots blasted the side window. He raised his hands high and slowly turned around.

Calvanese aimed the gun at his face. "I'm out of warning shots," he said. "The next one you won't hear."

Henderson rose groggily and took pieces of lawn out of his mouth, his face covered in mud.

Calvanese shook his head in exasperation. "Hey, Al Jolson, you still got your gun?"

Henderson looked at his holster. Fortunately, the gun was there. He glanced at Calvanese who clapped twice as the members of SWAT stood in silent amusement.

TWENTY

Calvanese and Henderson handled Nixon's preliminary interview in the interrogation room at headquarters. Calvanese loved this part of the job, a battle of wills that could be crude one moment and sophisticated the next. It represented the ultimate contest between predator and prey, except the current rules excluded the use of weapons or any form of overt violence.

Attorney Nelson Price, dressed in a pale plaid suit and seriously scuffed brown shoes, sat next to his client.

"You don't need to answer anything, especially from these wannabe detectives," advised Price, who avoided Calvanese's harsh glare.

Nixon ignored the advice. "I'm in America," he declared arrogantly. "I got a right to free speech. And I got a right to own firearms." He stuck out his chest and leaned back in his chair. He looked at Calvanese and then smirked. "You got a problem with that, go fuck with the N.R.A."

Calvanese wanted to rip out the man's heart and shove it down his lawyer's throat. Come to think of it, the old methods weren't so bad. He suddenly longed for the days of his father where these rooms were used for a little discreet persecution—a justifiable chamber of fear and coercion that elicited confessions from the guilty and saved the state the expense of a trial. Sure, a few innocent suspects might fall into unconsciousness protesting the charges and the city would have to settle out of court, but attribute that to the price of justice and then write it off as a legitimate business expense. In times of war, violations of personal liberties came with the territory. The judicious infliction of punishment, carried out for the common good, was still the most efficient and effective way to separate the wheat from the chaff. A.C.L.U. be damned.

"Why'd you need so many weapons?" asked Henderson.

Nixon cleared his throat, making a disgusting sound in the process. "I live in a bad neighborhood," he commented dryly and exchanged smiles with his attorney. "Never know when a cop's gonna break in, start some trouble. You guys really need to exercise self-control, stop hasslin' decent citizens like myself. Lucky for you I'm good-natured and willin' to let bygones be bygones." He grinned at Price then shifted his attention to Calvanese. "If you promise to say bye, I'll do my part and promise to stay gone."

"That's the one promise I can help you to keep," said Calvanese. "You're gonna stay gone a long time for killing a cop."

"I ain't killed nothin' but some time," said Nixon, calmly.

"You also gonna deny that you caused a lot of damage on that freeway? The good news is that you won't have to attend traffic school. The bad news is the only driver's seat your ass will ever touch is gonna have leather straps and enough electrical current to melt the gold in your rear molars." Calvanese leaned close to Nixon and spoke softly. "I recommend you steer that little wooden chair straight to hell."

"I recommend you go fuck yourself. You ain't got shit on me.

I didn't off no cop," he protested. "And I sure as hell ain't caused no damage with my car. My ride was stolen last week."

"You file an insurance report?" asked Henderson.

"Don't know how to file. Ain't got a secretary." Nixon gazed at the ceiling. "Now that I think about it, ain't got insurance either."

"What about the police, you notify them?" followed up Calvanese.

Nixon shuddered. "I break out in a rash just thinkin' about y'all." He scratched under both armpits and then picked at a fresh scab on his wrist.

"Yours were the only fingerprints in the car," declared Henderson.

"Really?" Nixon raised both eyebrows in feigned astonishment then gazed at his attorney. "Must mean the car was mine." He returned his attention to Calvanese. "Next you're gonna tell me you found my piss in and around my toilet bowl."

"Why'd you kill him, Derrick?" asked Calvanese, no longer interested in playing games.

"I was home with the flu."

"Anybody there with you?" asked Henderson.

"Yeah," answered Nixon, confidently. "A bunch of germs and some roaches on my sandwich." He tapped the side of the table with both hands. "I think it was ham and cheese, but I can't swear to it."

The attorney looked at his watch. "Are you charging Mr. Nixon with anything beyond weapons possession?" he inquired, and then closed his briefcase. "I've got a court appearance in forty-five minutes, and I hate to keep justice waiting." Price removed a soiled handkerchief from his shirt pocket and dabbed his forehead.

Calvanese slowly rose from his seat and approached the attorney. He despised most defense lawyers. This one was a real lowlife who'd made a living representing the scum of the earth.

"You enjoy his sandwich?" he asked with disdain. "'Cause only an insect would represent a piece of shit like him."

"The wrong cop got his head blown off," stated Nixon. "Lucky for me there's still plenty of bullets left," he threatened, then pointed his index finger at Calvanese mimicking firing two shots. "When I make bail, I'll sell them discounted to the right people."

Calvanese took a step away and then lunged across the table and grabbed Nixon's throat. Henderson pulled his partner off the amused suspect who leaned back in his chair and balanced himself on its rear legs.

"I can put you up on charges," Price informed Calvanese.

"Do that!" replied Calvanese. "I'll volunteer to share the cell with your client."

Nixon leaned back further. "If you wanna suck my dick, you ain't got to become an inmate," he said, pleasantly. "All you got to do is smile pretty and we can do it here."

Henderson's foot pushed the base of the chair and Nixon crashed to the floor. He looked up at the culprit.

"Had a cramp in my foot," Henderson said innocently.

Calvanese looked at the lawyer and shrugged helplessly. "I get those sometimes, too. Real painful. Last time it happened I had multiple spasms. By the time I managed to cure my problem, I kicked out an inmate's teeth and cracked four or five of his ribs." He smiled at Nixon. "What kind of sauce you like on broken ribs?"

Against the objections of Nixon's lawyer, who wanted the session to end, two detectives took over the interview and Henderson and Calvanese headed to their locker room.

"Finally did something that wasn't by the book," said Calvanese admiringly. "Maybe there's hope for you yet."

Henderson looked at him curiously. "Could this be a compliment?"

"No. It's an observation. But now I'm about to give you a

warnin', and it's the last one I'm gonna give." He stopped and thumped Henderson on the chest. "Don't ever interfere with me when I'm chokin' someone. Capisce?"

Henderson attempted to respond but Calvanese resumed his march down the police corridor.

TWENTY-ONE

Calvanese worked out his tensions on the abdominal machine, five sets of crunches, ten to twelve reps adding ten pounds of weight each set then he reversed the order, heavy to light, light to heavy. Although he didn't possess a six-pack anymore, he still turned heads at the health club. He touched elbows to knees then slowly eased the machine to its normal position. Sitting upright, his feet straddled the lower bars which were cushioned by torn leather repaired by duct tape.

It was true that Mike Stevens could be a bit of an asshole, maybe more of a redneck than required for the job, but he was also a good cop. Calvanese would want him on his side in times of war and a safe distance away during those rare interludes of peace. Then again, most cops weren't of any use during a truce. Like militant ducks out of turbulent waters, the transitory calm usually drove cops crazy, made them lose their bearings. It really messes with you not to be able to trust your fellow citizen. But when you can't trust your fellow officer, your brother in arms, well, that'll rip out your heart and any semblance of courage that went with it.

He watched the three televisions hanging overhead, all

tuned to different channels: ESPN, MTV, and CNN. Sports, music, news, what else would a reasonable person need in life? Maybe Disney for the kid in us. He read the scroll at the bottom of the screen on the news station. Some Black group had written the *L.A. Times* and taken credit for the police murders. They warned the retaliations would continue until "the oppression of people of color by uniformed assassins ceased." There was that phrase again, "people of color." Calvanese wondered if all white folks were colorless. Transparent? Sometimes. But clear? Never.

They called themselves the Black Liberation Army—B.L.A. Who the hell was going to be worried by a group named "bla?" Blah-blah-blah-blah... They could either talk you to death or bore you to tears, but terrify you? Come on. At least, that's what he was attempting to convince himself—it was just a prank of no consequence and would be seen as such by an informed and rational public. But he knew otherwise. Whether true or not, this newest revelation would serve to increase the paranoia within the force as well as throughout the city. He could almost hear the pundits shouting: *The race war is coming! The race war is coming!*

Calvanese had worked up a good enough sweat for two workouts. He listened to the sounds of his feet hitting the treadmill and quickened his pace. His arms pumped faster with each stride. What was he running from, or to? Like all treadmills, this one would take him nowhere. It would simply give him the sense, the illusion, that he had made some progress. Sometimes, that was all you needed to make it to the next day, the next exercise session, the next terrorist organization, or the next drink.

He jumped, spread-eagled his legs until his feet were balanced precariously on the edges of the treadmill, and then turned off the machine.

* * *

Max Oliver sat with two dozen other police candidates at the L.A.P.D. testing site. He was almost finished with the multiple-choice test. He had met the minimum qualifications for prospective officers last month, completed a background investigation, and passed his physical abilities exam. Once he passed this test, he'd attend a personal interview with an L.A.P.D. panel. After that he'd take the final step and complete a medical and psychological evaluation. His lifelong dream finally would be realized.

He had practiced at the gun range all week and had achieved a perfect score twice. He enjoyed shooting with police officers, had made some friends that encouraged him to apply, as if he needed any encouragement. He had given his condolences regarding the recent murders and thanked them for their service, telling them he would be proud to join them one day as a fellow officer. He wanted to attend some of the funerals but didn't think he had the right. So, he watched them on his television. It was the least he could do.

He completed the test, placed his pencil on the desk, said a quiet prayer hoping that he did well and waited to be dismissed.

TWENTY-TWO

Jasper Campbell poured Calvanese another cold draft and placed the tall glass in front of him. "You're usually not here so early," the bartender said, concerned.

"I heard business was down and I felt guilty. Thought I wasn't doin' my share of drinking." Calvanese looked at him with puppy eyes. "I'm gonna make up for all that, I promise." He lifted the glass, gave Campbell a toast, and then took a sip of beer.

Edward Poole, a young, handsome first-year cop walked past the bar. "Gentlemen," he said softly, and proceeded toward a table in the back of the restaurant.

Campbell gave Calvanese a weird look.

"What?" asked Calvanese.

"You think that rookie's a little strange?"

"All rookies are strange," replied Calvanese.

"I don't mean like that," answered the bartender. "He got a tender side," he said effeminately. "Might be hidin' the ole baton in the buttocks, if you catch my drift."

"You think he's gay?"

Campbell lined up a row of glasses. "I think he's wearin' pink underwear."

"With thoughts like that you might be the tender one," joked Calvanese.

Campbell wiped the counter clean with a damp cloth, not trying to avoid Calvanese's hands which he simply brushed aside. "You worry me sometimes, you know that?"

"I'd be worried if I didn't."

Campbell looked at Calvanese suspiciously. "You ain't got a problem workin' with a limp gun?" he asked, annoyed.

Calvanese gave a half-hearted shrug.

"You know, Calvanese, I didn't know you were such a liberal."

"I'm not. But I think if a person can do the job they ought to be allowed to fail or succeed based on their God-given talent. Anyway, I think about gays same way as I think about vegetarians—more meat for me."

Campbell laughed. "Now, that's the Tony Calvanese I know and love."

"You love me, Jasper?" Calvanese asked excitedly. "You really love me?"

Campbell flicked the damp cloth at Calvanese, hitting him on the arm. "I'm officially shutting you down for the night. No more drinks until you learn to behave decently in a fine establishment."

"If I'm ever in a fine establishment, I'll try and remember that." Calvanese dropped a ten-dollar bill on the counter. "If there's any change left over, you can buy the rookie a drink."

Campbell grumbled and then muttered an obscenity as he watched Calvanese exit the place.

Calvanese walked down the block toward the parking lot and took a quick glance at his watch. Still early. *Maybe there's a good movie on cable.* He didn't have time to complete the thought when the mysterious blond from last week pulled up in a Mercedes convertible and tapped the horn. He approached her, placed his hands on the vehicle, and leaned over.

She extended her hand. "Gabriella Morgan, but my friends call me Briella."

He took her hand and held it for a moment. "Nice car."

"You want to check the registration to see if it's mine?"

"I'm off duty," he informed her.

"You want to check it anyway, so you'll have my address."

He felt like a schoolkid and hoped he wasn't grinning or, if he was, there weren't any tiny pieces of pretzel stuck in between his teeth.

"I guess I could always follow you home," he said without thinking. and then worried that he seemed too suggestive or needy. "Just to make sure that you got there all right."

"Is that a special service the police provide free of charge?"

"We're here to protect and to serve."

"I promise not to drive too fast. Wouldn't want to lose you in traffic."

"If there's a problem, I'll use my siren."

"You might draw attention to yourself."

"Right at this moment"—he looked at her and smiled—"I want the whole world to notice."

She smiled back. He thought he saw her blush, but maybe that was his blood rushing to his face.

TWENTY-THREE

Geraldo sat behind his studio desk looking terribly distraught. He straightened his eyeglasses, stared into the camera, and released his trademark desperately tragic sigh. "Ladies and gentlemen, I'm reporting from Los Angeles, a city that has suffered through the Rodney King trial and its violent aftermath; endured the racist views of Mark Fuhrman and the racial divide caused by the O.J. verdict; been engulfed in the national reawakening following the death of George Floyd; and confronted widespread corruption in its once highly honored police force."

Nicole ate potato chips and sipped lemonade as she made herself more comfortable on the couch. She turned up the volume on the television and listened to Geraldo moan and groan.

"Now, we face the most challenging crisis yet to be confronted by the citizens of this beleaguered city."

The front door snapped open, and Henderson entered. He immediately took off his gun belt and placed it on the top shelf inside the closet.

The television voice droned on. "Racial tyranny, a police department divided... *The War between the Races*. That's what we're calling tonight's provocative program."

Henderson grabbed the remote.

"Stay tuned. It just might save your life." Geraldo released another pessimistic sigh that was terminated prematurely by Henderson.

"Hey," complained Nicole, "I was watching that."

"If Geraldo can save our lives, we don't deserve to live." Henderson plopped down near his wife and propped an extra pillow behind his head.

"I can't believe the stuff they put on air," Nicole munched a handful of pretzels. "Sherri had a brother with more gold teeth in his mouth than Fort Knox, bragging about all the white girls he's knocked up and agreeing to take DNA tests, the results to be announced by the end of the show. Wendy had on Black women who hated all Black men. Tamron had a segment about 'gangsta sistuhs'. Phil interviewed Black transsexuals who abused their children."

Henderson studied her curiously as she casually drank some lemonade.

"What?" she asked, defensively.

"Have you noticed you're on a first-name basis with talk show hosts?"

"Are you implying something's wrong with that? That I'm not allowed to have close personal relationships with my television friends?" She curled up on the couch and started sucking her thumb.

"Fetal positions really turn me on," said Henderson.

"Next on *Oprah*," she announced seductively.

"I thought all those shows were cancelled?"

"Reruns are forever. That's why we pay so much for all our streaming services."

"Streaming services? That sounds nasty."

He grabbed her affectionately and kissed her lightly on the lips. "Don't lose any sleep worrying about those programs," he said, comforting her. "No one takes them seriously. It's like wrestling, everybody realizes it's fake."

She pulled away, startled. "What do you mean, wrestling's fake?" She shoved him in the chest. "You better take that back."

Dexter returned from school and slammed the door. He wore a fresh bandage over his left eye and had several minor bruises on his face and chin.

"What happened to you?" asked his father.

Dexter hurried toward his room but was quickly intercepted. Henderson held Dexter and went down to one knee. Nicole rushed over and lightly touched her son's face. He winced in pain.

"Dexter, who did this to you?" Henderson asked, his concern quickly replaced by a father's bubbling anger needing to be directed at whoever hurt his son.

"Are you all right, baby?" asked Nicole.

"Two white kids jumped me at school. They called me that word you won't let me say." Dexter stifled his tears. "Daddy, I don't want you to be a policeman anymore."

"I thought you liked me in a uniform."

"They said the Black cops were gonna get killed next. Except they didn't say 'Black,' they said—"

"I know what they said, Dexter," Henderson cut off his son. "You go on and wash up. I'll come in later and help you with your homework."

"I don't want to go to school. I hate white people! I hate all of them!" He ran off crying and disappeared inside his bedroom.

Henderson and Nicole exchanged worried looks. "Got advice from any of your talk show friends?" he asked.

"Not even Oprah could fix this one. I better go in there and see to those bruises."

He grabbed her arm to stop her. "I got it."

"You sure?"

"No. But I'm a dad, so I have to fake it."

She watched him head to Dexter's room.

TWENTY-FOUR

Briella lived in a luxury high-rise in Marina del Rey with views of Catalina Island and the ocean on one side and the marina on the other, but Calvanese didn't get to see much of it. As soon as they set foot in the condominium, they began kissing passionately, starting at the front door, moving through the living room, proceeding down a hallway, and arriving inside the master bedroom. He fumbled with her blouse as she undid his trousers. He pressed her body against the wall and then stopped, uncertain, unsure.

She looked at him, concerned. "What's the matter?" she asked.

He shook his head, a slight motion of doubt and worry. "I don't know if I can touch anymore." He glanced away, felt foolish. "The only thing I've become good at lately is slamming people against the wall." He looked at her tenderly. She touched the side of his face, stroked his cheek, and ran her hand down to his shoulder. She held him in both hands and then suddenly spun him around and shoved him against the door.

"How do you like me now?"

He hadn't thanked God in ages, but before this night would

end, that record would be broken several times. He thanked God. He thanked fate. He thanked Briella's parents, and he even offered silent kudos for whoever designed her perfume. He hoped that scent would last forever but if it didn't, he would settle for the memory of tonight, even if it competed with other memories, other fragrances, and other loves.

* * *

Henderson sat on the bed next to a downcast Dexter, and used some antiseptic on his wounds which caused his son to flinch. He replaced the bandage.

"Am I gonna be punished?" his son asked apprehensively.

"Yes," he answered lovingly. "But not by me."

Dexter lowered his head until his chin was planted firmly into his chest. "By Mom?" he muttered.

"Not by her either." Henderson put his index finger under his son's chin and gently lifted until they made eye contact. "By you," he said with conviction.

"Me?" Dexter swallowed hard.

"When you hate, you hurt yourself, sometimes even more than the people you're angry at." Henderson fluffed his son's pillow.

"I didn't mean what I said about hating white people," Dexter said, his lower lip quivering slightly.

"I know," Henderson said reassuringly. "I'm going to watch a movie on demand. You want to watch it with me?"

"What is it?"

"*In the Heat of the Night.*"

"The television show?"

"The movie."

"They made a movie from the television show?" Dexter asked incredulously and then grimaced noticeably. "That was dumb. Don't people have any new ideas?"

"Dexter, work with me on this, all right?"

Dexter gave in. He got off the bed and marched to the door. "Can we make popcorn?"

"What would a movie be without popcorn?" announced Henderson.

"And order pizza?"

"It's already on the way," his father replied.

"With cheese bread?" Dexter asked eagerly.

"A double order, along with spicy Buffalo wings and ranch dressing."

Dexter flashed a huge grin then decided to push it. "Can we have ice cream after?"

"Not unless you want to eat it in the emergency room."

Dexter considered it. "Mom can take us there."

* * *

"It's been a while, hasn't it?" Briella asked as she gently stroked Calvanese's chest.

"Why, did I forget something?" he asked defensively, and then braced himself, leaning on the two pillows resting against the headboard.

"You forgot to talk."

"I was afraid if I said something I might wake up and discover none of this was real."

"I know the feeling," she said with a degree of sadness that surprised him. "But I've learned you've got to make your own reality."

"You sound like you learned that lesson the hard way."

She looked away for an uneasy beat. "You playing cop or detective?"

"We both do the same thing, only the uniform changes."

She pulled the sheet off him and gave him a quick overview. "I'm kinda partial to what you're wearing now."

He re-covered his naked body with the sheet and added a bit of the blanket.

"Modest?" she teased.

"Cold," he answered, untruthfully. He studied the penthouse suite. *God, how rich is she?* He'd never seen a room so tastefully and expensively decorated and in his twenty-plus years of service. He'd been in the homes of the fabulously wealthy many times. Granted, his visits usually followed a burglary, domestic violence call, or a homicide, but he'd still managed to see the inside of some splendid estates.

Recessed lighting soothingly illuminated two original oil paintings perfectly positioned on either side of the wide-screen plasma television built into the mahogany-paneled wall. If those weren't museum pieces, they would be the next best thing. The frames alone would fetch a pretty penny. And that stereo system she owned. Surround sound, state-of-the-art home theater in every room. He prayed they were still seeing each other once the football season began.

Then, there was the furniture—had to be one-of-a-kind designer. The table lamps were exquisite, made of crystal and marble and dark rosewood. He'd had one bare foot on the plush carpet for less than two seconds, but it was more than enough time for his toes to realize that up until that glorious moment, they had been deprived of true luxury for their entire existence, forced to walk the face of the earth in extreme discomfort. Had the king-sized bed not beckoned so urgently, he would have gladly remained standing and giving both feet the pleasure of sinking further and further into the carpet's sumptuous fibers. But then he would have missed the sensation of floating on a silk-and-cashmere mattress that seemed to undulate with each tiny movement of his body—or was it hers?

The floor-to-ceiling windows throughout the bedroom provided an unobstructed view of the marina. Oversized yachts rested peacefully in their berths and could have passed for another original painting—serene at night, lively in the morning, beautiful always. Smaller boats glided across the shimmering water, their masts supporting colorful sails that flowed freely in the gentle breeze. The tranquility outside stood in stark contrast to the world he had come to know too well. That place consisted of gunshots and screams and police sirens in the middle of the night, and doors splintering under the force of battering rams, and the final pleas of the dying followed quickly by the anguished sobs of those notified that their loved ones had perished. Was it possible that these two worlds, so different, eliciting such conflicting emotions, could coexist?

Briella reached across the night table that had a thin layer of inlaid jade, grabbed her purse, and removed a coin, extending it toward Calvanese. "Penny for your thoughts," she offered.

"Then you've come to the right man." He took the coin. "Getting paid that much is in my league. But, Briella, I can't compete with all of this." He gave a sweeping gesture and quickly surveyed the stunning condo, once again.

"Did I ask you to? Look, if I wanted to compete with you, we'd be playing chess right now."

"I don't know how to play chess."

"I didn't say it would be much of a competition."

"Thanks, that certainly helps to soothe my feelings of inadequacy."

She sat up on the bed and covered her breasts with the chocolate satin sheet. Calvanese couldn't tell which was smoother; he finally chose her skin.

"Tony, I make a lot of money helping other people get rich off the stock market."

"How much?" he asked.

She gave him a mysterious look. "You really want to know?"

He thought about it for a moment then replied with a weak "No." He reconsidered. "Just tell me, is it somewhere between Bill Gates and Elon Musk?"

"Not as much as Jeff Bezos, before the divorce. Listen," she said, ready to put an end to this. "I don't feel guilty about the money I have, and neither should you."

"Briella, that's a nice theory but I don't feel guilty about what you have, I feel guilty about what I don't. What can I give you that you already don't have?"

"My father was a school bus driver. He died when I was six. My mother was a receptionist at a dental office and worked at a café at night so my sister and I wouldn't go hungry. But hunger, real hunger that makes your heart ache, is something you feel when the person you love is unable to be with you when you need them most." She leaned against Calvanese.

"This is what you can give me: not money, but the ability for me to be held." She nudged him with her foot. "Now, is there anything else you want to know?"

He hesitated then joined her in sitting upright. Their bare shoulders touched, and he almost forgot what he wanted to ask. "That night at the bar, when we first met, I... was that... have you..."

She put him out of his misery. "Ever done that before?"

He nodded. "It's all right if you lie to me and say no. In fact, I'd really appreciate it."

"The answer is no. I've never gone into a bar to hit on a man. I've never come back after I've left."

"Why'd you do it for me?"

"The first time I saw you wasn't at the bar. I was driving. The sun hit my windshield. I reached for the shade and just as I pulled it down, you drove by me in your patrol car. Then I saw you a week later, same street, same car, same feeling. Only the light wasn't coming from the sun this time. It was coming from you. So, I did what any normal person would do, I followed you and then hoped you would follow me."

He smiled and realized that he had to look like some silly kid with a grin. She reacted to his expression. "Yeah, I smiled too. Thought it was one of those hormonal flashes you get when the biological clock starts ticking too loud. I dismissed it as momentary madness rather than destiny or divine intervention." She leaned against him more purposefully. "I make a lot of people money. I study the data. I research international markets. I double- and triple-check my information, but in the end it's all a risk. In the final analysis, you go with your gut, rely on your instincts. And so, I did that with you. I took the risk. Made an investment in a future that I hoped would last more than one passionate night."

"After you left the bar, how come you didn't wait for me?"

"I did, but you took too long. I started getting nervous, thought you saw me as some kinda—"

"Amazing woman," he said, quickly and gallantly.

"Actually no, but that will do." She looked at him. "That will do nicely."

"I've only known you for a few hours, and yet somehow I can't imagine tomorrow without you." He was stunned that he had made the statement, even more amazed that it was true.

She slowly ran her index finger across his forehead and stopped to point it at his temple. "Consider your mind completely incapacitated."

"This doesn't happen, does it?" he asked.

"What?"

"I mean, in the movies it happens all the time. People meet and the fireworks go off, and you see all kinds of different colors you never knew existed, and you throw away your little black book because you'll never need it again. But movies aren't real life. Are they?"

She lightly touched his face. "Why do you think they made the movies in the first place? If it was all a lie, no one would sit for two hours in the theater to not see themselves represented on the big screen."

He thought about it. Wanted to believe it. "What if it's an alien movie or one of those slasher films?"

"That's life, too. You more than anyone should know that, Officer Calvanese. Or do you wear a badge and carry a gun just to show off?"

"You're an amazing woman. Anyone ever tell you that?"

"Yes, but it bears repeating." She kissed him hard on the lips then rested her head against the pillow and waited for him to share it with her. "You think you can put your words together with your actions?"

He shook his head in wonderment. "You really are incredible."

"Keep that thought."

He would keep that thought and so many more. When he touched Briella for the first time, his hand trembled, not from nervousness but from fear. He wanted to trust that he could feel again. He wanted to believe that after all this time, it was still possible to find joy in the possibility of love. And if not love, then certainly happiness, whether brief or not. After his wife had left him, he went through the typical range of emotions: anger, grief, self-pity, a sense of betrayal, blaming her, his job, himself, in that order. It took a long while before he allowed the memories to overtake the loneliness. In those memories, he found happiness, even if bittersweet.

He feared that the memory of tonight would last longer than his time with Briella. But if that was the case, he'd accept it, no matter the disappointment and pain that came with unfulfilled expectations, real or not.

Calvanese saw the last sailboat glide by and then felt the distant movement of the ocean; or maybe it was the earth that shook.

TWENTY-FIVE

"Damn—just look at the L.A. smog," Calvanese said with renewed enthusiasm. He took a deep breath, expanding his chest, releasing a broad smile as he exhaled. "Ain't it wonderful to see what you're breathin'?"

Henderson studied him mysteriously. "What'd you have, a colonic?"

"There's more than one way to clean out the old system, pal."

Henderson chuckled knowingly. "What's her name?"

"Briella," Calvanese answered proudly. "How'd you know it was a woman?"

"Lottery's not till Saturday, so it was just a wild guess." Henderson glanced at his partner. "Plus, you've got little red marks on your neck, and they're not razor burns."

Calvanese pulled down his collar and searched his neck in the rearview mirror of the patrol car. "I know you think of yourself as a detective, but have you considered they might be an allergic rash?"

"You might have a rash, but it's not from an allergy and it wouldn't be on that part of your body."

Calvanese flashed a sign of aggravation but quickly let it pass. "Saying something like that would normally get under my skin."

"No pun intended," Henderson quickly added.

"But nothing you do or say is gonna upset me today. I've got a 'do not enter' restricted area that repels anything that might interfere with my total sense of contentment." Calvanese whistled joyously.

"We'll see how long that lasts," Henderson muttered.

Calvanese switched from whistling to humming a happy tune.

"You wanna tell me about her, before you break out in song and dance?"

"No."

"Fine."

"She's the most amazing woman I've ever known," he said, radiating happiness. "I can't stop thinking about her. I feel like I'm in high school."

Henderson raised his hand to stop Calvanese from going further. "That's more than I wanted to know."

Calvanese continued, undeterred, oblivious to everything other than his newfound excitement. "She's perfect. I didn't think it was possible to feel that way for a person, except..."

"Except what?"

Calvanese's mood changed dramatically. He became concerned, worried. "I think of doing crazy things for her." He looked at Henderson, seeking understanding and guidance. "I mean really strange things."

Henderson studied his partner for several moments. "How strange?" he finally asked.

Calvanese bowed his head, more embarrassed than ashamed. "I thought of sending her flowers."

Henderson's face went blank then slowly came back to life

in disbelief. "No," he said, cynically. "You couldn't do something so craven, so despicable."

"I'm afraid I could," admitted Calvanese, continuing his confession. "And you know what else?"

"I'm not sure my sensibilities can withstand any more shocking details, but go ahead, purge yourself of any remaining demons."

"You're really enjoying this, aren't you?"

"You have no idea," Henderson grinned.

Calvanese shifted his weight in the seat and tried to find a comfortable spot. He wound up leaning against the door, which was as far away from Henderson as he could get. "I almost bought one of those silly cards that says: *Thinking of you.*"

"That's it?"

"Yeah," responded Calvanese, flustered. "You won't tell nobody, will ya?"

"Tony, I know you'll find this hard to believe, but all that stuff is normal."

"Yeah, for regular people."

"We're making progress. You're finally admitting you're not normal."

"You don't understand. I'm not referring to me." Calvanese sounded desperate. "I'm talking about her. She's got a bidet in her bathroom."

Henderson arched his left eyebrow. "It would look pretty ridiculous in her kitchen."

"She owns a yacht!" he exclaimed. "You don't send a shoebox greeting card to a woman who owns a yacht. Last time I sent a card like that, it was to a woman who owned an eight-speed combination blender and food processor."

"So, what happened?"

"I married her." Calvanese stared out the side window and spotted an elderly couple, holding hands and walking slowly.

"The blender had a lifetime warranty, the marriage didn't." He sighed. "I can't believe this is happening to me. Don't get me wrong," he added quickly. "I'm glad it's happening. I'm ecstatic it's happening. I just don't believe it."

"*You* don't believe it. I'm the one that ought to be in absolute shock." Henderson gave him a quick look. "Next, you'll be telling me you have a Black friend."

There was a heavy silence that permeated the car. Calvanese slid down his window.

"Tell me something, Tony..." Henderson hesitated, appeared uncomfortable, then decided to go for it. "You ever had any Black friends?"

Calvanese considered the question in earnest. "First guy I busted. I was kinda fond of him. But then..." He dismissed it with a brief shrug. "The first time is always special."

Henderson did a sharp U-turn that forced Calvanese's body to slam against the door and then jerk back toward the center console. "Why the fuck do I bother asking you anything serious?"

"I didn't know you were being serious," Calvanese responded smugly. "But that's a positive sign. It's good to seek counsel, bare your soul to the world. Emote, emit, and embarrass yourself like I just did for the past five minutes." He rubbed his hands together and caught a glimpse of himself in the side mirror. "Plus, self-reflection can be a lonely and empty feeling." He turned toward Henderson. "Keeping things inside can cause one to fester and rot, creating an odor worse than soiled underwear tossed over a warm radiator on a dark wintry night." He paused to congratulate himself. "I'm usually not so poetic but I think I'm in love."

"If you ever put in for a mental disability, I'll definitely testify on your behalf."

"This is so meaningful," Calvanese said with great emotion. "I think I might actually be making a Black friend, after all."

"Be careful what you wish for," Henderson threatened.

"Not today, amigo." He leaned back against the chair and closed his eyes. "Not today," he whispered.

Henderson stopped the car at a red light, shook his head slightly, gave a trace of a smile, and then whistled softly.

TWENTY-SIX

They screamed on the roller coaster and crashed into each other's bumper cars. She knocked over all the cans and was awarded a giant stuffed lion while he received a tiny key chain as a consolation prize. He told her that the arcades at the Santa Monica Pier amusement park were rigged in favor of women and children. She challenged him to use his authority as a cop and shut them down or stop complaining and lose like a man. They ate soft ice cream cones dipped in chocolate, topped off with multicolored sprinkles, and then shared a large cotton candy. She ordered fried onions on a grilled Polish sausage while he selected a double cheeseburger with steak fries. They rode a two-seater along the bike path and once they reached Venice Beach, exchanged the bicycle for rented rollerblades. And for the last three and a half hours, Calvanese had maintained one continual smile that only grew wider whenever he looked at Briella, and he looked at her as often as possible.

He couldn't recall smiling that much in a single day. The last time he was on rollerblades—well, now that he thought about it, he didn't remember ever being on rollerblades. But if he had been, he was certain he never enjoyed it as much as he did right now.

"What are you thinking about?" she asked as they strolled down the boardwalk near Muscle Beach.

"Being a kid," he quietly responded. "That's what you've made me feel like, a silly kid that thinks anything and everything is possible."

"You should ride the Ferris wheel more often. When you're up that high, the world seems a lot smaller, much more manageable."

He released a questioning grunt.

"If you don't believe me, we can try again," she teased.

"Not a chance," he said.

"What's the matter, you a bit queasy at the thought of heights?"

"Being up high never bothered me," he answered with a seriousness the question had not called for. "It's the coming back down to earth that concerns me. You get to see the world for what it really is—a dangerous and violent place."

She hesitated and then asked the question. "You want to talk about your job?"

"Not a good idea to discuss politics or religion."

"Which one applies to your job, the politics or the religion?" she wondered aloud.

"With me, like most cops, it's a double whammy. You've got both bases pretty much covered."

"Oh dear," she uttered softly but loud enough for Calvanese to hear.

He watched two children splash each other with ocean water until their mother intervened. The sailboats were out in full force, gliding effortlessly with the aid of a mild breeze. The sun playfully bounced off the waves as they crashed harmlessly off the boulders sprinkled along the shore. White foam embraced the sand clinging to seaweed and other debris like a protective blanket that would gently sweep all the material back out to sea.

"You have any idea how long I've been alone?" he asked, suddenly.

She took his hand and squeezed it tightly. "To be honest, I'm not thinking about your past—my thoughts are about the future. And that's a place where being alone is no longer an option... unless you want it to be."

They continued walking but this time Calvanese had little to say. His smiles had given way to anxiety, the fear of commitment to another human being and all that it entailed. The one good thing about his divorce was that he didn't have to worry about his wife anymore. That gave him the freedom to take chances on the streets. He never hesitated, not even in the face of extreme danger. Calvanese's great strength was his willingness to be the first in and the last out of any hazardous situation. He wasn't reckless, as some of his fellow officers had charged, or crazy as others suspected. He was fearless; in truth, he simply had no one to leave behind, so, he wouldn't be missed, except by his parents and a few friends on the force who had grown accustomed to bidding farewell to fallen heroes.

And now, amid his invulnerability, this absolute feeling of security, along came this woman to give him a reason to play it safe, to avoid risking his life unnecessarily, not because he mattered, but because she did. After all this time, he'd found someone else, someone who wouldn't take his ex-wife's place but would make a new one—someone who might share his life, and in so doing make it more worthwhile and meaningful, perhaps even precious. And when that happens, as any good and honest cop will confess, you're in deep trouble because once you've got an important reason to get home it makes you more reluctant to take risks out on the street. And that's the greatest risk of all.

"Was it something I said that made you go away and hide behind that so-called blue wall of silence?"

He smiled, but this time it was bittersweet. "That's a myth, you know."

"You mean cops don't protect each other when they've done something wrong?"

"Oh, we do that, all right, to the death. We're just not silent about it to the people we can trust—the people who wear blue."

She took his hand and led him to a bench where they both sat, staring at the ocean. Calvanese was nervous about the silence because he knew it wouldn't last and he was concerned about what Briella might ask that would force him to answer in a way where he couldn't conceal the truth.

"You don't have to be afraid of me," she said, then looked at him. "You know that, don't you?"

"Who said I was afraid?"

"I don't wear blue. And if that means you can't trust me, then there must be a reason, and the only one I can think of is fear."

"I can't afford to care as much as I'm beginning to care for you. I can't be thinking of you when I should be thinking about what danger is around the corner that could kill my partner or end my life before I've had the chance to spend it with you."

"You don't think I'm afraid? I may not be a cop that wonders if I'll come home at night. But caring's not easy and sure as hell isn't safe. I don't really know you, and yet it seems I've known you all my life. That seems crazy, I know. But isn't that what little girls, and maybe boys, think about, hope for? The magic that we know only exists in fairy tales, but somehow doesn't stop us from believing it could happen to us. That it could be real." She lightly touched the side of his arm. "That's trust, Officer Calvanese. Whether or not you wear blue."

"I think we should go."

She stood, disappointed. "Where to?"

He stood close to her. "There's this clothing shop on the boardwalk next to where we had lunch. I noticed this little blue T-shirt that I believe would look great on you."

She smiled, and that was all he needed.

* * *

That night he dreamt about falling—a seemingly endless out-of-control descent that lasted until the alarm clock intervened, offering a much-needed safety net: his bed. Prior to being rescued, he remembered tightly closing his eyes and opening his mouth as wide as it would go but the sheer speed of the dark plunge drowned out his screams. Calvanese usually didn't put much stock in dream interpretation, but this was more like a premonition—a billboard-sized revelation or warning. He didn't need a psychology degree to accurately evaluate the deeper meaning of this nightmare, especially when it included flashing lights and postings of impending dangers.

Officer Calvanese, a highly decorated veteran of the L.A.P.D., no longer found himself on sure footing. The earth beneath him had moved, a seismic shift of epic proportion. In other words, he'd fallen in love, a steep fall, apparently bottomless. But even in this conflicting state of bliss and fear he knew there'd be a bottom; there was always a bottom. He just didn't know if he'd find it before it found him. He wondered if he'd have sufficient time to break the fall, minimize the damage and the pain. Probably not. Definitely not!

He gently caressed Briella, who awoke at his touch wearing only her recently purchased T-shirt, which he quickly removed. He made love with a desperation he'd never felt before and when they finished, he felt more alone than ever.

Briella studied him for a moment and then snuggled next to him, draping her arm across his chest. "So, you're still afraid, too," she whispered.

Terrified, he thought but didn't answer. He simply nodded, grateful that the loneliness had not lasted.

TWENTY-SEVEN

Wallace Reeves drove a restored metallic blue supercharged 1968 Pontiac Firebird 400 that, with a recently tuned engine, might eke out eight miles per gallon. Luckily, he didn't care a whit about gas mileage or any other form of conservation. He craved power, the roar of the engine when he floored the accelerator, the heat from the catalytic converters when he dangled his arm outside the driver's window. The two air ducts on the hood reminded him of a woman's breasts, perky and erect, needing to be let down easily rather than slammed. He took decent care of his cars; his women were another matter. It all depended on how they performed, if they'd been reliable in the past—never let him down in a tight spot or when unexpected rough curves disrupted the natural harmony in a man's life.

Unlike his vintage automobiles, he preferred his women young. If they were also dumb, so much the better. He treated them as if they were leased or rented, drove them to the ground, and then got rid of them: no hassles, no long-term obligations, and no sense of loss. Put the pedal to the medal and his foot up an ass. That's how he liked it and what he liked he generally got, one way or the other.

He stuck a non-filtered cigarette into his mouth but didn't light it. He'd given up smoking ten years ago but wouldn't give up the ritual. It reminded him of the battlefield, the lull either before or after the storm when he and his fellow soldiers would go through a pack in one sitting. Dirty hands with bloodstained, chipped fingernails would pass them around like tiny sticks of dynamite or an Afghan whore they'd captured and shared, in tribute to the universal spoils of war. Whoever lit the first cigarette would use it to light the others. Unwilling to wait for his nicotine fix, he positioned himself next to the guy with the match. For the men in his platoon the practice served as another rite of passage. Tightly wound white paper trapping shreds of shit-colored tobacco stuck in the mouths of grimy-faced soldiers likely to die at any moment.

He liked the way it dangled from a man's lower lip casting off glowing hot embers and billowing smoke that could have been emitted from a crematorium. The effects were particularly impressive at night, outside under a star-filled sky, especially when you took into consideration the risk they were willing to put themselves in for two minutes of pleasure. He knew enemy combatants could more easily focus their weapons on the burning tip centered in his or any other grunt's face. At least the poor son-of-a-bitch would be allowed a last cigarette before his head exploded, splattering brain matter on those unfortunate souls who survived to smoke another day. But then, no one really survived back then, did they?

He turned the radio to his oldies but goodies station and then removed the cigarette drooping from his lips and crushed it in the overflowing ashtray. He stopped the car at a traffic light, opened his glove compartment, pushed aside his .38 and removed a pint of Tanqueray.

"I appreciate the ride," said Max Oliver, who sat impatiently in the passenger seat. Reeves had ignored him the entire ride, treated him as if he didn't exist, because to Reeves, he didn't, not in a way that mattered. He surreptitiously concealed the bottle underneath his seat and quickly closed the compartment. He casually turned to the side and looked at the two Black police officers who pulled up beside him in their patrol car. Reeves gave a noncommittal nod to the driver and, as he expected, the cop never returned the acknowledgment. He just stared right through Reeves as if he wasn't there or didn't matter —a bug on a dirty windshield. *Fuck 'em*, thought Reeves. *He's just a nigger in a uniform.*

The light changed to green. The patrol car drove through the intersection. Reeves remained at the light and then turned left. He hated anyone in a position of authority, didn't give a damn what color they were. Give an ordinary man a gun and a badge and you've created a monster waiting for an excuse to do what monsters do best: destroy the innocent and terrorize the weak.

"You take a left at the light. It's about a mile up the street on the right," said Oliver.

Reeves's daddy hated authority more than he did and as it turned out, authority hated him back with a vengeance. He'd especially detested Blacks who had some "little bit of power" and needed to prove to the white man he could be trusted to use it appropriately. And the way you gained the trust of your enemy, his father always used to say, was adopt their evil ways. "They're all a bunch of self-hating bastards," his old man preached. "You wanna confuse that type of nigger? Give 'em a choice between a Cadillac and a white woman. The damn fool would be permanently paralyzed for life, unable to decide between drivin' a car or ridin' some pussy." Then he'd laugh, one of those deep, baritone sounds he made whenever he wanted to punctuate the truth with his own brand of biting cynicism.

As far as it went with Reeves, he'd inherited his father's sarcastic sense of humor but not the cause of "a nigger's confusion." He never had to think twice about what was better, the car or the cracker. If you drive the right automobile, you can always get a white woman—just race the engine. He'd always thought he'd come home in a casket paid for by Uncle Sam, and he was mistaken about that prediction as well. He'd cheated death by helping it along, that's how he looked at it. If you stand in death's doorway, it's got no choice but to take you with it when it leaves. Step aside and get out of its path or, better yet, point it in a new direction, and then you've got a chance: the only one you're ever going to have.

Yeah. Give the Grim Reaper what it demands, and your own life will be spared. Lord knows, Reeves had given it a healthy supply of corpses in the name of his government, enough to last a long time, but not forever. Nothing lasts forever. Not even the deal you've made with death. He tried to tell Oliver that, but the boy shrugged him off. Didn't want to hear anything about dealing with death. He had thought about firing him a few times, but he didn't have the heart. Plus, the more he learned about him, the more he thought the boy would become useful for a lot more than working in the shop. Even a pathetic dude could serve a purpose.

He pulled into Oliver's driveway and finally looked at his passenger. "What you gonna do, now?"

"Try again," replied Oliver.

"Once you fail the psychological test, that's your ass. Try all you want but the result's gonna be the same."

"I'm never giving up. The force needs good cops. And I was born to wear that uniform."

Reeves knew there was no point in trying to make sense to some dumb ass who had no idea how fucked up he was.

"I really appreciate the lift."

"Yeah. Get a new car and a better attitude, one that gives you some sense."

Reeves watched Oliver enter his apartment. He removed

another cigarette from the pack and let it dangle from his lips, unlit.

TWENTY-EIGHT

Calvanese finished the daily special and studied his mother, who sat across from him in the corner booth. It was obvious she hadn't enjoyed the meal, other than the fact that she shared it with her "heart." That's what she had called him as a child: her heart. She loved cooking almost as much as she loved him, which partly explained why she was the world's most severe food critic. No woman was quite good enough for her son, although she had grown fond of Susan after she left. And no restaurant meal was worthy of her time, let alone her stomach. Despite that, she never missed an opportunity to be with him, even if it meant she had to swallow her pride and taste food made for the masses.

"How was your veal?" he asked anyway.

She rolled her eyes. "To be tortured for the good of man is a sacrifice. To be poorly prepared is a sin." She sipped her coffee, black no sugar. "That poor little animal suffered in a small cage, confined all its life so that it would be tender enough to give pleasure to our taste buds. Then some chef comes along and turns its little body into shoe leather."

"To be fair," suggested Calvanese, "they probably don't have chefs here, just cooks."

"Crooks is more like it, and that would be paying them too much of a compliment." She lowered her voice. "Americans," she said with a degree of pity. "They are so obsessed with speed."

"They?" He pointed his finger at her. "Mama, you were born here."

"But not *my* mama, and that makes me a second-generation immigrant." She arched an eyebrow and frowned. "What was I talking about?"

"Foreigners and speed."

Her right hand gave the air a mild chop. "It works for cars, planes, and trains but you can't put the word 'fast' next to the word 'food.' That's not possible. You either want food or you want fast. You can't have both."

"I wish he had come," Calvanese mused, unaware he had shared the sentiment aloud.

"He's a proud man, your father."

Too proud for his own good, thought Calvanese.

"He keeps thinking he'll run into somebody he once arrested."

"I know," Calvanese said with a sense of resignation. "And he doesn't want to give them the satisfaction."

"You have to be pretty sick, even for a criminal, to get satisfaction that way."

Calvanese smiled at the innocence of his mother. Even after all these years, she had no idea what her husband or, for that matter, what her son had experienced on these streets. *Guess we did a good job of protecting her from the truth.*

"Lock 'em up, throw away the key. That's what I think," she declared.

"You've gotten softer, more lenient over time. You used to advocate torture," Calvanese reminded her.

"Between you and me," she confided, "for the cruel ones, I'd feed them this veal for the rest of their lives. That'll teach 'em a lesson." She sat back and waxed philosophical. "What goes around comes around." She then blessed herself with the sign of the cross, twice.

"Why don't you and Dad get away? Sell the house. See the world."

Her eyebrows came to full attention. "My house is my world. It's my home. It's the place we raised you." She relaxed and spoke nostalgically. "We still have those marks on the wall of your room. The ones your father made each birthday to measure how much you grew."

"Why'd he stop at sixteen?"

"You became a man that day."

"He should've waited until eighteen. I grew a lot taller."

"You don't measure a man by how tall he is," she responded, acting the sage. "If you did, there'd never be any giants when you needed them."

An attractive waitress approached their table. "Can I get you anything else?" she smiled warmly.

"Married?" his mother asked, as if ordering off the menu.

"I beg your pardon?" the waitress blushed.

"Mom? Don't go there," warned an embarrassed Calvanese, and quickly reached for his wallet.

"You're so lovely," Mrs. Calvanese continued, turning on her charm while pointing to Calvanese. "My son wanted to know if you were married."

Calvanese sank into his seat and thought about crawling under the table, but then he'd be tempted to grab his mother's ankles and yank very hard.

Mrs. Calvanese tossed back her hair with the flair of a young schoolgirl and touched the waitress on her wrist. "You know how shy men can be," she confided.

The waitress smiled and assessed Calvanese with growing interest. "I'm single and very much available."

Mrs. Calvanese couldn't contain her excitement. "How wonderful," she exclaimed. "Pretty girl like you could use the protection of a member of the L.A.P.D."

The waitress turned suddenly distant and cold, staring at Calvanese with a combination of disappointment and contempt. "You're a cop?" she exclaimed bitterly.

"Twenty years," he answered proudly, knowing his response would annoy her even further, a discomfort he'd take great pleasure in causing.

"Excellent pension and benefits," Mrs. Calvanese intervened, still trying to broker the deal.

"My sister tried to join the force a few years ago. They really made her life miserable." The waitress placed her hands on her hips and challenged Calvanese. "You guys threatened by women, or you just don't like working with them?"

"If the Pope has problems with women becoming priests and handling the body of Christ, maybe we should give some thought to them handling a convicted felon." He grabbed a roll from the breadbasket. "But I'm not infallible on these matters. I only have experience to guide me—that, and my faith in people."

"I guess those views created the Mark Fuhrmans in your department?"

He used his steak knife to slice the roll and then cut a large tab of butter, which he spread generously on both halves. "My department didn't create Mark Fuhrman," Calvanese said calmly. He'd been through this enough times and no longer allowed his anger to get the best of him. "People like you did," he said calmly.

"We'll take the check now," Mrs. Calvanese said, throwing in the towel.

"And just how did I accomplish that?" the waitress said, demonstrating greater defiance.

"If some six-foot-five, two-legged animal is about to break into your daughter's room and the only thing that matters to him in this world is satisfying his vile and violent urges, you tell me, lady, who would you want protecting her, Mark Fuhrman, or F. Lee 'Fat-ass' Bailey?" He waited for a response but delighted in the knowledge she wouldn't have one in sufficient time to make a difference.

Mrs. Calvanese looked at her son. "Coffee?" she suggested.

"That's my only choice?" the flustered waitress finally replied.

Calvanese pounced for the kill. "You don't have a choice anymore. And, while you were wasting time thinking about it, now neither does your daughter."

Mrs. Calvanese shifted her body toward the waitress. "Why don't you two exchange numbers? Get together? You both seem to be so—"

The waitress ripped off a slip of paper from her pad and slammed the bill on the table. She left abruptly.

"Passionate about your views." Mrs. Calvanese completed her thought with resignation. She looked morose. "I'm never gonna have grandchildren," she mumbled to herself then stared at her son. "Am I?"

Calvanese gave a playful grin. "Actually, you might," he said coyly.

Mrs. Calvanese placed her left hand over her heart, her right hand on her forehead, and shivered dramatically. "I've never given up on the power of prayer. Never." She hesitated uncomfortably. "Maybe, once or twice, but never on this issue." She smiled gleefully. "You're in love? Tell me you're in love."

"We've seen each other every night for the last two weeks," he confessed openly and without any guilt.

"That constitutes betrothal in certain countries," she hastened to point out.

"I can't stop thinking of her," he further admitted.

"Is she Italian?" Mrs. Calvanese asked hopefully.

"No." He observed his mother's disappointment. "But she's rich."

She scowled then folded her hands together. "This ethnic thing is overplayed. We're all Americans."

Calvanese searched through his wallet to pay the bill but hadn't brought any money. His mother, fully prepared for such an eventuality, had her purse open and her money out.

"Don't leave a tip," he stated resolutely.

She left a large one. "When am I going to meet her?" she asked excitedly. "Next Saturday will be fine."

"Mom, I—"

"No later than Saturday. Bring her to the house. I'll make a feast fit for a king, a queen, and a marriage ceremony. Should I order a cake?" She erased the thought with her hands. "Wait till I tell your father."

"Mom, can you slow down a bit with the wedding invitations. I mean, it's not like I'm—"

"A young man, anymore," she said quickly before he could object. "Which reminds me, how old is she?"

"I think she's about—"

"You don't know?" she asked, surprised.

"I haven't had a chance to go through her purse and check out her driver's license and compare it to her birth certificate. Give me another day or two."

"But she's still child-rearing material, right?" She studied him anxiously. "Tell me she can conceive," she said, desperation rising in her voice. "If there's a problem, God forbid, I know this fertilizer doctor."

"You mean fertility?"

"Isn't that what I said? And don't correct your mother."

"She doesn't need a doctor, Mama. She's fine in that area, as best I can tell."

Mrs. Calvanese joyously flung her hands into the air. "Oh, Tony! I'm so excited. I'm gonna be a grandmother!"

Customers seated at adjoining tables overheard the good news and applauded happily.

She bowed humbly as if receiving a major award and then waved a heartfelt thank you.

TWENTY-NINE

Outside the 77th Street Community Police Station, Black leaders formed a protective semicircular line behind Reverend Wilson as he responded to a group of reporters. Allen Davis and John Dawson, the rookie whose partner had been murdered in the Hollywood Hills, were on either side of Wilson and another dozen uniformed Black officers stood guard behind the podium. Mike Stevens and a few other white cops remained in the background observing the proceedings, not bothering to conceal their dissatisfaction with the event.

"We're here in total support of our Black police officers who put their lives on the line only to be unfairly treated within their own departments," said Reverend Wilson to the approval of those surrounding him.

"Reverend Wilson," shouted a reporter, "do you have any comment on the recent murders of white policemen?"

Wilson considered the question, displaying a hint of a smirk. "Of course, those deaths are tragic," he answered dryly. "But you can't continue to act like an occupying army then be surprised when the citizens finally strike back."

"Are you justifying these acts?" asked another reporter.

"No one condones violence," he said unconvincingly. "But this is a nation well-versed in the art of retaliation. Yet it remains conspicuously silent when segments within our own society are mistreated by those in positions of authority. When chickens come home to roost, someone should have the courage and moral clarity to ask who drove them away in the first place."

The reporters scribbled feverishly, delighted with the quote. By the time they were finished, an *L.A. Times* journalist had made his way to the front, positioning himself adjacent to a nightly news camera, thereby ensuring televised coverage of his question. "In light of the murders of police officers, do you believe this is the appropriate time for Black police officers to bring a racial discrimination suit against their own union as well as the city as a whole?"

"Officer Davis, President of the Fraternal Order of African American Police, can respond to that, if he'd like. But I submit to you, had some of their issues been resolved long ago, perhaps we might have been able to avoid these tragic killings. In 2010 Black officers made up fourteen percent of L.A.P.D. Today, it's down to nine percent and falling. If Black officers are victims of racist police policies in their own department, imagine how the community must feel. It's only a matter of time before hopelessness erupts."

At the Reverend's invitation, Allen Davis moved to the microphone and rattled off several grievances along with a series of proposed remedies. By the time he recommended increasing the promotion rate of Black officers, Stevens and his white colleagues were angrily entering police headquarters. On their way in they passed Wallace Reeves standing alone at the rear of the crowd, listening attentively but without any positive expectations.

On the contrary, Reeves thought of this whole occasion as a colossal waste of time. These folks were a bunch of talk. Not one of them was prepared to take any real action, put their own asses on the line. It was all for show. *How long niggers been gettin' killed by the police? And what do we do*, he pondered. *Demonstrate. Have a rally here or there where most of the brothers come looking for some pretty young thing to fuck.* Not that he ever turned down the opportunity for a new piece of tail, but at least he was honest about his motives. And when Black folks finally were pushed beyond their limits, how did they respond? Reeves knew the answer: by rioting every ten or twenty years, burning down their own damn communities so they were left with less than nothing. He shook his head at the futility and ignorance of his people. *We deserve what we get*, he concluded. And then he waited for someone to say or do anything that would prove him wrong.

* * *

Davis entered the locker room and never saw Stevens, who charged him like an angry bull. He connected with a right cross to Davis's jaw, knocking him to the floor. Calvanese grabbed Stevens before he could do any more damage.

Davis rose quickly and tried to retaliate against Stevens but was restrained by Henderson. White and Black cops positioned themselves as human barricades, attempting to maintain a fragile peace.

"You're a punk, Stevens!" shouted Davis, still attempting to break away from Henderson's grasp.

"And you're a fuckin' traitor!" screamed Stevens. "They ain't even cold in the ground and you're capitalizing off their deaths!"

"If there's any capitalizing, I learned it from your sorry ass!"

The two men tried to get to each other again but were controlled by other officers now helping Calvanese and Henderson. Everyone stopped their activities as soon as Captain O'Ryan angrily entered the room.

"You boys got so much goddamn energy, I'll put all your asses on foot patrol, and you can walk it off!"

The officers surrounding the two men backed off as O'Ryan grabbed Stevens and Davis, shoving them to the side. "It's not bad enough the city's declared open season on us, now you two clowns wanna spill each other's blood in here!"

"Not all of us are targets," Stevens said, glaring at Davis. "Only those of us whose skins are white," he continued.

O'Ryan stepped closer to Stevens and forced him against the locker. "Long as there's a shooter out there aiming at a uniform, blue is the only color you need to concern yourself with! Do I make myself clear?"

Stevens didn't answer.

"I asked you a question, Officer!" O'Ryan stood two inches from his face. "Do I make myself clear?"

Stevens spoke reluctantly. "Yes."

O'Ryan turned his attention to Davis. "You want to sue your own protective league, that's up to you. But you sure picked one hell of a time to go public."

"Can't get anyone to pay attention unless the cameras are rolling," Davis responded.

"You know where my office is, and you haven't been in it. You need a camera to visit, I'll supply one. But, until then, I better not hear of any more problems between my officers, or you'll all be collecting your pensions from every parking meter in the city." He headed for the door. "Henderson, Calvanese," he barked, "my office in five minutes."

As soon as O'Ryan was out of sight, Stevens pointed his finger at Davis. "This isn't over."

"Maybe now you'll know what the fuck it feels like to be a target," said Davis. "Ain't pleasant, is it?"

"You don't know how unpleasant it can get, but something tells me you're about to find out. You watch your back out there."

"You threatenin' me?" Davis tried to grab Stevens but was intercepted by Henderson.

"Allen," said Henderson, "it's not worth it. Just stay away from him."

Davis pushed Henderson away. "If I want advice, I'll get it from a *real* brother. It's gonna be quite a shock when you wake up and find out the 'N' word you've been hearing all your life includes you." Davis glanced at Calvanese then returned his attention to Henderson. "Maybe you ought to ask your partner to explain it. I'm sure he's had enough practice sayin' it." Davis slammed his locker and left. Other police gathered their belongings and went back to business as usual.

Calvanese approached Henderson tentatively. "Well, you see," he said, tracing the letter with his index finger, "the 'N' word is an abbreviation which stands for—"

"Don't push it. All right?"

Calvanese shrugged. "Just trying to bridge the racial divide."

Henderson and Calvanese crossed the room and ascended the stairs. "Try jumping off a real bridge," suggested Henderson. "That might help."

"Do I sense a little hostility?"

"Go fuck yourself."

Neither Henderson nor Calvanese could make much headway with their captain, who sat behind his desk unimpressed with their arguments.

"He had an arsenal in his living room," argued Henderson to no avail.

"I got ground beef in my kitchen," commented O'Ryan, bored. "Doesn't mean I killed a cow." He rose from his seat and stepped in front of his desk. "Anyway, Nixon's landlord says he personally collected the rent from him when the shooting occurred. Two neighbors back him up."

"So, somebody stole his car and then coincidentally decided to murder a cop?" asked Henderson.

"You don't like my theory, give it to Oliver Stone. I'm sure he can find a conspiracy. Until he makes the movie, we got one or more cop killers out there, and I want them stopped before what happened downstairs begins to spread outside." O'Ryan opened a new bottle of aspirin and downed two tablets without water. "Once my cops no longer trust each other, this really will become the city of angels. That's why I want the both of you to do what you can to calm things down."

"Why us?" asked Calvanese, fully knowing the answer.

"Damn it, Calvanese, why do you always have to challenge me? Can't you, just once, nod your head in agreement without asking any questions?"

Calvanese nodded his head. "Is that what you'd like me to do, Captain?"

"That was a question, wasn't it, Tony?" O'Ryan approached Calvanese. "Even when you're agreeing, you have to find a way to break my rules and fuck with me."

"I—"

"Don't!" O'Ryan wouldn't allow Calvanese to continue. "Don't say another word unless I specifically point to you and order you to talk. You understand?"

Calvanese looked at Henderson who avoided eye contact. He held his breath and stared helplessly at O'Ryan, who finally pointed at him.

"Yes, sir." Calvanese exhaled the words.

"I expect both of you to be examples of how to get along. You see any problems starting to emerge, if you can't solve them, you two notify me, pronto. Keep your eyes and ears open and report any disturbances to me."

Calvanese, in disbelief, stepped closer to O'Ryan. "You want us to spy on our own people?"

"Unless you intend to give me a kiss, I strongly suggest you step the fuck back." Calvanese hesitated for a beat, then moved next to Henderson.

O'Ryan softened his tone. "I need the two of you to assume a larger role in keeping the troops in line. I want to nip this bull-shit in the bud before it gets out of hand."

"What exactly are we supposed to do?" asked Henderson.

"I just need you out there getting along and making sure everyone sees it. Work with your respective groups to tone down the growing hostility before it gets out of hand."

"Our respective groups?" said Calvanese.

"Yes," replied O'Ryan, annoyed. "Whatever groups you two have the greatest influence with. Get out there, be the public face of this thing."

"Won't our dynamic public relations folks be a bit annoyed?" asked Calvanese, sarcastically.

"Fuck 'em. I've got four dead cops and a bunch of L.A.P.D.'s finest wanting to kill each other!"

"First you want us to spy," said Calvanese. "Now you want us to be poster boys? L.A.P.D.'s racial experiment proving it's not as bad as it seems. Everyone really loves each other. I didn't sign up for that, Captain."

"Neither did I, sir," agreed Henderson.

"Every time the two of you put on that uniform you sign up to do public relations and any other goddamn thing this depart-ment needs. I don't care if you have to take pictures together holding each other's dicks and put them on Facebook, Insta-gram, and TikTok." O'Ryan leaned back his head and took a deep breath. "I don't have to tell you, there's a lot riding on this."

He was right, thought Calvanese. He didn't have to tell them, but he did. And that meant their asses were on the line. In the event the shit hit the fan, they were being set up to take the fall, and this little scheme went all the way up to the chief. And if it came from him then the mayor had to approve it, too. After twenty years on the force, he knew how these decisions got made. He and Henderson were going to be the public face of the L.A.P.D. Racial unity in action. Real or not, the police had to appear united. Public Relations 101—when in doubt, lie.

The alternative, the truth, would only frighten people, cause them to panic, and they were already anxious enough. If you want to accurately gauge a community's nervousness, you don't have to monitor letters to the editor or emails to your congressman. The best barometer to measure fear could be found in the daily receipts at your local sporting goods store.

Gun sales had dramatically increased since the killings. That meant there were a lot of nervous citizens out there, many of whom had never fired a weapon. But most had formulated firm opinions about who needed to be shot. Those views were being reinforced every hour of the day and night by talk radio, cable news, the internet, and the print media, all needing to lay blame somewhere. Under their analysis, or lack of it, everything had to be defined and discussed in the simplest terms—good versus evil, right versus wrong and yes, black versus white, especially that. He and Henderson would be used as poster boys that assured the public there was no reason to fear that racial hostility existed or couldn't be overcome. Wherever there's fear there must be an enemy responsible for it. Destroy the enemy and restore peace and harmony—what a perfect solution. If only it were that easy.

And now, in the middle of all this, Calvanese and his partner had been given an impossible task: Keep the dam from breaking, regardless of the pressure steadily building on the other side. They were expected to get their respective troops in line, prevent them from strangling each other.

How the hell did we become representatives of our individual races? Calvanese couldn't believe the irony. Hell, the two of them had enough trouble getting along with each other; now they were expected to cure the ills of the department and the city. No fuckin' way. He wanted to shout that to his captain, his chief, his mayor, anyone who would listen. But that was the problem, wasn't it? No one of any consequence was prepared to really listen.

O'Ryan crossed to the window and looked out on the city.

Calvanese knew that whenever his captain marched to the window and turned his back on the people in the room, jumping out that window would be preferable to listening to what would eventually be said. He prepared to make the jump once O'Ryan moved away and presented an opportunity to escape, but before he could do so, O'Ryan spoke, dooming his dive to freedom.

"You better carry pictures of your loved ones, so you don't forget what they look like."

Should've jumped while I had the chance. Too late now. He braced himself for the rest.

O'Ryan turned and faced the two officers. "You'll be workin' double shifts until I say otherwise." He waited for a moment then stared at the men impatiently. "Why are you both still here?"

THIRTY

Henderson and Calvanese wore protective eye gear and goggles as they stood next to each other firing their weapons during target practice at the police range. Both men never looked at each other but it was clear that they were in competition. Calvanese fired rapidly, emptying his chamber dead center into the target's heart. He lowered the gun and waited for Henderson to match the effort. Henderson raised his weapon and carefully took aim but was interrupted by Officer Davis who tapped him on the shoulder, motioning for him to follow.

Henderson removed his goggles, holstered his weapon, and watched Calvanese calmly reload and then fire six bullets, hitting all bull's-eyes. "Better go see what your brother wants," Calvanese said, "before you get disinherited from the family."

Davis stood in front of a soda machine waiting for Henderson to join him. He purchased a Coke and offered it to Henderson, who declined.

"I wanted to talk to you," Davis said, working hard to sound apologetic.

Henderson looked away for a moment then confronted

Davis. "You sure I'm Black enough, or would you rather continue this with a real brother?"

Davis opened the can and took a swig. "I blew my cool last week. Said some things I shouldn't have." His eyes darted to the side. "We need to stick together."

"It comes with the uniform."

"I'm not talking about us as cops," Davis said with urgency. "This city's nervous. It's gonna be open season on niggers—might be a good idea if you knew who the real enemies were. That's all." Davis took another drink and then threw the nearly full can of soda into the wastebasket. He scanned the area and then spoke confidentially.

"Some of the brothers are beginning to question your loyalty. Thought I'd let you know while you still had time to correct their misperception." He stepped inches closer. "That would be a misperception, wouldn't it, Paul?"

Henderson remained motionless for a moment then bought his own can of soda from the vending machine. "They say beauty's in the eye of the beholder." Henderson opened the can, took a long drink, and then looked at an impatient Davis. "But everybody can pretty much agree on ugly."

"I'm trying to help you, Paul. I really am."

"You wanna help me? Get the fuck out my face."

Davis didn't take the challenge very well but contained his anger to the best of his ability. "Don't say you weren't warned," he said as non-threateningly as possible.

"Have a nice day," Henderson said with a fake smile.

Davis shook his head and walked away, obviously unhappy.

Henderson watched him leave, then looked at the firing range. Calvanese was no longer there but John Dawson had taken his place.

"You got a minute, Paul?" asked Dawson.

"What's up?"

"I know both sides respect you."

"What sides are you talking about?"

"You know. You gotta know. This shit ain't right. I ain't been here long, but I know when I'm not wanted. They blame me for Matt's death. Felt it should've been me. We ain't no different than the niggers on the street when it comes to them. These white cops don't want us here. Never have."

"Did Matt feel that way?"

"Matt was different. He was cool. Maybe he didn't care 'cause he was leavin'. Maybe he didn't care 'cause he wasn't that type of dude. He was good to me. But he was the only one."

"And you think Allen Davis cares about you?"

"I was gonna quit after Matt got killed. Allen talked me out of it. Said the situation was to our advantage."

"The situation being four dead cops?"

"He didn't mean it like that. But every crisis brings an opportunity. They finally have to pay attention to our needs, what's been happening to Black officers every day for God knows how long."

"John, you're being used. Allen doesn't give a shit about you. The only Black cop he wants to help is himself. As far as what side I'm on, right now with four of us gone and buried, I'm on the side of blue. It's the only choice we've got left to protect us and the people we love."

He touched Dawson on the shoulder. "And you should know, Matt didn't care because he had to, he cared because he wanted to. He was that type of cop because he was that kind of man. What kind of cop are you gonna be? And after you answer that, you'll know what kind of man you are."

Henderson walked away leaving Dawson to contemplate the question.

Henderson caught up with Calvanese in the lobby of the police station where they proceeded down the corridor toward the locker room. "So, what did Davis want?"

"Some change for the Coke machine," responded Henderson.

"Probably the wrong machine for the type of coke he wanted," said Calvanese with obvious disgust.

Henderson stopped walking. "Why you have to say some bullshit like that? He's Black so he's got to be a cokehead, is that it?"

"He's a shithead, and he'd be that no matter what color he was. Tell me I'm wrong."

"I'd have to tape-record the message and play it to you every time you opened your mouth." Henderson went through the motions of rewinding an imaginary recorder and then played back a message in a monotone voice, "You're wrong." He rewound. "You're wrong." He rewound. "You're wrong."

Calvanese frowned and spoke using the most superior tone he possessed. "That's so childish of you." He walked away with Henderson following close behind, pantomiming rewinding the tape but without the playback feature.

"At least he wasn't trying to get you to join Reverend Wilson's church," Calvanese said without paying attention to Henderson's antics. "Assuming you aren't already a member."

Henderson rewound his fake recorder and hit the imaginary play button. "You're wrong, you're wrong, you're wrong."

"Speaking of Wilson, how do you go about becoming a civil rights leader?"

Henderson ignored Calvanese, choosing to increase his pace and walk past him.

"You take a course on how to get to the camera first, or is it something else?" Calvanese asked sincerely, now trying to catch up to his partner in a hurry to escape the taunting.

Henderson rushed down a set of stairs with Calvanese in rapid pursuit.

"It must pay well," Calvanese wouldn't relent, "'cause every time civil rights leaders from around the country visit L.A. they stay at the Beverly Wilshire."

Henderson entered the locker room with Calvanese on his heels.

"You know what two eggs cost at the Beverly Wilshire?" Calvanese asked relentlessly. "Thirty-six dollars, without toast!"

Henderson removed a fresh shirt from his locker and tried unsuccessfully to get away from Calvanese.

"For thirty-six bucks I want the eggs to be the firstborn. Plus, the hens should have had a minimum of three years' private schooling."

Mike Stevens entered with a group of boisterous cops, excited by a recent bust.

"Whew! Did you see that punch Miller threw?" Stevens slapped Red Miller on the back. "Way to go, stud!"

Miller, a big red-headed cop born and raised on his family's farm in Bakersfield, grinned and strutted across the room pounding his barreled chest. "I hit that motherfucker so hard his African ancestors had to reach for their drums and play: Whoomp! There it is!" He danced in ever-expanding circles, high-stepping to the laughter and encouragement of his colleagues.

Henderson blocked his path and Miller stopped abruptly. "What the fuck did you say?"

"Stay cool, Paul," intervened one of the officers. "We just made one hell of a bust, that's all."

"So?" responded Henderson angrily. "Does that mean I have to listen to his crap?"

Miller attempted to move away but Henderson wouldn't let it end. "Is that the only way you can get off, knocking somebody senseless?"

"Hey, asshole," interrupted Stevens, "in case you haven't noticed, they're shooting at some of us? Yeah. It felt good fighting back. Maybe you ought to try it!"

"I wasn't talking to you so stay the fuck out of my business."

Stevens made a move toward Henderson, but Calvanese signaled to back off.

"Paul," said Calvanese, reassuringly. "He didn't mean anything." He walked over to Miller and put his arm around his shoulder. "He worked Devonshire too long, that's all. You know the only excitement he had before he got transferred here was watching the sun attack Granada Hills." Calvanese put the tall cop in a gentle headlock and pushed him away. "Ain't that right, Big Red?"

Miller managed a weak grin. "Yeah," he said begrudgingly. "Guess all the excitement went to my head." He looked at Henderson. "No disrespect intended."

Henderson gave him a cursory look, grabbed his bag, a shirt, slammed the locker door, and left the room.

"What got his ass so tight?" Miller asked.

"My fault," said Calvanese. "I was talking about food while he had an empty stomach. Probably made him a little hungry."

"Well, somebody feed the nigger," said Stevens.

Calvanese grabbed a surprised Stevens and slammed him into the locker. "What'd you call him?"

Several cops pulled Calvanese off Stevens.

"What the fuck is wrong with you, Tony?" said Stevens. "You been sittin' too long next to a piece of black ass? You forget where your loyalties are? Well, you better remember which side you're on. You better do it quick."

"I remember what side I'm on, Mike. It's whichever side you're not on." Calvanese took his things and left.

Stevens looked around the room at the other officers and then punched the locker.

THIRTY-ONE

Officer Lawrence Porter kissed his two young daughters goodbye. His wife, not yet fully awake, stood near the doorway watching, waiting for him to leave for work. On his way out he paused and looked at her. Her face had once given him much comfort; her smile, now rare, had always warmed him, made him feel young, perhaps important. He searched her for a signal, something indicating that the feelings from the past weren't gone forever—a sign they might be resurrected, restored good as new. Was she waiting for a kiss, or for him to get out as quickly as possible? He couldn't tell or didn't want to.

"You'll be late again, tonight." It was more a statement than a question and she delivered it with a noticeable degree of resentment bordering on contempt.

At least he didn't have to wonder any longer. She definitely wanted him gone. Whether it was for the day or permanently remained unresolved. "Don't keep dinner warm if that's what you're thinking," he said, his eyes occasionally glancing at the floor.

"I wasn't planning on doing that," she said sternly, then walked into the kitchen to make breakfast for the girls.

"Bye, Daddy!" yelled the youngest, who had shocking red hair like her mother's and a volatile temper that thankfully lasted less than thirty seconds.

"Bye, Daddy," repeated the oldest, without as much exuberance. At nine years old she had reached an age where she could tell when things weren't right. But she was still too young and too afraid to ask why. She had freckles like her mom, but her other distinctive features came from him, along with the silence that often followed her insecurity or stubbornness.

He was tempted to kiss her goodbye, ruffle her hair, and tease out a smile, maybe a giggle. He needed to hear her laugh, wanted to know he was still capable of bringing happiness to his family, even if he had to resort to a tickle here and there. He chose to wait until tomorrow morning. He knew by the time he returned home, his daughters would be sound asleep, and his wife would be in bed, pretending she wasn't awake. The only thing waiting to greet him would be a third pillow dividing the bed in half, an artificial barrier creating a demarcation that could not be violated intentionally or by natural impulse. Although after all this time, those nighttime desires would need to be fulfilled some other way, in some other place.

He left, closing the door quietly, hoping that might signify peace or, at least, the beginning of a truce. He took a deep breath of early morning air and stood at his entryway for a beat. He wondered if he should go back and try to settle things with his wife, once and for all. He decided against it. Not because he didn't want to resolve their conflict—he just didn't know how. When he was perfectly honest with himself, which wasn't often, he had to admit he still loved her, although he wasn't sure if the feeling was mutual. Considering all the things he'd put her through, he couldn't blame her if she didn't.

He proceeded to his car and sat behind the wheel. He placed the key in the ignition but didn't turn it. He stared ahead at his home then shifted his attention to the front lawn, wondering if he should reset the automatic timer on the sprinklers. It could probably use more water than usual. It had been very dry lately, an apt metaphor for his marriage. He could fix one problem, but he doubted he could repair the other. He wanted to, very much. That was a start. Or so he hoped.

He put on his seatbelt, reached for the ignition key, and felt an excruciating pain to the side of his neck. His hand instinctively reached for the blade before it could stab him again, but the sharp knife sliced his hand on its way deep into his throat. He heard an awful gurgling sound and realized it came from him. He saw blood gush onto the dashboard and splatter his windshield.

The knife exited and violently re-entered a third time. As it was removed, he pressed the button releasing his seatbelt and managed to shove open his door. He collapsed to the ground, face down. Like a snake slithering toward his house, he used his body to crawl, his legs pushing him forward. He couldn't use his arms since one hand was firmly pressed against his wounds to stem the flow of blood from his neck and throat. With his other hand, he tried in vain to remove the gun from his holster.

He desperately thought of his daughters as he felt the knife strike him once more, giving him a fleeting moment to think of his wife but not enough time to pray for forgiveness.

THIRTY-TWO

Calvanese sat with the rest of the officers for a briefing by Captain O'Ryan on the hot spots in the city. It had become fashionable to phone in death threats every fifteen minutes to police divisions throughout L.A. The 77th had cleared out twice this week alone, after receiving credible information that the building would be bombed. What made the threats "credible," O'Ryan never said, but it added to the overall anxiety and general jitteriness of anyone wearing a uniform, particularly white cops who were singled out in the warnings.

Every racist crackpot or attention-seeking kook in the state was having a field day playing phone call assassin and racial avenger. While most of the threats were made by folks too cowardly to personally challenge a parking citation, the level of venom and pent-up rage displayed by these anonymous callers signified a greater danger. It wouldn't take much for this city to explode. The resentment from minority communities toward local law enforcement ran deep, and every local and national media outlet was now here to record it. Twenty-four-hour cable news had an insatiable appetite for negative stories and no matter how much it was fed, it demanded more, even if it had to generate the news itself by regurgitating what its competitors had initially, and appropriately, ignored.

Stick a microphone and a news camera in front of the average neighbor and you've created a spokesperson not only for the entire community but the whole country. All the major networks had dredged up every shooting incident or excessive force allegation recorded on tape involving a white cop and a black suspect covering the past twenty years. They interviewed the families and loved ones of those allegedly "victimized" by an "out-of-control and abusive police department." The mother of a thirteen-year-old held the school portrait of her son, shot ten times by a cop, after the boy tried to run him over with a stolen car.

"They wouldn't have shot my son like a dog if he was white. You can be damn sure of that," she said, then wept as the camera zoomed close on the photo of an innocent-looking, smiling teen.

A fifty-five-year-old fledgling record producer wearing an old Fedora pulled down tightly over an oval-shaped head was a particular favorite of MSNBC. They used his ten-second soundbites as lead-ins to each of their nightly news segments and repeated them to tease viewers to stay tuned "to breaking news" during their commercial breaks. He wore multiple gold chains around his neck. The longest one held a bejeweled crucifix that dangled freely, occasionally bumping up against a rotund belly which shook noticeably when disturbed by any sudden movement. He was asked what he thought about the L.A.P.D.

"I stay away from 'em and hope they do likewise," he smiled, and then promoted a new album performed by a girl group he'd just signed to a long-term contract. "Gonna be bigger and better than Destiny's Child and the Supremes all rolled into one." He obviously wasn't up to date about the current girl groups or, for that matter, about contemporary musical tastes.

The owner of a dry-cleaning store was asked how he felt about the recent murders of white police officers. "They get paid to get shot at," he replied diplomatically. "Maybe now they won't be so quick to harass innocent law-abiding citizens."

Nearly every Black person living in a poor neighborhood seemed to remember at least one instance of a cop misusing his authority. And that one incident overshadowed every good and courageous deed by the average L.A.P.D. officer who placed his life on the line, willingly, to save the very people who mistrusted and too often despised him.

All of this was true, but Calvanese couldn't concentrate on the problems confronting the city or the status of the multiple task forces investigating the police assassinations or the involvement of the F.B.I. or anything else covered by O'Ryan. Instead, he thought about the way Briella looked standing naked underneath the fluorescent lights in the kitchen. Those lights made everyone else look like extras in a *Dawn of the Dead* movie, but not her. Somehow that yellowish-blue-green tint that accentuated veins, underscored dark circles, and highlighted other defections in the average person only served to make her lovelier; she was like a beautiful image captured through a backdrop of filtered strands of illumination, more mysterious and magical than any he had ever seen. So what if the lights were a gloomy haze that made your eyes go bad? For that one moment when Briella made them shine differently, he'd gladly risk total blindness.

"Yes, Captain," he answered to one of O'Ryan's questions that appeared directed at him but could have just as easily been targeted to the whole group. In his current state of mind, he would have answered yes to anything, if it bought him additional time to be left alone with his thoughts of Briella.

He recalled her lips, succulent and inviting, and how there was no wrong way to kiss them. They were always in the right spot, tender when they needed to be, firm when necessary, moving sensuously and then passionately in perfect rhythm with whatever music their lovemaking was generating at the time.

"No sir," he replied when asked if he wanted to report on whatever he was daydreaming about.

And then there was her skin—smooth except for the goose bumps that would appear when stroked by his fingers at a particular angle using a slow but steady pace. She had a small birthmark in the middle of her lower back, as if God wanted to leave his own personal fingerprint on a body that had to be divinely inspired. Or maybe nature simply wanted to identify the separation point between two halves, to show it could create and then duplicate sheer perfection, proving once and for all that genuine beauty did not occur by accident.

"Calvanese, are you listening to me?" asked O'Ryan.

"You have my complete attention, Captain," he replied with a degree of credibility that almost convinced O'Ryan Calvanese was taking special note of every word.

When they made love that first night and he had brought Briella to the edge, she moaned, "Right there, right there." He stayed in that spot, doing what pleased her, feeling her body ride with his, a gentle wave, then more abrupt and explosive, a powerful storm followed by an incredible serenity.

The room became quiet when O'Ryan took a slip of paper from his assistant and made an announcement that instantly brought Calvanese back from the place he had hoped to remain for much longer.

"We just lost another officer," announced O'Ryan, concealing both his anger and his grief, "stabbed in front of his home while leaving for work this morning. His wife and kids discovered his body."

Calvanese surveyed his fellow officers. Many had their heads bowed in sadness or a quick prayer while others stared aimlessly around the room. He closed his eyes and tried to imagine Briella's face, her touch, her voice, anything that would take him away to a different place, a better world. No matter how hard he tried he couldn't recall a single feature. He could no longer see the two of them together, smiling, laughing, making love. Every pleasant memory he had relived only seconds ago was now gone, completely erased from a memory bank that moments before had overflowed with intimate details, vivid recollections, extraordinary hopes, and unlimited possibilities.

When he opened his eyes, he noticed O'Ryan slowly balling up the message inside his closed hand.

Calvanese glanced at his own hands that by now were also formed into two tight fists. He watched his captain move slowly toward the window and look outside. O'Ryan, after several silent moments, turned toward his officers and said, "He was white."

Calvanese felt an enormous sense of frustration, followed by a surge of anger which didn't dissipate when he turned to the side and discovered Henderson watching him.

THIRTY-THREE

"You come up with some leads and I don't care how you do it, just do it!" screamed an agitated Chief Gibbs surrounded by police brass from each of the major divisions, including an equally miffed Captain O'Ryan. Gibbs slammed a thick file of reports on his desk.

"Put pressure on the gangs, the pimps, the junkies! Put money on the street. Do anything it takes! Just get me information and get it quick!" Gibbs contained his emotion and scanned the faces of his men and women. He spoke very deliberately and succinctly. "I want everyone out there to know: nobody declares war on the L.A.P.D."

Calvanese drove the patrol car, exiting the police garage. Henderson watched dozens of black-and-whites pull out, heading in various directions. The noise from the legion of motorcycles was deafening. "Haven't seen this much police action since the president was in town," he remarked to Calvanese, who was busy looking somewhere else, a group of protesters whose chants were temporarily drowned out by the roar of engines.

Reverend Wilson led the small group of demonstrators marching in front of the 77th Street entrance. They carried signs that read: MORE BLACK POLICE = LESS VIOLENCE. Calvanese was tempted to drive his vehicle up onto the sidewalk and scatter the crowd. If he timed it right, he could clip Wilson, just enough to get the Reverend's attention—nothing major, a mere spanking administered for disciplinary reasons—offered lovingly, of course, for the minister's own good. *Seemed like the Christian thing to do.* He thought better of it and drove past the group but not before tipping his hat to the Reverend, who glared back in disdain.

He noticed all the Black Lives Matter signs that were being waved like cardboard flags. He spoke without looking at his partner.

"You think white lives matter, or am I a part of the cancel culture?"

"You can't cancel a culture that doesn't exist," replied Henderson. "Although I admit I feel sorry for you."

"I appreciate it."

"I imagine it's not so easy for you anymore to share your limited misogynistic, homophobic, racist views without being called out about it."

Calvanese finally looked at Henderson. "I realize you can only care about those who are a darker shade but for your own safety you better learn a valuable lesson: You either bleed blue or you just bleed."

"Is that a threat?"

"That's the problem with your people, you can't tell the difference between a threat and friendly advice." He pointed to a mural of George Floyd plastered on the back of a liquor store. "That right there is a perfect example. If he hadn't been passing a fake twenty-dollar bill and just listened to some helpful guidance, he'd be alive today."

"Actually, he'd be alive today if a cop hadn't knelt on his neck for more than nine minutes."

"The jury found him guilty. Ain't that enough?"

"The video found him guilty. If it hadn't existed, he'd be riding around in a patrol car with the insignia on his door that reads 'to protect and to serve.'"

They got a radio call directing all available vehicles in the vicinity of 89 and Central to report to the scene of a disturbance at a local high school. He glanced over at Henderson. "Got your grenades ready?" he asked.

"Left them with my son," Henderson replied, glibly. "He wanted to take them to school, show 'em to all his friends."

"At least one male member in your family has got some cohonies."

Henderson's jaw tightened. "Speaking of having some balls, you read any more Baldwin, big fella?" he asked, trying unsuccessfully to get on his partner's last nerve.

"Decided to wait for the movie," answered Calvanese. "I figured even if he's dead, sooner or later someone would make a film, turn it into a comedy or a teen horror flick. Not that I would go see it or anything like that, but I might borrow the DVD from you, assuming you'd let me."

"When hell freezes over," said Henderson.

Calvanese wrapped his arms around his chest and rubbed his shoulders rapidly while making a shivering sound. "Ooohooo, it's sooo cold in here."

Henderson slid open his window all the way, allowing the air to rush in. "Anything else I can do for you?" he asked.

Calvanese looked at him and gave him a devilish grin. "Don't make it that easy for me, Henderson. You eliminate all the fun."

* * *

Additional patrol cars were assigned throughout the entire region covered by the L.A.P.D. They were expected to make their presence felt in the most obvious and persistent ways, disrupting the activities of petty criminals who earned their living hustling the streets. Motorcycle police trailed behind the patrol cars ready to offer protection and handle any minor disturbances, including arresting anyone with outstanding warrants, no matter how minor. The orders from on high were to make it miserable for any lowlife who might have names, addresses, rumors, or facts. It didn't matter what it was as long as they gave up information that might lead to something useful. And if they didn't have information, they needed to get some quickly or face the consequences. It was made clear that the pressure and harassment from the police would continue until they got the cooperation they needed.

In a matter of a few hours there were more arrests made than in a normal week, maybe two. To say nothing of the number of cars pulled over, licenses and registrations checked, vehicles searched at the first opportune moment. Teens weren't allowed to congregate. Prostitutes couldn't work in their normal territories. Shop owners were losing business having to answer questions from police who lingered around their stores longer than necessary. And forget about buying or selling drugs with impunity. No transaction, whether an expensive stolen T.V. or a bag of crack or a piece of flesh, could be bought and sold easily in this police-infested marketplace.

The community was now safe from ordinary criminals but not necessarily secure from those considered "outside preda-tors." Tempers flared quickly between resident and intruder, especially when that intruder wore a blue uniform. The city remained on edge, distrustful of police motives and resentful of their presence. The tension escalated after two Black men, allegedly engaged in drug activity behind a local 7-Eleven, were handcuffed and then beaten with nightsticks and a large metal flashlight.

The police claimed one of the suspects had reached for the arresting officer's gun. An onlooker said the man was simply complaining that the cuffs were cutting into his skin, raising his hands behind his back to show the police the severity of his condition. According to the witness, that's when the cops started beating the men, "for no damn reason, other than they could."

The two men were arrested but not before dozens of angry neighbors surrounded the police in protest. The police hastily left with the suspects firmly in their custody. By then, the gathering had swelled to well over a hundred men and women, blocking entry into the store and preventing access to the parking lot. The owner called 911 but was told his situation didn't constitute an emergency and he should phone the local police division. "They told me to call you," was his frustrated response. He slammed down the phone and swore in three different languages.

Henderson and Calvanese had arrived at their destination and were immediately issued riot gear. A dozen patrol cars were lined up in the school's main driveway, shielded by the yellow buses that had sustained damage to their windshields and side mirrors, along with a few sliced tires. Half a dozen other units were en route, sirens blasting. Inside the main courtyard, Black students engaged in a series of battles with Latino students. Whites, feeling left out, demonstrated their impartiality by throwing bottles and rocks at both groups. The only thing unifying all these students was their shared animosity now fiercely directed against the teachers and the police as well as their use of cell phones recording every action.

The teachers barricaded themselves in the locked cafeteria and hid underneath tables or congregated near the kitchen or behind the lunch counters: anyplace that offered shelter from shattering glass and flying debris. The principal and assistant principal weren't as fortunate. After their unsuccessful bid to quell the violence, they escaped into the nursing office where they received stitches for numerous hand and facial wounds. The assistant principal then left the premises but not before resigning, effective immediately.

The police remained a safe distance away, planning their strategy of attack while distributing protective shields, mace, and batons the length of an oversized baseball bat. The only difference between the two was that these clubs didn't need to be corked to do serious damage.

Calvanese listened to the yelling and screaming in the background and calmly surveyed the surrounding area. From a distance, the series of one-story buildings and classroom trailers looked more like a penitentiary than a school. Although to be fair, both institutions offered educational opportunities. It was a safe bet that some of the kids, fighting less than a hundred yards away, had a greater chance of being awarded prison degrees than high school diplomas, and the graduation rates of both places would remain relatively low.

Calvanese glanced at Henderson. "You remember *High Noon*?"

"With Gary Cooper?"

"Yeah," answered Calvanese. "You think the town deserved to be saved?"

Henderson thought about it for a moment. "Probably not."

"Then why'd he do it?"

Henderson surveyed the area. "Because he knew it was only a movie and he wouldn't get killed in the end." He ducked, allowing a bottle to fly over his head.

The two officers fastened their protective shields around their waists and secured cans of mace in their vests. They reached inside the police van and selected their batons.

"I was looking for something a little more inspirational," said Calvanese.

Henderson checked his baton for the right degree of balance, slapped the end against the palm of his hand, and responded without much passion. "It was the right thing to do. He took a sworn oath to uphold the law. Someone had to step forth and do the job. It was getting late in the day, and he wanted to have lunch." He looked at Calvanese. "That just about covers all the bases."

"That's the best you can do?"

Henderson shrugged. They looked at the brawl that had now spilled out onto the front yard.

"What time you got?"

Henderson glanced at his watch. "A little before noon."

"I hear the train a comin'."

"Let's do it," said Henderson.

Henderson and Calvanese joined their comrades and were pelted with rocks, bottles, cans of soda, books, anything that could be flung easily. They pushed back the angry crowd using shields and nightsticks. A white cop slammed his shield into the face of a Black female student who had confronted him. A Black officer took umbrage at the action and pushed the offending cop away from the girl, now bleeding profusely from a nasty gash in her head. The white cop retaliated by punching the cop who had intervened.

Calvanese grabbed the white cop and locked him in a bear hug. Henderson went to the aid of the student, who hurled profanities almost as quickly as she was losing blood. Henderson took the girl's sweatshirt and wrapped it tightly around the wound. He motioned for one of the school's security guards to take her, but not before she broke free from his hold and attempted to kick her assailant.

The Black cop also tried to get past Calvanese to land a blow but was prevented from reaching his target. Dozens of students cheered the action, urging the police to fight among themselves. They all were using their cell phones to capture the events, which were now guaranteed to flood social media and cause additional disturbances throughout the city.

Calvanese snatched both cops, tempted to slam them together.

Instead, he held them apart, at arm's length from one another. "What the hell are you two doing? You wanna get us all killed?"

The white cop shoved Calvanese and broke away from the crowd. "I'm gettin' the fuck outta here! I ain't battlin' those people and his black ass, too!"

The cop marched to his police car followed by two other white officers in solidarity. They were cheered on by a group of white students. Calvanese released the Black cop who had now gained the admiration of the African American students, who were openly applauding him.

Calvanese looked at Henderson with a sense of hopeless resignation. "Who said we weren't appreciated by the community?" A full can of soda smashed against his shield, bouncing off and striking Henderson.

"You got your answer?" asked Henderson.

The remaining officers formed a protective line and slowly moved toward the crowd, dispersing them easily. Calvanese observed that the students had seemingly lost interest in this skirmish and were probably ready to move on to more fun-filled activities. He feared they wouldn't have to wait long to find out how dangerous those activities might be, but he had no way of knowing how accurate his premonition would be.

Less than a quarter mile away, sirens blasted as three police cars pursued a sedan occupied by five Black teenagers. The teen driving the car slammed on his brakes at the corner of a busy intersection. The lead patrol car rammed the rear of the car, pushing it into oncoming traffic, while a second car battered the side, confining the driver inside.

The back door was flung open, and three youths exited but remained near the car as several officers closed in on the disabled vehicle forming a wide but effective net.

Mike Stevens shouted commands as all the cops aimed their guns at the two remaining teens trapped inside the front seat. Residents exited their homes to observe the activity. Cars pulled to the side of the road, surrounding the disturbance, essentially encircling the police within a larger and more dangerous trap. Occupants abandoned their vehicles and marched onto the scene. A local video store owner ran out of his shop and started recording the activity, joining numerous bystanders who were using their cell phones to do the same. The gathering of angry citizens was clearly distrustful of the police, even though two officers were Black.

The teen behind the wheel climbed out of his window while his companion eased out of the passenger side.

"Nobody move!" screamed Stevens at the two teens. "Put your hands over your head!"

"Make up your fuckin' mind," said the teen driver. "You want us not to move, or you want us to put our hands up?"

Derisive laughter came from some in the crowd, egged on by the defiant teens now casually leaning against their car.

"You motherfuckers are in the wrong neighborhood to pull this shit," screamed someone from a third-floor window to the cheers and applause of those surrounding the police.

One of the white police officers, on the force for less than a year, searched the area, becoming increasingly nervous. He gripped his firearm with both hands, trying to keep it aimed steadily at the two teens standing at the front of the car.

"Get away from the vehicle and put your hands up over your heads. Now!" ordered Stevens.

The teens enjoyed being the center of attention, particularly since they had a supportive audience. The teen driver mockingly did a little dance, stood frozen for a moment, and then dramatically thrust his arms over his head. The sudden action caused the rookie white cop to fire three rounds, which set off a rapid succession of gunshots from other police. The driver was blown to pieces, his blood splattering all over the car. The other teen standing next to him was critically wounded. He fell to the ground, screaming in anguish.

The crowd panicked. Some ran for cover while others grabbed objects and threw them at the police.

One of the three teens standing near the rear of the car quickly reached inside the backseat and came out firing a weapon, striking one officer and two innocent bystanders. The police retaliated, firing at the gunman, killing him instantly.

The two remaining teens dived to the ground, lying on their stomachs, arms spread out above their heads. Several officers moved slowly toward the teens; guns aimed at the two prone bodies. One officer patted them down, searching for weapons, while a second officer cuffed them both.

"You killed those boys!" shouted someone from the crowd. "Murderers! That's what you are! Nothin' but a bunch of damn murderers!"

"You better not hurt those young men lying on the ground," warned an elderly woman. "We're watching everything you do."

Patrolman Robert Taylor, a young Black cop six months out of the academy, noticed a man recording the action with his iPhone. He snatched the phone from the startled store owner and threw it to the ground, smashing it to pieces, causing the crowd around him to react with increased hostility.

"You had no right to do that!" screamed one irate woman.

"You fuckin' traitor," yelled a young man. "You're worse than the goddamn gangbangers that terrorize our neighborhoods."

Stevens grabbed his radio transmitter and called for immediate backup as his fellow officers made hasty arrangements to exit the area as quickly as possible.

Within an hour, all hell had broken loose throughout much of the inner city. Buildings were on fire. Firefighters tried to regain control but were attacked with rocks, bottles, and sporadic gunfire. Looters emptied stores, destroying anything they couldn't steal. Police marched the streets in full riot gear but were primarily assigned to protect banks, hospitals, and gas stations, fearing rioters would burn the places down, causing massive explosions in the area.

Chaos ensued the rest of the afternoon, extending throughout the night and lasting until the early hours of the morning. The tenuous calm hadn't occurred because of any intentional desire for peace. More likely than not, it could be attributed to the fact that there was little of value to salvage and virtually nothing left worth damaging. All that remained was for the news cameras to invade the deserted landscape, fervently capturing the desolation and destruction for the civilized world to see.

THIRTY-FOUR

Calvanese drove the patrol car. Henderson leaned against the passenger seat, totally wiped out. They had worked non-stop for nearly thirty-six hours and still had two hours remaining on their extended shift. In the riot's aftermath, there were few buildings unscathed, only devastation for miles around. Calvanese had grown weary of smelling smoke, tasting soot, and looking at ruins. He hadn't eaten in a day, but his belly seemed full, maybe from swallowing all the hopelessness and anger that still lingered in the air. He drove down Crenshaw and thought about its namesake, a sweet melon; it wasn't so sweet, now. Once he reached King Boulevard he reflected on the slain Black martyr.

You'd think an avenue named after a man who'd sacrificed his life advocating for peace would be the safest place in the city. It was often the most violent, not just in this part of L.A., but anywhere in the country that happened to honor his legacy with a street sign—which just as easily could be a noose symbolizing his perpetual lynching. Ironic, he thought, like killing him repeatedly or, at least, defaming his memory. He shook his head in disgust and looked at Henderson who placed his hand up in a gesture that said: "Don't go there."

"What are you so depressed about?" asked Calvanese, not attempting to conceal his annoyance. "You own property around here? Don't worry," he said dismissively, "there'll be other slums to invest in."

"Pull over," Henderson said weakly.

"What?"

"Just pull the fuck over," he said with more energy and far greater anger. "Stop the car, 'cause I know you can't stop your wise-ass mouth!"

Calvanese pulled over the car at the nearest intersection and turned off the engine. He sat patiently and appeared as innocent as a newborn baby.

"What's your problem, Tony?"

Calvanese lightly rubbed the bridge of his nose and looked away.

"You always got something smart to say. You treat these people like they're animals."

Calvanese turned his attention to Henderson. "You talking about these nice folks who just burned down and looted their neighborhood?" he asked innocuously.

"You don't know a damn thing about the people in this neighborhood, and you don't want to know!"

"We finally found something we can agree on. I don't want to know them. As a matter of fact, I'm not sure I want to know you right now. So just stay the fuck away from me!"

Calvanese pointed his finger at Henderson which resulted in his wrist getting slapped hard. He lunged at Henderson and the movement of his upper body coincided with a gunshot blast to the windshield that blew a hole through the driver's seat. Henderson held down Calvanese's head, shielding him with his body.

"You all right?"

"Yeah," confirmed Calvanese. "But if I live, I'm kickin' your ass. And, if I die, it better not be with my head between your legs."

More gunfire erupted from an automatic weapon. Bullets struck the hood and the top of the car in rapid succession, forcing Henderson and Calvanese to slide out of the seat and seek shelter behind the opened door. Calvanese crawled back inside the vehicle just long enough to remove the shotgun as Henderson searched the surrounding rooftops.

On the tallest building, a lone figure stood in the shadows holding a weapon that gleamed for a moment, then disappeared into the darkness. Henderson pointed toward the movement and he and Calvanese opened fire. Bullets tore into the façade, exploding large chunks of brick and demolishing a satellite dish. Calvanese rushed into the building. Henderson provided cover using up a full clip of ammunition which he quickly replaced. Once in the archway, Calvanese motioned for Henderson to follow.

They rushed up several flights of stairs. When they reached the top floor, they burst open the door leading to the roof.

A young boy stood at the ledge firing his Uzi. When he ran out of ammunition, he tossed the weapon to the side and removed an automatic pistol from his coat and fired again.

Henderson and Calvanese aimed their guns at the youth.

"Put it down!" screamed Calvanese.

The boy stopped shooting and stood, frightened, unsure.

"Don't look at us!" shouted Calvanese. "If I see your eyes, I'll put an extra hole in your head!"

The boy looked down; his body shook nervously. He appeared on the verge of tears.

"We don't want to hurt you, son," said Henderson sympathetically, "so, please, just put down the gun and then place your hands up in the air where we can see them."

The boy hesitated, too afraid to move.

"Put the fuckin' gun down!" ordered Calvanese.

The teen dropped the gun. He tried not to cry but tears appeared. Henderson and Calvanese converged on the terrified boy. Calvanese grabbed the teen's shoulders, yanked his arms behind his back, and cuffed him.

Henderson picked up the two weapons and then studied the teen. He didn't look terribly different from his own son, just a bit older with a slightly darker complexion.

"What's your name?" Henderson asked.

The boy didn't answer.

"I'm not your enemy, son. What's your name?"

"Deion," the boy replied, his mouth quivering, his body now trembling.

"How old are you, Deion?"

"Eleven."

Deion looked at Henderson, ashamed. Calvanese checked the cuffs and turned the boy toward him.

"You almost didn't make it to twelve," said Calvanese calmly. "But I got faith in you. Your mama will be grieving soon enough." Calvanese studied the boy and had to admit he didn't look like a gangbanger. Not yet. "You do have a mama, don't you, Deion?"

"Back off him, Tony."

Calvanese glared at Henderson for a long beat and then retreated, placing his hands up apologetically. "Don't mean to be so insensitive. You want me to reload his Uzi and let him go?"

Henderson started to respond but stopped himself. "Just read him his rights," he said, too tired to do anything but walk away.

Calvanese looked at the adjacent buildings burning and listened to the gunfire and sirens in the distance. He leaned close and spoke softly to Deion. "When I was eleven, I didn't have any rights."

. . .

Outside the building two Latino cops took Deion into custody,
shoving him unceremoniously into the back of their van. The
boy stared through the rear windows, briefly holding onto the
steel bars as the van drove away. Henderson watched him disappear as the van traveled several blocks and made a turn. Once
the boy was out of sight, he observed the damage to their patrol
car. He leaned against it, exhausted emotionally as well as
physically.

Calvanese tentatively approached his partner. "I guess I
should thank you for saving my life," he said, without much
gratitude in his voice. "If I wasn't trying to choke you, the bullet
would have hit me."

"Of all the times for me *not* to take your hands off somebody's neck," Henderson said dejectedly. "I had to pick that
one."

The two cops exchanged a quick look. The sarcastic
attempt at humor eased the moment. Calvanese relaxed and
leaned against the patrol car next to Henderson.

"I asked you before, but you avoided answering me," said
Calvanese. "With all the options you had, why'd you choose
this? Why'd you become a cop?"

Henderson studied him for a moment. Calvanese knew he
was trying to figure out if he was being set up for a joke or some
type of flippant response. Henderson exhaled deeply, not
having enough energy to protest.

"When I was a kid, I saw the movie where Bambi's mother
got killed by the hunter." Henderson searched the rooftops,
looked at the ominous sky filled with dark smoke. "I think it
started there."

A sudden silence dropped heavily around the men, an invis-
ible curtain that separated them from the outside world.
Calvanese felt his left eye twitch slightly then both eyebrows

rose in confusion, arching higher in astonishment. Gradually, he turned his head toward Henderson. He tried to speak but words refused to come out of his contorted mouth. He gestured toward Henderson, who still hadn't looked at him. Finally, with great effort, he forced out a response.

"You..." he stammered in utter disbelief, "you became a cop because of Bambi's mother?"

Henderson slowly turned and faced Calvanese but had nothing to say.

Calvanese said, "You don't know shit about *Heat of the Night*, but you're some kind of Disney freak?" He folded his arms across his chest. "What? You can tell if somebody's lying if their nose grows like Jiminy Cricket's?"

"Pinocchio," Henderson quietly defended himself.

"What?" The question lifted Calvanese's body away from the patrol car.

"It was Pinocchio's nose that grew when he told a lie, not Jiminy Cricket."

Calvanese glared at Henderson. "Pitiful," he shook his head sadly, "absolutely pitiful."

Henderson gave a trace of a smile as the two men stood side by side and once again leaned against their patrol car, confronting the dangers of the city, together.

By the time Calvanese made it home the news had reported the capture of the person allegedly responsible for the murder of Officer Lawrence Porter. Christine Lorraine Peterson, his mistress, five months pregnant with his child. The salacious details of his murder and their two-year adulterous affair now dominated every news station. The riot had taken a backseat to a sexual relationship, proving the well-known adage that love indeed conquers all—even the news coverage of communities burned to the ground, resulting in millions of dollars lost and countless lives destroyed.

News cameras were staked out in front of the dead officer's residence hoping to catch a glimpse of the grieving and/or outraged widow. Interviews were conducted with her neighbors. "How well did you know the family? Did they seem to be having problems? Have you ever seen the alleged murderer, the adulteress, in the neighborhood? Did she visit the Porters' home? Ever try to interact with the wife or children? Can you tell us how Mrs. Porter is handling it, the death and now the news of his unfaithfulness? Were you surprised? Did you ever have problems with the two girls? How old did you say they were? Did they seem well adjusted? Were they anxious or depressed? Did they have many friends at school? How do you think all this will affect them?"

Within forty-eight hours, cable national news would no longer be interested in the riot or its aftermath other than a quick review of the devastation. For better or worse, social media would assume that role of race baiting and showcasing the burning and looting to keep the citizenry nervous and the protesters active.

For the moment, nothing more would be mentioned about the murders of the other police officers, or the dangers the L.A.P.D. continued to confront. The omnipresent, ever-intruding media had a singular obsession but unlike other more honorable fixations, this one wouldn't last long. The fickle nature of news would eventually cause it to move on to the next big story and then the next. It might even return to the police murders, assuming another one would be committed soon.

For now, it was content to dwell on the lurid nature of sex and murder until it would invariably drown in the rancid pool of its own making. Then, like always, it would be resuscitated to create another pool, bigger, better, maybe a stream this time, so that it could continue the never-ending cycle of swimming and drowning, swimming and drowning, swimming and drowning—until the viewing public simply refused to watch. *Fat chance of that ever happening*, thought Calvanese.

He rested his body in a bathtub filled with aching bones and overflowing with scented bubbles, a habit he had recently and most fondly developed. Wasn't quite as good as sharing the Jacuzzi with Briella but that would come later—not soon enough for his newly acquired taste, but when it finally did occur, he'd appreciate it even more.

He suddenly thought of the boy on the roof, the one trying to kill him. What was his name? Deion. He'd probably get juvenile detention, where he would learn to be a hardcore gangster. Maybe he'd get probation and be assigned to the streets where he had less of a chance to make it, where he would find it almost impossible to survive and become a responsible, well-adjusted adult.

Calvanese placed a wet washcloth over his face and wanted to disappear, or barring that, at least feel clean, if only temporarily.

THIRTY-FIVE

The demonstrators, led by their indomitable leader, Reverend Wilson, chanted the familiar refrain: "No justice, no peace!" At the rear of police headquarters, dozens of mounted officers dressed in full riot gear with AK-47s and AR-15s pointed toward the sky, sat perfectly still atop their mounts, forming one long, impressive line. To Wallace Reeves, who stood quietly near the back of the modest crowd, they looked like ominous statues ready to come alive at the appropriate signal. But he knew the real danger didn't rest with these pathetic horsemen, nor did it lie with the police snipers sprinkled across the rooftop of the famed Parker Center. No, the dangerous ones carried not weapons but iPhones and other state-issued recording devices, and the media that they captured from those devices were potentially far more deadly than any bullets fired from a mere gun.

For in a few short hours, their photos and film would be studied, distributed to other police and governmental agencies and wherever possible the people filmed would be identified, then placed into a series of active files. If necessary, some among the gathering would be marked for surveillance, branded a "suspect" or "person of interest" in God knows how many past or future crimes. These were the methods the police used, part of a widespread pattern of intimidation and harassment that Reeves had spent a lifetime witnessing or experiencing firsthand. If you dared exercise your rights of assembly or free speech or were bold enough to protest authority and speak truth to power, then you risked paying the ultimate price. Who knew better than he? Not a damn soul.

"What do we want?" the crowd asked. "Freedom!" they responded. "When do we want it?" Reeves smiled faintly as they answered, "Now!"

He studied the mostly Black and Latino crowd, now dwindling in the oppressive heat, and couldn't make up his mind if he should admire or pity them. Their once strong voices were reduced to quaint sloganeering and their actions reflected nothing more than outdated strategies. They thought they were making a profound statement by announcing that Black lives mattered. Mattered to who? The police? The government? Certainly not to Blacks themselves, at least not the ones who roamed his neighborhood each night killing each other with drugs or bullets. Mothers told their children not to play outside at night or stand in front of windows in their own homes; homes that were supposed to be protective havens but that had more iron bars on their front and rear doors than most jail cells. They couldn't even live in their living rooms, not safely. No; these protests amounted to little more than foreplay with an idea that could never be satisfied and would never allow you to reach the desired goal.

Yes, a few faces within the crowd appeared frustrated, he thought, enraged even. But for all the antics, public posturing, and fruitless expenditure of energy, this could be just another group of aggrieved citizens, protesting the lack of health benefits or demanding a pay increase or wanting better schools or, for that matter, seeking entry into an oversold music concert. In other words, they were polite, powerless, and therefore totally irrelevant. And at the head of this emasculated group of misfits, orchestrating, perhaps controlling, their every move, was his pastor, the Reverend Donald J. Wilson—Dapper Don, in the flesh.

Reeves had to admit that this man was a bit of an anomaly. Like most preachers, Reeves wasn't quite sure how much he could be trusted to serve any purpose other than his own self-aggrandizement. Every Sunday these prophets or profiteers actively engaged in the art of pimping for money, or if you liked the more righteous term, "ministering for offerings." Then, when the end was near and the time came to meet and greet your maker, they delivered the eulogy and oversaw the interment, or to use the technically accurate description, they "buried your pitiful dead ass." And, even in that quiet moment of grief, they still found enough spiritual enlightenment to demand a handsome fee for the privilege of sending you to "a better place." They had you comin' and goin'. Sunday mornin' service or Saturday mournin' funeral. *You pray, you pay. You live. You die.*

"No justice, no peace!" The crowd had returned to their favorite and more easily repeatable chorus. "No justice, no peace! No justice, no peace!"

Reeves thought about his father, the strongest man he ever knew, and usually the quietest, except when he should have been. They said his father didn't know his place. The truth was he never had one. Not in this man's world. The day he was buried was also the day Reeves celebrated his ninth birthday. Quite a gift for a child, seeing your old man in a pine box covered with dirt, the type of cheap soil that would sustain nothing but death. If it hadn't been for that birthday, his father would never have gone out to buy milk to go with his son's cake and he'd be alive today. But Reeves had gone over that in his mind a thousand times, and it hadn't changed a single thing.

So, he did his best to stop thinking about it, except on birthdays and other special occasions like holidays or Father's Day. Or whenever he saw police dressed in their uniforms; treacherous symbols that gave them unlimited power and control over a child forced to give up the notion that wishes really could come true. He knew that to be the case because he'd learned it the hard way—by blowing out those nine candles over and over, making the same impossible wish: that his father would come home to help him cut the cake and celebrate another day, another year. Since that was impossible, he gave up cake and no longer drank milk.

"What do we want?" shouted the crowd. "Freedom!" they answered in unison. "When do we want it?" they asked. Reeves raised his fist high in the air and uttered softly, "Now."

THIRTY-SIX

Chief Gibbs held his press conference in a designated room on the third floor of the Parker Center. He chose the smallest space available to limit access and make those in attendance as uncomfortable as possible. He had presumed, incorrectly, that his selection might shorten the session. Instead, it wound up making the reporters irritable, which was never a good idea if you were counting on having your quotes recorded accurately.

"Mayor Palmer has informed me he spoke with the governor earlier this afternoon and has received his full assurance that, if necessary, we will be provided assistance from the National Guard." Gibbs scanned his notes then put them aside. "We're on full alert and do not anticipate any further disturbances, but we are certainly ready, and capable of handling any problems should they occur. I'd be happy to take a few questions, but I advise you in advance that because of pending litigation I will be unable to address any issues involving the murder of Officer Lawrence Porter."

He heard grumbling from the reporters but chose to ignore it. "Because of our ongoing investigation into his death as well as out of respect to his family and their express wishes for privacy at this painful and tragic time in their lives, I ask that you refrain from pursuing the matter at this news conference."

"When will you be publicly addressing the matter?" asked a reporter who had a much-deserved reputation for obnoxiousness.

"At the appropriate time and in the proper place," replied Gibbs, tersely, "neither of which exists today."

"Can you tell us anything about the suspect, Christine Peterson?" the same reporter asked, proving that the best way to avoid questions on a delicate subject was to refuse to hold a news conference in the first place.

"I've already made it clear that I don't intend to answer any questions involving this situation, and if you persist in asking them, I'll be forced to end this session, immediately."

"Chief Gibbs!" a second reporter shouted. "As you know, the union for Black police officers maintain their own website and have alleged patterns of discrimination in the overall organization of your department. They've listed a series of complaints in their newsletter and have accused numerous members of your staff, including top-level area commanders, of racism. Have you investigated these charges?"

"I have not," Gibbs answered quickly.

"Do you intend to and, if so, when are you likely to conduct your own independent review?"

"I have absolutely no intention of reviewing their allegations now or anytime in the future. The Black Officers' Association is an advocacy group." He said the word "advocacy" as if it was a social disease. "They are entitled to write whatever they like in their newsletters and freely disseminate that information on the internet for the world to see, which is, after all, their ulterior motive: to embarrass the L.A.P.D. and gain as much publicity and notoriety for themselves as possible. However, if they intend to act responsibly and file a formal complaint, there are well-established protocols in place. All police officers are fully aware of the procedures they must follow to file any grievance, whether it involves discrimination or any other allegation of unfair treatment or illegal practice." He took a quick sip of bottled water.

"I might add that I find it highly improper and, considering the progress we've made in diversifying our workforce, extremely hypocritical, as well as counterproductive, to publicly charge the dedicated and hardworking members of our force with unsubstantiated claims of racial bias. I'm sorry, but as long as I'm chief, I will not countenance that type of intimidation designed to inflame hostilities rather than resolve them." He allowed the cameras to capture his most indignant and self-righteous pose.

"Chief Gibbs, will there be any disciplinary action taken against the officer involved in the shooting of the unarmed teenager that took place yesterday afternoon which apparently sparked or at least contributed to the citywide riot?"

"The riot was sparked by a group of out-of-control hoodlums and thugs who would use any excuse to wreak havoc on our city. These criminals wantonly engaged in rampant lawlessness, committing random acts of violence against innocent people, and in the process their destructive actions have caused millions of dollars in property damage. There was, and is, no excuse or justification for their aberrant behavior.

"As far as the officer who discharged his weapon is concerned, he did so as a direct result of a threatening action on the part of a violent gang leader with a history of felony convictions. He acted in accordance with proper police procedure."

"Will you be bringing charges against any of the police involved in the shooting incident?" another reporter asked.

"Patrolman Robert Taylor, a member of the Harbor unit within our South Bureau, damaged the personal equipment of a citizen recording the event. While we are still in the preliminary stages of our investigation, his action appeared totally inappropriate and was a clear violation of our professional code of conduct. Pending a final report into this matter, he has been suspended without pay. Since Mr. Taylor is a probationary employee, it is unlikely that he will be reinstated, no matter what the eventual outcome of our inquiry."

A Black reporter jumped to the challenge. "Are you saying that a white police officer who shot an unarmed teenager acted according to policy, but a Black cop who broke some iPhone will be punished by losing his job?"

"It's precisely that type of race-baiting journalism that has contributed to tension in this city! One policeman acted in self-defense. The other acted out of frustration. Their race is irrelevant. I hope all of you will responsibly report that."

* * *

Allen Davis stood on the stage in the police assembly room. Robert Taylor, the cop who destroyed the phone, addressed a group of Black police officers.

"The Protective League wouldn't even talk to me. Look, I know what I did was wrong, but that recording was gonna distort what really went down. I only wanted to help those officers."

Davis put his hand on Taylor's shoulder in support. "Most of those guys never wanted you to be hired in the first place. So, if you're looking for assistance, you're not going to get it from them."

Taylor lowered his head, dejected. He spoke with a great deal of frustration. "All my life I wanted to be a cop. Now that might be taken from me because of a damn phone."

"Brother Taylor," Davis said, "we'll do whatever we can to assist you. We'll include your situation in our list of demands." He ushered Taylor away from the podium. "Let's show some love and appreciation for our brother and fellow union member."

The group applauded. Henderson, who was seated near the front row, raised his hand, and was recognized by Davis.

"Paul, you've got the floor."

Henderson stood. "Have we tried to explain the situation to the owner? Offer to reimburse him, purchase a new iPhone? If he drops the charges, we—"

"I don't want to cut you off, my brother," interrupted Davis, "but if the bus driver had changed his mind and let Rosa Parks sit in the front, maybe the Civil Rights Movement would never have happened."

The audience laughed.

"We're presented with an opportunity to showcase racism," continued Davis. "I say we take full advantage of it."

"Regardless of the cost?" asked Henderson.

Davis appeared annoyed but contained his anger and offered a superior smile. "Freedom ain't free, Officer Henderson. Never has been. Never will be."

Henderson slowly retook his seat while Davis recognized another member.

THIRTY-SEVEN

As Calvanese fully anticipated, his mother had made a feast fit for the Pope and his most trusted cardinals. There was more than enough food to feed them all for a week with leftovers they could donate to the poor. Veal, chicken, roast beef with a special tomato and garlic sauce, stuffed shells, three varieties of home-made pasta, salads recently plucked from the garden and piping hot mozzarella bread basted with a coating of Parmesan butter, olive oil, and fresh basil. And the desserts were still in the oven, except for the sponge cake soaked in espresso and layered with mascarpone and chocolate. Gelato and spumoni would soon be removed from the freezer and allowed to soften at room temperature.

"Mrs. Calvanese, this is the most incredible meal I have ever had in my entire life," Briella gushed, seated directly opposite Calvanese.

Mrs. Calvanese brushed off the praise with a hand that cut across the air. "Just put together some last-minute things," she proclaimed modestly. "I wanted to find a nice leg of lamb, but this really isn't the season." She grated some Romano, sprinkled some on her husband's rigatoni and placed another piece of bruschetta on the side of his plate. "But you'll have plenty of opportunities to try each of my special recipes." She looked at her son. "Isn't that right, Anthony?"

She called him Anthony. That signaled she wasn't asking a question but issuing a command. He smiled sheepishly and gave a shy, awkward glance at Briella. "I certainly hope so," he said softly, to the amusement of his father who sat at one end of the table while his wife held court at the other. "But that's up to Briella."

"What a beautiful name for a beautiful lady," said Mr. Calvanese, flashing his considerable charm.

"Why thank you," responded Briella. "It's short for Gabriella."

"An Italian name," Mrs. Calvanese said proudly. "So, are any of your people from Italy?" she asked optimistically.

"I wish so, but unfortunately not," Briella replied. "I was named after my grandfather whose nickname was Gabby. I talk almost as much as he did."

"Isabella thinks any person whose name ends in a vowel must be Italian," said Mr. Calvanese.

"Only the lovely ones," corrected his wife. "Briella, Isabella, we could be an aria." She released a satisfied chuckle at her witticism and sang a few high-pitched notes from her favorite cantata.

Briella applauded.

"Please don't encourage her," pleaded Mr. Calvanese. "Otherwise she'll be doing that all night."

"It makes me regret not being Italian, even more," said Briella.

"That's sweet of you to say," remarked Mrs. Calvanese. "But it doesn't matter what a person's background is, as long as they're Catholic."

Briella laughed but stopped almost immediately after she realized no one else considered the comment funny.

"Stop with the religion thing, already," said Mr. Calvanese gallantly. "If a person's good and decent to the core, religion shouldn't matter."

Both his wife and son gave him a curious look.

"And when did you become an atheist?" asked Mrs. Calvanese, eyebrows fully arched.

"I believe in God. The Catholic church just isn't the same anymore, that's all," Mr. Calvanese said regretfully.

"You mean because of all the molestation scandals?" asked Briella as Calvanese closed his eyes and wanted to disappear. This wasn't a subject to discuss with either one of his parents.

"Heavens, no," exclaimed Mr. Calvanese. He pointed his fork at her and then moved it in a half-circle encompassing everyone else at the table. "I'll tell ya precisely when the church changed. When they—"

"Stopped performing the masses in Latin," his wife completed the statement.

"Exactly," said Mr. Calvanese, now pointing the fork at his son. "You remove the mystery; you kill the faith." He took some more stuffed shells from the platter. "Simple as that."

"Like sauce without any secret ingredients," said Mrs. Calvanese in solidarity with her husband. "Might as well heat it straight from the can or, God forbid"—she made the sign of the cross—"cook it in a microwave," she gasped. "Can't tell one meal from the other. Boiled leather would have more flavor and taste better. I make my sauce the same way my mother made her sauce and her mother and her mother before that. Tradition is not a thing you throw out with the trash. Once you've got the right recipe, you pass it on to the next generation."

She extended a platter of veal to Briella, who hadn't requested it.

"I'm full, thank you," Briella said politely.

"Have another piece," Mrs. Calvanese said firmly but with a gentle smile. "It'll pave the way nicely for dessert later."

Briella looked at Calvanese for support, but he simply shrugged his shoulders in surrender. She took the smallest piece of veal she could find on the dish and nodded her head in appreciation.

"What's good for a sauce should be good for a church," Mrs. Calvanese continued. "The church should never change, period," she said with growing conviction. "Once you start tinkering with dogma then nothing's sacred. All you're left with is a shaky foundation," she grunted quietly. "It's no wonder these kids today are confused and have no values. If they don't like the rules, they change them. I'm surprised we're not down to seven or eight commandments by now."

"I don't know, Mom," said Calvanese, treading carefully. "Seems like the church may have made some changes for the better."

His mother placed her knife and fork on her plate and gave Calvanese a cold stare. "Name one," she dared her son.

Calvanese didn't hesitate. "Used to be a time when you could go to hell for eating meat on Friday."

"What's your point?" asked Mrs. Calvanese, mystified.

"Mom, you can't be serious." He studied his mother, who seemed genuinely perplexed by the challenge. "A serial killer commits the same mortal sin as a person who swallows beef. You tell me, is it all right for someone to be condemned to eternal damnation for eating a cheeseburger?"

"Ask your father," she advised.

"Don't put me in the middle of this," Mr. Calvanese protested.

"You started it," she pointed out correctly. "I'm just trying to defend your position," she said innocently, now totally above the fray. "I think Anthony has a point." She smiled lovingly at her son then winked at Briella.

The conversation turned quickly to other subjects, with Calvanese doing his best to steer clear of religion and recipes.

Any discussions about the recent riots or the dangers of police work were also off-limits.

He learned Briella's parents were divorced when she was six years old.

"That's so sad," Mrs. Calvanese said sympathetically. "Leaves such a mark on the children."

It left the right one on Briella, who said she'd only marry when she was sure it was for life. Calvanese's mother grinned like she'd just won the lottery.

"You like children?" Mrs. Calvanese asked with a lump in her throat.

"Love them," Briella answered. She wanted at least two. Calvanese thought he saw his mother's hand tremble in excitement. If this conversation continued, he was going to wind up engaged by the time his mother made the cappuccino while the angelic voice of Luciano Pavarotti played in the background. She was probably contemplating converting the guest bedroom into a nursery for overnight visits from her grandchildren.

Calvanese marveled at how easily Briella got along with his parents, as if she'd known them forever, had been a part of the family. At one point, his mother commented that, "If I ever had a daughter, I would have liked her to be you." She said it so casually, and with such sincerity, that Calvanese thought he saw Briella's eyes mist over when his mother followed the sentiment with, "Maybe that can still happen." She gently touched Briella's wrist and then with her free hand touched Calvanese on his forearm. He didn't know if this was a prelude to a prayer, a sacred ceremony, or a secret séance. But if he saw any lit candles, smelled any burning incense, or noticed any dimmed lights, he was out of there.

Briella broke the spell before it could be completely cast. "Mrs. Calvanese, let me help you with the dishes."

"Not at all," she replied. "I wouldn't think of it," she added for emphasis.

"But it'll give me a chance to ask you questions about…" She nodded in Calvanese's direction, which elicited a broad smile from his mother.

"I'll wash. You'll dry." They rose from the table. She placed her arm around Briella. "There's so much to discuss."

"I should help you in the kitchen," volunteered Calvanese. "That way I can hear what the two of you are saying about me."

Mrs. Calvanese dismissed him with an abrupt wave. "Go play dogma with your father," she ordered. "Just leave the Ten Commandments as they are."

Calvanese didn't have to wait long for the evaluation he had sought. As soon as he entered his father's den, Mr. Calvanese spun around his wheelchair, looked at his son with sparkling eyes, and announced the verdict. "She's a keeper."

"I'm glad you approve."

Mr. Calvanese raised his eyebrows and smirked. "As if it mattered," he said.

"It always matters what you think."

"Then you do what you want anyway."

"Yeah, but I do it with a genuine sense of guilt," Calvanese smiled then turned more serious. "You really like her?"

"What's not to like?"

Calvanese released a deep sigh of relief. His father studied him curiously. "You're not kidding, are you?" He brought his wheelchair closer to his son. "She's that important to you?" He waited for a response and finally got a definite nod followed by an unequivocal, "Yes."

The next question wasn't necessary, but he asked anyway. "You sure?"

"Never been more certain of anything in my life."

His father rubbed his chin then moved his hand up slowly and massaged his forehead.

"Uh, oh," Calvanese remarked, uneasily.

"What?" his father asked.

"You've got reservations."

"What makes you think that?"

Calvanese imitated his father and rubbed his chin, and his hand made its way to his forehead.

Mr. Calvanese chuckled. "I guess even a man in a wheelchair ought to watch his body language."

"So, what's wrong?"

"Nothing's wrong. I just don't want my favorite son to get hurt."

"I'm your only son."

"Only and favorite are not incompatible."

"But you're thinking that she and I might be?"

His father shrugged. "You said she had money."

"I said she was rich."

Mr. Calvanese shook his head. "Always a problem when a woman makes more money than her man."

"Certain problems I can live with."

"For a while, lust is blind. Then you see."

"That's love," corrected Calvanese.

"Love's not blind. It just looks the other way, a lot. Sometimes it doesn't look at all, which is a form of forgiveness."

"Okay, fine. I'll forgive her for having money."

"She doesn't have money. She's rich. Money pays the rent. Rich collects it."

"Yeah," Calvanese answered, less confidently.

"That calls for a whole lotta lookin' away, something you've never been terribly good at."

"She makes me feel..." Calvanese searched for the right word.

"What?"

"I guess that's it. She makes me feel."

Mr. Calvanese smiled warmly. "Feelings can cut both ways, you know?"

"Considering the benefits," said Calvanese, "that sounds like a fair deal, even a bargain."

"What's that I hear about a bargain?" Mrs. Calvanese asked as she and Briella entered the den.

"I was telling our son what a bargain privacy can be and that it was increasingly a very rare thing. He should take advantage of it anytime he gets the chance."

Mrs. Calvanese nudged Briella with her elbow. "In case you should ever wonder where Anthony gets his sarcasm from," she pointed to her husband, "there's the source."

"I'm not sarcastic," Mr. Calvanese defended himself. "I tell the truth and it stings sometimes."

"I've got a bit of truth for you," Mrs. Calvanese countered. "Briella said she was going to take me shopping."

"For what?" asked Mr. Calvanese.

"Clothes," answered Briella. "Your wife's been admiring my dress and I offered to take her shopping at my favorite boutiques."

"Boutiques!" Mr. Calvanese exclaimed, now clearly alarmed. "As in, more than one boutique?" What the hell's wrong with Macy's?" He gave his son a look, and sadly shook his head, mumbling something in Italian.

"You boys finish up talking. The cappuccino's ready. Honey, put on Pavarotti. The album that has 'Ti Amo'." She and Briella left the room.

"You got a woman who shops at boutiques," he said to his son, and then made the sign of the cross.

Calvanese's parents accompanied their son and Briella to the car. Mrs. Calvanese kissed Briella on her cheek, and they exchanged a warm hug. Mr. Calvanese grabbed his son's head with one strong hand and brought him close. He whispered, "Find yourself a poor girl." He released his son and smiled at

Briella. He held his wife's hand and they both waved goodbye as Calvanese drove off.

He had driven more than a mile when Briella finally broke the silence. "You okay?"

"Much better than okay."

"Why are you so quiet?"

"I guess I'm still a bit nervous. I just wanted everything to be perfect, for you."

"Tony, I can't remember when I had a more enjoyable time. Your father is wonderful, and your mother is enchanting. Your parents are amazing."

"Well, you certainly made a great impression. I always knew you would."

"Can I ask, what was it your father whispered to you just before we left?"

"He was happy that I was in love."

She looked at him, surprised, then smiled. "Are you?"

"Am I what?" he asked.

"In love."

He pulled the car to the side of the street and stopped. He thought about it for a moment. Not because he had any doubt, but he wanted to be able to tell her in a way that would adequately describe the depth of his passion and how much she meant to him. He turned to face her and answered, "Yes."

THIRTY-EIGHT

Chandra lived in a predominantly Black and Latino neighborhood along with a sprinkling of poor whites, but the pretty seven-year-old got along well with just about anybody. Her parents taught her not to care about someone's color or religion or the way they dressed or sounded. "God doesn't make mistakes," her mother always said. "Only his people do," added her father. But at this moment, Chandra didn't care about any of that. To this playful Black girl with two precious dimples and a single long, braided ponytail, the only thing that mattered on this gorgeous summer day was her new beach ball. True enough, the ocean wasn't anywhere in sight from her street, but she had a keen imagination and her father had promised to take her to the Venice pier this weekend and from there to Muscle Beach. She'd saved up her allowance and would surprise her parents by renting her own rollerblades.

She bounced the ball and then kicked it into the air but had misjudged its trajectory. It ricocheted off the building and then hit a tree before finally rolling across the street. She rushed after it, ignoring the car that sped by, almost striking her.

Mrs. Briscoe darted out of her duplex apartment screaming

at her daughter. "Chandra! Chandra! Watch what you doin'!" She reached the girl and grabbed her arm more roughly than intended. "Child, how many times I got to tell you to stay outta the street?"

"Tell my ball not to go there," Chandra suggested respectfully but with the conviction and assurance of someone much older.

"It would do as much good as talkin' to your hard head." Mrs. Briscoe playfully tugged Chandra's ponytail then pointed toward their house. "Now, get back over there and stay put till I tell you different."

"But I gotta get my ball," Chandra protested.

"I'll get it. And I just might keep it if you can't take better care of your toys."

"Whatcha gonna do with a beach ball?"

"Same thing you do, 'cept I won't lose mine." She lightly spanked her daughter and they both laughed. "Now do what I told you and wait in front of the house. And look both ways before crossing the street."

Chandra observed the empty street and exaggerated the safety measures by carefully starting and stopping, testing the non-existent traffic every few moments.

"You keep playin' and I'll make you walk down to the corner and use the crosswalk," warned her mother. Mrs. Briscoe waited until her daughter had reached the other side and then proceeded toward the ball now stuck underneath the front bumper of a parked sedan. "Wait till your father gets home. Maybe he can convince your stubborn behind to stop all your foolishness."

"Daddy ain't gonna do nothin' but give me a big ole hug and toss me in the air just like he always do."

"Always does," her mother corrected, struggling to dislodge the ball. "You're gonna start second grade, better talk right." Mrs. Briscoe retrieved the ball and started to return across the street when she became distracted by a slow-moving car headed in her direction. The rear windows of the vehicle slid down, emitting gangster rap music blaring at full volume. She looked at her daughter who had started dancing tiny hip-hop moves to the music.

Further up the block two teenage boys exited their building and then suddenly froze at the sight of weapons protruding from the front and back windows of the car, now racing down the narrow street.

Mrs. Briscoe frantically yelled at her daughter, who joyously danced to the music while pleading with her mother to "throw the ball, Mommy! Throw the ball!"

"Chandra! Get in the house!" she screamed desperately. "Get in—"

Automatic gunfire exploded. The two teenagers dived for protection behind a parked car. Chandra stopped dancing and stared helplessly at the commotion. Bullets riddled her body. Blood stained her dress, giving an unimaginable, red-drenched color to its circular pattern of flowers and little puppies at play. Her tiny arms flailed but Chandra remained standing for what seemed a lifetime, and for the child and her mother, it was. She finally dropped to the ground and landed near the foot of the concrete steps leading to her home.

Mrs. Briscoe charged across the street, unconcerned about her own safety as the car sped past her. She screamed in anguish and held the body of her daughter as neighbors rushed to her assistance. She wouldn't let any of them touch her Chandra. "Call an ambulance!" she begged. "Somebody call an ambulance!" And then she noticed the expressions of those who had gathered around her and knew when nobody had moved, that an ambulance was unnecessary. Her fists balled up in rage and slowly uncurled in pain. She looked at her daughter and saw the face she had kissed to sleep each night. She turned Chandra to the side and noticed for the first time that half her daughter's head had been blown away. She sprang back in horror and then collapsed, unconscious of everything except the unrelenting hurt.

* * *

Police tape sealed off the area. A white coroner's van was parked on the sidewalk blocking entry into the building. Henderson and Calvanese kept onlookers away from the crime scene. Two patrol cars, each with a pair of white cops, were parked on the street, directly in front of the Briscoe home.

One of the patrol cars drove away, the driver signaling goodbye to the officers in the remaining vehicle as he left the scene.

Calvanese approached the other patrol car and spoke to the driver. "Where are they goin'?" he asked, puzzled.

The cop behind the wheel looked at his partner, started the engine, and then gave Calvanese a wink. "Same place we are." He tapped the side of his head with his index finger and then pointed at Calvanese. "If you had any sense, you'd get out of this neighborhood, too." The cop glanced at Henderson then returned his attention to Calvanese. "Let your partner handle it. He'll be safe."

The car pulled off as Calvanese stood motionless. After several uncomfortable moments, Henderson joined him. "Where they off to?"

Calvanese massaged his forehead. "Had another call." He looked around the neighborhood, stared at the blood on the concrete, the limp body of the girl now being covered by a coroner's sheet. "I don't know what the fuck is wrong with these people," he murmured. "Doesn't life have any goddamn value?" he continued more forcefully.

Henderson took a step back from his partner and surveyed the area. He noticed neighbors standing around helplessly, a recently painted portrait of people in shock and despair. He saw men and women in tears or else too angry to show any other emotion. Mothers and fathers clutched their terrified children. An elderly woman had cried so desperately she had made herself ill and was now wrenching out the last bit of sorrow. He saw Mrs. Briscoe sitting on the steps of her home being treated by paramedics. Suddenly, she stood, exhibiting a terrified look of concern.

Passengers disembarked an R.T.D. bus that had stopped at the corner.

A large Black man exited carrying a metal lunch pail and holding a rolled-up newspaper. He was the last rider to get off. He waved goodbye to the driver and the bus made its way to its next destination.

The man had a light bounce to his step, and he whistled happily as he emerged from the crowd. He stared ahead and then suddenly stopped. He looked at the disturbance near his home, the gathering of police and city officials and neighbors. He took two small steps forward, appearing to move against his will. He then assumed control of his body, stepping slowly at first, then gradually at normal pace, then faster, until he dropped both the paper and pail and raced toward the scene screaming, "Chandra! Chandra! No, God! No! Not my Chandra!"

Mrs. Briscoe rushed to her husband, as did Calvanese. Henderson grabbed the woman who became frantic and started sobbing.

"Tell that officer to get his hands off my wife," Mr. Briscoe ordered and then searched Calvanese's eyes. "Chandra?" His voice broke, his hand pointed unsteadily. "Is that Chandra lying there on the ground?"

"I'm sorry," Calvanese prevented him from moving farther. "I can't let you—"

"Chandra!" the man screamed, horrified. He pushed

Calvanese's hands away. "Get your hands off me. I'm her father!"

"Mr. Briscoe," pleaded Henderson, "please let us—"

"You gonna stop me from goin' to my daughter?"

"There's nothing you can do. Help us protect the crime scene. It's the—"

"Crime scene?!" Mr. Briscoe cried out. "That's my little girl! And I'll be damned before I let you or anybody else keep me from her!"

He pushed Calvanese to the side and quickly proceeded to the body of his daughter.

Calvanese nodded approval to the forensic staff, and they pulled back, allowing the father access to his child. Mr. Briscoe stopped a foot away from his daughter and stared at his wife who, unable to look at her husband, slowly lowered her eyes. He turned back toward the body on the ground. Blood covered the pavement. A small frame lay tortured and twisted in death beneath the covering. He dropped to both knees and pulled back the sheet.

The face still appeared alive, as if sleeping peacefully. There was a trace of a dimple now covered with a splattering of blood. Her hair, as always, remained tied into a single ponytail but it no longer hung properly. Mr. Briscoe attempted to straighten her hair and discovered a scalp made limp by the bullet-ridden destruction of his daughter's skull. His body jolted back, a primal sound escaped his lips, and he covered his mouth with trembling fingers.

Mr. Briscoe replaced the sheet over his daughter's face. He placed his hands underneath her body. He lifted her, stood motionless, cradling her. His eyes moved side to side but never fixed their gaze in any one direction or on any one person. Gradually, he moved, walking past the police, stepping over the blood and brain matter that had once contained his daughter's thoughts and memories. He stopped next to his wife and glared at Henderson, then Calvanese.

"You ain't gonna do nothin' about this. She ain't one of your cops killed. She ain't no rich white girl. But she ain't no crime scene. She's my baby. She's my world. And I'm takin' her inside where she belongs."

He crossed the front lawn holding his daughter close against his chest and took her inside their home.

Henderson spoke without looking at Calvanese. "Guess he must be one of those."

"One of those what?" responded Calvanese.

"People for whom life still has value." Henderson looked at his partner without any vindictiveness, then walked away.

Calvanese stood motionless and then felt something touch his foot. He stooped and picked up a beach ball, surprised to see it in this neighborhood.

THIRTY-NINE

A full plate of food remained untouched. Henderson stared at it aimlessly while Nicole finished her meal. Dexter was now anxious to leave the table.

"Dad, can you help me with my math?" He waited for a response, but his father never gave him one.

Henderson quietly rose from the table and touched Nicole on her shoulder. "I'm going out for a while. Get some air." He looked at his son as if seeing him for the first time. "Dexter, have you done your homework?"

Dexter glanced at his mother, bewildered.

"I helped him before you got home," she said, and gave a look at her son to hush.

Henderson nodded and kissed Dexter on the cheek. He gave Nicole a peck on the lips and then left.

* * *

Calvanese sat at his usual place at the bar, but the cold draft remained in front of him untouched. Henderson entered the bar and took a seat next to him.

"Thanks for meeting me here," he said, without looking at Calvanese.

"You'd do the same for me."

Jasper Campbell tossed a white towel over his left shoulder and approached Henderson. "What you havin'?"

"Whiskey," he answered to Calvanese's surprise. "Anything with a kick will do."

"You sure you wanna do this?" asked Calvanese.

Henderson stared straight ahead and then he shifted his attention to the bartender. "Make it a double and be sure it's strong," he ordered.

Campbell glanced at Calvanese who nodded reluctant approval. Campbell shrugged, poured a mixture from two separate bottles, and placed the concoction in front of Henderson. "Drink it slow," he warned. "You drink it fast, and it'll burn a canyon down your throat."

Campbell walked away after giving Calvanese a look of concern.

Calvanese studied Henderson who held the glass as if contemplating suicide. "Thought you didn't drink."

"I don't." Henderson placed the glass to his lips, threw back his head and swallowed hard.

Calvanese didn't see an expression at first, then noticed Henderson's nose flare slightly, followed by his eyes opening wider in a silent scream. His lips trembled. He appeared to stop breathing. His grip tightened around the edge of the bar.

Campbell returned. "You want another?" he asked, barely concealing a smile.

Henderson spun off the barstool and headed directly to the restroom.

Campbell chuckled and turned to Calvanese. "That his first?"

"No," he answered respectfully, "just his youngest." He pushed Henderson's empty glass toward Campbell, who filled it to the brim and placed it in front of Calvanese. He took the glass and drank it slowly then went to check on his partner.

Henderson stood at the sink running water, the faucet turned on to full pressure. He scooped two handfuls and splashed his face, then repeated the action. Calvanese entered and signaled to another officer who was waiting to get to the basin. The message was received and understood. The officer left giving Calvanese a good luck nod.

"You gonna be okay?" Calvanese asked.

"If you came in here to fuck with me, I'm not in the—"

"First child I saw murdered, I rushed home to hold my wife," Calvanese said without emotion.

Henderson turned off the faucet and dried his face with a paper towel. He didn't turn to face Calvanese, watching him instead in the large mirror which was in definite need of replacement.

"To tell her every detail," Calvanese continued, matter-of-factly. "I wanted someone to understand." He wondered if Henderson was following him. "To hurt as much as me," he said, more honestly.

Henderson turned and the two men stood face-to-face.

"Did it help?" Henderson asked with a sense of urgency.

Calvanese shook his head. "I never told her." He took Henderson's place at the sink and turned on the faucet. He wet his hands, tapped the liquid soap container, and scrubbed. "I decided if I didn't speak about it, then it never happened. After a while, I couldn't talk to her about anything. Couldn't touch her. I was afraid I'd feel something I couldn't afford to feel." He rinsed his hands and turned off the water.

Henderson tore off a long section of paper towel and handed it to Calvanese.

"Go home to your wife, Henderson." Calvanese dried his hands. "While you still want to." He balled up the wet towel and tossed it into the wastebasket. "While you still can."

They exchanged a look of understanding and remained silent for several moments. Henderson nodded in appreciation and left. Calvanese returned to the sink and turned on the faucet. He cupped both hands, held as much water as he could, and then brought the water to his face.

* * *

Nicole sat alone quietly at the table. She looked at her watch, concerned. It was after three in the morning. Her husband had never stayed out this late outside of work. She heard fumbling at the back door and experienced a sense of relief. Henderson walked in, unsteady and disheveled.

"You wanna talk?" she asked.

"Can I throw up first?" was all he could manage to utter.

"I'm not going to clean it up," she warned.

"Then I'm not going to do it."

He sat down next to her but avoided making eye contact. She leaned in close and smelled his breath and quickly pulled back, overwhelmed.

"Oh, my," she exclaimed. "Did it smell that bad going down?"

"I didn't hold it all that long," he answered dejectedly, then looked at her for the first time, trying to hold back his emotions. "When I left the bar, I intended to come straight home but I..." He had difficulty finishing the sentence.

"Didn't." Nicole completed it for him.

He shook his head. "No, I didn't. I went back to the place where that girl was murdered. I sat in my car, staring at the spot where it happened, where she laid lifeless, like a doll waiting to be picked up."

She touched the back of his hand and rubbed it gently, soothingly. Her tenderness made it more difficult for him not to cry. He spoke as if he was in a church or a cemetery.

"When her father knelt beside her, I remember this trickle of blood on her lips. I keep thinking about it. If she hadn't been dead, I might have thought it was lipstick. But she wasn't old enough ever to have..." He stuttered and stumbled over his words. "I mean, she probably thought about it, maybe even took her mother's and played with it, but I—"

His voice broke. He fought back the tears by rising violently, swiping his right hand across the table, knocking a glass bowl onto the floor, shattering it to pieces.

Nicole tried to approach him, but he pulled back, holding up his hands for her to stay away.

"She looked so beautiful. I know she was dead. I saw all the blood. But, her face, it... it... was so damn beautiful. Nicole, how could somebody do that? How could—"

She placed her arms around him. He resisted at first, then surrendered to her touch. He knew he needed her even though he realized that letting her come close would overwhelm him. He rested his head on her shoulder and wept.

FORTY

Allotted seven minutes on the FOX cable news network, Reverend Wilson had extended his interview beyond a second commercial break. He visibly enjoyed frustrating the conservative talk show host by spouting inflammatory statements about justice and validating his arguments with selective quotes from the Bible. What was not nearly as obvious to the susceptible viewer was that the host secretly enjoyed the battle even more than his guest.

"Please don't use the holy book to justify your views, Reverend," the host fumed with righteous resentment, throwing up his hands in disgust. "I don't think you'll find Matthew, Mark, Luke, or John advocating violence against the police."

"Clearly, you don't understand your history or your Bible, especially the Old Testament," Wilson retorted. "Philistines were out of control 1,200 years before the arrival of Jesus and I can assure you that no one, back then, suggested turning the other cheek in the face of their unrelenting oppression."

"Are you comparing the police..." The host forced himself to pause, released a tragic sigh, followed by a long somber breath.

"The very people we rely on for our own protection, the brave men and women who risk their lives every day on our behalf... Are you seriously comparing them to Philistines?" The host probably didn't know what a Philistine was, but he managed to transmit shock and outrage at the arrogance required to suggest such a despicable thing. To punctuate his indignation, he quickly ran his fingers through his thick mane of black shiny hair, leaned forward, and with a fury that would be the envy of any great orator, he bellowed, "How dare you." He waited for Wilson to take the bait but instead was confronted with a wry smile from this incredibly smug guest. His leg shook out of sight of the camera and his eyes reflected a man becoming unhinged by circumstances no longer under his control. "You really don't give a damn about police being murdered, do you, sir?" His face, now fully contorted with genuine ire, wouldn't allow his mouth to form the more respectable word, "Reverend."

Wilson remained surprisingly calm and steadfast. "You know how many Black children were killed last month in Los Angeles?" he asked, his voice conveying a measured indictment directed more to the national audience than his outgunned interviewer.

"No, I don't," the exasperated host shot back, "but we're not talking about that problem."

"That's exactly my point. Nobody wants to talk about Black people dying. You want to look the other way and pretend it's not happening. Black people get murdered every day, and I'm not just talking about being shot unjustly by police. Only the other week a young Black man, college student on the honor roll, a star athlete, was shot to death while he was walking his younger sister home from Bible study. You didn't cover that on your network, now did you?"

"Reverend Wilson, we give a lot of coverage to those types of crimes."

"How much time did you devote to it, assuming you devoted any at all?"

"I'm not here to answer your questions. I'm the host and you're the guest. Plus, I'm not going to let you change the subject. You're very good at avoiding the real issue, but you were invited here to address your outrageous and belligerent comments regarding the murders of police officers, all of whom happened to be white, which is why you haven't expressed any concern over their deaths. I wonder if you'd feel the same if those were Black officers being assassinated."

"If those were Black officers being killed you wouldn't be devoting so much time on your show," argued Wilson passionately. "They'd be treated just like any other Black homicide, which is to say they'd be ignored."

"You have no idea what you're talking about," the host said dismissively.

"I know one thing."

"You're nothing but a demagogue."

"Coming from you, that's a compliment. But regardless of what you say or how you say it, I'll tell you that if conditions don't improve for the masses of Black people, not only in this city but throughout the country, these killings shall continue, and I predict right here and now they will escalate into something you and the rest of this racist nation won't be able to ignore."

"Now you've shown your true colors," the host shouted, incensed. "You're actually inciting people to violence. I'm ending this interview right now!"

"You've long ago lost the power to silence this or any other Black man!" shouted the Reverend.

"You can scream all you want," replied the host, "but you won't be getting any more airtime on my program. I'm not going to allow you the forum or the platform to disseminate your insidious views, not on this network." The host then looked directly into the camera, regaining his professional demeanor, and conveying total control of the circumstances. "We'll be right back after this brief commercial break. Please rejoin me for a special interview with Mayor Palmer." He stared at the camera and waited for the red light to go off.

He got out of his seat with a huge grin and shook Wilson's hand. "Well, that generated a little heat," he said, pleased with the interview. "They'll be talking about that at the water coolers in the morning, you can put your money on it."

"Will you send me a copy of the tape?" asked Wilson.

The host, now displaying genuine charm and graciousness, placed his hand on Wilson's shoulder. "Just check with any of my producers on the way out, leave the address you want it mailed to. They'll be happy to get in touch."

A technical assistant removed the microphone from Wilson's lapel while a producer congratulated the Reverend on his performance. "Really nice job. You did wonderful."

Wilson noticed Palmer. They shook hands and exchanged pleasant greetings. The Reverend left after receiving a souvenir coffee mug inscribed with the show's title and stuffed with chocolates and other sweets.

A make-up artist provided the host with a handheld mirror which he used to observe his face. He checked his tie and then quickly evaluated his overall appearance. The make-up artist used a cosmetic puff to apply bronzer, a spot here and there around his mouth and neck while reassuring the vain man that he looked great.

"Was that good?" he asked.

"You were terrific," she responded while other employees in the studio nodded in agreement. The cameraman gave the host a huge thumbs-up while a second assistant carrying a white towel echoed the sentiment. "Fantastic segment," he gushed, and then removed some perspiration from the host's forehead.

The executive producer accompanied Mayor Palmer to the

set and directed him to the proper seat. The make-up artist now focused her attention on Palmer, applying additional foundation. She also added a light coating of mascara and a few finishing touches just underneath the eyes, concealing night shadows and morning wrinkles. The technical folks swarmed over the guest, straightening his jacket, positioning his back, checking the lighting, attaching his microphone, and conducting a sound test.

The host gave the mayor a friendly wave. "How you doin', Alex?"

"Can't complain," answered the mayor. "Where's your partner?" He was referring to the liberal co-host who usually cowered in the presence of his more forceful and articulate headliner.

"Home with a backache," answered the host with a smirk. "If anybody should have back troubles it should be me. I've been carrying him for the past three years."

The mayor laughed. "You gotta at least try to make it look fair and balanced."

"I do my best." A hairstylist eased his head back carefully, quickly applied some spray to both sides, and ran a hot comb through an uncooperative curl.

"Ten seconds." The warning came from somewhere in the shadows.

The staff cleared the set. The host returned to his seat looking refreshed, a bright sparkle to his eyes.

"Five." The second advisory announcement was made by the head cameraman who counted down the remaining four numbers using his fingers. When he got to one, the host smiled on cue.

"Now to bring some much-needed sanity and rationality back to our program, I'm pleased to welcome to the show L.A.'s favorite son and a frequent guest on my national radio broadcast."

The camera widened to include a two-shot of the host and Mayor Palmer.

"Mayor Alex Palmer, thanks so much for joining me tonight."

"It's nice to be here. I appreciate the invitation."

The two men shook hands.

"You're more than welcome to visit anytime. We're honored to have you here."

"It's always my pleasure," replied the mayor pleasantly.

"I assume you had a chance to listen to the ranting of my previous guest. I don't really want to dignify him by referring to him by name, let alone using the title, Reverend."

"Unfortunately, I did hear much of what he had to say."

"Tell me, and our viewers, honestly—and I've known you a long time, so I can say you're always very frank and truthful, which is why I love talking with you—tell us what was going through your mind as you were listening, and you already know how I felt about his outrageous comments, but give us your impressions of what Mr. Wilson had to say." The host squished up his nose momentarily, as if attempting to alleviate a sinus problem or track the scent of where his question would inevitably lead.

Palmer nodded respectfully and then quickly found the camera angle that would capture his best profile. "My response to you and your viewers is quite simple. To those who have used these tragic incidents to further their narrow and self-serving political objectives, I have this to say. I, along with every law-abiding citizen, personally hold you responsible for your violent rhetoric that has directly contributed to the tensions in this great city." He leaned forward as if offering a prayer or casting a judgment. "Make no mistake, the blood of these officers is clearly and unequivocally on your hands."

The studio camera moved in close on Palmer while the host

added his comments. "Well said, Mayor Palmer. I couldn't agree with you more."

* * *

The choir sang quietly, respectfully, a soothing lullaby that caused their bodies to move slowly from side to side as if surrendering to a light spiritual breeze. Then, like the onset of a shifting storm, the tempo changed. The movement had a more dramatic ebb and flow. Bodies swayed deliberately, snapping waves off the rock of ages, embracing the shores of salvation, and uplifting the song into another heavenly gear. The standard gospel selection became a celebration. Hands clapped. Feet stomped. The members of the choir spun around in tight little circles then swung side to side. Their colorful robes twirled and flapped and appeared to float, simultaneously revealing the souls of the cleansed while concealing aroused bodies whose sins of the flesh were being washed away by their collective devotion.

Reverend Donald Wilson stood at the pulpit urging the choir to take the spirit higher. They did so, with unparalleled dedication and enthusiasm. The organist played, divinely inspired, his instrument reaching a new crescendo. All but the infirm and incapacitated were now on their feet. A few of them were even assisted by ushers and holy rollers who gladly replaced nurses and other secular caretakers. All that their pastor could see among his devoted congregation were smiling black faces lifted in glory and jubilation.

The gospel had reached its most feverish pitch when the rear doors of the church burst open, allowing the devil to enter uninvited. Two white skinheads rushed down the center aisle screaming, "White power!" They tossed Molotov cocktails in every direction setting off fiery explosions and forcing members of the congregation to climb over pews in their haste to make it to the side exits. Some jumped through stained-glass windows, shattering the images of angels and saints. The two attackers rushed past the altar and into the rectory where they accomplished their escape.

Reverend Wilson and some deacons assisted the children. One woman's clothes caught on fire. She immediately fell to the floor. Several worshipers went to her aid and managed to smother the flames using nothing but their own hands and their unwavering faith in the Almighty, whose name they praised throughout their trials and tribulations.

Screams of terror and cries for help were drowned out by the intensity of the flames rapidly consuming the interior of the church. Windows exploded from the heat. Most of the congregation fled to safety and were now using garden hoses to contain the fire and save the exterior structure.

The security sprinkler system started belatedly within the four corners of the church, having minimal effect on dousing the flames but succeeding in flooding the area, making the marble floor slick and treacherous to maneuver.

Wilson was the last to reach the exit door. He stood for a moment, watching his sanctuary engulfed in flames. He stared at the silver metal cross of his Lord and Savior and then he felt a hand grab his shoulder, forcefully pulling him out of the inferno.

FORTY-ONE

Six hours later, all that was left of the building's front entrance was covered in hate-filled graffiti. The side windows of the church were shattered, debris scattered across the adjacent parking lot. A homemade explosive had blown away part of the rectory. The large smoldering cross atop the steeple had been set ablaze and was now reduced to blackened wood and ash. To remove any doubt, the symbolic message of the burned-out cross was made clear by the letter "K" scrawled three times in red on the sidewalk where Reverend Wilson now stood. He ordered his supporters not to clean up the spray-painted warning. "Leave it there," he shouted, in front of the news cameras. "Let the world see that racism is alive and well in the city of Los Angeles."

Henderson and Calvanese requested a private moment with Wilson, who obliged by leading the officers to the rear of the church. Calvanese removed a notepad from his shirt but didn't appear terribly anxious to record the Reverend's words.

"A church can be firebombed, the lives of Black men, women, and children threatened, and there's no outrage about that," Wilson said as if delivering a Sunday sermon.

"You think you may have brought this on yourself?" asked Calvanese. Henderson gave him a signal not to go there, but as usual, his partner ignored it. "Maybe you were targeted because of some of your earlier remarks?"

Wilson glanced at Henderson then displayed an expression of disgust. "When Black folks speak out, we're labeled trouble-makers, rabble-rousers, and told we deserve what we get." He took a step closer to Calvanese. "Well, I don't believe in turn-the-other-cheek redemption. I'm an Old Testament eye-for-an-eye preacher. Get used to it. There's a new Black man in town. And you created him."

"Reverend," Calvanese responded softly, "if I had created any Black people, I'm sure I would have remembered." He glanced at Wilson's feet and spotted a pair of multicolored alligator shoes: lime green, yellow, brown, dirty gold, and a pale blue. "You know, I hate to be the one to tell you this, given your recent loss and all, but somebody threw up on your gators. And based on the evidence, I'd guess the perp had lunch at an all-you-can-eat buffet."

Henderson took a safe step away from the two men. Calvanese wasn't sure if his partner was attempting to conceal a smile or a look of disappointment.

"These are Pradas, you impertinent ass." Wilson shoved both elbows to the side in a release of tension, which also served the purpose of expanding his chest in proud defiance. "Although, looking at you, I doubt you'd know anything about designer fashions."

"Prada, huh?" scoffed Calvanese. "What's the matter, Stacy Adams too Black for you?"

"I've had enough of your insolence," Wilson said, angrily. "Your superiors will hear from me, you can be certain of that."

"You talkin' God or someone higher, like the chief or mayor?" asked Calvanese, innocently.

"Get off my property!" demanded Wilson.

"I just have one or two more questions, then we'll—"

Wilson sharply cut off Calvanese. "I'm not answering any more of your questions." He turned away and faced Henderson. "Brother," Wilson spoke warmly, "I'll talk with you." He pointed dismissively toward Calvanese. "Not him."

Calvanese didn't relent, offering a compromise. "I'll make it'll real brief, I promise."

Wilson reluctantly turned toward Calvanese and waited with his arms folded across his chest. "Just remember who you're speaking to, Officer," he warned.

"You're a hard person to forget," Calvanese responded, taking the edge off his reply. "First, I'd like to say, and I really do mean this, that I'm grateful no one in your church was seriously injured."

"That was God's will," responded Wilson. "It was His mighty hand that provided protection and guaranteed the miracle of my safety."

"I'm sure that's true," replied Calvanese, unconvincingly. "But what I'd really like to know from you is..." Calvanese paused, demonstrating great effort to properly form the question. "And let me ask this in the most respectful way," he continued while Henderson braced himself for the inevitable. "I've always been curious, which benefit of the job do you enjoy most—talking directly to God or having a one-hundred-percent tax shelter?" Calvanese readied his pencil to his pad and waited to record the response.

Wilson walked off in a huff as Calvanese shouted, "Holla at me later!" He turned toward Henderson with a satisfied grin, looking like a cat that had just swallowed the canary.

"That was really quite impressive," commented Henderson, tersely.

"You mean the way I handled the Reverend?"

"No. The fact that you knew about Stacy Adams. I must admit, that was startling, maybe even a little frightening."

"Hey, I just peep at the billboards in the 'hood, my uptight brother," quipped Calvanese. "Those shoes be da bomb!"

* * *

Within ten minutes of leaving behind a furious Reverend Wilson, Calvanese had received the notification summoning him back to headquarters for a "come-to-Jesus meeting" with his captain.

"Who the hell told you to go there?" asked O'Ryan, unable to contain his anger.

Calvanese and Henderson attempted to rise from their seats but immediately froze halfway up at their captain's order. "Sit down! You move when I tell you to move, is that understood?"

The two officers retook their seats and answered together, weakly, "Yes, sir, Captain."

"Now answer my damn question. Who told you to go there?" O'Ryan moved to his desk and grabbed a silver and bronze clock paperweight with the insignia of the L.A.P.D. Calvanese feared he was about to fling it.

"That was my idea, Captain," Calvanese responded calmly. "I thought—"

"Oh," snapped O'Ryan, shifting the paperweight from one hand to the other, "you had an idea and then you thought. And you were able to do that all on your own, were you?" Now the weight was being transferred more rapidly between hands.

"Well," Calvanese sounded almost childlike, "Officer Henderson helped a little."

Henderson's eyes searched the ceiling.

"How lovely," remarked O'Ryan. "And let me hazard a wild guess." He paced in front of the two men. "Officer Calvanese, I take it you acted mostly on your own initiative?"

"We were only doing what you asked, trying to present the best public face for the department."

Henderson looked away, smiling.

O'Ryan suddenly lost his temper and exploded, "Does your best public face include insulting the man just after his church had burned to the ground?"

"I asked him a simple question," Calvanese responded professionally.

"He's a community leader!" snapped O'Ryan.

"Who made him one?" Calvanese asked in a more defiant tone.

"Television," O'Ryan answered calmly, then his anger resurfaced slowly. "He was on it twice and he announced he was a community leader. I'll take his word for it!"

"You can't believe everything you see on T.V." suggested Calvanese.

"No? Well, you can believe this," stated O'Ryan, his face flushed beet red. "Because of this racial bullshit, now every damn bureau got to attend some ball-bustin', touchy-feely seminar where we've got to bare our black and white souls, hold hands in a big happy circle, and sing 'Kumbaya' while we jerk each other off! As if that's not bad enough, now we got the Women's Police Officers' Association joining hands with the union representing Black officers, both demanding an investigation into hiring, promotions, and workplace harassment!"

He pointed the paperweight clock at Calvanese. "You got any idea how much I hate attending sensitivity workshops? I'm already fuckin' sensitive! I've had sensitivity rammed up my ass so many times I'm afraid to look at a woman below her eyes or compliment a Black cop by saying 'thatta boy, great fuckin' job!'" He slammed the paperweight clock on his desk and heard the glass shatter. Both hands on the clock popped off. He inspected the area more closely and realized he had also gouged out a healthy chunk of wood. He stared at the damage he'd inflicted on his desk, showing absolutely no expression.

Calvanese and Henderson exchanged a look of quiet desperation.

O'Ryan turned around and addressed the two officers as if nothing unusual had happened. "Do either one of you happen to have the correct time?"

Calvanese looked at his wristwatch. "Three twenty-five," he answered.

O'Ryan nodded and then asked wistfully, "Didn't I throw both your asses out of my office once already?"

Henderson answered respectfully, "And we'd be proud if you did it again, sir."

O'Ryan walked slowly to a metal cabinet and removed a stack of files. He spoke without looking at either officer. "I got a meeting in five minutes I don't want to be at, with a man who's more of a pain in the ass than the two of you could ever hope to be."

"Thank you, Captain," replied Calvanese.

O'Ryan turned and faced Calvanese. "That wasn't a compliment, Calvanese."

"No, sir," agreed Calvanese, "but I appreciate the sentiment." He looked at Henderson for an endorsement. "I believe we both do. But to be sure let—"

"Get out!" shouted the captain.

Both men jumped out of their seats and exited the room.

O'Ryan approached the desk, picked up the shattered clock, studied it sadly, and then dumped it into the wastebasket.

FORTY-TWO

O'Ryan sat on the stage, perched high above the proceedings, giving him the perfect vantage point to monitor the activity below. He was joined by the top brass from the Office of Operations. Three of its four bureaus, Central, South, and Valley, had commanders or assistant commanders in attendance. The deputy chief from the West Bureau arrived early but had to leave when he got a message that his wife went into labor. A representative sampling of bureaucrats from the various advocacy units within the massive organizational hierarchy of the L.A.P.D. were also prominently showcased.

Specialists from the chief's P.R. operations were assigned specific oversight duties. Media Relations, Public Communications, and Community Relations each had at least one representative present. The Consent Decree Bureau sent three employees: a Black man, an Asian man, and a Latina who all worked in the Civil Rights Integrity Division. The women's coordinator was in attendance on loan from the Ombuds Office. Two commissioners from the Board, including the vice-chair, were on stage overseeing the session and taking copious notes.

All these illustrious, powerful, and highly paid servants of the city were gathered for the express purpose of observing and participating in the much-touted, and very well publicized, "sensitivity training session" designed to root out political incorrectness, racial bias, and what police officers valued most: gut instinct.

The first half of the workshop was devoted to the women officers, who spoke in reverence to the history of their struggles that forced them to create the Los Angeles Women Police Officers' Association in 1925. They stood on the shoulders of those who came before who were utilized as babysitters to handle cases involving children. Many argued that little had changed, and they were still not given the respect that their male counterparts received. They were forced to contend with their inferior assignments, lack of promotional opportunities, and were constantly having to deal with a misogynistic department where sexual harassment was viewed as an employment benefit for the males.

Everyone listened respectfully, thanked the speakers for their candid comments, then offered strategies, policies, or programs that would provide solutions to their legitimate issues. After a brief break, the workshop on race was moderated by Ms. Irene Shaw, a human resources director who asked for honest conversation and got it, in spades.

"You didn't want us," shouted Allen Davis. "Once we got hired you wouldn't support us! And now that you feel threatened, suddenly you want us to stand by your side!" Davis took a moment to observe nods of agreement from fellow Black cops and elicit additional support from those not yet willing to commit. "Well, you're not gonna use us as shields to hide behind. We're not puttin' our asses on the line to protect the likes of you."

"Don't talk protection to me," countered Mike Stevens. "You're too damn chicken-shit to go in your own communities. You bitch and moan and groan about needing more Black cops, then you don't wanna get assigned to the very areas you're supposed to represent."

The two officers were surrounded by a roomful of other police from the 77th Street Station. This "experiment" in conflict resolution sponsored by the mayor's office had been degenerating into an increasingly loud shouting match for the last thirty-five minutes. Irene Shaw, considered an expert on racial sensitivity, had decided to physically isolate the Black and white officers on either side of the room, as if they needed any additional encouragement to remain divided. The few Latino officers were stuffed in between the two opposing sides and for the most part had remained relatively quiet.

"Very good," Ms. Shaw said as if reading from a prepared script. "We're starting to make some real progress. Gentlemen, why don't you have a seat, and we can discuss what just happened."

"Weren't you listening?" asked Calvanese from the back of the room.

"I beg your pardon," said a perturbed Shaw.

"You wanted to discuss what just happened. So, I asked you if you were listening."

She searched her sheet of paper and located his name on the prepared seating chart. "You're Officer Calvanese?"

"Guilty as charged," confessed Calvanese to the amusement of his fellow white officers.

"Actually, I was just going to call on you and your partner." She studied the sheet of paper again. "Officer Henderson. Could you both share with the group how the two of you manage to work together so well?"

Calvanese didn't answer.

The Black officers looked at Henderson, who showed no expression.

"Come on," encouraged Ms. Shaw, "you must have difficulties. How do you go about resolving them?" She waited for a moment and then looked at O'Ryan for assistance.

The captain nodded at Calvanese and threw in a stern look for good measure.

"Since you obviously have so much you wish to contribute to our workshop, please stand and give us your advice, your recommendations for racial harmony," she said with a tinge of sarcasm and a great deal of annoyance.

Calvanese rose, twiddling his hat in his hands. "What was your question?" he asked, respectfully.

"I wanted to know how you managed to get along so well with your partner, Officer Henderson. I'm sure your insights will be very revealing."

Calvanese looked around the room. He had everyone's rapt attention. He answered as if sharing the solution to world peace. "I ask him politely not to spit his watermelon seeds on my side of the patrol car."

The white officers, and a few Hispanic ones, laughed. The Blacks looked as if they were attending a funeral or wanted to cause one. Henderson simply lowered his head and sank a few more inches into his chair.

Shaw walked slowly toward Calvanese who stood perfectly erect. She held the sheet of paper so tightly with both hands that Calvanese thought she'd either rip it down the middle or use it as a taut trampoline, vaulting herself to a higher level of unrestrained, uncontained fury. "Do you find humor in what we're attempting to do here, Officer Calvanese?"

"No," he answered, politely. "I can't say that I do. I don't think there's anything funny about what you're attempting to do here. Not only isn't it funny, but it's also not helpful, not necessary, and not worth our time!"

"Well, Mr. Calvanese, I find your outburst—"

"I'm not Mr. Calvanese. I'm Officer Calvanese. And while I'm at it, lady, let me correct you on a few—"

"Tony, that's enough!" commanded O'Ryan, who had now made his way down the stage to the floor.

"Damn right it's enough," Calvanese responded angrily. "You wanna play these games, put us in groups and treat us like we're some social experiment! It's wrong, Captain. It's dead wrong, and you know it!"

"I know something else, Calvanese. I know if there's another word out of you, you'll be facing a suspension without pay!" barked O'Ryan. "When you're asked to participate in this program, I expect your full cooperation! You will show Ms. Shaw the respect she deserves. Do I make myself clear?"

Calvanese glared at Shaw who matched his stare but complemented it with an obvious satisfied smile.

"I'll show Ms. Shaw the respect she deserves," he said, as if issuing a threat, which had the immediate effect of wiping away her smile.

"Now sit down and keep your mouth shut," ordered O'Ryan.

Calvanese sat down and noticed Mike Stevens give him a supportive nod. He shifted his attention to the other side of the room and discovered Allen Davis who displayed a "you got what you deserved" smirk, followed by a smug wink.

Calvanese then searched the room for Henderson, who was glaring back at him.

FORTY-THREE

Henderson walked toward his patrol car, distancing himself from Calvanese who followed several yards behind. At the conclusion of the workshop Calvanese had been taken aside and chewed out again by his captain who was joined by two deputy chiefs and one commissioner. He knew it wouldn't be long before his so-called "disruptive and offensive behavior" would be reported to the chief and probably the mayor. Miss Irene "I-can-ream-you-a-new-one" Shaw, expert seminar leader and self-proclaimed race relations specialist, would make certain of that.

How come conflict resolution mediators and group facilitators never possessed a sense of humor? He'd have to figure that one out some other day. Right now, he had more urgent matters to resolve. He needed to concentrate on repairing the damage his "off-color humor" had caused to his relationship with Henderson. He wasn't in the mood for a likely confrontation with his understandably angry partner but, on the other hand, he wasn't exactly looking forward to eight hours of frigid silence.

Henderson got behind the wheel and started the engine. Calvanese entered the passenger side and turned toward Henderson, whose body language spoke volumes, none of which could be read aloud to children.

"You got anything to say?" asked Calvanese.

Henderson pulled out of the parking lot and drove past a large church. "Fuck you," he replied.

"You just used profanity in front of a house of worship."

"Am I past it now?"

Calvanese looked back. "Yeah."

"Good. Fuck you."

Calvanese massaged his chin and spoke quietly, his words slightly muffled by his hand rotating over his mouth. "I didn't mean to embarrass you with the watermelon joke."

"I don't give a shit about your dumb-ass, juvenile, ignorant, incredibly lame, and extremely racist jokes."

Calvanese drummed his fingers against the dashboard. "My jokes are not lame," he defended himself, more hurt than annoyed.

"Maybe I should have dropped you off at the church, because if anybody needed Jesus, it's you."

Calvanese took a deep breath and released all the honesty and sincerity he could muster. "Look, I apologize." He placed his hand over his ear. "I'm sorry. I was pissed, and because I couldn't hit anybody or strike out any other way, I joked. That's what I do when I get frustrated or nervous or angry. I made light of that bullshit back there because—"

"At my expense!" snapped Henderson. "You made light of it at my expense! And it's not the first time but I'm telling you now, it better be the last."

Calvanese considered the statement and knew Henderson was right. "Okay, sometimes I might say things the wrong way," he admitted sheepishly.

"Sometimes!" Henderson responded incredulously and stopped the car at an elementary school crossing.

"You gonna listen, or you gonna make things more complicated than they need to be?" asked Calvanese, desperately seeking a truce, since a resolution seemed out of the realm of possibilities.

"I wonder if you really know how complicated things already are." Henderson watched the young students cross the street. Black students walked with other Black students. Latinos had their group. And the few whites kept to themselves, straggling a safe distance behind.

"Maybe I do, maybe I don't." Calvanese shrugged. "But I'm trying to find out. Reach a place of common ground. That's gotta be worth something, doesn't it?"

The crossing guard signaled for Henderson to proceed. He drove through the intersection. "It's not worth the price of absolution, if that's what you're looking for."

"What is that supposed to mean?"

"Nothin'. It's just I get a little nervous when white folks try to appear reasonable and concerned. Especially when they attempt to make me feel comfortable, like suddenly I'm surrounded by hostile strangers who are looking out for my best interests. I think you people are more interested in being forgiven than taking responsibility for your behavior."

"That's a racist statement."

"No. It's a fact."

"And I'm not a white person. I'm your partner."

"The only thing you know how to be, the one thing you've mastered from birth, is how to be a white person." Henderson pulled into a small outside mall and parked in front of a coffee and doughnut shop. He and Calvanese exited their car.

"See, if I had said some shit like that, you would have cut me no slack whatsoever," said Calvanese, miffed. "How come

Black folks can get to say whatever they want and there's no problem, but a white person comes along and—"

Henderson put up his hand, displayed his palm to Calvanese. "It's far too complicated for you to comprehend so don't go down that road." He put down his hand and nodded. "All right?"

They approached the order window and waited in line.

"Oh, okay," said Calvanese, refusing to let it drop. "I forgot —you only want to travel in the same self-pitying circle that you create on your own terms where you're always the victim while everyone else is a—"

"What don't you understand about a palm in your face signaling the command, stop?"

"I thought that was code." Calvanese snapped back his head and rapidly shook his shoulders side to side, stuck out the palm of his hand in imitation of a Black woman. "For talk to the hand!"

Henderson looked at him in disbelief and then chuckled to himself. "You know, you did that pretty good, for a racist," he added.

"I'm not a racist."

"Of course, you are," insisted Henderson. "You're not brain-dead, so that makes you a racist."

Calvanese pondered that for a moment or two. "First you insult me by calling me a racist. Then you give me a back-handed compliment by sayin' I'm not brain-dead. I don't know if I should feel insulted, flattered, or depressed."

"I agree," said Henderson. "Why don't we leave it at that— you don't know and, most likely, you never will."

An elderly Asian man who stood in line in front of Henderson, turned around and gave the two officers a quick look over, then faced the window and stepped up to give his order.

"I don't want anything," said Calvanese, who walked away and sat at one of the patio tables.

Henderson waited patiently for the customer in front of him to neatly fold his bag containing an apple fritter. He took extra napkins from the silver holder and poured cream into his hot tea. As he turned, he nodded respectfully at Henderson and confided quietly, "Caucasian people don't understand." He nodded again, then patted Henderson on the arm.

Henderson moved up to the window and placed his order. Calvanese wondered how far he should push this—if he should push it at all. Henderson joined him at the table and gave him a coffee and muffin.

"I said I didn't want anything."

"I knew you didn't mean it."

"Did you know to bring extra sugar?"

Henderson dumped several packs in front of Calvanese, who appeared pleased. "Thanks."

"You're welcome."

Calvanese ripped off the tops of three packets and poured the sugar into his coffee. "What'd you mean when you said I wasn't brain-dead, as if that was proof I was a racist?"

"You learn to be racist, Tony. From the moment you're born to the moment you die. If you're capable of learning, then that's what you're programmed to become." Henderson sipped some coffee. "If you're smart or just plain honest with yourself, you try to overcome those lessons of a lifetime. But you gotta want to do it. And you gotta try really hard."

"You know all that Pavlov stuff we were talkin' about?"

"Yeah, and I'd appreciate if you didn't bring it up again." Henderson took a bite of his blueberry muffin.

"I've been thinking about it a lot."

"Good. Another year or two of study and you'll be a certified campanologist."

"A what?" asked a mystified Calvanese.

"Campanologist. Someone skilled in the art of ringing bells," explained Henderson, using a slightly superior tone.

A blank expression overtook Calvanese's face and then gradually a look of exasperation replaced it. "You know, there's such a thing as too much education, especially when you use it for the sheer pleasure of confusing a situation."

"I'm sorry I interrupted your train of thought," replied Henderson, sounding anything but apologetic. "Jump back on whatever track you were traveling and get to your point."

"You know, you're beginning to sound like me, and I don't appreciate it."

"Imagine how badly I must feel."

Calvanese turned serious. "Look, I don't wanna play tit for tat, right now. The thing I was trying to tell you about Pavlov was this. I realized it's not the bell that's dangerous and causes all the problems. It's the one who designs the experiment, the one who rings the damn thing."

"Halleluiah," replied Henderson. "You've finally discovered who had the power all along."

"I also learned there's only one way to get the power back." Calvanese paused and became extremely still, as if trying to identify the location of a faraway sound. "You hear that ringing in the distance?"

Henderson listened for a moment. "No."

"There you go," answered Calvanese. "Ignore the signal and the whole experiment fails."

"You think it's that easy?" replied Henderson.

"Yeah, I do."

Henderson leaned closer to Calvanese.

"We've got God knows how many years of mistrust between us. We live in completely different worlds where we see everything shaped by our own separate experiences. We can't tell the truth to each other, assuming we even know it. And if we stumbled upon it, we wouldn't believe it anyway, so what's the use?" He leaned back and studied Calvanese. "You tell me, Tony, what the hell is the use?"

Calvanese stirred his coffee and then put the cup to the side. "You know what I thought you were describing, Paul?" He spoke with disappointment. "Us."

"I was."

"No, I don't mean the difference between you and me as people. I meant you and me as cops, any police officer in a Black neighborhood. Hell, more and more, it could be any neighborhood. So, we're not trusted by the community and now we don't trust each other. Where's that leave us?"

"It leaves us at the same place we began," answered Henderson.

"Yeah," Calvanese answered dejectedly. "I suppose it does." He took his coffee and uneaten muffin and dumped both inside the waste container. He walked toward the patrol car and entered the passenger side. Henderson didn't finish his food either. He tossed it in the trash can and headed for the car.

Once he got behind the wheel, he placed the key in the ignition but didn't turn it. He faced Calvanese. "When you look at me you don't see a cop, you see a color just like you said about all Black folks. We're not people, we're potential criminals. You remember saying that?"

"When I don't know someone on the street, that's what everyone is. That's what I've got to see if I want to stay alive!"

"Fine. Then look at me and see the same color you always do. The enemy."

"Bullshit."

"You gonna sit there and tell me I'm wrong?" asked Henderson.

"No. I'm gonna tell you you're one hundred percent right."

"Thanks for finally admitting it." Henderson started the engine and pulled out into oncoming traffic.

"You wanna know why I agreed with you?" asked Calvanese.

"No."

"When I look at you, I *do* see a color. Wanna know which one it is?"

"No."

"Fuchsia."

Henderson turned toward Calvanese in disbelief. "Fuchsia?"

"Yeah. You wanna know why?"

"Oh, on this, yeah, I really want to know how you came up with that one." Henderson sped up and moved into the left lane.

"Because I have no fuckin' idea what color that is. If I didn't know it was a color, I would've guessed it was some type of stomach virus or a faraway exotic vacation island where you go to catch a stomach virus."

Henderson's mouth opened slightly in stunned amazement. "That makes absolutely no sense."

"Then we're having the same discussion because when I look at you, of course I see a color, but the hell if I know what it is or what it means and, therefore, *it does not matter*. You understand? It doesn't matter, Paul. Now you tell me if you can look at my skin color and say the same thing."

Henderson thought about it for a second then pulled a rapid U-turn in front of a no U-turn sign.

"You just broke the law," Calvanese notified him.

"That should make you happy," replied Henderson.

"It's a start," Calvanese said, grim-faced. "But what would make me happier is if you just got over playing the 'power to the people' cop and just did your fuckin' job."

"And how do you expect me to do that when I'm in the middle of a bunch of troglodytes who just because they're wearing uniforms and carrying guns instead of clubs act like—"

"You're doing it again," interrupted Calvanese, "using your education to fuck up a meaningful conversation. I just got through telling you I didn't know what fuchsia was, now you're gonna use some word like troglodyke, throw it in my face, and—"

"Dyte," corrected Henderson. "Not dyke, dyte."

"Man, how are we ever gonna communicate if we don't speak the same language?"

"Neanderthal," offered Henderson. "Is that better?"

"Much. Until you clarified it, I thought you might have been accusing me of being a Communist," confessed Calvanese. "Now I know you were only calling me something very old that belongs in a cave."

"See? Our language isn't that difficult to understand, after all." Henderson pulled the car to the side of the road and parked in a handicapped space.

Calvanese pointed to the sign. "You're breaking the law again."

"It gets easier the more times you do it," replied Henderson. "You know, that symbol up there sort of explains our working relationship."

"You're exaggerating, something you do well. Granted we may strain each other's patience from time to time. But we're hardly disabled from doing our job."

"Disabled? No. Handicapped? Yes. You're blind, Calvanese, and you don't even know it."

"My vision's just as good as yours, Paul. Except when you've got difficulty seeing, you blame it on someone else. You've got nothing to complain about. In fact, you've got it pretty damn good, a lot better than most. Any white cop on the force would give their left arm to have your advantages."

"Would they want to be forced on the ground spread-eagled, with their face in the dirt, while some kid stares at them like they're some type of wild animal who needs to be caged?"

Calvanese shook his head in disbelief. "You still haven't got over that?"

"There's no reason for me ever to get over it. And, if through some miracle I just managed to forget about it for a minute or more, there would be something else that would come along and take its place. Some overweight security guard who'd follow me around the store while the white folks were having a field day robbing the place. Or some woman named Karen who clutches her purse as soon as I get on the elevator." He pointed at Calvanese. "Or my partner who used me to make some damn watermelon joke."

That stung Calvanese, but he wasn't yet prepared to show it.

"Or someone who wants to touch my hair to see how it feels or gets amazed that I might sunburn in summer."

"You sunburn?" asked Calvanese, appearing surprised.

"A goddamn automobile changes color underneath the sun, why shouldn't my skin?"

"Don't get so sensitive. I just never thought about it that way, that's all. And what's so wrong about someone wanting to touch your hair?"

"Because the woman who asked was in law school with me at the time, and I kind of figured that after someone received nineteen years of formal education, they might think of Black people as human and not as some exhibit at the zoo to be fed and patted with amazement." He studied Calvanese for a long beat, looking for a clue that what he had just said was making any sense. "But then maybe that's too much to hope for, let alone expect that you might understand."

Calvanese looked away for a moment. "She was ugly, huh?"

Henderson rolled his eyes in confusion. "Who was ugly?"

"The woman who asked to touch your hair," Calvanese explained. "If she had been attractive, it probably wouldn't have bothered you that much."

Henderson closed his eyes briefly, his body tensed and then relaxed, almost at the same time. "You're unbelievable, you know that?"

"Not really," responded Calvanese. "I just find a way to laugh when it hurts. Wouldn't be a bad idea if you could do that, once in a while, for yourself."

Henderson looked straight ahead, lost in thought, when he was suddenly jolted back to his senses by a loud banging on his vehicle.

An angry woman in a wheelchair used her cane to strike the patrol car near its front tire, alternately hitting the bumper and the chrome around the headlight. "You ought to be ashamed of yourselves, parking in a space you got no right being in!" she screamed. "You need to be driving around looking for someone to arrest."

Calvanese slid down his window. "You hit this car one more time, I'm going to arrest you."

"I'd like to see you try," she said defiantly, and then tapped her cane against the car as a direct challenge to his authority.

Calvanese turned toward Henderson. "What do you think we should do?"

"Tell her a joke, or shoot her," answered Henderson.

"I've run out of clever things to say." Calvanese reached for the shotgun attached to the center console while Henderson stepped on the accelerator and drove off.

Calvanese glanced at the side mirror and saw the woman flip him the middle finger while a group of onlookers enthusiastically applauded her efforts.

"Now that," he said to Henderson, "was some funny shit."

Henderson shrugged. "It was all right," he admitted reluctantly. "Would've been better if she hit you instead of taking out her frustration on the car, but there's always tomorrow."

Calvanese leaned back, closed his eyes, and spoke whimsically. "And as long as there's a tomorrow, there's always hope."

Henderson turned on the siren and pursued a car that had just run through a red light. "Not for this guy," he muttered. "He is sooo busted."

The first sign of a genuine smile appeared on Henderson's face.

FORTY-FOUR

Henderson sat on his lounge chair in the backyard and gazed hypnotically at a dark gray sky. He had hoped to see some stars, but he couldn't find one tonight. He and Nicole had bought their home when he was in his last year of graduate school. Well, it was supposed to be his last year, but once he completed his master's in criminal justice, he started law school the very next fall. Three years later, while he was studying for the bar exam, he enrolled in the police academy, a decade older than his fellow recruits, and to the ongoing disappointment of his wife.

Now, after residing at the same address for a record six years, he couldn't imagine living anywhere else. For a while, it had seemed as if owning this or any other house would remain a distant pipedream. If it hadn't been for the generous loan from Nicole's parents, who lived in Rhode Island, they would never have been able to afford the down payment. Nicole made a decent salary as a telecommunications specialist, whatever that meant; after all this time he still wasn't sure. But it wouldn't have been enough to qualify for the home of their dreams, a four-bedroom colonial in upper Ladera Heights, Mecca for the upwardly mobile Black professional.

The real estate agent told them that on a clear day they had an ocean view from every room on the second floor. That sold them on the house, as if they needed any additional incentives. They'd managed to see the water a total of seven times, and on at least two of those occasions, it was raining. Rain and severe wind are about the only elements of nature that eliminated the smog and haze long enough to see more than a quarter mile in any direction. But ocean view or no ocean view, it was their house and he loved coming home to it. Wait. Was that a star he saw twinkling brightly? He stared more intently. It turned out to be just a light glowing in the vast horizon from one of the jets leaving LAX.

The rear door to the kitchen opened and Nicole exited carrying a book of children's stories. She sat down next to him.

"What's the matter?" she asked.

"Nothing," he said unconvincingly.

"You usually don't come out here this late unless you've got something on your mind." She kissed him on the cheek. "Wanna share?"

"It isn't anything major," he said. "I just had a long discussion about race with Tony Calvanese, earlier today."

She chuckled. "That must've been worth the price of admission."

"We were trying to figure out which one of us was the biggest racist."

"And he won hands down."

"I'm not certain."

She studied him, taken aback by his answer. "There's not a racist bone in your body," she said, trying to ease his anxiety.

"You sure?"

"Positive," she answered.

"You think we can ever see each other as fuchsia?"

"I have no idea what you're talking about."

"It's a way of making color immaterial. Seeing a color but

not giving it any weight, any meaning. That you can't define it beyond what it is, so you can't be afraid of it."

"I don't understand."

He looked at the rear of the house, noticed a nightlight in his son's bedroom. "Is he asleep?"

She thumped the cover of the book. "Made me read *The Lion King* three times." She moved closer to him. "It was the abbreviated version."

"You were lucky. He usually makes me sing the musical."

She smiled and stroked his leg. "That's 'cause his daddy has such a marvelous voice," she said seductively.

"I think it has more to do with the fact that I dance all the lead parts. That, and I die magnificently."

She pulled away suddenly, repelled by the joke.

"Sorry," he said. "I know you're a bit sensitive about that subject."

She folded her arms across her chest. "Not anymore," she declared confidently, much to his surprise. "Not since I increased your life insurance policy."

His face squished up in distress, a cartoon character about to pitch a fit.

"Only kidding," she confessed, then slugged him hard in the arm. "We're even."

"I didn't hit you," he whined pathetically then rubbed his arm in earnest.

"There're a lot of ways to inflict damage," she stated firmly. "And the most devastating abuse doesn't require physical contact."

He thought about a time, long ago, when he had a chance at physical contact and didn't take it. He decided to leave that subject for another day. "You ever marvel at the things Dexter does?"

"What things?" she asked.

"Everything," he answered quickly. "The way he giggled

when he was a baby. It sounded like he had swallowed a rattle and was trying to spit it out." He searched her face for a clue, trying to discover if she understood what he was saying, if she knew how he felt about his son, and about being a father.

"The way he laughs now, like the rattle has become part of his personality, his soul. He's growing up so quick, Nicole, learning so much so fast. He jumps from one shoe size to another in the course of a week. His vocabulary increases with each new television commercial. And his body and even his face, it changes, Nicole. I mean, his face really changes. It's his face, that's obvious. I can recognize it. Pick it out of a line-up. But I was looking at the photo album, with all his pictures, and it's amazing! Do you understand what I'm getting at?"

She looked at him tenderly, her eyes slightly misty. "You're a great father, Paul." She touched his hand and held it. "You're a wonderful father."

"My father never told me he loved me," he said softly, without any resentment. "The few times he was around, he never told me."

"I know," she said. "But your dad's from a different era. When you don't feel that you can speak out, you suppress all your emotions and you remain quiet, even when it's the last thing a son needs. Your father was in pain, Paul, unable to express the gift he had. People handle disappointment and heartache differently."

"Don't give me that suffering artist shtick to excuse him as a father, or for that matter, a man."

"The only reason you're so angry at him after all these years is that you loved him. And you wouldn't be able to do that if he wasn't a man who deserved to be loved. I think all the things you've accomplished were to make him proud. And whether you believe it or not, I think he always has been. I know deep inside the reason you became a lawyer and then a cop, was you wanted people to be treated fair, something denied your dad."

"Whatever the reason he couldn't tell me he loved me, Dexter's always gonna hear that from me. He's always gonna know how much I love him. I swear to God, he'll always know. Do you understand?"

"What I think doesn't matter. It's what Dexter thinks. And he thinks he's the luckiest boy on the face of the earth to have you as his dad."

"I want him to see fuchsia. I want him to be able to see people for what they are, what they can become. Not what any color defines them as being. I'm afraid that can never be. I'm afraid Dexter will see what every other person makes him see, including myself when I take him aside to have *the talk* every Black father is forced to have with his son. Even though I wear the same uniform as those I warn him about. The talk is still necessary. It will never change, never get to a place where race doesn't matter. He deserves better."

Nicole kissed him on the cheek. "We all do."

He held her hand. "We all do."

FORTY-FIVE

Mrs. Calvanese visited all the fashionable boutiques on the Westside, an extravagant tour if ever there was one, led by the extremely knowledgeable and incredibly delightful Briella, girl-friend to her one and only son. Change that to potential fiancée. No strike that, likely wife. Yes, that was much better: Briella, her future daughter-in-law.

Halfway through purchasing three dresses, two sweaters, a silk skirt with two matching blouses—one solid and one with a light floral pattern—four pairs of shoes, and a cute little purse that fit inside a bigger one, they took a well-deserved break and ate lunch at an outdoor café on Rodeo. Actually, it was brunch—imagine that, and it wasn't even a weekend. Surprisingly, Mrs. Calvanese approved of the food. Although it may have had more to do with the company she kept, rather than any item on the twelve-page leather embossed menu. Briella was an absolute doll, the daughter she never had but soon would. *Just wait and see*, she promised herself.

Mrs. Calvanese couldn't remember the last time she had enjoyed herself so much. In addition to sharing an exquisite meal in Beverly Hills with a wonderful companion, it didn't hurt that she had seen at least three celebrities, including her favorite actor since the glory days of Humphrey Bogart and Jimmy Stewart: None other than Tom Hanks himself! She could hardly wait to get home to tell her husband. Of course, she'd have to delay the news until he came to. Once he realized how much she had spent on clothes, he would have no choice but to faint.

Briella wanted to pay for all the purchases, but Mrs. Calvanese would have none of that. "Absolutely not," she said.

Briella protested. "But, Mrs. Calvanese, I really want to."

"And that makes your generous offer even more gracious," she had replied. "But you've done more than enough, already."

"Can I at least buy you lunch?" she asked as a reasonable compromise.

Mrs. Calvanese happily agreed, and here they were, hobnobbing with the movers and shakers of Hollywood, and based on the designer outfits and expensive jewelry on display, there were probably more than a few financial titans of the banking industry thrown in for good measure. Given the number of patrons with earbuds or those white things that looked like tiny worms trying to get in or out of their ears, they all could have been mistaken for members of the secret service providing protection to only God knows who.

She thought, in the middle of her meal, what did people do before cell phones? Nobody should be that important. She told Briella it was rude to eat while speaking into a metal object.

Briella laughed. "It's the new status symbol. They're probably leaving messages on their own answering machines." And she laughed again, causing Mrs. Calvanese to understand, as if she needed any more evidence, why her son would have fallen for this woman. You couldn't fake a laugh as genuine or as contagious as that one.

After they ate, they did some more shopping—a lot more. Hats, scarves, jewelry—nothing too expensive, just some faux pearls and an interchangeable fashion watch that came with a set of different colored faceplates. Imagine that! It was late, but Mrs. Calvanese had left two plates of food for her husband with detailed heating instructions. "What would that man do without me?" she confided to Briella, then admitted, "I hope I never find out."

Briella said it was wonderful to see two people still in love after so many years.

"The secret's in the sauce," Mrs. Calvanese advised her. "Add the spices at the proper time. Don't overcook. Keep the ingredients fresh and whatever else you do, don't stir too much or too hard."

"You think you can teach me how to prepare that meal?" asked Briella.

Mrs. Calvanese smiled, lightly touched Briella on the wrist. "I wasn't talking about food."

Briella smiled and returned the touch. "I know."

They took in a movie, a romantic comedy, that wasn't particularly funny and showed too much flesh for Mrs. Calvanese's taste. The popcorn was great, though, served in a bucket that she thought could hold ten pounds of cooked pasta. For the price, you should be able to go back and fill it an unlimited number of times. By the time they left the theater, it was dark outside and a bit chilly.

Briella put up the convertible top and stopped at an ATM machine. "I'll only be a minute," she said. "Just need some cash to leave for my housekeeper. Might as well get it now."

"Leave the heat on," Mrs. Calvanese responded. "Also, the radio."

Briella walked up the ramp and stood in front of the money machine. She looked around and then placed her card inside the slot and entered her PIN.

Mrs. Calvanese felt warm and tried to figure out how to manage the temperature controls. So many buttons! After several failed attempts, she slid down the window and stuck her face outside, breathing deeply. She listened to a song. It was nice. She tried to think of the name of the singer.

The car door opened.

"That didn't take long," she said. She turned around and felt a heavy blow behind her ear. She fell forward, striking her head against the dashboard. Carmen McRae, that was the singer and the last thing she remembered before blacking out.

FORTY-SIX

Jennifer Goode sat on the couch in her living room and took a sip of coffee. "You sure you don't want any?" she asked Calvanese and Henderson, who had been interviewing her for the last fifteen minutes.

"No thanks, ma'am," said Henderson.

Calvanese smiled politely and shook his head no.

"I've been told my coffee's better than the stuff they sell at Starbucks, but I ain't gonna spend six dollars to find out. Shoulda called the place too-many-bucks if you ask me."

"Couldn't agree with you more, ma'am," said Calvanese.

"We won't take much more of your time, Mrs. Goode," said Henderson. "I know it's getting late."

"You can stay for dinner if you like. Plenty of chicken, and my macaroni and cheese ought to be against the law." She winked. "In a manner of speakin'."

"It sounds very tempting, but I'm afraid we can't do that," said Henderson. "Maybe another time."

"I'd like to help you, I really would. But I've told the detectives everything I seen."

"We're sure you did," said Henderson, "but occasionally

with the passage of time, memories improve, events get a little clearer, and you recall things you may not have noticed or given much thought to before."

"My memory don't get no better with time, don't matter how much so-called passage goes by and, truth be told, neither do my waistline."

"If you think of anything," said Calvanese, "no matter how small, will you give us a call?"

Her two youngest daughters ran into the area, jumping onto the couch into their mother's arms.

"Didn't I tell you to stay in your room?"

They buried their faces into her chest. She comforted each one. Her oldest daughter entered the room and at the sight of the two policemen, ran into her room crying.

"I'm sorry, Mrs. Goode," apologized Henderson. "We didn't mean to frighten your children."

"They haven't forgotten what happened to those other two officers, may they rest in peace. My oldest took it the hardest. She still has nightmares, wakes up screamin'. It's a shame what happened to those men. I've prayed every night for their poor families." She rose from the couch. "I better go take care of her."

"You mind if we come with you?" asked Calvanese.

"I'm not sure that's a good idea," she responded.

"I don't want her to be afraid every time she sees someone wearing this uniform," Calvanese replied. "Mind if I give it a try?"

Mrs. Goode considered it. "Come with me." She walked toward the bedroom with her two daughters in tow. The officers followed behind. "I'm warnin' you, though. She can be stubborn when she wanna be."

"My partner can be like that, but I've managed to grow on him."

She glanced at Henderson and smiled. "He don't look too pleased about it. Maybe you growed in the wrong places."

"You're very insightful, ma'am," remarked Henderson.

"I'm even better when I'm wearin' my glasses."

They entered her daughter's bedroom which she shared with her younger siblings. As soon as Calvanese stepped inside, the girl rushed to the corner and hid behind the curtain, trembling.

Her mother reached her and moved the curtain aside. "It's all right, baby. Nothing bad is gonna happen. I promise." She held her close and listened while the girl whispered something in her ear.

Mrs. Goode's other daughters quietly observed their sister's discomfort. They both held hands to reassure each other.

"Are we frightening her?" asked Henderson.

"She doesn't want you to leave."

"Why not?" asked Calvanese.

"She thinks the same thing's gonna happen to you happened to those other officers."

Calvanese approached the little girl still clutching her mother's side. He got on one knee. "What's your name, precious?"

Her expression of fear suddenly changed. She giggled a bit, then looked at Calvanese and smiled.

Calvanese glanced at Henderson. "See? She likes me. I have a way with children."

"That's not why she's smiling," responded Mrs. Goode. "You guessed her name."

"I did?"

"Precious."

"Precious?" he asked.

The girl giggled again.

"Well, I'd have to say that's the perfect name for you," Calvanese said. He curled his right arm tight. "You want to feel my muscle?" he asked.

Precious looked at him, and then at her mother, who gave

permission. She touched his arm and smiled. Her two sisters rushed over and grabbed a free spot.

"Will y'all let the man alone?" complained their mother.

"That's all right, Mrs. Goode. I just want them to see that no one's gonna hurt me. Know why?" Calvanese smiled at the little girls.

Precious nodded yes and pointed to Henderson. "'Cause you're with him," she answered.

Calvanese's smile faded. Henderson's smile appeared.

"We've taken enough of your time, Mrs. Goode," Henderson said. "Come on, Officer Calvanese, I'll let you feel my muscle in the car."

"I'm sorry I couldn't help more," she said. She accompanied the officers and her daughters back out to the living room and walked them to the front door. "I think about those two men all the time. Don't know what this world's come to. But it does my heart good to see the two of you workin' together. Praise Jesus."

Henderson and Calvanese exchanged an uneasy look.

"Renews my faith in humankind," she said. Mrs. Goode opened the door. The youngest daughters waved goodbye.

"Bye-bye," said Precious.

"Take care, everybody," said Calvanese.

Henderson tipped his hat to the girls.

Mrs. Goode leaned closer, spoke softly. "I'll say a prayer for your safety," she said.

"Thank you, ma'am," said Henderson. "We could use as many of those as you could spare."

Calvanese nodded appreciation and waved goodbye to the girls, finding it difficult to leave them.

Calvanese and Henderson walked down the alleyway.

"Nice lady," remarked Henderson.

"Cute kids," added Calvanese.

They turned the corner and entered their patrol car. Henderson got behind the wheel.

"You religious, Paul?"

Henderson thought about the question for a moment. "Not as much as I should be," he confessed. "What about you? You believe in God?"

"I don't discuss religion," replied Calvanese. "And after learning the hard way with you, I've also eliminated race and books about Baldwin from my conversation list."

"Lucky for you, you've got a fairly limited vocabulary so it shouldn't present too much of a problem." Henderson drove off. "It's probably a blessing in disguise. Oh, I forgot you don't want to discuss religion, which considering how you treated Reverend Wilson after his church burned down, is quite understandable."

"Look, I felt lousy about what happened to his church. I hope we catch the two cowards that started the fire so I can personally put their asses behind bars and throw away the key."

"I think I sense a qualifying *but* coming soon," said Henderson.

"But just because he's a reverend, doesn't mean he's right. Believing in God doesn't mean I have to believe in all his self-proclaimed representatives."

"I agree," said Henderson. "And just because you're a cop doesn't mean you're right and, by the way, you just admitted you believed in God."

"Did not."

"Did."

"Did not."

"Did."

"You're just jealous because those little girls liked me more than they liked you. Wanna feel my muscle?" Calvanese laughed, but his moment of levity ended when his cell phone rang. "Hi, Dad," he said with a huge smile that ended as the blood drained quickly from his face. His father's call would now test far more than his faith in the creator.

FORTY-SEVEN

Mrs. Calvanese's unconscious and battered body rested motionless in a hospital bed. Tubes ran down her nose and an I.V. protruded from the back of her right hand. A host of machines monitored her condition spitting out technical and medical information on her vitals, blood pressure, heart rate, respiration, everything but what her husband and son most needed to know: Would she be all right? Would she survive? And who did this?

Calvanese stood near the foot of her bed. His father had pulled his wheelchair as close to her as he could get it without physically taking her place, something both men gladly would do. Mr. Calvanese held her hand and wouldn't let it go, forcing the African American nurse to move to the opposite side to administer an injection.

"Was she raped?" he asked without ever taking his eyes away from his wife.

"Haven't completed the exam yet, but she was found naked and..." The nurse hesitated. "She had signs of trauma in the lower region of her body," she answered sympathetically. "Your

wife put up one hell of a fight, Mr. Calvanese. Either that, or..."
The nurse stopped herself.

"Or what?" asked Mr. Calvanese, in a manner that gently
demanded a response.

"It was a crazed-out animal who did this to her. I just don't
understand how someone could be so vicious to another human
being."

"Where'd they find her?" asked Calvanese.

"A deserted lot in South Central," she replied, then noticed
Calvanese's face flush a dark red.

He walked slowly toward his mother's bedside and stopped
near her pillow. He lightly fluffed it, then touched her face,
pushing back her hair, trying unsuccessfully to style it the way
she liked—the way his father loved. His eyes fought back tears,
but it was a fruitless battle that he eventually lost. He touched
her arm, now violated by a needle, and softly stroked her skin,
surprised to discover it was still so smooth. She had long slender
fingers. *Better to tenderize the veal*, she always joked. *Among
other things*, her husband would add with a sly grin that caused
her to blush. She'd then brush away his comment with a modest
wave of her hand, followed by an Italian expression that needed
no translation.

He heard a small choking sound, more a stifled sob. It came
from his father, fighting desperately to keep his emotions
contained. Mr. Calvanese's eyes filled with tears, and his lips
trembled, which caused a similar reaction in his son.

Calvanese looked at the nurse and signaled for some
privacy.

She nodded in agreement. "If you need me, just press that
buzzer next to her bed. I'll check back in a few minutes." She
waited for some acknowledgment from Calvanese, but never
got it. She left, closing the door behind her.

"Dad, I can stay here with Mom," he studied his father who
showed no expression, just a dead and vacant stare in the direc-

tion of his comatose mother. "Might be a good idea if you went home and got some rest. I'll come by later and—"

"All those years I was out there protecting everybody else," Mr. Calvanese said with a detached coldness. "Now, I can't even protect the only woman I ever loved."

He loosened his grip on her hand and touched each individual finger. He stopped on her ring finger, now badly swollen, and bruised. He caressed the spot where her wedding ring had once been.

"Forty years," he said softly. Calvanese thought he heard a sense of deep pride in his father's voice. "Forty years," he repeated, emphatically. "In all that time, she never once took off her wedding ring. I used to ask her, Isabella, how much tomato paste you got stuck underneath that ring by now?" He looked at his son. It was the first time Calvanese had ever seen his father afraid, totally lost.

"I wanted to get her a new one," he said, just above a whisper, then he spoke more forcefully. "She said only if she got a new husband. One ring for one marriage. That was her golden rule." A bittersweet smile crossed his lips, ever so briefly, and then his expression turned to unrelenting hate. "The bastard took her ring," he spewed out, his breath deserting him. "He took her..." The floodgates opened and a monumental, ghastly grief released itself into the room. His body shook. The sobbing grew louder. The muscles in his upper body convulsed.

Calvanese pressed the buzzer then raced to his aid, holding him, trying to bring comfort to his father even though he could find no such consolation for himself.

The nurse entered and quickly dampened a towel with cold water. Calvanese watched her methodically, professionally, but with a surprising degree of tenderness and genuine care, dab his father's face and forehead with the compress. She poured a glass of water and helped him take a sip, followed by a swallow. His father gripped the glass with both hands, reinforced by the nurse, who had placed her hands around his. He eventually managed to drink half the contents with her assistance.

Calvanese moved away from his father, but it wasn't to give the nurse more room to work. He needed to find a space, a tiny spot somewhere, anywhere in the confines of this antiseptic chamber that had suddenly become claustrophobic. He wanted to release his own sorrow, even though it likely would shrink the room further, suffocate everyone in it more quickly. He looked around, carefully studying every corner, finding not a single solitary place where that potentially self-defeating goal could be accomplished.

He felt a sharp pain in his stomach and feared that every awful thing that had ever happened to him during his entire life was being forced back up and out of his throat, for him to taste and relive again. This time the memories would be more concentrated, intense, the product of being allowed to fester and rot, year after year, until they cumulated into the worst form of sickness and despair creating this unbearable moment of anguish.

He thought of Briella. If he hadn't met her none of this would be happening. How stupid could she be, leaving his mother alone that time of night? Especially in front of a bank. He suddenly found a space on the wall, a target, where if he couldn't release it all, he could at least begin the process. His fist went through the plaster aided by a guttural sound loud enough to alert security guards several corridors away. But despite the overwhelming alarm set off by his emotional emergency call for help, it didn't bring an end to his desolation. For the moment, all it could accomplish was to silence his pain.

FORTY-EIGHT

Calvanese sat on his couch in the darkened living room and opened another bottle of beer. He'd never drunk this much without passing out or getting sick. But then he had never felt this helpless, and this hurt. He gazed around the room and could no longer recognize it as his own. Briella had eliminated the memories of his wife from his home and replaced them with a ghost that he feared would haunt him in ways he'd never survive. It had been so long since he'd allowed himself to feel again, to love despite all the internal warnings to the contrary. For the first time in years, he could see the future and he wasn't alone in it, until now.

His mother had survived for the moment, and he was grateful for that miracle. But he also knew it would be a while before he could look at Briella and not see his mother lying in that hospital bed, battered, and bruised and violated. He feared he couldn't touch Briella without being reminded of the horror his mother must have felt. He was terrified at the thought that she might not make it, that she would die with those tubes connected to her frail body. If that happened, he would surely grieve twice, first as a loving son who'd lost his mother, and then as a man who could no longer be with the woman he would blame, fairly or unfairly, for his mother's death. *How the hell could she leave her alone in an expensive car, engine running, inviting horror to happen?*

No. He'd never forgive Briella if his mother should die. And he'd never forgive himself for being unable to forgive her. She'd called him a hundred times in the last three days, but he wouldn't speak to her, wouldn't allow her to visit the hospital. Her last message, left on his recorder, was that she wished with all her heart that it had happened to her instead of his mother. The tape beeped and cut off her crying, but not his. He listened to the message over and over and wondered if he agreed with it or not. He concluded that he didn't, and that tormented him more. He had fallen in love with a woman who would be the cause of the violence against his mother. He knew if he were a cop visiting a victim of a crime, he wouldn't be blaming anyone other than the criminal who perpetrated the crime. But he wasn't a cop now. He was a son. And he blamed the woman he loved for being responsible for victimizing the mother he loved.

His father had called him earlier this afternoon, before the drinking binge started. Hearing his broken intonation was all the incentive he needed to reach for the first bottle. His dad wanted to let him know they'd found the car, or what was left of it, behind a high school off Avalon Boulevard in Compton. The guys from the lab lifted plenty of prints, but they could belong to anyone who'd stripped the car. "At least it wasn't torched," his father said, temporarily restoring the vitality and self-assurance to the voice Calvanese had grown accustomed to hearing. "So, we still got a chance to I.D. the driver." Conveying the news made his father sound like a cop again, which was certainly far preferable than sounding like a devastated husband.

In his hour of need, he'd been able to revert to a profession that provided more than a badge—it gave him a shield to hide behind, protect his true feelings. But Calvanese knew that no matter how seasoned a cop, you could insulate yourself from the heartache for only so long. And then the truth, in all its power, would deliver the crushing blow. It wouldn't score a knockout. That would be too kind. It would simply leave you staggered and defenseless, groping for time and hoping to be saved by the final bell. But not even Pavlov, with all his fancy experiments, could help you get through this crisis. The crime against his mother had left behind more than one victim; it always does. Calvanese wondered how many more victims this random act of violence would claim, how many more lives would be left shattered in its wake?

He'd never seen his father so helpless and heartbroken. Even after the accident, when he was unable to move and unsure if he'd be paralyzed for the rest of his life, he still managed to appear in control, joking about fixing the television's reception. "It looked good while I was falling," he'd said to the doctor who had performed the surgery. He invited all the nurses to watch the game he'd been taping before his fateful trip to the roof. "Don't tell me who won!" he pleaded. "I'd hate to think I sacrificed my body for nothin." *My dad, the jokester repair man.*

The doorbell rang several times, but Calvanese made no effort to leave the couch. He heard the fumbling of the doorknob followed by the door creaking open. He knew it was Henderson, long before he heard the voice. "Tony?"

Henderson entered the room, turned on a set of lights, and stood before Calvanese waiting to be acknowledged. Calvanese finished drinking and tossed the bottle aside. He looked at Henderson, his eyes glazed over in a drunken stupor, but not yet drunk enough to conceal the pain and the terror.

"I'm sorry," Henderson said softly.

Calvanese closed his eyes for a moment then looked away.

Sorry was the last thing he needed to hear. Any form of apology right now sent a dagger through his heart.

Henderson sat next to him. "Is she gonna be all right? Your mother."

"Some fuckin' nig..." He stopped himself from saying the word. He looked at Henderson, hesitating briefly. "Animal— attacks my mother. You wanna know is she gonna be all right?" He slammed his fist into the palm of his hand. "Yeah, she's gonna be just fine and dandy!"

He rose quickly, unsteadily. Henderson stood next to him and tried to provide balance, but Calvanese slapped away his hand. "Keep your fuckin' hands off me!"

Calvanese took a step away but then turned suddenly, standing face-to-face with Henderson. "Was he another one of your poor victims you feel so sorry about?" Calvanese balled up both hands into tight fists and tapped them against the sides of his legs. "Answer me!"

Henderson took a deep breath and swallowed hard. "I came by to see if I could help, to see if you need anything. If you don't want me here, then—"

"Need?" Calvanese replied in disbelief. "If I..." Calvanese felt the grief surface to his throat where it collided with the rage inside his heart, now both boiling over with the urge to strike out at anything or anyone. "You wanna know what I need?!" His stomach churned, but whatever sickness he felt was not going to be relieved anytime soon. "I need my mother to be home where she belongs! Safe and secure and with the man she's loved all her life! I need her to be cooking in the kitchen and tasting whether the sauce is ready or if it could use some more spices or if..." He forced back the tears and anguish, but the effort took his breath away. His chest expanded, making room for a cruel, more excruciating pain. He cleared the vile taste from his throat and lungs, tried to speak. "I need—"

"Tony," Henderson made another attempt to place his hand

on his partner's shoulder, but the effort caused a swift violent eruption.

Calvanese charged Henderson, decking him with one fierce punch. They both crashed to the floor. Calvanese jumped on top of Henderson and struck him again. He reared back and tried for a third time. Henderson blocked the next punch and flipped Calvanese over his head.

Both men rose quickly and attacked each other with a flurry of punches. Henderson spun Calvanese around, throwing him forcefully into the wall. A mirror crashed to the floor and shattered. Henderson pinned Calvanese against the wall but received a furious shot to the rib cage, another to the stomach.

Calvanese followed the combination with a right cross to the jaw, knocking Henderson over a coffee table, breaking the furniture, and sending glasses and table lamps flying. Calvanese dived at Henderson but was met with a kick to the chest that lifted him up and then drove him backwards.

Henderson threw two clean shots to the face and Calvanese returned the favor. He charged Henderson, a wild bull driving him across the room into the opposite wall. Trapped, he kneed Calvanese's midsection, knocking the wind out of him, bending him over in pain.

Calvanese sprang up, driving his forearm into Henderson's neck and then swung his elbow into the side of Henderson's head.

Henderson whipped his leg around, delivering a powerful kick to Calvanese's kidney.

The two men exchanged blow after blow, neither man willing nor capable of backing down, fully engaged in an emotional release as much as a physical one.

After several brutal exchanges, sheer exhaustion tried to settle the matter but both men refused to be defeated by mere fatigue. The punches were now slower, heavier, but equal in force and effect.

Henderson struck Calvanese in the jaw then prepared to hit again. Calvanese offered no resistance, apparently wanting to be struck. Henderson grabbed him by the shirt and then cocked his other fist for one last mighty blow. He stared at Calvanese who stood helplessly, waiting for the punishment. Gradually, Henderson's fist opened, and his fingers eased off Calvanese.

It was over.

The two men looked at each other, defeated warriors.

"You want somebody to hurt you?" Henderson asked. He let go of Calvanese, who didn't move. "You have to find somebody else."

Henderson stepped over the broken glass and destroyed furniture and left through the front door. Calvanese remained motionless, before collapsing to his knees, covering his face with his hands, and sobbing.

FORTY-NINE

"We got over a thousand homicides in this city every year," the male caller's voice was interrupted by some static over the car radio as Henderson decided to take the long way home. He stopped at a crosswalk, his thoughts still on his fight with Calvanese. Nearly every part of his body was sore or bruised. He coughed up some blood and spit it out the window. He wondered if one of his ribs was broken, then he assumed his wife would break the rest once he got home and told her what he'd done.

"Most of the victims are Black and poor," the radio caller continued. "A couple of white cops get killed and suddenly we got a major problem. Hey, they get paid to risk their lives. That's their job."

Henderson watched a homeless man push a severely damaged grocery cart that contained his belongings. Hunched over, the man stared at his feet as he maneuvered the wobbly cart through the crosswalk. He reached the sidewalk and continued past a homeless woman who stood on the corner next to a young child who held a dirty cardboard sign asking for food.

Henderson motioned for the woman, and he gave her five dollars.

"Thank you," she said. Her teeth showed signs of decay and her nails were infected with a fungus that had discolored the tips of her fingers. She took the money and rejoined her daughter, who gave Henderson an appreciative wave. Henderson winked at the little girl, and she giggled, and then flashed a perfect smile. He smiled back, which caused his right side to ache.

"This is K.N.Z. 710. You're on the air," announced the host in a friendly manner.

Henderson stepped on the accelerator and drove further down the avenue.

"I'm a white woman." The voice conveyed a discernible tremble. "I've had Black friends all my life. I've never thought of myself as prejudiced. But I've had enough. If you ask me, Black people are the ones who are racist."

Henderson switched the radio to a soothing jazz station on Sirius XM and stopped the car at a traffic light. A bearded Black man wearing a green army jacket approached the car, walking unsteadily.

"Can you spare some change for food?" the man asked, his head bowed.

Henderson removed two dollars from his center console and handed the money to the man, who placed a knife to Henderson's throat. "Just give me your fuckin' money or I'll kill ya! I swear to God I will!"

Henderson remained perfectly still, speaking slowly and quietly. "You can have everything I've got. Just be calm." He moved his hand a few inches from the steering wheel. "Look, I'm reaching for my money."

"Smart move," the man said, then hurriedly surveyed the area. "Just don't try nothin' foolish or it'll be the last thing you ever do."

Henderson secretly grabbed the inside handle and thrust the door open, knocking the man down. Henderson quickly exited his vehicle. The man got to one knee and wildly slashed his knife several times. Henderson waited patiently for the man's arm to extend backwards and then he drove the toe of his shoe directly into the man's exposed underarm. The knife fell to the ground and Henderson kicked it away.

Henderson lifted the man up and slammed him into the side of his car. He punched him in the face twice. The man collapsed only to be lifted and punched again and again. Possessed by some demon, he released the fury of his fists. His screams of anguish would go unheard by the man, already unconscious.

"You're gonna kill me?!" Henderson shouted as he pummeled the man, continuously striking him in the face, now a bloody mess. "For some fuckin' money that I was gonna give you anyway!"

Henderson heard police sirens, but the noise made him angrier, gave him a sense of greater urgency. "That's what my life's worth to you? Some fuckin' change!"

Two cops exited the police car and grabbed Henderson, pulling him off the man who remained propped against the side of the vehicle for several seconds before slowly sliding to the ground. The cops were shouting commands at Henderson, but the voices didn't seem real. Nothing seemed real, not the flashing lights from the patrol car, not the intersection that gave the impression of being eerily small, not the handcuffs about to be placed around his wrists. He suddenly had the presence of mind to identify himself as a cop, and then reality quickly reappeared.

The fire department's paramedic truck pulled up at the scene. Henderson looked at the man sprawled out before him. He thanked God when the man's eyes flickered open and his legs came to life, moving aimlessly from side to side.

"We're gonna need you to file a report," one of the cops said.

Henderson nodded agreement and asked to use a cell phone to call his wife. He received the phone, started to dial, and then studied the blood on his hands. Was it from this man he almost killed? Or was it from his partner who he had intended to comfort? He wondered, for a moment, if it mattered.

FIFTY

Henderson stood quietly at the bedside of his son and watched Dexter's small body curled up under a superhero blanket. The blanket had numerous heroes plastered together, an animated quilt of comic book characters, all sharing the same essential cartoon trait: immortality. The figures glowed in the dark, glistening under the moonlight that filtered through the bedroom window, giving the impression that they were alive, providing protection, offering eternal vigilance. Perhaps their presence contributed to his son's peaceful sleep. Life should be that easy, he thought.

Nicole stood at the doorway dressed in her blue cotton bathrobe and watched her husband gently pull up the blanket and cover their son's shoulders. She took a quiet half-step into the room but then decided to leave.

Henderson sat in a chair next to the bed and gazed at Dexter. He wanted to wake him, needed to hear his voice, and hold him. But his son had school in the morning, so he would simply remain at his side until the boy awakened on his own. He'd then tell Dexter that he had just entered the room a moment earlier to turn off the alarm. He knew his son would sleep through it for at least the first two minutes. Usually, about then, the boy would reach for the clock radio and hit the snooze button, at which point his father would grab his wrist, lift the arm high into the air, and softly tickle good morning.

Henderson and Nicole had lost their first child shortly after his birth. The boy had been born almost three months prematurely. To complicate matters he was breech, and the delivery created additional health problems. The doctor told Henderson there was virtually no chance of survival, but he stayed by the infant's side for thirty-six continuous hours. His vigil failed to protect his son from the inevitable. He had saved numerous citizens from violent predators but couldn't protect his little baby from something as simple as early arrival. Ironic—he and his wife couldn't wait for their first bundle of joy and evidently their son couldn't wait to be delivered. Now their impatience would lead to a sorrow that only became more bearable with the birth of Dexter. Yet, the death of his first child still left a hole—a large one. And Henderson tried to fill it every day in the only way he knew how: working hard and loving harder.

The nurse on duty had told Henderson that he could touch his son while he lay in the incubator fighting for life. She said his skin was so soft, and it would be all right to massage it lightly. But Henderson declined, indicating he didn't want to risk hurting the boy. Both he and the nurse knew the truth. He was afraid to touch him. Didn't think he'd ever get over the loss if it turned out to be the last time he was able to do that—touch his son while he was alive. As it turned out, he never got over his decision not to touch him. That's what he had thought about the other night in his backyard when Nicole had told him there were many ways to inflict damage, and that the most devastating abuse didn't require physical contact. He wondered if she had any idea just how right she had been.

How could a baby so small leave such a huge emptiness? But that's what happened; a veritable canyon devoid of memories that should have developed over years of watching his son grow older. No first steps, no learning to eat on his own, or dress by himself, tie his shoes, catch, and throw a football, play a favorite video game, or experience the thrill of being tossed in the air and safely caught. Henderson would never be called Dad by this boy or have his son fall asleep in his arms or be able to teach him math or tell him scary stories that would compel them to stay up all night eating hot buttery popcorn and watching Cartoon Network. And that explained just a small part of the hole—a very small part.

Sometimes he regretted not agreeing to a burial. That deprived him of the opportunity to visit the graveside on special occasions, leave flowers and offer a prayer. But he didn't feel it right to place his son under the earth when the boy had never walked upon it or felt the wind or rain on his face or seen stars and sunsets and summer clouds. So, he and Nicole had their firstborn cremated, scattering the ashes across the Pacific Ocean, like a thousand pirates on a voyage for secret treasure that they should have discovered together.

If the ocean had a memory, and Henderson believed it did, then he hoped it would share a child's newfound freedom and relieve a father's everlasting grief whenever tears and ashes met to consider dreams that might have been.

Dexter released a groan and then something that sounded like quiet laughter. If he ever lost this boy... He quickly forced himself not to think about that possibility because the hole left from that devastating loss would devour Henderson's entire world.

Dexter had a way of placing the side of his face against Henderson's cheek whenever they sat next to each other on the couch, watching television. The boy would climb partway up his father's leg, place his knee at Henderson's hip, slide his body against the man's chest and rest his face cheek to cheek. To the outside observer this arrangement might have looked just a tad uncomfortable but, to Henderson, it felt like riding on the surface of a cloud. At moments like that, they were one person, inseparable, with thoughts melded together, sharing much more than the football or basketball game being televised.

When they smiled it was a single joint muscle forming two half-moons on faces connected by their actual proximity and Henderson's absolute conviction of the power of unconditional love. He'd do anything to bring this child happiness. He knew there were bruises Dexter would make on his own. But he'd try to find a way to help his son heal faster, better, without leaving behind any permanent scars. Isn't that the role of a father?

As an infant, Dexter was susceptible to ear infections; like all illnesses they occurred most frequently at night, on the weekends, when the pediatrician wasn't readily available. Henderson would rush out to fill a prescription at the nearest twenty-four-hour pharmacy. Dexter screamed the most God-awful cries and Henderson could only hold him, walk with him, whisper it would be all right and wait for the medicine to achieve the desired goal—to relieve the pain. Henderson had learned early on what all parents experience with great dread: There's absolutely nothing in this world that gives you a greater feeling of helplessness than when your baby is ill.

Unconcerned for your own health, you hug your son or daughter as tightly as possible all the while praying to absorb into your own body whatever infection is attacking theirs. Your prayers are partially successful. You usually wind up getting sick, too. Of course, that does nothing to cure your child but now your empathy has been rewarded—you share the same condition and the identical fate of your loved one. The family that hugs together stays sick together.

Henderson was more than willing to pay that price. What he feared was the day the hugs stopped, the moment when a son got too old for cheek-to-cheek face time. He strove to make

Dexter independent and knew with all his heart he would rue the day when it finally happened.

He smiled, recalling the Saturday afternoon he removed Dexter's training wheels from the boy's bike. His son was hesitant, a bit fearful, maybe even frightened, but Henderson reassured him in the way only a father can. "I'm not going to let you fall, Dexter," he had said, convincingly. "It's a lot easier than with the training wheels on, you'll see."

Dexter started pedaling, his father holding on and running alongside the bike.

"You can do it, Dexter!"

"Don't let go."

"I'm right here, son!"

"Don't let go."

"That's it, you're doing great!"

"Okay, you can let go, now."

Henderson held onto the back of the bike's seat, running along as Dexter pedaled faster and faster. "I will, I will," he told his son, but managed to hold on a few more yards.

"Let go, Dad. Let go!"

Henderson's fingers finally loosened their grip and Dexter was free to maneuver the bicycle, unencumbered by the safety net his father tried so hard in vain to supply.

The moment of release brought smiles to both Henderson and his son, albeit the grin on Dexter's face gleamed ear to ear. Henderson's expression remained more contained, his body leaning forward and his hands attempting to control the direction and movement of the bike from a terribly long distance away.

"Not so fast!" he yelled; his body arched to the side as if trying to keep a baseball from going foul. "Slow down, Dexter. Take wider turns!" Henderson gripped imaginary handlebars and turned them carefully. "You're cutting the turns too tight!" He contorted his body to follow the uneven path being made by his son and then, he simply stood still, studying the accomplishment from afar.

He watched his son ride his bike at his own pace, with growing confidence. Henderson had felt a mixture of pride and trepidation that made his heart race, alternating between exuberance and panic. Then, it happened... a minor crash, but the way Henderson ran toward the fallen boy, you would have thought it was a major collision requiring an emergency call to 911, along with a command to send all available fire engines to the scene of the accident.

Dexter jumped up in celebration.

Henderson asked, "Buddy, are you all right?"

"I did it, Dad!" Dexter gave his father a high five. "I rode by myself," he proclaimed proudly. "I wasn't afraid or anything, not even when I fell!"

"That's great, Dexter. Didn't I tell you that if—"

"I wanna do it again! I wanna do it again!" Dexter righted the bicycle and straddled it before Henderson could object.

"Should I hold the bike this time?" asked his father, hoping the answer would be yes.

"Just push and then let go."

"You sure?"

"And don't hold on so long this time."

"Okay," Henderson agreed reluctantly. He steadied the bike until he felt his son gain control and then gave him a light push.

"Thanks, Dad! Wooo-weeee!"

Woo-wee, indeed. Henderson saw that magical look on his son's face—the moment when you discover you're better than the thing you were afraid of; when you finally realize you've conquered the fear you thought you'd never overcome. He understood that this bicycle represented much more than a pivotal learning experience. Sooner or later, Henderson, like all fathers, had to push and then let go, had to sit back and watch his son make it on his own, mistakes and all. But thank God, not yet. Not now.

He leaned back in the chair and closed his eyes for a moment. When he opened them, the room appeared brighter as he slowly wiped away a few isolated tears from his cheeks and waited for morning to come.

FIFTY-ONE

Max Oliver wiped his brow and realized he'd done so using a cloth drenched in grease. "Fuck!" He threw the rag across the garage and kicked the tire on a beat-up Buick. "Ow!" He felt a sharp pain in his ankle and rubbed it, annoyed with himself. Everything had gone wrong today. The parts he needed weren't available, so he fell deeper behind in his workload. He'd forgotten to bring both his lunch and his wallet.

Reeves had business to attend to and left him alone for most of the day handling irate customers, phone calls from creditors, and a visit from a disappointed Black woman wearing yellow hot pants and a purple tank top, looking like a broken-down used-up Laker cheerleader. She wanted to know if Reeves would be back soon and when he told her he had no idea, she left a card with a brief message. She sprayed some cheap perfume on the envelope and sealed it with a kiss, leaving behind a bright red imprint of her chapped lips.

"Just give that to him," she had said, smacking her chewing gum and straightening her platinum wig. "He'll know who it's from." He watched her leave the shop, wondering how she managed to move on high heels the width of a sidewalk crack.

She'd been gone for more than three hours, and he could still smell her perfume, which easily defeated the scents of burned rubber, oil, grease, and other mechanical fluids.

He searched for something clean, found a blanket in the backseat of the Buick, snatched it, and wiped oil and grease off his forehead. He evaluated his face in the side mirror, dabbed the blanket on his chin to remove as much of the grime as possible, then folded the blanket so the stains wouldn't show. He placed it back inside the rear of the vehicle and glanced at his watch—twenty minutes past closing.

He figured Reeves wouldn't be returning, so he decided to straighten up the place before leaving. Tools were put in their proper place, cans of paint were lined up and arranged by color, tires were neatly stacked on top of each other, and he even replaced the towels and toilet paper in the restroom. Reeves had gone ballistic last month when there wasn't enough toilet paper left on the roll to complete the task.

"How the fuck am I supposed to wipe my ass with two sheets of toilet paper left on the goddamn roll!" he had screamed from behind the locked door. He'd then burst into the garage, pants down around his ankles, and pointed to Oliver who, at the time, was busy with an elderly female customer. "Were you the last one to shit?" he demanded to know.

"No," the frightened and confused woman whimpered.

Oliver gently took her aside. "He was talking to me, ma'am," he told her reassuringly.

She didn't know what to say or where to look, so she excused herself and quickly left without a receipt.

Reeves grabbed a stack of paper towels. "Don't leave me with no empty toilet roll, you understand me, boy?" He hadn't waited for a response, just showed his naked behind as he retraced his steps into the stall, not bothering to close the restroom door. Since that day, Oliver made certain there was always a full roll of toilet paper readily available. Not only didn't he want to incur his boss's wrath again, but he had also absolutely no desire to see Reeves in that state of half-nakedness. Once in a lifetime was one time too many.

He organized some papers on Reeves's desk then took a handful of paper clips and pencils, slid open the center drawer, and dumped them inside. He noticed a long album, a scrapbook of some kind. He removed the book and when he flipped the cover, his fingers trembled. He remained frozen for a moment, then he turned a page, and then more quickly another, and another. He read the headlines, scanned the articles, and stared at the photos in disbelief. Reeves had saved all the clippings about the murdered police. Why would he do that? What did he know? His stomach churned. He felt ill; perspiration formed on his brow. He closed the book and pressed it hard against his chest, hoping that might slow down his heart now beating rapidly in fear.

He had to get out of this place, and for good. Luckily, he already had given his notice. Now he had to find a way to move it up a week. What in God's name was Reeves doing with a scrapbook filled with murdered cops?

"Jesus Christ," he uttered aloud.

"Jesus had nothing to do with it," a voice responded from behind.

Oliver turned and discovered Reeves standing only a few feet away. How had he managed to walk in through all this mess without making a sound?

"What you doin'?"

"Just cleaning up," Oliver's voice sounded like a child about to be punished.

Reeves pointed to the scrapbook in Oliver's hands. "Strange place for you to dust."

"It fell off the shelf, just wanted to make sure I didn't damage anything."

"Damage?" Reeves offered a sick, twisted smile. "Bit too late to worry about that, don't you think?"

Oliver glanced around the garage, searching for the nearest exit that wouldn't bring him in contact with Reeves.

"I ever tell you about my father?"

Oliver shook his head.

"Of course not," Reeves said. "Why would I? Really didn't have a reason to, until maybe now." He looked at Oliver still clutching onto the scrapbook, as if it offered protection. He appeared like a frightened kid trying to hide behind a see-through curtain.

"The police killed him, murdered him. Said he was resistin' arrest, but why shouldn't he resist? He hadn't done anything wrong."

Reeves took a step toward Oliver. "Know what his crime was? He went to the store to buy me some milk. I wanted it for my birthday cake. It was fudge and everybody knows you need to drink milk with a fudge cake, especially when it has creamy whipped chocolate frosting. That's funny, ain't it? I just had to have that milk. Didn't think I could eat that cake without it."

He took another slow, deliberate step toward Oliver. "As it turned out, I could live without milk or, as it turned out, that damn cake, but my daddy..." Reeves shook his head, sadly. "My daddy couldn't live long enough to bring that milk home or light the candles on my cake. All because he wanted to do something special for me on my birthday. Something I asked him to do, begged him to do, just so I could eat some cake and celebrate another lousy year on this god-forsaken earth."

Oliver hesitated, unsure what to do, and then he said, "I'm sorry." He swallowed hard and spoke softly. "For what happened to your father?"

"You mean for what those police made happen," Reeves countered sharply.

Oliver stood motionless as Reeves continued his steady approach.

"You ever heard of John Brown?"

"The abolitionist?"

Reeves chuckled. "That's what some people called him. Others said he was the devil, Satan himself, some evil madman that needed to be destroyed." Reeves took a step closer to Oliver and sensed his nervousness, enjoyed it, found it amusing.

"To me?" He gave a noncommittal shrug. "He wasn't good. Wasn't bad. Don't much give a fuck if he was a hero or a coward. I guess you could say he was just bein' practical. A white man who would do for slaves what the slaves wouldn't or couldn't do for themselves. You can put the scrapbook back on the shelf where it belongs. Unless you want to keep it for yourself? A goin'-away gift from me to you. Something to remember me by."

Oliver shook his head but held onto the book.

Reeves smiled and slammed the drawer shut causing Oliver to recoil, startled.

"You know what John Brown wrote the day he was hung?" Reeves spoke less than a foot away from Oliver, who now had his back against the wall, in more ways than one. Reeves wanted the man to feel his breath on his face when he talked.

"Got no idea," Oliver responded.

"It's one of the few things of any use I remembered from school. He slipped his jailer a note that said, 'The crimes of this guilty land will never be purged away, but with blood.'" Reeves stepped back to study Oliver, see if the story was having its desired impact. "Then the jailer walked John Brown to his death. That's the mistake Brown made, didn't finish the job he started. Know why?"

Oliver gave an empty stare.

"The damn fool didn't have a plan, an exit strategy. He wanted to be a martyr. So that's what he became. Poor dumb bastard." Reeves sat down in the chair next to the desk, looking up at Oliver. "Whatcha think of that? Interestin', huh?"

Oliver avoided Reeves's cold stare. "I suppose," he muttered.

"You ain't got a stronger opinion than that?" asked Reeves, demonstrating some impatience.

"Yeah," replied Oliver. "I think it's interesting."

"You know what's even more fascinatin' than that?" asked Reeves. "If only some Black folks had helped him back then, maybe this world would've been a much better place. Now everybody's payin' for the sins of their fathers, or the sins committed against their fathers." He stood, positioned his body face-to-face with Oliver. "Either way, got a lot of unnecessary sufferin' still left to handle. But I ain't no martyr, and I hope for your sake, neither are you." He put his hand on Oliver's shoulder and felt it flinch. "You understand what I'm sayin'?" Reeves waited for a response.

"Not really," Oliver finally answered.

"You will," commented Reeves, dryly. "I truly believe you will. But you're gonna need to be a man and not just act like one. That means you got to be better than John Brown. You got to have a plan. You need an exit strategy. I can help you with that. I know how." He moved closer to Oliver. Spoke gently. "Scrapbooks are for memories. But the memories ain't finished yet. Know what I mean?"

He took the scrapbook from Oliver, placed it on the counter, and opened it to the last page. "You can finish cleaning." He glanced at the scrapbook. "Looks like you're almost done." Reeves left his auto shop. Oliver touched the scrapbook. "The motherfucker knows," he said, then closed the scrapbook.

FIFTY-TWO

Henderson and Calvanese sat next to each other and patiently watched O'Ryan fumble through some paperwork on his desk. "What the hell happened to you two? You look like both of you were in a plane crash."

"Tripped getting out of the shower," answered Calvanese. "Or maybe while I was trying to get in. It's all a blur."

"Maybe it was both," replied O'Ryan. "By the look of it, you tripped more than once." He shifted his attention to Henderson. "What about you? You get assaulted by unruly bathroom tiles?"

"Yard work, sir," he replied weakly. "Slipped on the wet grass."

"I'm sure the guy who tried to rob you feels the same way. Although from the report I got, he won't be feeling much of anything for a few weeks."

Calvanese looked at Henderson then back to O'Ryan. "Some guy tried to rob Paul?"

"You really need to learn to communicate better," responded O'Ryan. "How you expect to protect each other if you don't open up and share?"

"Did you get a chance to review my request?" Calvanese asked, changing the subject.

"Considering what you've been going through, I think you should ask for some time off." O'Ryan removed his reading glasses and lightly massaged his brow.

"I didn't ask for time off," Calvanese answered sharply. "I asked for a new partner."

O'Ryan made no effort to conceal his disappointment. He removed a pipe from its rosewood rack and packed it with cherry-flavored tobacco. He inhaled the aroma, savoring it. "You believe I used to chew this stuff back in the day?" He shook his head, gave a wry smile. "You do a lot of foolish shit when you don't know any better." He turned toward Henderson. "Paul? You feel the same way? You want a new partner, too?"

Henderson took a moment to respond and then nodded agreement.

"Fine," O'Ryan said determinedly. "But not now."

"When?" asked Calvanese.

O'Ryan tossed a file folder to the side of his desk. "When we have racial harmony. After that, I'll split you up and segregate you by age, sex, ethnicity, religion, and any other damn thing that'll make you happy. Until then, you're partners whether you like it or not." He pushed back his chair and moved to the file cabinet. "You got a problem with that? Find our cop killers and I'll pin the medals on you myself. I'll even let you pick out your favorite color ribbons."

He wheeled the chair around again and faced the two officers. "I want a written report on the racial progress, if any, within the department. I want it by the end of the day." He stared directly at Calvanese. "You're to prepare the report... together."

Calvanese glanced at Henderson and neither one looked pleased.

O'Ryan drummed his fingers against the edge of the desk

and then stopped suddenly. He took a sip of water from a plastic bottle and replaced the cap, twisting it tightly. "Look, Tony," he said, eliminating the previous harshness or any obvious sign of authority. "I know you're going through a really difficult time."

"Do you?" asked Calvanese, dismissively.

"I worked with your dad, Tony," O'Ryan reminded him. "I'm not a stranger to your family and right now, I'm not just your boss. I'm your friend. And in that capacity, I'm asking you to take a couple of days off. Think things over."

"And if I say no," replied Calvanese, "you still gonna be my friend?"

"No," said O'Ryan. "If you say no, I'm gonna be your boss and order you to take a full week." He studied Calvanese. "What's it gonna be?"

"I appreciate your friendship. Let's just leave it at that." Calvanese stood, anxious to leave. "Is that all, Captain? I've got some free time I need to use up."

O'Ryan nodded his permission to leave. Calvanese hustled out of the office before Henderson could follow.

Henderson rose but O'Ryan motioned for him to sit. "I'm gonna ask you a question. I want an honest answer."

"Go ahead," responded Henderson.

"I know those bruises didn't come from any yard work."

"I got in a confrontation with a mugger, remember? Could have happened then."

"From the report filled out at the scene, he never laid a hand on you." O'Ryan touched a file on his desk and eased it closer toward Henderson. "You wanna read it?"

Henderson shook his head.

"I said I wanted honesty. You gonna give it to me or not?"

"I'll give you all you can handle."

"You want a new partner?"

Henderson hesitated. "I don't know."

"Can you still work with him?"

"We got our problems but he's a hell of a cop." Henderson glanced away and then returned his gaze to O'Ryan. "Yeah. I can still work with him."

O'Ryan took a whiff of his pipe tobacco. "It smells a whole lot better than it tastes. I guess it doesn't matter how you take it, it'll kill you if you use too much. The problem is it's hard to know exactly how much is too much. In the end, it's probably wise not to take a risk." He dumped the tobacco into his wastebasket. "It wouldn't be a bad idea if you also took a couple of days off. Give you a chance to finish cleaning up your yard." He unscrewed the cap on his water bottle. "The sooner you start, the better." He took a drink.

Henderson rose and headed for the door.

"Paul?"

Henderson turned to face his captain.

"Watch out for those slippery spots. I know how dangerous wet grass can be."

"Thanks, Captain."

"You're welcome." He finished the bottle.

* * *

Calvanese spent his time off at the hospital or at his parents' home helping his father, or at his own residence refusing to answer his cell or landline when it rang. He rewound the tape countless times, listening to Briella's voice. The message was always the same, but it elicited different responses each time he played it. She pleaded for him to call her. Asked him to change his mind, if not about them and their future together, then at least about her being able to visit his mother, if only once.

At first, hearing her voice brought him great torment. Now it gave him comfort, even though his heart ached whenever he pushed the stop button. He knew he was being cruel to her by not returning the calls, and he regretted that. The only consolation he had was the knowledge that he was punishing himself far more than he was hurting her. At least, he hoped that was true. If it wasn't, he'd have to add that to a growing list of reasons why he would never forgive himself. He wanted to see her. Wanted to hold her. He wondered if that was a sign of progress or weakness.

In some ways, this separation was a convenient excuse. He should decide it was over before she did, and he was desperately afraid she would one day make that decision. How could she not? They lived in different worlds. It was just a matter of time before she realized that and left. Susan had left him the way most cops' wives always had, after too many nights of worry and anger and fear. He and Briella were still in the early stages of lust and love, and not looking too closely or thinking too hard to consider all the reasons why this would never work. But reason and love were often incompatible. They cancelled each other out. Reason had no choice but to give in, deny itself when confronted with the need to be together. Still, he realized it wasn't just blaming Briella for his mother's condition that kept them apart. It was the fear that someone as successful and independent as Briella would discover what Susan had learned long ago: that love wasn't enough to remain a cop's wife.

The home phone rang again but this time the caller left no message. He had hoped it was her, needed it to be her, but like their first encounter at the Outlaw Bar & Grill, he had waited too long to follow her lead. He wondered if history would repeat itself and provide a second chance. Or if he really wanted one. He took the phone off the hook and placed the receiver on the coffee table. After a few seconds, it started to make that annoying buzz or beep or series of little belches. He rested his body on the couch, closed his eyes and like the cop he was, ordered the noise to cease and desist.

FIFTY-THREE

It was a particularly peaceful Sunday afternoon in Santa Monica. The elderly from one of many local retirement homes had staked out their favorite spots on Ocean Boulevard and were actively involved in their typical weekend rituals: checkers, cribbage, dominoes, gossip, and drinking plenty of iced tea or freshly squeezed lemonade. Cardboard tables were lined up across the edge of the park for the participants to take full advantage of the mild ocean breeze. A few eschewed playing games and swapping stories, choosing instead to sprawl out on blankets under the protective shade of a friendly cluster of trees. Others rested in lounge chairs soaking in the sun, tanning oil and arthritis lotion in abundant supply.

Teenagers maneuvered skateboards in between overflowing grocery carts pushed by the homeless. Children chased each other coming perilously close to upending several chessboards. A newly married couple walked their dog and shared a kiss. A young woman, wearing a revealing two-piece bathing suit, rode her bicycle, leaning forward over the English handlebars, chest fully exposed, to the delight and cheers of some interested onlookers.

This idyllic scene was briefly interrupted by the flashing lights of a patrol car parked in the middle of the bicycle lane. The driver of a Jaguar convertible had been pulled over and was being handed a speeding violation after pleading unsuccessfully for the officer to give him a break.

In the distance, a pounding, deep bass could be heard blaring from expensive car speakers. Violent rap lyrics attacked the surrounding area, immediately eliminating whatever tranquility had existed moments before. The source of this intrusion was now visible, moving slowly with the glare of sunlight shining from behind—a metallic cherry-red, custom-made, gangbanger special, with chrome wheels, heavy-duty suspension, oversized tires, the general circumference of two round speakers stuffed inside the trunk. Five-Dollar-Rock's car bounced to the beat of the music.

Some of the elderly grimaced, demonstrating their dissatisfaction with the noise. One woman looked at her male companion and shook her head in disgust. "Sarah Vaughan would turn over in her grave," she said and then moved her red checker across the board. "King me."

"Just turn down your hearing aid," suggested her playing partner. "It's a gift from God." He turned down his hearing aid to demonstrate and then pointed to his ears, indicating he couldn't hear anything.

She smiled, nodding her head in agreement. Suddenly, her eyes filled with terror at the sight of an automatic weapon protruding from the passenger window of the shiny red car. The awful music was now replaced with something much worse. Gunfire erupted with deadly consequence, a barrage of bullets striking indiscriminately, wounding or killing innocent pedestrians.

Her companion couldn't hear her scream but was startled when he saw her mouth open wide, contorted in fear. He tried to reach for her, but she turned in the direction of the violent popping sound and saw a police officer trapped against the side of his car, like a helpless boxer held up by the ropes, unable to fall. But these weren't fists pummeling his body but rather a bombardment of bullets ripping into his torso. The driver of the Jaguar was struck in the onslaught. His speeding ticket flew out of his bloodied hand.

Just as quickly as it had begun, the gunfire ceased, the weapon disappearing behind a darkly tinted window. The car sped away. The officer sank to the ground, remained on both knees for a moment, and then collapsed backwards, partially propped up by his patrol car's front end, his face to the sun.

The elderly woman moved as quickly as she could toward the fallen officer, joining dozens of other stunned citizens wanting to provide aid. Her companion stood mesmerized, staring in absolute silence at a piece of paper, the traffic violation, floating high in the air, drifting slowly over the beach toward the ocean. He reached behind his earlobe, turned on the hearing aid, and was thrust into the middle of the maelstrom, assailed by dissonant screams and shouts for help and desperate howling that didn't end, even after he tried to escape from the turbulence by completely removing the medical device from his ear.

* * *

Inside the mayor's office, Gibbs, O'Ryan, and other high-ranking police administrators sat around a conference table and listened to Palmer vent his displeasure. "What am I supposed to tell the news media?" he asked, his outrage rising to the surface. "You're beginning to look like the Keystone Cops! You can't protect the public. You can't protect yourselves! And you keep arresting suspects that can't even spell 'cop' let alone have the smarts to kill one!"

Chief Gibbs attempted to deflect attention away from his

operation. "The Feds think this might be either orchestrated or financed by some international terrorist group."

"The Feds think everything's international. That's so they can fly all over the goddamn world and charge it to Homeland Security." Mayor Palmer popped two breath mints into his mouth and chewed rapidly. "Bunch of pretentious assholes. Do they really think that some Middle East terrorist rides around in a souped-up, iridescent low-rider, playing rap music through a high-tech ghetto blaster, firing off an Uzi?" He slapped a gnat that had landed on his yellow pad of paper. He tore off the sheet that contained the smashed remains of the tiny bug, rolled it up and tossed it at the corner wastebasket, missing the "hoop" by a considerable distance. "Fuckin' morons."

"I've made sure they don't do anything without coordinating their efforts with our Counter Terrorism and Criminal Intelligence Bureau," stated the chief.

"Do you think this is still the work of the B.L.A.?" asked the mayor.

Chief Gibbs turned to O'Ryan for his view on the matter.

"Far as we've been able to determine, they don't exist," answered O'Ryan. "That doesn't mean some other Black group or radical organization isn't behind the killings. We've got no shortage of people willing to take credit for shooting police officers."

"Then ask them to come forward so they can have their pictures taken while you arrest them," snapped Palmer. "We sure as hell won't learn much from a bunch of old half-blind witnesses scared to death. They couldn't identify which bottle of medication to take without the help of a registered nurse."

"We got several good I.D.s on the car," said Chief Gibbs. "Something that distinctive should be fairly easy to trace."

"Nothing about this case has been easy," replied Palmer, running his fingers through his hair. "As if I didn't have enough problems, I got a stack of complaints from Reverend Wilson and his congregation alleging mistreatment from your office. What's the cop's name?"

Gibbs glanced at O'Ryan, who reluctantly gave up the information. "Tony Calvanese."

Palmer's eyes lit up in anger. "Isn't he the same one who acted up at the sensitivity training session?"

"I had a long talk with him about that," responded O'Ryan.

"Evidently it didn't work," replied Palmer. "You need to suspend him for a week or two. Tell him if he keeps his nose clean and his mouth shut, it'll be with pay. Otherwise hang him out to dry and use him as an example."

"We're already stretched pretty thin," protested O'Ryan. "Everyone's working extra shifts. Plus, he's a good officer, and has been through a lot recently. His mother—"

"We've all got mothers," the mayor sharply interrupted. "Give him my condolences and then suspend him." He turned to Gibbs. "Chief, you need to be able to issue a press release that makes it clear you can handle proper discipline within your force. Are we clear on that?"

"If he takes it up with the union, he can fight it, and probably win," warned Gibbs.

"He's a popular cop," added O'Ryan. "This won't go down well with the rank and file."

"Then that makes it even more important for you to act firmly. Show the public we're serious about..." The mayor hesitated, attempting to find the proper words. "Whatever the hell it is we're supposed to be serious about. Listen, I just want Reverend Wilson off my back! So, do it! And do it quick."

Palmer's administrative assistant entered the room and whispered into Palmer's ear and handed him a message slip.

"Send him in," he said, with a combination of resignation and fatigue setting in.

She crossed the room and opened the door and stepped aside for Allen Davis to enter.

Gibbs motioned for Davis to have a seat next to him.

"I appreciate you meeting with us, Officer Davis," said the mayor, pleasantly.

"Thank you for taking the time to hear my concerns," Davis responded cordially.

"I asked the chief to arrange this meeting because we both wanted to reassure you that we take your concerns seriously."

"That's very good to know, sir," replied Davis. "The men and women I represent take them seriously as well, or we never would have raised them, particularly during such a sensitive time."

O'Ryan diverted his eyes from the group and glanced at the floor. Chief Gibbs picked up a cold pitcher of water, poured a glass, and offered it to Davis, who declined. The chief then drank it himself.

"I'm glad to know that you also recognize how delicate things are at the moment," stated Palmer. "If we're unable to exercise good faith and resolve the issues confronting us, then we will have done a major disservice to the public that we serve. I hope you agree."

"I do," responded Davis.

"It's not too late to salvage something good from this tragic situation." Palmer looked to his officials and received affirmation from those present. "If calmer heads prevail, we have an excellent chance of dramatically increasing police resources. That means more officers, better equipment, and supporting much-deserved promotions. All of that will be exceedingly difficult to achieve if there's a division within the department. Can we avoid that?"

"Everything is negotiable, Mayor," Davis answered. "After all, we want the same things."

"Then we can anticipate your support?"

"I'm as anxious to settle this as you are, sir."

"I'm certain we can work out something that's satisfactory

to all parties. But let me have Chief Gibbs and Captain O'Ryan address this more specifically."

Palmer looked at O'Ryan, who wasn't ready to cooperate. The mayor then shifted his attention to Gibbs.

"Chief, you have any recommendations or questions you need clarified?"

Gibbs hesitated and then turned to Davis. "What demands on your list did you want to address first?"

Davis paused for a moment, removed a pen from his uniform and slid a notepad closer. "Promotions are always a good place to start." He surveyed all those at the table as the room fell silent.

FIFTY-FOUR

In the night sky, police helicopters hovered over the city. Their searchlights focused unsteadily on the same immobile object on the ground below, illuminating a metallic red vintage automobile parked haphazardly in the middle of a driveway. The pilot of the lead copter barked instructions into a handheld radio transmitter. "Suspect's car located. Vermont and Third. All units proceed with caution. We'll light the way. Copy."

Patrol cars surrounded the area. SWAT members took up their positions across the street from the targeted home. Henderson and Calvanese wore protective vests and coordinated their activities with Mike Stevens who was supervising his team of officers. The copters aimed their spotlights at the house, flooding the front lawn and entryway with a bright yellow glow.

Another team of officers sealed off the rear entry and had shooters covering every window. Stevens held a bullhorn and signaled SWAT to act. They aimed their high-powered rifles at the front door.

Stevens issued the command, his amplified voice booming throughout the neighborhood. "All occupants in two-eleven, this is the police. You are ordered to exit the premises peace-fully with your hands over your head. This is your only warning."

Henderson and Calvanese stood next to each other, shielded by a police van. Their weapons were drawn and aimed at the entrance. The helicopters pulled back higher, their lights becoming more concentrated and intense. There was no discernible movement or activity in the home and then a porch light came on. A second or two later, the front door opened. Calvanese's finger lightly squeezed the trigger.

Five-Dollar-Rock, half asleep, totally whacked out and still taking a hit on the pipe appeared at the doorway, bare-chested. He emerged from the home, took a single step outside, and then stumbled to the ground. Police rushed him. Henderson and Calvanese were the first inside the house, followed by a group of fellow officers.

C.J., a nineteen-year-old Black gang member, remained sprawled out on the couch. A naked woman was asleep on the floor next to a sizable quantity of drugs. Three other young men in various degrees of drug-induced euphoria were too confused to protest their arrests.

Officers moved in and out of rooms conducting a quick search. All the inhabitants of the home were cuffed and escorted out of the house. The naked woman was handed over to a female officer who wrapped her in a blanket and led her to a separate police car.

Stevens crossed to a walk-in closet, opened it carefully and searched inside. When he exited, he appeared sick, disgusted. He shook his head at Henderson. "You don't wanna look inside, trust me."

Henderson gave him a concerned look. "What is it?"

Stevens shook his head again, with far more distress.

Henderson slowly approached the closet, tentatively placed

his hand on the doorknob, pulled back the door and cautiously stepped inside.

Stevens grinned at the cops who had remained inside the house. They waited for the joke to be completed. Calvanese didn't enjoy this but did nothing to prevent it. Henderson came out of the closet and looked around, confused.

He stared at Stevens, who appeared totally innocent. "I've always wanted to do that," he said, then broke into laughter.

The other cops laughed. All Henderson could do was stand there and take it like a man.

Stevens mockingly opened and closed the closet door several times, acting increasingly nervous with each attempt to look inside. He pointed at Henderson and then laughed even harder.

Calvanese crossed to the closet and slammed shut the door. He turned to Stevens and issued a warning. "You've had your fun. That's enough."

Henderson intervened. "It's all right, Tony. I actually enjoyed it." He paused for a moment then looked at Stevens. "Not as much as I enjoyed being with your wife. Speaking of which, being inside her closet is really frightening." Henderson nodded and then walked off.

Stevens glared at Calvanese as the other officers observed the two men. "He had no call to go there."

Calvanese shrugged. "Maybe you've lost your sense of humor." He opened the closet door and then motioned for Stevens to enter. "You better check it out again. You might find important evidence before we leave."

Calvanese walked away, leaving the door wide open. Stevens looked at his team for support, but they glanced away, amused.

FIFTY-FIVE

Henderson parked the patrol car at police headquarters. Calvanese grabbed the passenger's side door handle, about to exit.

"Are we ever gonna talk about it?" asked Henderson.

Calvanese eased off the handle and sat back. He didn't know what to say, wasn't sure if he wanted to say anything at all.

"How is she doing?"

Calvanese wasn't prepared for that question. "Better," he said quietly. "A lot better." He looked at his partner for the first time. "Thanks for asking."

Henderson nodded. "I know this is none of my business—"

"Then you probably shouldn't go there," Calvanese abruptly cut him off.

Henderson folded his arms across his chest. Both officers sat in silence for a moment. "I'm glad to hear your mother's recovering."

Now it was Calvanese's turn to provide a slight nod of appreciation.

"It would be a tragedy to lose her."

Calvanese looked at him.

"Briella, I mean." Henderson exited the vehicle. Calvanese remained behind for a moment, considered the advice, and then left.

Henderson and Calvanese reached the interrogation room just as the detective was leaving.

"How's it going?" asked Henderson.

"Open and shut," answered the detective. "He confessed to everything."

"Mind if we talk to him?" Henderson requested.

The detective hesitated. Calvanese assumed he was about to get the brush-off or else a condescending remark. But surprisingly, this guy was okay, didn't look down his nose at his uniformed brethren. He stepped away from the door and waved his hand signaling permission to enter. "I got what I need," he said. "But, if you beat his ass, hit him once or twice for me."

The two officers entered and nodded to the prison guard who was about to escort Five-Dollar-Rock out of the room. "We've got a few more things to cover before you leave," said Calvanese. "Is that all right?"

The guard pointed at his prisoner, "He ain't got nothin' to do and I'm getting paid overtime, so take as long as you need." The guard retreated to a seat in the corner.

Five-Dollar-Rock sat with his hands cuffed and his legs shackled.

"You look good in that orange prison suit," remarked Calvanese. "It brings out the color in your bloodshot eyes."

Five-Dollar turned to the prison guard. "Do I got to deal with Nick Nolte and Eddie Murphy?"

"You in a hurry to get back to your cell?" asked Henderson.

"I don't wanna miss lunch."

"You're probably gonna be somebody's lunch soon enough," remarked Calvanese. "I'm sure they're waiting for you with open arms."

"Motherfucka, I been to prison before," Five-Dollar said indignantly. "I owned it then and I'm gonna own it now. Same rules, different territory. Ain't no biggie. So, if you're tryin' to mess wit' me, go find some white boy to mind-fuck. It don't work here. Go ask anybody. Five-Dollar-Rock don't scare easy, hard, or at all. If you ain't wastin' your time you sure as hell is wastin' mines."

"Five-Dollar-Rock, now that's an interesting way to be introduced," said Calvanese. "It's appropriate, too, a low price for a bad high. Your daddy give you that name?"

"My daddy ain't gave me shit. I earned this name."

"Now they can call you cop killer," said Henderson. "Seeing as how you earned that name, too?"

Five-Dollar smiled proudly. "I like that." He thumped his chest over his heart. "I can handle it."

"Seems a bit out of your league," said Henderson. "All you've been is a two-bit drug dealer." He moved closer to Five-Dollar. "And some punk that gets off slapping around young girls."

"They weren't that young, and they never complained. Some bitches like it when you treat 'em rough. You ought to try it sometime. Might get your lady off, assumin' you got one."

Henderson sat on the table, his knee not far from Five-Dollar's face. "Whatever rep you think you might have; it hardly qualifies you as a big-time revolutionary."

"Don't you believe in growth?" Five-Dollar asked smugly. "First, I gave my people the drugs to free their minds, then I supplied them the guns to free themselves."

"You kill all those cops?" asked Calvanese.

"All six."

"There were five," corrected Henderson.

Five-Dollar smiled at Henderson. "You take these chains off, and I'll reach over and kill me one or two more."

Henderson leaned close. "Even me?"

"Especially you."

Calvanese watched this mystery unfolding with increased interest. He'd never seen Henderson act this way. *He's acting like me*, he thought and then held back a smile.

"You wanna tell us how you killed them?" Henderson asked.

"With bullets."

"Did you plan it out, follow any of them around, or was it all spontaneous?" Calvanese followed up.

"I don't believe in plans. And I don't follow nothin'. I'm a leader. People follow me."

"How many of your gang members helped you?" asked Henderson.

He smirked. "You think I'm stupid?"

"No. I think you're a complete idiot," replied Henderson.

Calvanese braced himself for more. This really was a complete transformation.

"If you need a further recommendation," continued Henderson, "you're also a punk who hides behind a bunch of thugs more ignorant than you. Now that I've been kind enough to answer your question, why don't you return the favor and answer mine?" Henderson moved closer.

Calvanese began to worry. His partner wasn't used to playing it recklessly. He positioned himself so that he could keep sight of Five-Dollar's hands. He knew Henderson wanted to bait this kid into action, tempt him into some type of foolish assault. The only thing he didn't know was why.

Five-Dollar glared at Henderson but then relaxed, spoke casually. "I don't do your work for you. You need some assistance, take a walk in the sewer and ask the first rat you come across. Shouldn't be long to find one." He pointed at Calvanese. "Just take him with you."

Henderson stood up, leaned over until he was inches away from Rock's face. "In addition to being a punk, you're also a coward." Henderson eased back. "You don't have the balls to go after a cop when he's facing you. Even when I make it easy." Henderson turned his back on Five-Dollar, stood a moment as both the guard and Calvanese watched uneasily.

Five-Dollar stared at the gun handle sticking out of Henderson's belt. Calvanese readied himself to pounce on the suspect if he made a move.

Henderson walked away telling the guard to "take this sorry excuse for a human being to his new home."

Henderson and Calvanese proceeded to the main elevator. "You wanna tell me what that was all about back there?" asked Calvanese. "Suddenly you're Clint Eastwood and Al Pacino rolled into one. You wanted him to make a play for your weapon, didn't you?"

"I wanted him to try," answered Henderson. "But I knew he wouldn't."

"Any reason you wanted him to kill another cop?"

"I don't think he's killed any."

"What's that mean?" Calvanese pushed the elevator button and they both waited.

"You saw for yourself. He didn't even know how many cops were murdered."

"Hate to break this to you, but I don't think someone like him actually bothers to keep count."

"You think that scumbag would take a leisurely ride through Santa Monica in a customized cherry-red entertainment center on wheels, blow away a cop, park the vehicle on his front lawn, and do enough cocaine to pass out while he waited for us to arrest him?"

"He confessed, remember?"

The elevator door opened, and they entered.

"He's a two-time loser who'll do life without parole," said

Henderson. "If you were him, would you rather go in bragging about being busted for possession of dope or let everyone think you were there for being a revolutionary terrorist and cop killer?"

"You got a better suspect?"

Henderson pushed a button. The elevator door closed. "If you wanted to start a race war, how would you go about it?"

"I'd outlaw barbecue and make rappers listen to Barry Manilow."

"Forget it," Henderson snapped.

"Don't get so touchy. Go on and give me your U.F.O. theory. I promise not to be judgmental."

"Divide and conquer. You turn the police against each other, the people against the police, you commit a few random killings, make 'em appear racially motivated, and then you just sit back, let nature take its course."

"Condition us to expect the worst and then ring the bell?"

"Ding-dong," Henderson said.

"You're getting to be a real campanella."

"Campanologist," corrected Henderson.

"You say neither, I say nayther."

The elevator door opened on to the main lobby.

"Let's call the whole thing off." Henderson exited quickly, followed a moment later by Calvanese.

"Not yet, Mr. Vocabulary," replied Calvanese as he caught up to his partner. Both officers walked together down the corridor. "So, under your theory, who has the power to start something like that?"

"Anyone. For any reason. They don't have to know anything about Pavlov. And, they don't have to be Black."

Calvanese stopped and thought about it.

"What do you think?" asked Henderson.

"I think we need to get back on the elevator. Tell the captain about our theory." Calvanese turned around and headed toward the elevator. Henderson followed behind, aggravated.

"Since when did it become our theory?"

"Okay. If you wanna take the heat for this by yourself, by all means, be my guest." Calvanese pressed the button, and the elevator door slid open. He stepped aside and allowed Henderson to enter first.

"Bullshit!" barked O'Ryan.

Calvanese sat patiently in the captain's office and watched Henderson plead with O'Ryan.

"Why is it bullshit?" Henderson asked defensively.

"'Cause I got a nose for it. You know how I got it? By having to kiss a lot of politicians' asses." O'Ryan didn't look at Calvanese but addressed him anyway. "Calvanese, wipe that shit-eatin' grin off your face," he ordered.

"Consider it gone, Captain," answered Calvanese, running his hand across his mouth and feigning compliance.

"And that's precisely what I want both of you to be, in exactly thirty seconds. Gone! Now get the fuck out of here, and if I want any more theories, I'll call the psychic hotline."

Calvanese rose from his seat and spoke in a helpful tone. "Technically, those aren't theories, Captain. They're predictions."

O'Ryan approached Calvanese and stood close enough to bump chests. "My theory is, if you correct me again, I predict you're gonna be one unhappy, paper-pushin' patrolman."

"That's kinda redundant, isn't it, Captain?" offered Henderson.

O'Ryan turned to face Henderson. "You're starting to sound a lot like Calvanese. That's not good for your career."

Henderson was about to respond when Calvanese grabbed him by the arm and led him to the door. "We don't want to take up any more of your time, sir," said Calvanese. "No need to show us out, we know the way."

"Hold on a second," said O'Ryan. "Tony, I got to tell you something."

Calvanese sensed O'Ryan's growing discomfort. He had known this man for a long time, most of his career, and he had never seen the captain this uneasy.

"You want me to leave, Captain?" asked Henderson. "Give you two some privacy?"

"Yeah," answered O'Ryan. "I mean, no, that's all right, you can stay. Actually, never mind, you should leave. In fact, both of you go on and get out of here. I'll deal with it later."

The two officers exchanged looks.

What was that about, Calvanese wondered. "You sure?" he asked.

"Do I look sure?" replied O'Ryan.

Calvanese answered with a dubious arch of his eyebrows.

"Don't worry about what I look like," snapped O'Ryan. "Just do what I told you and get back to work."

Henderson and Calvanese left. O'Ryan crossed to his desk and picked up an envelope. He removed the letter and read Calvanese's notice of suspension. He placed the letter back inside the envelope, sealed it, and dropped it in the outgoing box on his desk.

FIFTY-SIX

In less than a week, Mrs. Calvanese had made considerable progress. Breathing tubes had long since been removed. From the moment she'd regained consciousness, she complained incessantly about the "dreaded I.V." until finally, at her insistence, two nurses took out the "damn contraption" from the vein in the back of her hand. "Get this meat thermometer out of me or I'm leaving this very moment!" she directed the doctor in no uncertain terms. Since that time, she had made her poor husband's life unbearable, conclusive proof that she was feeling much better.

Mr. Calvanese fed her some soup as their son watched with admiration.

"Never thought I'd see the day Dad would be feeding you," Calvanese said, forcing a smile.

Mr. Calvanese glanced dismissively at his son. "I taught the woman how to cook."

His wife rolled her eyes and shook her head slightly. "You should teach the people here how to run a cafeteria," she said weakly. "They shouldn't feed this stuff to sick people."

"It'll give you an incentive to get well," teased her son.

"It worked," she responded. "Take me home."

"Not so fast," interjected her husband. "You stay where I can take care of you." He gave her another spoonful of soup. "And where I can get that cute young nurse to stick a needle in you when you don't listen."

"Don't mention the word needle ever again," she warned. "That nurse of yours poked me with so many holes, I could rent myself out as a colander and drain spaghetti for a month." She released a long sigh. "Speaking of pasta, what I wouldn't give for some rigatoni Bolognese." She looked around the room and spoke secretly. "Which one of you will be brave enough to sneak some in next visit?"

Calvanese and his father both shook their heads, declining the offer.

"And if you manage to browbeat anyone else into bringing you any," warned Mr. Calvanese, "I'll report you to the doctor myself."

"Traitor," she responded sharply then looked at her son, combining a mixture of desperation, hope, and sweetness. "Anthony, my child, will you betray me, too?" She searched him for a sign.

Calvanese tentatively approached her. She studied his expression and then gave up, helplessly. "I take it from that sour look on your puss, your answer is yes."

"Mom, I know you don't want to think about it, but—"

"I don't remember anything, Tony."

Mr. Calvanese gave his son a signal to back off.

"It happened so fast. If I could tell you, I would, but it's all just a blur."

Calvanese remained intent on pursuing this. "Did you see his face, how tall he was, what he hit you with, what he was wearing? Mom, anything, any detail, no matter how small, could--"

"As ranking officer, I put an end to any more questions," his father insisted. "We'll find who did this. Even if I need to come out of retirement."

"That won't be necessary, Mr. Calvanese." Henderson stood at the doorway holding a small bouquet of red and white flowers. He took a hesitant step into the room and looked at Calvanese for any type of clue. Calvanese refused to give him one.

Henderson walked slowly toward Mrs. Calvanese's bedside, placed the flowers on her side table, and then addressed her husband.

"We'll find the person who did this to your wife," he said softly. "I promise," he said more firmly.

Mrs. Calvanese studied her son who showed no emotion and then she shifted attention to her husband, who rubbed his chin uncomfortably.

Henderson stepped back, unsure if he should stay or leave.

"You must be my son's partner." Mrs. Calvanese broke the ice. "I'm sure he was about to tell me that but wanted to come up with a proper introduction."

"Mom," Calvanese's voice cracked slightly. "Dad," he continued more formally, "I'd like you to meet Paul Henderson."

"And he is...?" She nudged her son with her eyes and a slight nod.

"My partner," Calvanese conceded.

Henderson nodded. Mrs. Calvanese provided a genuine smile.

"I didn't mean to barge in, I—"

"You like pasta?"

Her question threw him off stride.

"We were just talking about pasta and how it would be nice to sneak a little into the room when the nurses weren't looking. You know any good Italian restaurants close by?"

"There's this—"

Calvanese cut him off. "She's kidding, Paul."

"I never kid about pasta," she said sternly. She nodded at Henderson. "That would be sacrilegious." She quietly studied him head to toe. "You look a little thin," she said kindly. "If you're going to catch the bad guys you need to stop by the house and let me feed you."

She noticed the disapproving glance exchanged between her husband and son and then snatched the spoon away from Mr. Calvanese. "Cops nowadays need all the help they can get," she said, giving both her husband and son a declaration as well as a warning. She nodded at Henderson. "Consider yourself formally invited to dinner."

Henderson looked at his partner and noticed a grudging acceptance. He smiled at Mrs. Calvanese in appreciation. "I'd look forward to that," he said warmly. "Very much."

"Not as much as me," she responded. "I'd die for a home-cooked meal."

The three men exchanged uneasy looks.

"Well, not die," she corrected herself, "but I think you get my point."

Mr. Calvanese snatched the spoon from her hand, filled it with soup, and shoved it gently into her mouth.

She swallowed and rolled her eyes in exasperation. "What would I do without you?" she said. Cynicism dripped from her lips along with some soup.

Mr. Calvanese wiped her chin with a cloth. "You'd never want to find out."

"Actually, you're wrong," she informed him in all seriousness. "I'd like to find out right now."

"You want me to leave?" he asked, his feelings hurt.

"I want you to take that handsome officer over there and buy him a coffee and a nice doughnut."

He glanced over his shoulder at Henderson. "My wife thinks that's all cops do, drink coffee and eat doughnuts." He turned back to her. "You want Tony to come with us?"

"If I wanted our son to leave, I'm perfectly capable of telling him that without any help from you."

"Where's the nurse with her needle when you need her?" Mr. Calvanese grumbled.

"I'd like a moment alone with Anthony," she said, keeping her eyes glued on her son.

It's Anthony again, thought Calvanese, with some notice-able uneasiness.

"Paul," she smiled, "thanks so much for the lovely flowers. That was very thoughtful and kind."

"My pleasure, Mrs. Calvanese."

"And mine, too. We'll see each other again very soon, under much more pleasant circumstances, I hope."

"I'd like that," he said.

Mr. Calvanese motored his wheelchair toward the door and Henderson opened it. "Come on, Paul, I'm buyin'."

"And give him directions to the house," ordered Mrs. Calvanese. "We can plan a big dinner my first weekend back."

Mr. Calvanese shook his head in resignation and left with Henderson.

Mrs. Calvanese gave her son a suspicious look. "Seems like a very nice man," she said. "I think you're lucky to have him as a partner."

"Did you send them away so you can talk about him?"

"I sent them away because I wanted to talk to you about Briella."

"Mom, I—"

"I nothin'," she said sharply. "That one you don't want to lose," she said with conviction. "You let her get away, and you'll regret it all your life." She observed him then continued very dramatically. "Maybe not today. Maybe not tomorrow. But one day, you'll wake up and—"

"All right, Mama, stop with the Bogart stuff."

"I can't help myself. I love a good movie, especially a romance. You got that from me, you know. Not the romance, your love of movies." She smiled. "Did I tell you I ran into Tom Hanks?"

He looked stunned. "In the hospital?"

"No, silly." She waved him off. "At brunch with Briella. What a day! I dine with the stars one minute and then the next, before I can digest my food, I get mugged. All in all, I'd rather still be eating brunch with Briella."

"And Tom," he added.

"Tom is nice. Briella's better by a mile. But I didn't raise a fool, so you know that already, don't you, son?"

He didn't answer.

"Why did you tell her not to visit?"

He looked surprised. "She told you that?"

"She didn't have to. But I knew as soon as I asked you the question, you'd blame her. What I didn't know, what I couldn't have imagined in a thousand years, is that you'd blame her for this. For what happened to me. I never thought you could be that unfair or that selfish."

"Selfish?"

"What would you call it?" She waited for him to respond. "Some type of noble outrage or protective punishment?" She shook her head, sadly. "Whatever it is, I hope you're not doing it on my behalf because then I'd really need to stay here for another month or two."

"This would never have happened if it hadn't been for—"

"A sick, vile, and disgusting human being that should never have been born let alone allowed to walk the face of the earth hurting innocent people. That's who I blame. That's who you should blame. Not the woman who wanted to make a good impression on her boyfriend's mother." Her voice became less harsh, more concerned with her son's well-being, but not at the expense of what she had to say. "And you know what, Tony? She made a great impression, utterly fantastic. The only one that should ever really matter to a mother or to a son or to anyone really interested in the truth. She left me with the indelible impression that she's in love with you."

He motioned with his hand to stop but it caused her to be more animated.

"Yeah, I said the word. LOVE! Is that what you're afraid of? Not the reason I'm here. Not because you blame someone who doesn't deserve to be blamed. Because my son Anthony Calvanese fears the thing he needs most. The possibility of being loved and loving back."

He had the sense she was staring through him, into his heart, to his soul.

"What are you gonna do about it?" she asked, compassionately.

He looked around the room and answered softly. "I don't know."

"Well, you better figure it out quick because I told her to meet you downstairs in the main reception."

"You spoke with her?"

"On the phone," she gave a bittersweet smile. "The last thing I said to her made her laugh and then cry."

"What did you say?" he asked, really wanting to know.

"You can ask her yourself at two thirty."

He glanced at his watch. "That's in less than five minutes."

"So, what are you doin' here, wasting time? I'm a sick woman and I need my rest." She shushed him away. "Andare la fretta."

Great! She was ordering him to leave and be quick about it in Italian. *Can't get any more serious than that.*

. . .

The hospital lobby was unusually crowded but he had no difficulty finding her, almost immediately after getting off the elevator. She stood in the middle of the room staring directly at him. The surrounding noise disappeared. He heard his heart racing faster with every step he took that brought him closer to her. He heard something else, too: his mother's voice.

She's in love with you. Yeah, I said the word, LOVE. What are you gonna do about it?

He was about to find out.

"I've missed you," were the first words she said to him, but they could have been, should have been, his words.

"I'm so sorry," she said.

Those should have been his words as well, but for that moment he appeared incapable of saying or doing anything.

"The doctor said she was doing much better," she continued.

He knew she needed to talk, say anything to keep from crying. He was just the opposite; couldn't afford to speak for fear it would open the emotional floodgates.

"Is it all right if I go see her?" she asked.

He gave a slight nod.

As she started to walk away, he summoned the courage to speak. "My mother told me she said something to you that made you laugh and then cry."

Now it was her turn to nod and not speak.

"If you don't mind me asking, what was it?"

She took a step closer to him. He could smell her fragrance.

"She said that once she got out of the hospital we should go shopping again, but..."

"But what?"

"This time we should take the bus."

He laughed, then a moment later his eyes filled with tears.

"She's a remarkable woman, your mother."

"Yeah," he agreed proudly. "But she's not the only one." He looked at her, spread open his arms and she stepped into his embrace and cried, and then laughed.

FIFTY-SEVEN

C.J., one of the teens arrested with Five-Dollar-Rock, marched into a county jail waiting room led by his female guard. C.J. tugged at his prison shirt, which was too tight for his well-developed upper body, and then flopped down in his seat and stared across the metal table at Calvanese, who displayed a look of utter contempt. He shifted his attention to Henderson who slid him a pack of cigarettes.

C.J. smiled but didn't take it. "That supposed to make you my friend?" he asked, wryly.

Calvanese reached for the pack but C.J. quickly snatched it with both hands, manacled together by metal restraints. He placed the pack inside his prison shirt and tapped it proudly. "Got somethin' to negotiate with, now. Get me a favor here or there." He smiled at the guard who remained at the door. "What'll you give me for two smokes, sweetie?"

"A broken arm," she replied.

Calvanese nodded approval. "I think you'd be better off giving those to Five-Dollar-Rock," he said. "Trade 'em for something useful."

"I ain't givin' that crazy motherfucka nothin'."

"Is that what your life's worth?" asked Calvanese. "Nothin'?" He studied C.J. for some type of clue. "If you take the fall for him, it's the death penalty for your ass."

"Death penalty comes with life," C.J. said casually and then took a deep breath but never seemed to release it. "Niggers are born. Niggers die." He glanced at Henderson and gave him a slight salute. "If you plan it right, you don't go out alone. You take as many of 'em wit' you as you can shoot before you run outta bullets or time."

"You shoot that cop in Santa Monica?" asked Calvanese.

"Nope." C.J. cleared his throat and looked for someplace to spit. "Can I go home now?"

"Rock said you did," stated Henderson.

"That nigger was so high he couldn't have shot himself," C.J. said, more amused than disgusted. "Plus, we wouldn't do no drive-by in his car."

"Why not?" asked Calvanese.

"You see that paint job?" he exclaimed proudly. "Cost Rock over three grand. If we had put a tiny scratch on it while drivin' around he woulda killed us, sure 'nuff." He rested his elbows on the edge of the table. "He only had the car back from the paint shop a few days before you busted us."

Henderson glanced at Calvanese who never lost eye contact with C.J.

"He hardly ever uses it, 'cept when he wants to impress some ho. Usually keeps it locked up in his garage. No way he'd take that car out for a hit," C.J. stated emphatically. "That's why we got us a Toyota. Fuckin' Japanese killin' machine." He pantomimed rapidly shifting gears, the range of his hands limited by the cuffs. "Plus, it's got better gas mileage than a Mexican who just finished eatin' at Taco Bell." C.J. laughed, pleased with himself. "I just made a joke, ain't you two gonna show me some love?"

"Where'd he get the paint job?" asked Henderson.

"I look like the yellow pages to you?" He shrugged. "Some old brother in the 'hood." He paid special attention to Calvanese. "We believe in recyclin' dollars in the community," he explained and then glanced at Henderson, flashing him a gold-capped smile.

"And lives? You recycle those, too?" asked Henderson, not amused by C.J.'s antics.

"Gots to take the good with the bad, homie. Not everybody gets to wear a badge and get paid for shootin' niggers."

"C.J., I'd shoot you for free," replied Henderson with absolute sincerity.

C.J. studied him and then nodded approval. "Honesty goes a long way wit' me." He blew his nose on a rolled-up napkin. "You ever need bodywork, there's a dude named Wallace Reeves. Runs a paint and body repair shop off Exposition. You might wanna check him out."

"Any good with custom paint?" asked Calvanese.

C.J. rolled his eyes. "How you gonna repair a body and not put somethin' on it?" He got up, signaled his readiness to leave. "Come on, Mama, take me home."

He walked toward the guard who held open the door. He looked over his shoulder at Henderson. "But I don't do referrals, so don't tell nobody I sent you."

* * *

Henderson and Calvanese were intercepted in the hallway by O'Ryan. "I just got notified you two were down at county. What the hell were you doin'? I told you to leave it alone. It's in the hands of the D.A.'s office, now."

"Just had a hunch, Captain," answered Calvanese.

"The guy who rang the bell in Notre Dame had that problem till he fell off the chapel tower. Both of you straighten up. Your job is to put folks in prison, not get 'em out."

O'Ryan hustled off. Calvanese and Henderson met with Keela Castleton, assigned to the Administrative and Technical Services Bureau within the Records and Identification Division. She handed a thick file to Henderson. "This is what you asked for on Wallace Reeves. He's owned Star Auto for over twenty years."

"Any record?" Calvanese asked.

"Minor stuff. Got a bit of a temper when confronted by a dissatisfied customer. Been charged with assault several times, but the victims never testified against him, so the cases were always dropped."

"You find anything else?" asked Henderson.

"You didn't give me much time. I'm still running background. But, so far, I'm impressed."

"With what?" asked Calvanese.

"Evidently your boy was quite a hero in Afghanistan," she replied. "Served in special forces as a marksman." She noticed the look exchanged by the two officers. "Is he in trouble?"

"Just checking out a possible alibi," said Henderson.

"For that guy you busted?"

"What guy?" asked Henderson.

"The one you chased down the freeway last month. They still haven't repaired all the damage from that one."

"Not him," replied Calvanese. "Why'd you ask?"

"Thought that's why you wanted me to run a check on Reeves. A receipt for auto work done at his shop was found in the Cadillac."

Henderson and Calvanese look at each other. *Bingo!*

"Keela," said Henderson, "if I weren't married, you and I would—"

"Henderson," warned Castleton, "I'm gay."

Calvanese took her aside and spoke confidentially. "Well, if he was a single woman, who wasn't attracted to men, wouldn't the two of you give the neighbors something to talk about."

"How long will it take for you to run a complete check on him?" asked Henderson. "Where he lives or any organizations he belongs to. Anything that—"

"Whoa, slow down there, Deputy Chief." She raised both hands in front of his face. "I've already done you and Tony one favor. You know the procedures. Fill out a formal request and I'll get to it first thing tomorrow morning."

"Tomorrow!" said both officers.

"I'm off in ten minutes. Got a hot date."

"A date?" asked a surprised Calvanese. "I thought you were-" then stopped himself and realized it wasn't with a man. "Never mind. I was confused there for a minute about you and dating and, you know, stuff like that," he said, fidgeting uncomfortably.

She looked at him with some degree of amazement and pity. "That's why you're not a detective, Calvanese," interrupted Castleton. "You don't have a clue."

"Keela, help us out on this," pleaded Calvanese. "Or else," he added with a sinister warning.

"Or else what?"

"I'll start a rumor you became gay only because it was fashionable."

"It is fashionable, Tony. It's the way we wear our genes. Get it?" she asked, smiling effusively. "Not jeans with a 'J.' Chromosomes with a—"

"Keela, I've already heard a lame hunchback joke. I really expected more from you."

"You couldn't handle more," Castleton responded.

"I have no idea what you're talking about."

"I like that in a man, Tony," she said. "In fact, I've come to anticipate it."

"We'll check back with you in ten minutes," said Henderson, who handed back the folder to her.

Castleton took a deep sigh. "That's why I don't date men."

Henderson and Calvanese look at her confused.

"They want everything finished in ten minutes or less," she said, and then tapped Calvanese on his behind with the file as she walked past.

Calvanese stared at Henderson; a bit mystified. "I thought ten minutes was doin' pretty good."

"That explains why you've been living alone for so long," responded Henderson.

"Thanks," said Calvanese, turning serious.

Henderson spoke with regret. "I didn't mean—"

"For visiting my mother," clarified Calvanese. "And," he cleared his throat, "trying to help." He extended his hand.

Henderson looked at it for a moment. "You'd do the same for me," he replied and then extended his hand.

"Yeah, but I'd be better at it."

They shook hands with a little more force.

FIFTY-EIGHT

It took less than ten minutes for Henderson and Calvanese to reach the auto shop. Henderson decided to look in the back while Calvanese headed for the front entrance. Before opening the door, he took a moment to observe the surrounding area. The primary lot was enclosed by a tall iron fence with barbed wire strewn along the top. The shop itself was a small brick structure with the customary grime and debris associated with these types of places—cans, trash, discarded auto parts, and badly worn tires.

Reeves stood behind the counter as if he had been waiting to greet someone. Once Calvanese entered, Reeves extended no courtesies and generally ignored his uniformed guest.

"You Wallace Reeves?"

Reeves located some paperwork and started writing some information as Calvanese stood in front of him, a few feet away.

"I asked you a question."

Reeves looked up and answered derisively. "Thought you were makin' a statement. Next time you ask a question, ought to make it sound more polite." He returned to filling out his forms.

"Are you Wallace Reeves?" Calvanese asked less forcefully.

"For fifty-two years, not countin' the time I spent inside my mama's womb." He peeked at Calvanese. "That would add an extra nine months, give or take."

"You got a customer that goes by the name of Five-Dollar-Rock?"

"Is that a question?" Reeves asked, moving on to the second page of his form. "Couldn't tell."

"Don't play cute with me. Or we can move this downtown, and you can have your lawyer help you figure out if I'm asking a question or giving an order."

"Don't got a lawyer. But I got lots of customers, and most of 'em have fucked-up names. Five-Dollar-Rock might be one of 'em, then again, he might not."

"You did a cherry-red metallic paint job for him. Cost over three grand. Does that refresh your memory?"

"Cherry red's a popular color, and I don't keep in touch with my customers after they've paid me."

"What happens if their checks bounce? You stay in touch then?"

Reeves pointed to a sign that read: NO CHECKS—CASH ONLY. Calvanese looked around the office. Reeves placed the paperwork on a shelf underneath the counter, next to a sawed-off shotgun.

Calvanese looked through the rear window and spotted Henderson rummaging in the back lot. Even from this distance, Calvanese could see cars in various stages of repair. Some were obviously wrecked and used only for parts. The place looked like a huge yard sale of hazardous material. The shop's work area wasn't much better organized. Stacks of sheet metal were leaning against the walls, jagged pieces of steel jutted out of every corner. Cans of oil, paint thinner, grease-stained rags, and other combustible materials were piled together near an old iron compressor, an oversized factory compactor.

"How about a guy named Derrick Nixon? You serviced his Cadillac several weeks ago."

"Cadillacs are popular here, too."

"Mind if I have a look around?"

Reeves pointed to another sign: CUSTOMERS NOT ALLOWED IN WORK AREA. "My insurance don't cover personal injuries."

"I'll be careful."

"Long as you don't try and hold me responsible when you get hurt," Reeves said.

Calvanese heard an implied threat or, at the very least, an expressed wish. "When?" he asked. "Didn't you mean to say: if I got hurt?"

"A place like this can be dangerous for your health, if you don't know what you're doin'." Reeves gave the officer a cold stare.

"Thanks for your concern," replied Calvanese. "But I've been in more dangerous places than this one."

Reeves smiled. "We'll see."

Before Calvanese had put his hand on the latch to open the screen door separating the work area from the lobby entrance, he had already decided to find a reason to arrest this guy. If he had to write him up for a fire hazard, expired license, or unsanitary restrooms, whatever the excuse, Reeves was going to spend at least one night locked up. That should do wonders for his sense of humor.

Calvanese flipped up the latch on the screen door and entered the work area while Reeves remained behind the counter, watching his every move. He noticed a small rectangular cabinet that had some metal filings at the base.

"You got a search warrant?" Reeves shouted.

"Tell you what, you don't complain about me looking around and I won't notify your insurance company to terminate your policy. Fair enough?"

Reeves didn't answer but glanced underneath his counter and eased the shotgun forward so that the barrel stuck out a few inches over the shelf.

Calvanese opened the cabinet door and discovered equipment to duplicate keys. He picked up a blank key. "Must come in handy to be able to make your own keys. You keep extra copies for the cars you work on?"

"Why would I do that?"

"In case your customers lose theirs," Calvanese shrugged. "Or because you enjoy driving their cars," he smiled at Reeves. "With their permission, of course." He stepped away, still observing the area. "You know," Calvanese continued, "it's funny, and I'm sure it's a mere coincidence, but it's possible some of the cars you've worked on have been driven by someone who likes to murder police."

"You don't say?" Reeves shook his head. "Guess that is funny." Reeves slipped his right hand underneath the counter and gripped the shotgun. "If I had known that mighta given the customers a discount."

"Maybe you still can," replied Calvanese as he headed back toward the lobby area. "Might be a good idea if you came with me and we can finish our conversation at my place of work. But let me give you a warning: once we get there, you need to be extra careful with what you say." Calvanese opened the screen door. "It can be dangerous for your health, if you don't know what you're doin'." He repeated Reeves's advice and allowed it to linger for a moment.

Calvanese moved toward the counter and then instinctively ducked as Wallace fired the shotgun at the officer's head.

Henderson heard the blast and tried to break through the rear entrance. The thick reinforced steel door wouldn't budge.

Wallace swung the shotgun at Calvanese and missed, striking the glass cabinet that contained his war medals and memorabilia. Calvanese drew his revolver, but Reeves struck him on the hand using a wrench. Calvanese's gun dropped to the floor. He tried to retrieve it with his good hand, but Wallace rushed him and pinned him against the wall. He was about to strike again with the wrench.

"Drop it!" ordered Henderson, pointing a weapon at Reeves's head.

Reeves slowly brought down his hand and dropped the wrench to the floor.

Calvanese grabbed his hand in pain.

"Tony, you all right?"

"I'll never play banjo again."

Calvanese pushed Reeves away from him. Henderson retrieved his partner's gun. He was about to hand it to him when he pulled it back for a beat. "Aren't you the least bit embarrassed?"

Calvanese wasn't amused. He grabbed his gun and holstered it.

Henderson mumbled under his breath, but clear enough to be understood. "I swear you'd lose your dick if it wasn't attached."

Calvanese shot him a deadly glare. Henderson ignored him, more than content to whistle a congenial tune.

Calvanese removed his handcuffs from his police belt. He shoved Reeves's face against the wall, placed a cuff on his right wrist, and snapped it locked, then snatched the left arm, brought it around Reeves's back, and completed the task. He tested the restraints, tightening them enough to cause discomfort.

He glanced over his shoulder at Henderson. "You took your sweet time gettin' here. I know how you like everything neat and in its place, but did you really have to choose this moment to clean up his backyard?" He spun Reeves around so they were facing each other and read him his rights, ending with an ad lib: "And you got the right to breathe until you don't."

Henderson placed a call requesting a team of investigators. After conducting a cursory review of the premises, the two officers escorted their prisoner outside where a group of interested onlookers had gathered, peering through the shop's windows.

"You just gonna leave my place unlocked?" Reeves complained.

Calvanese spoke loud enough for the crowd to hear. "Officer Henderson, you think we should leave this fine establishment unlocked and risk having it looted and stripped bare?"

"We better send someone back to guard it," replied Henderson. "In a few hours."

Several young men in the group looked at each other and smiled, but their smiles faded quickly as a series of black-and-whites pulled up along with police forensic technicians.

Calvanese made an announcement to all those gathered near the front door waiting to enter. "Sorry, my friends. As much as I'd like to offer you a five-finger discount, this is a crime scene, so back off! If you're that interested in police procedures, there's plenty of room in my rear seat and I'd be happy to arrange a ride and a semi-private jail cell."

People demonstrated their displeasure but moved away from the entrance as crime scene investigators took over.

Calvanese shoved Reeves into the back of the car and shut the door. He got behind the driver's wheel while Henderson entered the passenger side and buckled his seatbelt.

He turned to Calvanese and studied him closely.

"What?" Calvanese asked.

"Just checking to see if you've still got your gun?"

Calvanese started the engine. "You're really starting to annoy me. You know that?"

The patrol car pulled off. Reeves looked out the rear window at the crowd, discovered Max Oliver in the background observing the event, and gave him a brief nod.

FIFTY-NINE

Wallace Reeves bit down on his lower lip as if he were attempting to hold back a smile and surveyed the interrogation room. "Nice place you got here," he said, smugly. "Could use a little color, maybe a few pictures, a potted plant. I can cut you a deal on the paint, won't charge you much for labor."

"Yeah, the going rate paid by your new employer is about five bucks a day," replied Calvanese. "But it might be a good idea if you saved your decorating ideas for your six-by-eight cell. You'll be there for the rest of your life."

"You think so?" asked Reeves. "I don't stay anyplace too long."

"I didn't say you were gonna be there long," commented Calvanese. "I said you'd be there the rest of your life." Calvanese couldn't tell what if any emotions the man had. He appeared soulless, unflinching, as he sat calmly without a care in the world.

"You sure you don't want a lawyer?" asked Henderson, who stood in the corner opposite O'Ryan and three other high-ranking L.A.P.D. officials, including the head of public information.

"Don't need one," said Reeves. "What's he gonna tell me? I'm in trouble." He picked at his finger, dislodged something, a speck of dirt or hangnail and flicked it away. "I'll save the money and figure that out on my own."

"Why'd you go for the gun?" asked O'Ryan.

Reeves pointed at Calvanese. "Thought he was goin' for his," he answered, tersely.

"And why would I do that?" Calvanese replied, expecting a flippant response.

"You're a cop. That's what you do."

"Any reason you make duplicate keys on the cars you work on?" asked Calvanese.

"Things get misplaced. Always a good idea to have a spare just in case. Is that a crime?"

"No. But stealing the cars and then using them to go on a rampage murdering police officers might qualify as breaking the law." Calvanese moved closer to Reeves and leaned near the man's face. "Don't you think?"

Reeves didn't blink. "I think I can smell what you had for lunch, and since I don't eat pussy, get the fuck out my face."

Calvanese took a step back but clenched his fist tightly to the amusement of Reeves.

"You'd like to hit me, wouldn't you?" asked Reeves quietly.

"No," answered Calvanese. "I'd like to put a bullet through your head."

Reeves leaned back and studied Calvanese. "I bet you'd like to have a bigger dick, too. But that ain't gonna happen either."

"Why'd you murder those cops?" asked Calvanese.

"I don't know what you're talkin' about. I ain't got nothin' against cops." He winked. "I'm even gettin' fond of you."

"Don't play games with me!"

"Last game I played was who could kill the lieutenant in the mountains of Afghanistan and make it look like enemy fire. I won that game, too." He smiled. "Now that I think about it, you kinda remind me of him. A real smart ass, but without his uniform that he wore like some damn peacock, he'd be just another ignorant white boy lookin' for somebody to do his dirty work." Reeves removed a cigarette from a fresh pack and tapped the table with it.

"As it turned out, he kept the uniform, but he lost his head, unlucky bastard. You ever see what an artillery shell can do to a human skull?" He flipped the cigarette over and tapped the opposite end.

"You confessing to killing a soldier, Wallace?" asked Henderson.

Reeves glared at Henderson with disdain. It was the first time he'd shown any intensity, raw emotion. "They let you speak, now?" Reeves ran the side of the cigarette across his lips then crushed it in his hand, letting the tobacco spill out of his fist forming an uneven pile on the table. "And, he wasn't a soldier, he was a Marine."

"Which means what?" asked Henderson.

"Which means you don't kill a Marine, you sit back and watch him commit suicide." He finger-painted the tobacco, forming a question mark. "Sooner or later they all do."

"You were a Marine, weren't you?" asked Calvanese.

"Kinda proves my point, don't it?"

An assistant entered the room and handed O'Ryan a file. He scanned it quickly. The captain's expression changed dramatically. Calvanese thought it signaled a sickening realization that they had, indeed, captured their man.

O'Ryan stepped away from the corner and moved closer to Calvanese.

"Thought you said you liked cops," O'Ryan said to Reeves.

"I said I didn't have anything against them, in particular."

"Not even after they killed your father?"

Calvanese and Henderson exchanged a look.

Reeves never changed his expression. "Actually, they

murdered him. Probably doesn't make a difference to you, but it made a big one to me."

"That would give you a pretty good motive," said Calvanese.

"If I was that type of person," replied Reeves.

"What type of person are you?" asked Calvanese.

"Just a hardworkin' stiff. Don't dwell on the past, don't look to the future." Reeves folded his arms across his chest.

O'Ryan handed the file to Calvanese. "They found a scrapbook at his garage, filled with articles about the cops murdered." He crossed to the door. "The mayor and chief are waiting to hold a joint press conference. I've heard enough from this piece of trash. If he changes his mind and wants a lawyer, let him call one. I don't want anything he says thrown out because his rights were violated."

O'Ryan motioned for his three colleagues to follow him. "Tony, get at least two, no, make that four, officers to take him back to his cell. He can get there in time to watch the evening news."

O'Ryan left with the others.

Henderson looked at Calvanese. "You want me to request the detail?"

Calvanese hesitated, shook his head.

"You gonna give me all this attention just because of some stolen cars and extra keys you got a problem with?" asked Reeves.

"You think you're here because of that?"

"That and the fact I thought my life was in danger and acted in self-defense against a cop, a white cop, who was comin' at me in a threatenin' manner. Why else would you be hasslin' me?"

"If you didn't kill those cops, you should talk to us. We might be able to help," said Henderson.

"Last cop that helped me took my dope and the money for himself and still turned me in."

"That's why you hate cops?" asked Calvanese.

"I already told you, I ain't got nothin' against cops. Even hired me one at the shop."

"You got a cop workin' for you?" asked Henderson.

"Kinda, sorta. He's a rent-a-cop. But his daddy was a real one. Leastwise, he was till he went bad and got caught."

Calvanese and Henderson let this sink in.

"Used to be a time you couldn't buy a West Coast cop, that was strictly an East Coast thing. You guys were corrupt as hell, didn't give a fuck about how you enforced the law, but you couldn't be bought off. Now, you could empty all the cells of convicted felons and fill 'em back up with L.A.P.D."

"This guy still works for you?" asked Calvanese.

"Quit last week," replied Reeves. "Went back to S.C. as a wannabe cop. Fuckin' universities let anybody in nowadays."

"Why were you keeping a scrapbook of murdered police officers?" asked Calvanese.

"See, that's the funny thing," Reeves responded. "I hired this boy, almost a year ago. Real broken-wing type. You know, fucked up, emotions all fragile and shit. I could tell the minute he walked in the shop, lookin' like a lost puppy, he wasn't regular. Seemed like the type of dude shoulda been workin' at the post office. Had that tickin' bomb thing goin' on." He stared at Calvanese. "Know what I'm sayin'?"

"But you hired him anyway," said Henderson.

"Cats like that need a job more than normal folk. Never can tell what they're likely to do if they get down and out on their luck. I tried to do the right thing and give 'em a break."

"Still doesn't explain the scrapbook," said Calvanese.

"I'm gettin' to that." He pressed two fingers against his left nostril, breathed in hard, trying to clear a stuffy nose. "When I interviewed him, asked him about his past employment, what type of trainin' he had, typical bullshit, that's when he turned all weepy and dejected. Told me the whole story how he'd always wanted to join L.A.P.D. until his dad was fucked over by his own friends on the force. He even mentioned a couple of the cops who ratted out his dad. Something about the way he said those names, I guess they stuck with me. So, when they started turnin' up dead, I figured I should keep a record."

Calvanese looked away, stunned.

Henderson shook his head in disbelief. "Why didn't you report this?"

"What was I gonna say?" asked Reeves. "Didn't have no proof. The boy been through enough, didn't want to accuse him of something coulda been a coincidence." He shook his head dismissively. "Wasn't none of my business, anyway. I figured you guys were on top of it. Everybody knows you can't get away with killin' a cop. Police always take care of their own. Ain't my fault if you were a little slow this time."

Calvanese took a seat opposite Reeves. "And you didn't mind, did you?"

"Mind what?"

"That cops were being killed."

"I kept a scrapbook, didn't I?"

Calvanese wanted to reach across the table and gouge out those eyes that stared back at him, filled with mockery and arrogance.

"Did you also help him?" asked Henderson.

"I'm helpin' you, ain't I?" He closed his eyes for a moment and took a relaxed breath. "You ought to be grateful, show a little more appreciation. How you expect to have decent people come forward and do their civic duty, if the only thing you know how to do is mistreat 'em when they try?"

"You egged him on," replied Calvanese. "I can tell just by looking at you that you did a lot more than collect newspaper clippings."

Reeves placed both hands in the air, gave a helpless shrug. "Lookin' and provin' is two different things. Anyway, why would I encourage him? It's like watchin' somebody else get laid. If I ain't the one fuckin,' then I ain't the one gettin' off."

"I think you're getting off now," said Calvanese.

Reeves chuckled. "I guess that means I must be the one fuckin' while all you can do is watch." He leaned back in his chair. "Either one of you got the time? Don't want to miss the news conference."

"Why's that?" asked Henderson.

"Might have a lawsuit to file," Reeves answered and then smiled. "I think they call it defamation."

Calvanese leaned closer. "Don't bother. Before you can sue, you'd have to have a character worth defaming and you don't qualify."

"What if I cooperate and lead you to the real killer?" Now it was Reeves's turn to lean closer and he did, remaining only inches away from Calvanese. "Will you vouch for my character then?"

"You never told us the name of your former employee?" Calvanese responded.

"You never asked." Reeves removed another cigarette, briefly smelled the aroma of the tobacco, and then stuck it in his mouth, letting it dangle in his favorite position. He stared at Calvanese with renewed interest and raised his eyebrows in anticipation of a question.

"What's his name?" asked Calvanese, giving in reluctantly.

Reeves nodded as if accepting a small victory and then answered, steadfastly. "Max Oliver."

SIXTY

Henderson and Calvanese were officially off duty, but instead of heading home, they had signed out their patrol car and were now proceeding to the police garage to retrieve it. Before they left, they asked Keela Castleton to get as much information as possible on Max Oliver's father, who he worked with on the force, when he was arrested, and what cops testified against him. Henderson had the information in a file Keela had quickly put together.

"Shouldn't we notify the captain or at least request some backup?" asked Calvanese.

"You heard him," replied Henderson. "Reeves is guilty, and the chief and the mayor are going to announce that at a joint news conference where they can have their pictures taken and bask in the glory of their achievement." He patted Calvanese on the shoulder. "Far be it from us to rain on their parade."

"What if we're right and they're wrong? The chief's not gonna appreciate having egg on his face. I think we better protect our asses and let him know what we're up to."

"We're off duty. Technically we're not up to anything," said Henderson, sounding more and more like his partner.

They entered the car. Henderson got behind the wheel.

"I still think this is a bad idea. We could get in a lot of trouble. Better play by the rules on this one."

Henderson started the engine. "You know what your problem is, Calvanese?" Henderson shifted in his seat and began his lecture. "You wanna be loved. I trust cops who wanna be loved as much as I trust politicians who wanna get elected." He rotated his head side to side imitating Calvanese's earlier rant. "Except the cops are a lot more dangerous."

Calvanese rotated his tongue inside his cheek, trying hard to maintain a positive perspective. "Are you through now?"

Henderson thought about it. "Not yet," he answered. "You also concern yourself too much with rules." He leaned closer and offered personal advice. "Good cops, like good chefs, don't give a fuck about checking with the captain. They make up their own recipe." He reflected further and then added, "Or some shit like that."

Henderson glanced at Calvanese. "Briella has gotten to you, made you want to play by the rules, follow procedure. Wouldn't be surprised to see you marching with the Black Lives Matter supporters." He turned on the siren and floored the accelerator, snapping back Calvanese's head.

Calvanese read sections of the file aloud as Henderson drove.

"Twenty-four years on the force. Busted eight years ago, three weeks before his retirement. Sentenced from fifteen to twenty-five for stealing drug money and other assorted crimes."

"He's still doing time?" asked Henderson.

"Did less than six months then hung himself in his cell." Calvanese glanced over at Henderson. "Guess who his partner was?"

"One of the murdered cops?"

"Matt Hoffman. Shot in the Hollywood Hills. He was the

one who turned him in, so I guess he got the distinction of being first on the list."

"What about the other cops, any connection?"

Calvanese quickly went through the file. "Two testified against him. Another set him up. Don't know about the last one shot in Santa Monica, but he doesn't appear to have any connection. Wasn't even on the force until three years ago." Calvanese slammed the file against the dashboard. "Goddamn! All this is about revenge!"

"Not race," replied Henderson. "Not war. Just one dirty cop and his incredibly angry son."

"We're getting close, better turn off the siren. No need to give advance warning, just in case."

Henderson turned off his siren and pulled up at a stop sign at Exposition then quickly went through the intersection.

"If this pans out, we should put in a word for C.J.," suggested Henderson.

"Too bad he won't be able to hire Johnnie Cochran. When Cochran died, so did his only chance to get off."

"You won't let it rest, will you?" responded Henderson. "You can't stand it that a Black lawyer won the case of the century. Get over it."

"You're crazy," snapped Calvanese. "Everybody knows Scheck and Shapiro won the case."

"It was Johnnie all the way." Henderson cut off a truck, causing the driver to slam on his brakes, blow his horn, and angrily shout a litany of profanities.

"Hey, Pavlov, stop the ringing in your ears and get a grip on reality," said Calvanese. "Even that truck driver you almost ran off the road knows you're full of shit."

"He probably didn't watch the trial. Cochran's closing argument was brilliant," responded Henderson.

"It was a subliminal message to the Black jurors about penis size," stated Calvanese adamantly.

"What are you talking about?"

"If the glove doesn't fit, you must acquit." Calvanese paused and studied a confused Henderson. "Tell me that wasn't sexual."

Henderson turned the car into the driveway leading to the main entrance to the University of Southern California. He smiled in earnest. "Gee," he said, impressed. "I guess Johnnie was even better than I thought." He pulled up at the security booth. A young female guard slid open her door.

"We're looking for Max Oliver," said Henderson. "He's a security guard."

She checked her records. "He's doing patrol. Probably down at the football field. You want me to call him for you?"

Henderson sped off. The guard picked up her phone and dialed a number, waited for a moment, and heard Oliver's voice over her transmitter. "Max. What the hell's goin' on? Some cops are lookin' for you! And they're in a real hurry. You read me?"

Max Oliver sat in his campus patrol car; his face expressionless. He listened to the voice crackle on his speaker, "Max, you there?" He turned off his communication device and started the ignition when he noticed an L.A.P.D. patrol car heading his way.

Oliver floored the accelerator and raced across the football field. Players in the middle of their practice scrimmage dived out of the way. Henderson crashed through a meshed-wired fence trying to cut off escape. The patrol car closed in but swerved as Oliver stuck an automatic weapon out of his window and fired a series of shots, ricocheting off the front and side of the police vehicle.

Football players and coaches raced off the field into the stands or toward the tunnel, anywhere they could find safety.

Oliver's car reached the road and then veered onto a narrow walkway. Students jumped out of its way as the car obliterated trash cans, bulletin boards, and part of the campus's famous rose garden.

Henderson's car followed behind, kicking up dirt and crushing a row of colorful flower beds. Calvanese pulled out his revolver and leaned out of the window, aiming his gun at Oliver's back tires.

"That's against regulations," warned Henderson.

"Not when we're endangered," replied Calvanese. "And the way you're driving, our lives are definitely at risk."

A student riding his bicycle and listening to music on his headphones casually rode down a steep incline. Oblivious to the danger, he cut in front of the patrol car. Henderson quickly maneuvered his vehicle down an embankment, sideswiping several bicycles locked in their rack and then barely missed running over a study group sprawled out on the lawn in front of the large Trojan statue.

Oliver's car broke through a construction barrier onto a temporary walkway. Henderson whipped around his car and raced across a large patch of dirt and gravel, positioning himself parallel to Oliver. Henderson's car skidded past a patch of wet cement, careened off a tree, raced up a ramp, and went airborne over a pile of sandbags.

Oliver headed for the main security booth and smashed through the guard gate, causing more student pedestrians to dive for safety. He rushed into early evening traffic onto Exposition Boulevard where his vehicle got broadsided and spun completely around. It was struck several times, rear, front, and driver's side. Immobilized and trapped inside the wreckage, Oliver was about to be attacked by some incredibly angry accident victims.

He grabbed a rifle and a backpack and fired a weapon into the air, causing panic at a scene that had already become chaotic. He ran across the street forcing drivers to slam on their brakes, resulting in a series of additional rear-end collisions.

Henderson and Calvanese, unable to negotiate through the maze of disabled cars jammed together on both sides of the boulevard, had no choice but to abandon their car.

Calvanese kept an eye on Oliver, sprinting toward the Natural History Museum. The suspect rushed down a ramp toward a side employee entrance. Discovering it locked, he smashed the glass and entered.

Calvanese and Henderson raced after him, jumping on top of damaged cars to get through the traffic mess caused by the accidents. They heard police sirens, but patrol cars had no chance of getting past the metal and rubber junkyard.

SIXTY-ONE

The two officers entered the dark building, rushed through a pair of swinging doors, and headed down a long corridor. They climbed a spiral staircase leading to the main entrance of the museum.

Blue lights reflected off various exhibits, most of them showcased behind thick glass enclosures. Henderson and Calvanese cautiously proceeded past the lobby, weapons drawn and aimed at potential target areas. Their footsteps off the marble floor echoed throughout the large room as they walked past the dinosaur exhibit and into the prehistoric caveman area.

Calvanese surveyed replicas of extinct animals and birds, displayed in their imagined settings, recreating what life must have been like thousands of years ago. He looked for signs of contemporary life, searching for a dangerous two-legged animal that had the potential of making either himself or his partner extinct with just one well-placed bullet.

Calvanese called out, his voice booming inside the massive hall. "Max! Give it up. It's over!"

Oliver responded with rapid gunfire forcing both officers to dive for cover. Glass booths shattered. Dinosaur bones exploded, splintering onto the floor.

Calvanese raised his head from behind a huge Brachiosaurus and discovered Henderson lying underneath a much smaller—but during that period, far more dangerous—Tyrannosaurus. "I think he's not surrendering," Calvanese said to his prone partner then glanced at the two exhibits. "Bet you my dinosaur can beat your dinosaur."

"I'll take that bet," answered Henderson. "Especially since my pet devours meat while yours nibbles on plants."

Both men rose slowly, carefully surveying the area. "Don't think I'm takin' your word for that."

"Fine," replied Henderson. "You can look it up for yourself after we catch their more primitive counterpart."

Calvanese called out a second time. "You hear that, Max? We're going to put you in your own private exhibit and all your fellow inmates can come by at night to feed you!"

Shots were fired from the area behind the staircase, destroying the skull and beak of an Iguanodon.

"I don't think it was a good idea to yell at him," said Henderson. "Look at the damage you caused."

Calvanese looked at the ruined exhibit, shrugged at the damage. "The stuff was old."

They heard footsteps, rapidly moving up the stairs. The two officers pursued Oliver to the second floor, where they found themselves in the middle of an exhibit on Ancient Egypt.

"I've always wanted to visit Egypt," said Calvanese, speaking quietly, spying the precious stones and jewelry locked behind a glass case.

"Cleopatra was Black," Henderson notified him.

Calvanese rolled his eyes. "Just 'cause Elizabeth Taylor's best friend happened to be Michael Jackson, doesn't mean that she—"

Henderson heard a noise, put up his hand to quiet

Calvanese. He turned rapidly, firing into the statue of a pharaoh.

Calvanese released a deep sigh, shooting Henderson an annoyed look. "I think you got him. He'll never see his mummy again." Calvanese realized both he and his partner were using humor to cover their own anxiety, like surgeons who joked during a complicated operation to relieve their tension. Only with cops, it's more than just putting the patient's life at risk.

Gunfire blew away the glass exhibit. Calvanese and Henderson ran for cover, slamming into the structure and tumbling it over, spilling precious stones and jewelry across the floor and setting off security alarms. Both officers charged down the corridor firing their weapons at the fleeing suspect.

Oliver turned and fired, barely missing Calvanese who dived to the floor and rolled to safety behind a large column. Henderson fired several shots at Oliver who disappeared behind a large doorway.

Henderson rushed to his partner's aid. "You all right?"

Calvanese brushed off his uniform. "I just had this cleaned, too. Twelve-fifty down the drain."

Henderson checked his weapon. "I'm out of bullets." He helped Calvanese to his feet, who thanked him by criticizing the situation.

"Great. This time you hold onto your gun but it ain't worth a damn."

Henderson started reloading his weapon when Calvanese stopped him. "We ain't got time for that. Here use mine. Calvanese gave Henderson his gun and then reached down his leg and removed another weapon from an ankle holster. Henderson gave him a suspicious look.

"I got thin legs," said Calvanese defensively. "The extra gun helps keep my pants from flapping."

"Don't tell me what you've got stuffed in your shorts," remarked Henderson.

Calvanese took a step but winced in pain.

"What's the matter?"

"First, he messes up my uniform then he fucks up my knee. Now I'm really pissed."

"Are you able to move?"

"Play the right music and I'll be able to dance."

Henderson and Calvanese went through the door Oliver used to escape and entered the planetarium auditorium. The exhibit had been turned on, filling the massive domed ceiling with a magnificent array of stars and other planetary phenomena. Colors and bright lights floated through the moving image of the solar system. Henderson slowly walked down one aisle, his weapon pointing at every possible danger spot. Calvanese moved slowly along the opposite aisle, both officers searching each row of theater seats.

"Life's a stage," Calvanese uttered loud enough for Henderson to hear.

"Break a leg," replied Henderson. "But not mine."

"Stay where you are!" a voice shouted from the front of the auditorium. Oliver appeared from behind a large maroon curtain and walked onto the stage holding a gun to the head of a terrified woman, a custodian. "Or she dies."

"Your beef's not with her, Max," said Calvanese. "It's with us. Let her go."

"I ain't got a beef with anybody anymore."

"You think you settled the score?" said Henderson.

"My dad put his ass on the line for nearly twenty-five years. Got shot twice, injured a dozen or more times, and still wouldn't retire. My mother left 'cause she couldn't take it anymore. But he always tried to find time for me, no matter what else was going on in his life."

Calvanese and Henderson continued walking very slowly, watching Oliver's every move.

"He promised he was going to put the family back together,

retire and take a long vacation, the entire family. And when he finally got the chance to be with us again, they took everything away from him, from me, for one fuckin' mistake."

"He took an oath, Max," Calvanese said calmly. "He broke it."

"One time!" Oliver screamed. "That's all! He took drug money that never should've been on the street in the first place. What harm was that gonna do? He deserved something for all he gave the department."

Calvanese lengthened his stride and took another step.

"I told you to stop!" ordered Oliver.

"Why'd you shoot the cop in Santa Monica, what connection did he have to your father?" asked Calvanese, trying to keep Oliver talking and preoccupied with him rather than with the hostage.

"None."

"Then why'd you kill him?" Calvanese asked.

"Thought, sooner or later someone would find a pattern between the cops, trace it back to the trial. I needed a diversion." Oliver moved slowly to the side, ensuring that the woman was positioned in front of him, preventing any opportunity for the cops to take a clean shot.

"And the people in Santa Monica that you shot, were they a diversion, too?" asked Henderson, who took a small step closer toward the front of the auditorium.

"Write that off to the media. They needed the extra tension, wanted to start a race war so I thought I'd give 'em a little help."

"You think that up all by yourself, or did Reeves give you some advice?" asked Calvanese.

Oliver responded by tightening his grip around the woman's neck.

"Who else was in the car with you?" asked Henderson.

"Nobody!" he screamed nervously, trying to keep track of the two officers.

"The shots were fired from the passenger side. Somebody had to be riding with you," said Calvanese, wanting Oliver's attention to be split between himself and Henderson.

"If you were the shooter, somebody had to be the driver. Did your boss help you out on that one, too?" asked Henderson.

"Did Reeves help you, Max?" Calvanese asked, demanding to know the answer.

"I ain't got to tell you shit!" screamed Oliver, about to lose control.

"He told you to do the Santa Monica shooting, didn't he?" continued Calvanese. "You got the idea from him, cover your tracks, maybe even start a little race war in the process. Admit it, you weren't smart enough, maybe you weren't even evil enough, to think of that on your own."

"You wanna talk about evil? You got any idea what they did to my dad in prison?" Oliver shook in anger, or fear.

Calvanese wanted him to be unsteady but not unhinged— that would make him unpredictable and, therefore, far more dangerous. He sought to calm him down. "I don't know, Max," he answered. "Why don't you tell me?" Calvanese spoke calmly, almost compassionately.

Oliver let the rifle slide down the hostage's face a few inches, stopping at her neck as if the weight of the weapon or the burden of the story was too heavy. He needed to find a place to rest his hand and the only one available happened to be her shoulder.

"Bunch of prisoners got to him one night," he said, with a combination of bitterness and heartbreak. "Probably with the aid of one of the guards who couldn't care less about my dad. All the fuckin' guards there treated him like dirt."

Calvanese kept his eyes glued on the weapon pointing away slightly from the terrified woman. He took another step closer and to the left, wanting to get a better angle in the event he needed to fire his gun.

"You know what they do to ex-cops in prison?" asked Oliver, his voice breaking. "No human being deserves that." Oliver moved to the side and looked at Calvanese while Henderson inched closer. "They raped my father. Beat him so bad I couldn't recognize him." He lifted the rifle back to the woman's head, just in front of her ear. "They castrated him and made him swallow his own—"

"I'm sorry for what they did to your father, Max, I really am," Calvanese said, wanting to dissipate the anger, but only for a moment. He saw Oliver's hand relax again.

"Given what happened to your father, why'd you want to be a cop, Max?"

"That was his dream for me. I wanted to do that for him. Prove he was a good cop by being one myself."

"You're a sick puppy, you know that, Max? You're killing cops but now you want to be one?"

"They had to pay for what they did to my dad!"

Calvanese decided it was time to turn up the emotional pressure. "Whatever happened to your father, he brought on himself. He wasn't good. He betrayed his friends, his uniform, and his duty!"

"Say that again, and I'll blow her fuckin' head off!"

"You don't wanna hurt her, Max. Truth is, you want to kill me, too. Wanna know why?" He took one small step to the side but couldn't find a clear path to Oliver, who was fully shielded by the woman's body.

"I don't wanna hear anything you got to say."

"'Cause I'm honest like those others you murdered?"

"They turned on my dad! Set him up. They were like family to him, and they betrayed him! He would've taken a bullet for anyone of them and they—"

"They took a bullet from you, you sorry piece of shit!" screamed Calvanese. "But it wasn't their choice."

"Shut up or she's dead!"

"Tony," warned Henderson. "Back off."

"You better listen to your partner," said Oliver, "or there's gonna be a lot of blood and pieces of her skull for somebody to clean up."

"You really wanna know why you killed those cops, Max?"

"I already know."

"Because they did their job!" exclaimed Calvanese. "A job your father couldn't do anymore. That's why you killed them. Not out of revenge. You were jealous of them."

"Shut up!" screamed Oliver. "I ain't gonna tell you again. Now put your fuckin' guns down or I'm blowing this bitch away! I mean it."

Oliver's anger and rage were precisely what Calvanese needed. The greater his agitation, the less attention he paid on his human shield. The side of his face was increasingly more visible, but Calvanese needed a bit more of a target.

"You want me to get rid of my gun, Max?" asked Calvanese. "That's not a problem. If I get rid of it, will you let her go?"

"Just do it!"

"Whatever you say." Calvanese slowly moved his arm to the side, pointing the gun away from Oliver, and then with a flip of his wrist, tossed his weapon to the floor, a few feet in front of where he was standing.

"Tony," called out a concerned Henderson, but Calvanese's attention remained frozen on Oliver.

"Satisfied?" Calvanese asked Oliver then started walking toward the stage.

"Stop!" screamed Oliver, and pointed his rifle at Calvanese, which was exactly where the officer wanted it aimed.

Calvanese stopped but only after moving closer to where he had tossed the gun. "What's the matter, Max?" he asked. "I'm unarmed. That should make it easier for you, shouldn't it? Or you want me to turn my back, so you'll have the guts to do to me what you did to all those honest cops you murdered?"

Calvanese turned his back, spread out his arms wide, and gave Henderson a wink. "That's what they were, Max. Honest cops, something your father couldn't be. So, you murdered them all to revenge a lowlife traitor like your dad." He made eye contact again with Henderson, and gave him a slight nod, signaling him to be ready. "That's exactly what your punk ass daddy was, a traitor that deserved what happened to him."

Enraged, Oliver tossed the woman to the floor.

"Now!" Henderson screamed.

Oliver fired his weapon at Calvanese, who had already dived behind some seats, reaching for his gun.

Henderson fired three times, striking Oliver in the chest with all the shots. Oliver fell off the stage to the floor. The terrified woman ran behind the side wing of the stage, screaming hysterically. Henderson rushed to Calvanese and noticed a pool of blood underneath his body, streaming down the aisle.

Henderson cradled his partner in his arms. "Tony? Tony, talk to me." He tried to search for a pulse: his throat, then his wrist. Henderson tended to Calvanese's lifeless body when he noticed the trace of a smile.

Calvanese opened his eyes. "Have you noticed how tender my skin is? I apply cocoa butter at night, just before I go to bed. It does wonders. I can loan you a bottle if you like."

"You're an asshole, you know that?"

Calvanese grinned. "This time, I get the medal."

"Congratulations," replied a relieved Henderson.

"In the movies it's the Black guy who gets shot trying to save his white partner," declared Calvanese. "I guess you didn't remember that part."

Henderson moved his hand over his partner's face and using the tips of his fingers, gently lowered both of Calvanese's eyelids until they were completely shut. "Dream on, Gary Cooper. Dream on."

SIXTY-TWO

Henderson walked down the police corridor with Calvanese, who shifted his left arm uncomfortably. The shoulder harness made him feel trapped like a wild, albeit injured, animal. His unopened bottle of prescribed pain medication had been discarded before he left the doctor's office three nights ago. He didn't believe in artificially numbing the senses. He'd managed to accomplish that goal on his own for most of his life and saw no reason to change now.

As the two men proceeded toward the assembly room for the morning briefing, fellow officers lined up on either side of them, standing in mock attention reminiscent of a British Royal Guard unit. As Calvanese and Henderson passed through the formation, the officers in both lines saluted, extending their right arms, creating a protective overhead tunnel for the two heroes to march under. As if this wasn't enough tribute, the men started humming a bad version of "Hail to the Chief."

Calvanese hammed it up, bowing to the overplayed adoration and using his one good arm to pump his fist in the air.

Henderson accepted the homage with feigned humility. "Thank you, thank you, it was nothing, really. Any true hero would've done the same thing." He smiled politely and gave a slight wave of his hand.

Even Mike Stevens and Allen Davis were able to put aside their differences, if only temporarily, and stood together participating in the celebration, enjoying it immensely.

Suddenly Captain O'Ryan appeared wearing an extremely serious expression. All the officers stopped clowning and stood silently. He raised both hands, halting Henderson and Calvanese dead in their tracks.

O'Ryan directed his comments to Calvanese. "I'm pleased to inform you that you're no longer suspended."

"I didn't know that I ever was," responded a surprised Calvanese.

"You'll get the formal notice tomorrow."

"Thanks, Captain," Calvanese said sincerely.

"Thanks for what?" asked a mystified O'Ryan. "For the record, you were never suspended, the notice was obviously sent in error, someone in my office mailed it out by mistake. So technically we never had this conversation."

"What conversation?" replied Calvanese.

O'Ryan smiled. "You've finally decided to play by my rules?"

Calvanese shrugged. "Technically we never had this conversation, so I don't know what the hell you're talking about."

"It's not the first time, probably won't be the last," declared O'Ryan. "But just to make sure there's no misunderstanding, what I'm about to say is definitely *on* the record." He placed his hands on the shoulders of both men and spoke solemnly. "In case you're still wondering..." He studied them for a beat then issued his solemn edict. "I'm not separating you, so don't ask."

Calvanese and Henderson exchanged satisfied looks.

O'Ryan hinted at a sly smile then grinned broadly. "Great

job, men!" He patted them on their backs. "You're a credit to your color—L.A.P.D. blue."

Around them, their colleagues laughed, some more genuinely than others. Calvanese winced in pain, either from the lame joke or his tender shoulder.

Calvanese and Henderson walked away from the gathering but stopped on O'Ryan's voice. "Hey, Tony," he said with a distinct tone of accomplishment. "Got a call a few minutes ago. We found the guy who assaulted your mother." He nodded respectfully. "You might want to tell her the good news yourself."

"Where is he?" asked Calvanese in a lethal voice, more a command than a question.

O'Ryan hesitated then offered a response that caused Calvanese to rip off his shoulder harness and march away, a man on a singular mission.

O'Ryan looked at Henderson, concerned. "He's your partner," he said with conviction. "You better go with him."

* * *

Calvanese sat in the passenger seat, staring silently ahead. Henderson drove down 108th Street in Watts and turned into the entrance of the Southwest Community Police Station. He parked the car near the front of the building.

"You sure you wanna do this?" asked Henderson, sounding as if it was futile to say any more.

Calvanese shoved open his door and exited.

They entered through the main entrance and checked in with the officer on duty, who had been expecting them. They took the elevator to the third floor and were greeted by two uniformed officers standing guard outside the interrogation room. Calvanese explained his situation and sought permission to enter but was denied access.

"Wish I could slip you the key to his cell," said the older of the two guards, "so you could pay him a visit tonight." He gave Calvanese a helpless shrug. "Unfortunately, I can't do that, no matter how much I'd like to."

"I just want to see him. Hear what he has to say," pleaded Calvanese. "Won't be any problems."

"None for you, but for a lot for us should something go wrong," stated the other guard.

After an uneasy beat, his partner offered a compromise. "You can check it out from the observation room." He looked at his colleague who nodded agreement. "That's the best we can do." The men waited for a response.

Calvanese didn't like the option but finally agreed. "Thanks," he said. "I appreciate that."

Calvanese and Henderson were led to the adjoining room, shown how to handle the controls, and then left alone.

Henderson stood in front of the one-way mirror separating him from the proceedings occurring in the next room. He looked at Calvanese, who remained a safe distance from the glass.

"You want me to turn on the sound?" asked Henderson.

"I want to see him first." Calvanese moved slowly, seemingly against his will, toward the mirror. His heart raced with every step. He stopped at the control panel and observed the interrogation. A huge Black man stood with his back turned toward the mirror. He was poorly dressed, ripped sneakers without laces, long, unkempt hair, dirty and tattered clothes, undoubtedly the result of the struggle to get away. His short-sleeve shirt clung tightly to his muscular arms. He had broad shoulders and an unusually small waist for a man that big.

Calvanese thought about his mother and knew she had no chance against this animal. A uniformed white cop leaned against the table and said something to the man, who didn't appear to respond. Calvanese wanted to put his fist through the mirror and grab the back of his neck, jerk it around so he could see the bastard's face. *Turn, goddamn it! Turn!*

Calvanese's expression was full of hate, as the man turned slowly, directly facing the observation mirror. Calvanese studied the man's face, which was hard, indifferent. He didn't look the least bit troubled or concerned, as if he had no soul or conscience, no regret whatsoever. And then Calvanese discovered the handle of a gun peeking just outside of the man's police-issued holster, a detective's shield attached to his belt.

The detective moved away from the window and crossed to the other side of the room, revealing another person, the handcuffed suspect now in custody—a teenager, frail, drugged-out, disoriented, sniffling, scared, and most of all... white. The man who had so viciously beaten his mother was seated less than ten feet away, and he looked nothing like Calvanese had imagined. His face turned blank at the sight of this pathetic-looking creature.

Henderson observed the proceedings from behind Calvanese and leaned over to flip a switch. They could hear the man pleading over the two speakers hanging on either side of the wall in front of them.

"I wasn't planning on hurtin' her. I just wanted the purse and the keys to the car." The man brought his cuffed hands to his face and wiped his nose with the back of his sleeve. "I was lookin' for a place to drop her off, but she came to and started screamin' for help. I told her to stop, but she went crazy, fightin' me, scratchin'. She almost put out my eye. I had to punish her, teach her a lesson. I didn't have no choice."

"And then what'd you do?" asked the uniformed officer.

"I just made plans to get away."

"You almost did," commented the detective. "But then you tried to sell her credit cards to me." He paused and studied the man with growing contempt. "Wasn't very smart now, was it?"

"You didn't look undercover, I'll give you that much," replied the suspect. "Certainly fooled me."

"You're not exactly a rocket scientist," responded the detective.

The man chuckled. "No. I ain't ever gonna be mistaken for that, no matter how high I got."

"How long you live in the Valley?"

"All my life."

"Why'd you dump her in South Central and not someplace closer to home?"

The man looked at the detective, appeared embarrassed. "You know why," he said, softly.

Henderson flipped off the switch and watched Calvanese move slowly toward a chair and sit. He put both elbows on the edge of the table and gently rubbed his eyes.

"Wasn't what you wanted?" Henderson said.

"What?" Calvanese responded without looking at him.

Henderson leaned against the table as if he were starting to interrogate a prisoner. "You wanted him to be Black. Expected him to be."

Calvanese stared at Henderson then looked away.

"I saw it in your face," Henderson continued. "All that anger. All that rage. Maybe even all that hate." Henderson waited until Calvanese looked at him again. "It needed a target. And when he wasn't what you thought, all you had left was the pain."

"Leave me alone, Paul."

Henderson nodded and moved silently toward the one-way mirror. He turned and faced Calvanese. "You know what's sad, Tony?"

Calvanese ignored him. Henderson watched the interrogation continue without the audio. "I wanted him to be white."

Calvanese rose slowly and joined his partner at the mirror.

They both stared at the man as he was led away by the detective and the uniformed officer.

"No matter what either one of us wanted, it wouldn't have changed what happened to your mother." Henderson faced Calvanese. "So, you tell me, Tony, why was it so important for one of us to be right?"

Calvanese didn't respond. Henderson proceeded to the door and opened it. "You remember when you asked me if the town deserved to be saved?" Henderson asked the question without turning around.

"Yeah," Calvanese answered.

Henderson turned and stood in the doorway. Calvanese saw the teenager being escorted down the corridor.

"We are the town," said Henderson, and then left.

Calvanese considered the statement. He stared through the one-way mirror, showing no expression, feeling no emotion, as he silently studied the interrogation room, now empty.

SIXTY-THREE

Multicolored balloons decorated the crowded auditorium filled with police officers, city officials, and community leaders from around the state. The national as well as local news media attended the event sponsored by Chief Gibbs to pay tribute to the L.A.P.D. and to give awards to a carefully selected group of officers who would best serve the political interests of the department and the mayor's office.

"We are indebted to the brave men and women of Division Seventy-Seven," Mayor Palmer's voice boomed over the loud-speakers, as he addressed the large assembly from behind the city's official ceremonial podium, "and indeed, all members of law enforcement, who despite the difficulties of the last few weeks, placed their personal differences aside and remained committed to each other as well as to the people of this great city."

Calvanese and Henderson shared the same platform on stage with other police officers waiting to receive their medals attached to red-white-and-blue ribbons. Calvanese's wounds were now completely healed, but he longed for the arm sling.

Left to his own unrestrained impulses, his arm might find its way around his commander's neck.

Gibbs, once again assisted by Captain O'Ryan, placed commendations around the necks of Mike Stevens and the recently promoted Allen Davis. Both men were selected for awards because of their "unique contributions to unity within the division." Palmer didn't seem to recognize any inherent contradiction or irony in his words of commendation, but Calvanese thought "unity within the division" was a phrase worthy of inclusion in Bartlett's. After the mayor had made his statement, he displayed a certain smirk which elicited a smattering of applause from the audience.

Before the smirk had completely vanished, Calvanese took the opportunity to wink at Reverend Wilson, perched in the front row along with a group of his devoted followers. The Reverend mouthed two words which probably had their origin in the Old Testament. Calvanese chuckled and then responded by mouthing the words, "You, too," followed by a slightly concealed one-finger salute that he hoped had certain biblical connotations.

Gibbs and O'Ryan stood several feet away from Henderson, preparing to present the next award. Calvanese leaned close to Henderson and spoke conspiratorially. "What would Gary do right now?"

Henderson didn't turn toward Calvanese but whispered, "Gary who?"

"Cooper," answered an agitated Calvanese, but he knew Henderson still didn't get it. "*High Noon*," he insisted.

"Tony, it was only a movie."

"So? Movies can't be about life?"

Henderson thought about it. "Only the comedies," he answered.

Gibbs placed the award around Henderson's neck and then

stepped in front of Calvanese and did the same, completing the awards presentation.

"Ladies and gentlemen," Mayor Palmer announced, "I present to you the men and women of Division Seventy-Seven, who brought peace to our community and great distinction and honor to our department. We owe them all a great debt of gratitude." The mayor stepped away from the microphone and led the audience in applause.

Nicole and Dexter sat in the same row as Calvanese's proud parents. Mrs. Calvanese reached over to the seat next to her and held Briella's hand.

Henderson had finished adjusting his medal when Calvanese nudged him in the ribs. "Will you leave me alone?" Henderson said harshly.

"This is all bullshit, you know that don't you?" replied Calvanese.

"Just accept the award," Henderson pleaded. "I shot the white man, didn't I?"

"I'm not playing this game anymore. I've had enough."

"Jesus called. He wants his cross back."

Calvanese gave him an innocent look. "Gee, I didn't think he wanted to hang onto it."

Mayor Palmer raised his hands to quiet the audience. "Chief Gibbs and Captain O'Ryan, will you please join me at the podium?"

News crews moved their cameras closer to the front of the auditorium to capture the three officials together. Gibbs and Palmer displayed smiles con men would envy. O'Ryan's expression was more restrained, but once he received an encouraging tap on the shoulder from the chief, he managed to beam from ear to ear. The three men stood shoulder to shoulder, forming a unified coalition of the politically expedient, basking in the glory of their victory against the forces of evil while upholding the virtues of loyalty and duty regardless of race, ethnicity, or the truth.

Calvanese sang quietly, "Do not forsake me, oh my darlin'." He looked at Henderson, nodded encouragement for him to follow suit.

Henderson made an expression that suggested he'd just swallowed something awful. Calvanese wouldn't relent, his jaw jutted forth as he moved his head forward and back like a horse suggesting it was time for its rider to get a move on.

Henderson, seeking an end to this before it got any more embarrassing, reluctantly sang. "For I..." He hesitated, uncertain, then regaining his composure continued with, "Da da da da da daaa."

Calvanese's mouth dropped open slightly in disbelief and he nearly doubled over in pain.

Henderson shrugged. "I don't know the words," he confided, ashamed.

Calvanese took a deep breath and then shook his head sadly. "Pitiful... absolutely pitiful."

Palmer separated himself from his two colleagues. "I'd like to present to Chief Gibbs and Captain O'Ryan these awards that will forever stand as a testament to a job well done." Palmer handed Chief Gibbs an award—a crystal bowl with the insignia of the L.A.P.D. etched in gold. He then handed O'Ryan a plaque with a proclamation from the city. All three men posed for photos. Flashbulbs exploded throughout the building. In the middle of this happy family portrait a voice rang out from behind them on the stage.

"Hey, Captain!" yelled Calvanese.

O'Ryan slowly turned toward the voice, maintaining a loose grip on his award.

"I thought you had a nose for bullshit!" Calvanese concluded as the photographers now aimed their cameras directly at the source of the disturbance. Henderson turned his body to the side in a failed effort to disappear.

The smiles faded from the faces of O'Ryan, Gibbs, and the mayor. The jammed auditorium went dead silent followed eventually by a murmuring throughout the crowd.

Calvanese walked across the stage as if he had been invited and stood in front of the mayor. He took a quick sniff then repeated the gesture toward Gibbs. He looked at O'Ryan, whose blue eyes had turned a turbulent black.

"Can't you smell these guys?" asked Calvanese.

"Calvanese," muttered O'Ryan, "if you don't get—"

"I can smell 'em, too!" chimed another voice. Henderson approached his partner and stood on the other side of Palmer. Calvanese nodded in appreciation. Henderson acknowledged the gesture with one of his own.

"Gentlemen," asked Chief Gibbs with great restraint that forced his neck muscles to protrude, "I take it you have an explanation for your conduct?"

"This award ceremony isn't for us," answered Calvanese. "It's for the public. Why don't you tell these people the truth?"

"Perhaps we should leave that to you," said Palmer as if he was accepting a resignation. "Since you've obviously taken it upon yourself to disrupt these proceedings, you might as well use up your remaining fifteen seconds of fame." He stepped away from the podium but managed to position himself further from the microphone and to within earshot of Calvanese. "Be sure to enjoy it," the mayor threatened, "for I assure you, you'll never have another opportunity."

Calvanese didn't flinch and matched Palmer's stare. He then faced the audience and took a step toward the podium, his voice amplified by the microphone, just slightly louder than his rapidly beating heart.

"Maybe this doesn't make any sense to any of you out there, or maybe you don't want it to. But after you've put these

uniforms on enough times, you don't have good cops anymore,"
he said respectfully. "You don't have bad cops. All you have are
time bombs waiting for a victim to break your heart, or a suspect
to put a bullet in it."

He turned toward Chief Gibbs and spoke without anger or
bitterness. "And before you became a politician, instead of a
cop, you used to know that."

Calvanese reached for his badge and glanced toward
Henderson, who reached for his. They simultaneously removed
their badges and exchanged a knowing look. They measured the
weight of the badges in their hands and did so in a way that
suggested they were considering far more than the physical heft
of the shields. They looked at each other again and thought
better of it. They pinned their badges back on their uniforms.

Calvanese brushed against Palmer hard enough to push
him aside. He spoke defiantly. "We're not giving up our badges,
no matter how much you'd like us to."

"But you can take the chief's award and stick it up your next
press conference," added Henderson.

Henderson and Calvanese twisted their right feet on the
floor of the stage as if extinguishing a cigarette or crushing an
imaginary badge à la Gary Cooper. Henderson stepped off the
stage and descended the steps leading to the stunned crowd.
Calvanese turned and followed but stopped on O'Ryan's voice.

"Calvanese!" demanded O'Ryan. "Where the hell do you
think you're going?"

Calvanese replied innocently, "He's my partner, Captain. I
thought you wanted me to be with him." He flashed a killer
smile and hurried to join Henderson, marching down the center
aisle of the auditorium.

Palmer's lower lip trembled furiously. Gibbs stared into
empty space, dumbfounded. O'Ryan stood expressionless and
then tried hard to conceal a smile.

News crews fell over themselves collecting their equipment

to get an interview. Photographers rushed toward the exits, taking numerous pictures along the way.

Calvanese and Henderson strolled in lockstep. Officers seated on both sides of them looked stunned. Guests watched them in disbelief, except for Nicole and Briella, who smiled proudly. Dexter didn't know what to think, but he was definitely impressed. He stood and applauded. Nicole and Briella also stood and followed his lead.

Calvanese and Henderson continued their journey out of the assembly area, walking side by side.

"You think they can fire us for that?" asked Henderson.

"What do I care? I got my pension."

A few officers stood and applauded, which started a chain reaction of fellow officers, who become increasingly enthusiastic. Mrs. Calvanese and her husband held hands and smiled proudly. He gently stroked her wedding ring, which was back on her finger where it clearly belonged. Briella remained standing, her head lowered and her body nearly convulsing in laughter.

"If we lose our jobs," offered Henderson, "maybe we can start a detective agency."

Calvanese nodded in agreement. "Good idea. We'll name it Calvanese and Henderson. We'll take turns shootin' the bad guys regardless of race."

Members of the Black community stood and applauded. Reverend Wilson reluctantly joined them, eventually providing the loudest cheerleading.

"The sign on the window will read: Henderson and Partner. I want a big bell over the door," proclaimed Henderson

"But no dogs," said Calvanese.

"Definitely no dogs," agreed Henderson, as both men reached the rear doors, leaving to a rousing ovation.

A LETTER FROM THE AUTHOR

One of the things I find most satisfying as a writer is hearing from readers who have seen themselves in my work, or who have been exposed to a different perspective that may have contributed to a greater understanding of each other. For those of you who are familiar with my work, either as a novelist or playwright, you already know that I attempt to explore our shared humanity: the goals, aspirations, and dreams that make us human, regardless of our perceived differences and any obstacles that are placed in the way of our finding the truth. For my first-time readers, as always, I offer my heartfelt gratitude to each of you for investing your time in reading my novel, *The Killing Season*, and more importantly, my sincere appreciation to you for supporting the literary work of writers everywhere.

If you would like to join other readers in hearing all about my new releases and bonus content, you can sign up here:

www.stormpublishing.co/jeff-stetson

Writers, if honest, leave a little bit of their soul on each page so that the reader will better understand that writer's truth as well as their own. I'd love to hear your truth, so I hope we will remain in contact. And if you find *The Killing Season* merits your support, I invite you to provide reviews and hope you will recommend the novel to your friends and colleagues. Regardless of your decision, I wish you unlimited wonderful novels on all your future reading lists.

Some years ago, a big-city mayor at a news conference, following the police shooting of an unarmed African American teen, announced that when it came to police shootings, he would always give the benefit of the doubt to his officers. But the benefit of the doubt is almost always influenced by the biases we have or the group affiliations we share. How can we ever be confident of the truth when the truth is affected by the racial, religious, or political prism through which we see the world?

This question is at the heart of my novel *The Killing Season*. Following the police shootings of several innocent African Americans, white members of the Los Angeles Police Department are being murdered. Tony Calvanese, a hard-edged, seasoned white cop, is paired with Paul Henderson, an idealistic thirty-year-old Black rookie, who holds a graduate degree in criminal justice as well as a law degree. After earning the degrees, he decides the best way to help the community is to join the force and make it more sensitive and humanistic in the way it responds to minority communities. He's partnered with this twenty-year veteran, third-generation cop, who has seen too much violence and desperation on the streets and has become jaded, appearing at times to be racist, or at best, highly insensitive.

These two men, from very different backgrounds and sharing opposing perspectives, must transcend their own personal differences and hostilities and find the person or persons responsible for the police murders before the city erupts in racial violence. The murders have caused enormous polarization inside the LAPD. White officers no longer trust their Black counterparts. Black cops, long feeling that they've been discriminated against and denied promotions, use the murders to push forth their own agenda, increasing the tension between the two groups.

Throughout this growing crisis, conflicting views, and

mistrust between the races in the community and police force threaten that justice will be compromised and truth will remain elusive. The conflict between Calvanese and Henderson in doing their duty is intensified by their respective tribalism that prevents them from seeing beyond the limitations of their inherent bias. *The Killing Season* hopes to underscore that the world is more complicated than we like to admit, and that reducing it to black and white inhibits the opportunity to understand each other or resolve the problems we face.

In the end, I hope that the reader not only wants Tony Calvanese and Paul Henderson to solve the crime before the community is irreparably harmed, but just as importantly, that both men remove the barriers that preclude the chance for mutual understanding and the possibility for friendship.

facebook.com/jeff.stetson.5

x.com/JeffStetson

instagram.com/jeff_paul_stetson

linkedin.com/in/jeff-stetson-356b7818

ACKNOWLEDGEMENTS

It always takes a leap of faith to write a novel and place it in the hands of a new publisher. But when that publisher is comprised of many gifted and talented people with a history of success and a passion for what they do, then it creates a rewarding and lasting partnership. I offer a special thanks to Claire Bord, deputy managing director, for her editorial vision, assistance, and ongoing support for my last two novels. I'm grateful to Alexandra Holmes, editorial operations director, Anna McKerrow, publicity manager, as well as to the entire team of Storm Publishing for providing an environment that nurtures writers and creates opportunities for them to flourish under the leadership of Oliver Rhodes, managing director.

My deepest gratitude to those who have supported my work throughout the years, whether in theatre, film, television, or novels. I left my position in higher education in order to truly educate. If I've managed to accomplish that, and at times inspire, then that will be my greatest reward. Continue to support the arts and fight those who would restrict or obstruct the right to do so.

Made in the USA
Las Vegas, NV
07 November 2024

11299253R00231